A TALENT WITHIN

Visit us at www.boldstrokesbooks.com

A TALENT WITHIN

by

Suzanne Lenoir

2023

This Trade Paperback Original Is Published By
Bold Strokes Books, Inc.
P.O. Box 249
Valley Falls, NY 12185

First Edition: June 2023

Credits
Editor: Barbara Ann Wright
Production Design: Stacia Seaman
Cover Design by Fred Miller

Acknowledgments

Pretty much everything I do starts with my sister Holly, who in response to my worrying about my grammar when I was twelve, said, "That's what an editor is for." Once I got over that hurdle, the next step in my writing journey was trying to get the attention of my first girl crush (who never knew!). A few dozen very short stories later, I'd discovered how fun it was to write.

So on to the thanks...

Thanks to my good friends, who read a lot of bits and pieces of my work over the years and encouraged me to keep trying.

Thanks to the GCLS Writing Academy program and to the instructors for giving of their time and knowledge. Thanks to the Class of 2021 for their continued encouragement, and particularly to classmate Nan Campbell for helping me decide it was time to submit my manuscript.

Thanks to Wynn Malone and Beth Hawkins for a lot of writing discussion Zooms that grew into two-hour random and fascinating philosophical debates. Thanks to librarian Maddy Wells for reassuring me it would fit the YA category and making me change the title. Genius, I tell you. And a huge thank you to Chris Sandusky, who read every single version of the story. She's read my story as many times as I've written and rewritten it. That is a best friend.

Finally, thanks to all the folks at Bold Strokes Books for taking a chance on a queer YA fantasy novel by a first-time writer. And a special thanks to my editor, Barbara Ann Wright, for convincing me I'm a legitimate author now.

For Brianne, who always believed I could do this. I love you.

CHAPTER ONE

Annika dreaded market days. She preferred staying near her cottage, safe and alone. But she tapped her staff on the ground, driving the gaggle of geese onward as she and her father, Steffen, approached Byetown. Lord Cederic's flock produced a record number of goslings, and now fattened, twenty of the best ones were ready to sell at market. They had walked half a day to arrive in time to sell the birds.

On the edge of town, two men cleaned muck from a cart, dumping the filth into a stream. Their tunics shabby and stained, they stood ankle-deep in shite and offal. As Annika and her father passed, both men stopped their work and watched her. The taller one rested his arm on his shovel and eyed her. There was nothing kind in his expression.

Now that she was seventeen and with her hair uncovered, signifying her unmarried status, men leered at her. Her pale skin and fair hair, rare for Valmorans, always made her something of an oddity, but now the stares were filled with the sin of lust. She touched the Maiden hanging at her neck, hoping for protection from the men's evil thoughts. She reached back and pulled her hood over her head, shielding herself from their prying eyes.

In town, the houses along the street were mud brick and wood structures, some with thatched roofs, others with wooden shingles. None seemed to be square; some had a unique angle or a crooked doorway. Others had second floors jutting out over the street, nearly touching the buildings across from them. The road felt restricting. The smells of rotten vegetation and human shite hung in the air, overwhelming Annika's senses.

On a typical market day, people moved in a flurry of activity. Women and men carried large rolls of rough fabric on their backs or yokes with clay jars of butter or loads of hay, wool, and wood, much of it bound for the Royal Court in Tarburg. Today, there were fewer people, and Annika was thankful. She hated being in a town—any town—with a crowd.

When she and her father stayed home in their cottage outside their tiny village of Marsendale, she felt safe. As soon as she left the familiar sights and sounds of the open fields and the wide horizon, she withdrew into herself. She felt it now. She hunched her shoulders to make herself smaller. And the discomfort didn't take into account her deepest fear, the one even her father didn't speak aloud. She couldn't return home soon enough.

The main street was empty except for a lone man-at-arms sitting precariously on a stoop outside a tavern. As they passed, he kicked at a goose that came close to him and leaned forward and honked loudly. His cup of ale spilled over its sides. Annika's father moved closer to the man and worked the gaggle. He always put himself between trouble and her. It was his way. He nodded at the man, and a sort of recognition in the man's eyes seemed to calm him. Did men who had been in battle always recognize each other? Annika wondered if her father could have ended up drunk on a stoop had he not met her mother, Hella.

The closer to the town center they traveled, the more uncomfortable Annika felt by the emptiness of the streets. Something wasn't right. "Where is everyone?" she asked.

Her father hobbled along, his stiff leg more apparent on the uneven, rutted street. "The square." He gestured ahead of them. "Hear the crowds?"

She was paying more attention to her thoughts and the honking geese, but now she listened carefully. She could hear an undulating noise from loud to soft. She looked at her father for reassurance. This wasn't a high holy day or any other day of celebration. His pinched face and furrowed brow told her he was concerned as well.

The sound grew deafening as they entered the large market square. Sales tables and wheeled carts were pushed against the surrounding buildings, and a raised platform sat under the watchful tower of the guildhall. Annika's heart raced. Everyone in town seemed packed in the space, yelling and throwing rotten vegetables at someone on the dais.

She drove the flock along the edge, close to the buildings, trying to navigate the crowds. Her fear bubbled to the surface. She didn't want to see what was happening, but she turned toward the dais anyway. She mostly saw the backs of heads, raised arms, and heard yelling.

"Traitor!"

"Heretic!"

When she reached the far side of the square, she pushed the geese into a large pen while her father engaged with the merchant to negotiate the sale. She moved out of the way of the crowd craning their necks for a view and willed her father to finish quickly. Something wasn't right. She felt it. She grasped her necklace and murmured a prayer.

A woman approached with a basket on her hip. "Maiden bless you, sir," she said to a man next to Annika. "What has the girl done?"

"A Talent," he replied, his face an angry red. "Her family hid her from the temple. Said she didn't want to serve. A heretic, I say. Heretic," he yelled at the platform and hurled something.

Annika felt cold. Maiden help her, it was a rogue Talent on the platform, and everyone around her was screaming and throwing things. How had they found her? Had she given herself away somehow? Or could the hunters sense her? Could they sense Annika? Fear gripped her. She glanced at her father. He continued to haggle with the distracted merchant.

When she turned her view back to the dais, the crowd in front of her parted enough that she could see the girl tied by the wrists to a tall post. She looked wealthy, her tunic embroidered, her hair in loose braids in large circles around her ears, her metal belt glinting in the sunlight. A tradesman or noble's daughter, maybe seventeen or eighteen, no older than Annika. And she looked terrified.

Annika felt nauseated. That terror was all she could see. Everyone was yelling profanity and curses. All she could think was it could be her tied to that pole. With all these people hating her for something she couldn't control. Something she never asked to be. Her father should have turned her over to the temple when she'd first showed her gift, as was the rule. Now she lived in constant fear of this moment. When someone found them out and tied her to a pole in the center of their village.

A man in a blue tunic appeared next to the girl. Annika could *feel* him, even at this distance. She'd never felt the presence of another Talent before, but his warmth spread out, touching her like a fire. He said something, but Annika couldn't hear him. The crowds in front went silent, and only a few of the townsfolk around her continued their barrage of insults. The lull seemed oddly respectful for a frenzied mob. The man in blue gestured at the girl, and an executioner opposite him raised a torch. As one, the entire crowd roared with a fearsome agreement, and the torch touched the girl's clothes.

Annika turned away in horror. She pressed her hands to her ears, blocking out the bloodthirsty roar, and looked desperately for her father. The crowd had filled in around her, and she couldn't see him. If she could feel the man on the dais, he might feel her. If so, she'd be burning beside the girl soon enough. She pushed frantically against people, trying to squirm through to find her father. A man blocked her way and grabbed her shoulders.

"You should watch this, missy." The veins in his neck bulged, and spittle rolled from his lips. "Wealthy bastard got his. Hiding her."

Tears welled in her eyes. She beat upon his chest. "Let go of me!"

"Afraid to watch?" He pushed his face closer. She could smell the ale on his breath. "Did you know the girl? A friend?" He twisted her around to face the platform.

Flames engulfed the girl, gray smoke curling into the sky. Annika tore her gaze away and twisted in his grip. "Let me go."

"She caused the spring crops to fail. And brought the plague last winter." He looked past Annika at the spectacle. "She's got hers now."

His grip loosened. She escaped him and rushed to a building at the back of the crowd, pushing people out of her way. She turned her back to the wall and scanned the crowd for her father. If the townspeople could do this to the wealthy daughter of one of their own, surely, they would do worse to Annika: a peasant, half-outsider, child of a Weyan. She reached for the hilt of the dagger on her belt. If they tried to take her, she'd fight.

The tight grasp of a firm hand on her wrist alarmed her. She turned to see a beggar woman squatted against the wall, her cloak ratty, full of patches and frayed edges. Hunched as if she were old, her hand was strong and youthful. Her dark ebony skin stood out against Annika's fair complexion.

Annika yanked her arm, but the woman held tight. "Let me go."

"Be still, young one. I know of what you fear." The woman's head was half covered by a hood, but Annika could see her mouth was not moving, and yet, Annika could clearly hear her. She looked around to see if anyone else noticed, but they were all focused on the platform.

Another Talent? Was she with the man in blue? Was this the end? Annika pulled again, but the woman held tight. No, no. This was not the way she wanted to die. She wanted to go home. Damn the gift. Damn her mother for giving it to her and leaving her alone. She looked around again for her father. Where was he?

"Stop. You'll bring attention to us." The woman's voice was

strained, but her lips still did not move. Was she afraid too? Annika stilled. "You are special, young one. More powerful than you know."

"How do you trick me, old woman?" Annika asked.

"No less and no more a trick than one you could do yourself if you tried."

Fear overtook her. She would never try. Never use her gift on purpose. The smell of burning flesh was filling the square. Sweet and sickly. That could be her flesh if she used her gift. She turned side to side, looking for her father. "I know nothing of what you speak," she replied, this time in a harsh whisper. She could grab the dagger with her free hand and cut the woman to make her let go, but if she did, they might both burn.

"I knew your mother," came the reply.

Annika whipped her head around. She stared more carefully at the beggar woman's face. A shimmer changed the visage of a crone to that of a beautiful woman and back.

"The time has come," the woman said. "You need to know who you truly are."

"You've made a mistake. You think me someone else."

The woman smiled. "Annika."

She stiffened.

"If you need me, think of me. Concentrate your thoughts, and you will find me. I am Zuri."

Annika felt a tingling warmth on her forearm. She reached to touch the spot, afraid a cinder had fallen on her. The fear of burning gave her the strength to yank her arm free. She felt nothing, but even so, her skin tingled. She took a few steps toward the animal stalls, and when she glanced over her shoulder, the woman was gone. A large hand took hold of her shoulder. She shrugged it off and turned to flee.

"Annika?"

Her father.

She grabbed him in a hug. He took her hand and guided her from the square, pushing people aside like he handled the geese.

"Don't look back," he said as they hurried down the street. His unease showed on his face, the same look in his eyes as when he spoke of battle or when he knew wolves were hunting the geese. Rushing, he limped more severely. "I've got the coin from the sale."

"I'm scared, Da."

"And right to be. We'll head home now."

"After dark?"

"I can kill what's in the dark." He looked side to side, watching for threats. "I can't kill what's in this town."

Did he mean the ones who'd hunted down the girl? The girl who was no longer a girl but a burned shell of bones? She shivered. "Da, there was a beggar woman. Her name was Zuri."

He stiffened and looked behind them. "What did she say?"

"She said she knew Mother." How much could she tell him? He never wanted to talk about her gift.

He dragged her at a faster pace. She ran next to him to keep up.

"Do you know her?" she asked.

"She worked at the castle for Lord Cederic…for a time."

She stumbled on the uneven lane, but her father didn't slow his stride. "She's a—"

"I know what she is." He spat the words. "Stay clear of her. Stay away from all of them. And don't talk about it." They took a few more steps in silence before he spoke again. "I can't lose you."

Annika's arm still tingled. The burning sensation was still there. "Da, I don't want to die." Not yet. Not here. She knew nothing about the world. Nothing about herself. What was she really? A girl with visions. A Talent, hidden from the temple. She didn't even know why she was a Talent, and there was no one to ask.

He paused, placed a firm hand on her shoulder, and looked her in the eyes. "I'm here with you. Nothing will happen to you."

He couldn't always be with her. Hadn't her mother made the same promise?

"Da, where will I go when I die?"

"You'll be with your mother, m'love. I'm certain. Now come, we must go."

Annika's heart rate didn't slow until they were through the town walls and well on the way back to Marsendale. And her dread didn't subside at all.

CHAPTER TWO

The castle loomed over Evelyne like a great gaping maw of a predator, the crenellations on the wall its teeth and the keep its tongue. Once back inside the walls, the freedom she felt on her ride would dissipate like morning fog settling in the valley.

She rode up the steep, winding approach on her father's favorite destrier. He foamed at the mouth, and sweat dripped down his shoulders, chest, and withers. He was fifteen hands high, a thick, brutish horse meant to carry a knight dressed in a full coat of mail, with helm, sword, and shield. Not her—daughter of a lord, dressed in her long tunic—meant to be anything but a knight.

She could see the bars of the portcullis, barely visible in its retracted position, as she approached the main entrance through the outer wall. She couldn't recall the last time they had lowered the gates. No one had attacked this deep in the heartland of Valmora in a hundred years. Vandals, rogues, and in-fighting, yes, but a siege? Not in Evelyne's lifetime.

The guards nodded at her as she passed through the gatehouse, the horse's iron shoes clattering on the flagstones. The guards were local men, born and raised in the village or one of the dozens surrounding the castle. Rumors of Evelyne's behavior had most likely found their way to everyone who worked at the castle, including these two. She had been breaking the rules since she was a little girl. Out of her bed early. Staying out late. Running through the woods. Curiously watching the workers in the village. Being reprimanded for getting dirty, trying to fight with the boys, being too aggressive.

Those days were ending. Lately, she'd been met with harsh reprimands and was expected to behave as her position and age demanded. But her soul only soared when she was outside the castle walls, alone, free to do as she pleased. At least, it felt that way, though she knew she couldn't really do anything she wanted. She wanted to ride through these gates in her own coat of mail, carrying the king's banner. She shook her head. Maybe if she lived in one of the border states. The barbarian tribes allowed women to fight but not Valmora.

She rode to the stable, a barn set against the shadow of the outer wall. As she came to a stop, a young groom rushed from where he was cleaning a bridle and grabbed the horse's reins. Evelyne dismounted and patted the horse's neck gently as she walked beside him. The smell of hay, manure, and dust mingled with the muddy morning earth.

"Pleasant ride?" the boy asked.

"Yes. Glorious. Give him an apple when you're done."

She strolled the expansive flat ground between the inner and outer walls, watching the young squires and men-at-arms practicing the art of war, some with swords, some grappling, some on horseback. Nearby, young women fulling wool pranced to their knees in great vats of stale urine, watching the handsome young men, giggling and gossiping. When she looked at the men, she watched their movements, strategies, and expertise, but she never felt the desire to giggle. Not once.

She stopped to watch a pair of particularly skilled fighters. She would never be allowed to fight, but in her mind, she swung and ducked and pivoted along with them. Taking a ride and watching the armed practice was certainly better than listening to the drivel of her sisters in their mother's solar, where each girl took turns reading religious texts out loud while the others worked their needles. The romances, hidden in the folds of the Book of Enlightenment, appeared when her mother left the room.

Romance and religion. Both useless to Evelyne. Geography, philosophy, astronomy, mathematics, all the subjects her brothers studied, were tenfold more interesting than a love story that ended with the brave knight winning the girl. But her sisters sighed and tittered and blushed at every word of love spoken in the poetry of romance. The only time Evelyne even remotely found the stories interesting was when she imagined herself as the knight. Odd, but being a knight was all she ever seemed to dream about.

Master Berin, master of arms, stomped his way across the ground toward her, his face red as boar's blood. He carried a thin birch switch in his hand. "What have I told you about riding the warhorses?" He came to an abrupt stop next to her and slapped his free hand with the switch.

"I am to go to the chapel and pray to the Maiden for my disobedience." She'd memorized this reply long ago. They'd discussed something like this almost daily for her entire childhood.

He shook his head. "You, m'lady, will never live long enough to do penance for all your transgressions."

"You are right, Master Berin," she replied without remorse. "I will not ride the destriers again."

"Good." He pointed at the fence rail in front of her. "Place your hands."

Evelyne turned her palms up and laid them against the rail. If he didn't punish her, her father would punish him in her stead. He brought the switch down with a crack. The pain was instantaneous and sharp. The shame struck her as sharply as the stick. All the fighters and even the servants could see her punishment. Their sideways glances and smirks hurt more than the strikes.

She winced and bit her lip. "I think I'll ride a palfrey next time."

He harrumphed. A second sharp stinging slap hit her palms. Now her hands pulsed with pain, and a long red line ran across them both.

Evelyne knew he would never hurt her, even though he was a bear of a man. He spent as much of his time protecting her from herself as he did teaching combat to the men and boys. He looked like he was about to say more about riding, but a young page interrupted him.

"M'lady…your lady mother…" His sentence broke as he caught his breath from running. "Wishes you to address her…in the main entrance hall."

Evelyne nodded to Berin and the page and made her way to the keep. She trotted up the few steps and through the great oak doors that stood open in the early summer air. Lady Wilhema stood near a window, examining several bolts of cloth. The merchant beside her nodded to Evelyne.

Her mother's gown was immaculate, heavily embroidered in golds and reds. A tight cap and a veil fell above her eyes and covered her braided and pinned hair. She wore rings on four of her fingers, and a heavy gold chain hung around her neck. At the bottom of the chain hung the likeness of the Harvest Maiden in solid gold, right above her enormously pregnant belly.

Evelyne felt inadequate next to her. Where her mother was elegant and stately, even when pregnant, she felt gangly and overly tall. She was as tall as her eldest brother, Witt. A good head taller than her mother, though she felt smaller when in her presence. Only her father stood taller than her. Her mother worried her unusual height would affect her chances of finding a wealthy husband. Her stature made her something of an oddity in the noble courts. Another reason Evelyne hated when they left the manor for the royal seat in Tarburg.

Her brother Erik, whose head barely made it to her chin, made her height a target of scorn. He had taken to calling her a pox and placing the blame squarely on her unnatural desire to be a man. She knew his jealousy came from the fact that he could no longer torment her with physical threats, as she had outgrown him.

"Which do you like?" her mother asked.

Evelyne stepped closer and drew the fabric between her fingers. She turned each of them over as if examining the weave for tightness, seeing if there were pills or mistakes, all the things she knew her mother looked for. To her, they just looked like fabric. Soft and colorful, but she didn't care about the details and never had. She pointed to the crimson one. The one closest to their house colors.

Her mother thanked the merchant. She moved toward the spiral staircase in the corner. Evelyne followed. "You'll need a new wardrobe. An arrangement has been made for your future."

"An arrangement?"

Her mother took her hands. She grimaced. "What have you done this time?" her mother asked as she examined the red welts forming on her palms.

Evelyne pulled her hands away. "What arrangement?"

"Lord Tomas has approved your marriage to his son, Samuel."

Evelyne's stomach plummeted. She felt cold.

Her mother continued, "This is a great honor. Lord Tomas is one of your father's closest allies."

Evelyne knew this day would come, but she wasn't ready.

"Tomas arrived this morning." Her mother nodded to a servant sweeping and changing the rushes on the floor. "He spoke to your father, and they bound you by seal." She touched her free hand to Evelyne's cheek. "I am so happy you will have someone to take care of you."

"I can take care of myself," Evelyne muttered. She was already several harvests past marriageable age, but she'd hoped her troublesome behavior might postpone this moment.

Her mother patted her wrist, careful to avoid her hands. "You cannot stay unmarried. Unless you wish to enter the service of the temple." She eyed her, waiting for an answer.

Evelyne shook her head. "I do not." Had she been one of her brothers, the temple would offer her scholarship, libraries full of knowledge, and even the opportunity to attend a sponsored university. But she wasn't a man. She'd be tucked away in a remote temple, serving the Maiden as one of hundreds of women, singing, chanting, meditating, and working on tapestries.

Deadly boring.

"I don't believe you have the right temperament for the temple." Her mother didn't say it spitefully, more a resigned statement. Everyone knew Evelyne would be a disaster in the temple. She could barely sit through a daily reading without fidgeting, much less devote her entire life to religious texts.

She winced when her mother took her hand at the entrance to the narrow, winding stairs. Her mother huffed as she climbed, her stomach so large, Evelyne worried she'd get stuck in a turn. "Ow." Her mother placed a hand on her belly. "Your brother is a feisty one. He's ready to be in the world."

Evelyne's eyes followed her hands to the swollen belly. "How do you know it's a boy?"

"Your father wants a boy. He always wants a boy."

Once on the first floor, her mother released her throbbing hand. Evelyne opened the heavy wooden door of the sleeping chamber by its circular pull. A lady-in-waiting was seated by the hearth, though no fire burned; this summer was warm. She leapt to her feet, laying aside the clothing she was repairing, and helped Evelyne's mother to her bed. Her mother gasped.

"Are you in pain?" Evelyne asked.

"Nothing I can't bear." She shifted her weight as she lay down. "In a few years, you will have children of your own, and you'll find out how strong you are. You will bear your husband many sons, I am certain."

Evelyne frowned. "I don't want to bear children."

"You say that now, but things will change once you marry. You will have a purpose." Her eyes closed, ending the conversation.

With her mother resting, Evelyne stared at the birthing chair tucked in the corner of the room. She walked over to it and sat. The wood was hard against her backbone, and she had to spread her legs to stay seated on the flat, horseshoe-shaped surface around the edge of the hole in the center, the hole a baby would emerge through.

She lightly grasped the carved ends of the arms, careful not to aggravate the welts on her palms, and felt the smooth rolls of the lion's paws. Just beneath her fingertips were several gouges left by a previous occupant. Perhaps even her mother when she gave birth to her last child, one of several siblings who had died.

Her mother's last three children had emerged from this chair stillborn, their tiny bodies limp and lifeless. Evelyne had held the last little girl in her arms and wept with blood and humors covering her hands and arms, the sounds of her mother's wailing forever embedded in her memory.

A baby. Evelyne ran her fingers across her abdomen. What would it feel like to be with child? She saw how large her mother had become. How she waddled when she walked and struggled to sit and stand. How odd it would be to feel the child's movement inside her own body.

She leaned her head back and stared at the ceiling. She could see a spiderweb between two of the rafters. If she was in the throes of childbirth, would she notice a spiderweb? Or would she merely see a dark mass closing in on her, heavy with stone?

She ran her fingertips carelessly along the outside of the seat and caught a rough edge. She hissed in pain and raised her hand to examine the damage. A large brown splinter was stuck in the skin. Blood welled underneath, threatening to spill on her tunic.

Rather than reach for a rag, she carefully pulled her tunic up around her thighs, making a space so she could see down through the birthing hole. She held her finger over the hole, and using her other hand, squeezed.

She watched the dark red liquid pool as a drop, barely clinging to the splinter, shaking and shimmering as it got larger until it eventually fell to the stone floor beneath her. The blood spread unevenly, making an imprint with several spindly arms and smaller dots farther from the center. Evelyne squeezed again, creating another drop of blood, this one falling and making a companion spot with more spindly arms.

The tip of her finger throbbed but didn't hurt, not with the angry soreness of her palms. That would not be the case when she bore children. She'd watched enough births to know this chair could be many things, but it wasn't a healer. She ripped the splinter from her skin and allowed a few more drops of blood to mix with the others.

Blood. Pain. Death. Childbirth on this wooden chair could mean many things. Elation was not one of them for her. She felt no desire to bear children. No desire to fulfill her feminine duty. And yet, she did not want to be relegated to the temple, either. She was stuck in her role as if a stone above her had fallen and pinned her to this chair.

She grabbed the bottom edge of her tunic and pressed the cloth to her finger to stop the bleeding. She leapt from the chair and rushed from the room. No matter what her mother told her, Evelyne could not imagine herself in that chair giving birth.

CHAPTER THREE

A formal feast was called to celebrate the official betrothal and required Evelyne to be sealed in clothing, as she liked to refer to it. A servant girl, not more than fourteen, pulled the many layers of garments over Evelyne's head. Long and billowy linen undergarments with ties at the neck and wrists. A long tunic with the elongated, drooping sleeves Evelyne despised. A sleeveless overgarment dyed in red and embroidered in gold thread. A simple leather tie in her hair, which was braided in two buns on either side of her head. A long, looped belt completed the outfit. Though the servant and Evelyne's eldest sister Miriam nodded in satisfaction, Evelyne felt constrained and bound, like a package to be handed to Lord Tomas the Elder for his son.

The windows and doors of the great hall stood open, allowing warm summer breezes, heavy with the perfume of flowers, to fill the room. Long wooden tables with benches stretched from the front entry to the dais. Evelyne and her sisters made their way through the room while the lesser lords, squires, men-at-arms, and their other retinue stared at the girls.

She hated this parade. Showing the wares of the household.

"Stand straight." Miriam yanked her shoulders back. Evelyne was already uncomfortable, but now she felt her cheeks flame with embarrassment. She towered over her siblings when she stood at her full height. They filed onto the benches along the wall, and servants pushed the trestle tables closer for them and brought out platters of food and trenchers of bread.

They ate while the temple elder stood above them on the gallery overlooking the hall. He droned on with his readings through several courses. The Book of Enlightenment held many exciting tales of battles and evildoers, but the story he picked for this meal was dull and wordy and brought on slumber quickly. Evelyne willed him to finish soon.

She chewed on a bite of lamb and stared at the tapestry hanging behind the dais where her parents sat, presiding over the meal. A woven tree, the length and breadth of the wall, was filled with the names of all the lords who'd ruled Marsendale, their part of Valmora, and also their wives' names, if they were of landed title, and occasionally, an important sibling.

Gregor the pious, who was the lord and priest to King Harold the First. Edgar, lord of the treasury to King Grandon. And so on and so forth. Beside the gnarled branches, next to each lord's name, hung the fruit of knowledge. Birds with arrows in their talons flew about the treetop, and rabbits with crossbows defended the roots.

The room's decor impressed and intimidated anyone called before his lordship. But Lord Cederic didn't need a tapestry to impress. He was a giant of a man, his full brown beard filled with flecks of gray. His eyes dark and brooding. A scar cleaved his face in two, running the length of his right cheek, given to him in battle when he was young. He told the tale at every celebration, usually after several glasses of ale.

How many times had she leapt on her pony as a young girl and ridden full speed to strike a cabbage with a practice sword, intent on proving her skills to her father while he trained her brothers? Instead of the praise she sought, he'd had her removed by Berin or someone else and punished for her indiscretion, punishment that included strikes, withholding of food, and endless hours on her knees in the chapel. No matter the castigation, she kept trying, hoping one day, her father would see she could be as good as, or better than, any of the boys. She wanted his approval, but he ignored her. His only focus was on her brothers. Now she practiced in secret, if for no other reason than to save herself from the soreness of the beatings, and one day, she still hoped she could display her skills to him.

"Lady Evelyne." A young squire stood in front of her. He offered her a small, square package wrapped in cloth. "Lord Tomas hopes your marriage to his second son, Samuel, will be fruitful."

Evelyne took the package, and the boy bowed and backed away.

"What is it?" asked her sister Winifred.

Evelyne unwrapped the gift and stared at the tiny portrait of her husband-to-be. Painted like an illustration in the margins of the Book of Enlightenment, flat, indistinct, and simple. All she could tell was he had brown hair and brown eyes.

"He looks...pleasant," Winifred added, obviously no more impressed than Evelyne.

She looked across the room at her future father-in-law. He had wide-spaced eyes and a weak chin which met his throat. Half of what he ate flew out of his mouth as he spoke, and grease spots covered his linen tunic. Did the son take after the father?

Her eldest brother, Witt, sat next to Lord Tomas. Witt looked much like her father, especially around the eyes and nose. The servants all seemed to think her father was a handsome man, scar or no scar, but Evelyne suspected his position and wealth were the attraction. She returned her gaze to Lord Tomas and grimaced. No amount of coin nor daring deeds would make that man attractive in her eyes. She turned the portrait of Samuel over and laid it facedown on the table.

"You should be excited. One more harvest and we'll be celebrating your wedding," Miriam said. She held her newborn on her lap. The birth had been hard. She'd lost two unborn children before birthing this one, so her husband had agreed she should visit family and recover. As if to make everyone aware of her presence, the child vomited breast milk on Miriam's tunic.

"Here." Miriam handed the little girl to Evelyne.

Evelyne held her like a shovelful of manure, up in the air at arm's length. They eyed each other warily. The little girl looked unsettled by Evelyne's visage instead of her mother's. She didn't have a name. No use naming her yet. Chances were great of her dying before she reached one harvest. And though her mother and Miriam kept saying Evelyne would feel differently when she had a child, Evelyne stared at this little bundle and felt nothing but awkwardness.

"Maiden's eyes, Evelyne." Miriam took the child back. "You'd think she was a wild dog the way you hold her."

Evelyne shuddered. She looked at the cut on her finger from the birthing chair. Pain still pulsed through it. At least she had time to adjust to the idea of being someone's wife, but being a mother seemed to take longer. Perhaps Samuel would be a perfect husband, one who ignored her and left her to ride and explore the countryside around his home. His manor was on the eastern edge of Valmora, the farthest edge of her father's demesne, along the Dragon's Back Mountains. She'd never seen the mountains, had only read about them in the journals of masters who had traveled there. There would be no valley of wheat and barley. Sheep and goats reigned supreme in the hills around the mountains. She would have to read more on them before she wed.

She glanced at Lord Tomas again. He choked on his wine, spewing a mouthful all over the table in front of him. After which, he stood and made his way to the corner where he pissed on the floor. Evelyne sighed and went back to dining.

Winifred and Birgitta, both younger than her, tittered and giggled, heads close together as if sharing unspeakable secrets. Whatever their conversation, they both appeared flushed, as if they had run through the halls. Evelyne followed their eyeline to the young squires of Lord Tomas, several of whom were of similar age.

Evelyne's youngest sister Matilde, nine harvests old, rolled her eyes. "Oh, if only he'd look my way. What a handsome fellow," she mocked, a hand across her brow feigning a swoon. "Blech." She pretended to retch on the table. Evelyne smiled conspiratorially and reached for a handful of goose meat.

"Just you wait," replied Winifred. "Soon enough, you will see things in a much different way."

"I hope not," Matilde replied with a snort.

"Agreed." Evelyne threw one arm around Matilde's shoulders in a quick hug.

"Lady Evelyne."

She could smell the wine on Lord Tomas's breath. He swayed slightly in front of her table. He reached across and pulled her arm toward him so he could kiss her hand. The long sleeve of her dress dragged across the goose fat in front of her.

"My son will be pleased. Your mother has given Lord Cederic many strapping young men in your brothers. I expect you'll be able to do the same." He frowned slightly as if trying to focus on her. "You're a tall one, aren't you?"

Evelyne's cheeks felt flushed. Trapped behind the table, she wrenched her hand from his grip and tried not to look at his pudgy red face.

"No matter." He waved a hand. "You'll make giant lords, is all." He guffawed and choked slightly on another sip of wine. It dribbled from his lips.

He looked like a horrible troll from a fairy tale. Maiden help her. She hoped his son was nothing like him.

"Does she speak?" he yelled over his shoulder to her father. "Or is she mute? You didn't tell me she was mute."

Evelyne couldn't decide what to say to the man. Tell him he was a drunken lout or pretend she was the doting wife-to-be for his son?

"She is not mute, Lord Tomas," Winifred said. "She is overcome with joy at the news of her marriage to Samuel. So much so, she has become bashful this night."

Thank the Maiden for Winifred. Evelyne was so angry, she knew anything she said would be misunderstood. All she wanted to do was push this oaf of a man over on his ass. Tall, mute, and could birth giant children? He knew nothing about her. Why had he arranged for her to marry his son? Was she such a valuable trophy on her own that he didn't bring his son with him to meet her?

"She'll talk to you, Tomas." Her father's voice raised in the way that men who led brought attention to themselves. He directed his gaze to Evelyne. "Would you prefer I send you to the temple of the Harvest Maiden to become an innocent? I can arrange it."

Ah, the only escape and the consistent threat. The temple. She was tiring of the choice.

"As you wish, my lord." Evelyne stood and made a grandiose and overstated bow to Lord Tomas and toward her father and mother. "I look forward to our future conversations with great joy. With your leave."

With that, she pushed past Miriam and stalked down the aisle between the great hall tables, ignoring the throng around her, and marched out the main doors.

Annika took the gittern down from where it hung on the wall, careful to cover the instrument's strings so she wouldn't wake her father. The summer sun was still on the horizon, but he had collapsed in slumber after their meal. His permanent injuries drained him as he toiled at daily chores, his limp more pronounced with each passing year. She tried to take on more of the work, but he was too proud to allow it. She looked at his face, serene in slumber.

I love you, she thought, and slipped out the door.

She followed the familiar path to the small woods, nothing more than bushes and copses of young growth trees, until she came to the one old-growth tree which hadn't been felled for timber. She caressed the bark as if greeting an old friend and settled into the hollow base. The music from the gittern usually soothed her mind, but tonight, she couldn't shake the images from Byetown.

As she tuned the instrument, she remembered the look in the other girl's eyes when the townspeople had hurled insults at her. People who knew her, perhaps had known her for her entire life, had turned on her because of something she had been born with. Would the villagers here in Marsendale do the same to her if they discovered she'd hidden her gift from the temple?

Being back in Marsendale, in her small corner of a big world, she expected to feel safe, but instead, she barely slept. For several days, she dreamed of being on the dais, burning, the smell of scorched flesh as strong as the day she was in Byetown. How long would she keep this memory? She still smelled her mother on a spring day, and her mother had been dead for years.

She wished with all her heart she could confide in someone. Someone to share her secrets. Someone to share her fears. Had the girl in Byetown felt the same way? Did she tell a friend, expecting understanding and instead receiving a death sentence? A slow and painful one. The thought clung to her like a cold wet shift in the snows of winter.

And why had Zuri appeared to her after all these years since her mother's death? Even if Zuri had known her mother, Annika had no way of finding her. And even if she knew where to look, she wasn't sure her father would help her get there.

There had to be a way to contain her fear. Tomorrow, she'd go to the village chapel and pray to the Harvest Maiden. But if the Maiden truly existed, would she listen or merely hasten her demise?

She lifted the gittern and played as her mother had taught her, willing the music to still her churning mind.

CHAPTER FOUR

Evelyne dug her heels into the courser with a viciousness that betrayed her anger. The flowing tunic with its lengthy sleeves was a detriment to this ride. If she had trouble holding on with her thighs, if she lost her grip on the reins or stirrups, she might as well throw herself off at full speed.

The only sounds were the snorting breaths of the horse and his rhythmic footfalls against the packed earth. The sounds were comforting, and the farther she rode, the calmer she became. As twilight fell, she swung back toward the castle, taking a shortcut past the water mill and through the small woods at the base of the castle's hill. In the woods, the light faded to near blackness.

The horse stumbled on something, and then a thin, low-hanging branch hit her in the face, both unseen in the darkness. It would be madness to continue like this. Either she would lame the horse or kill herself. Neither seemed like it would get her closer to what she wanted. Did she know what she wanted? She had no interest in marrying Samuel or having children. She wanted to fight, to ride, to feel the pride her brothers felt every time they rode through villages in their colors.

She pulled hard on the reins and brought the courser to a stop. Though not as large as the destrier, the hot-blooded warhorse wasn't meant for long, fast rides. She'd pay dearly when her father discovered she'd taken another expensive horse out for a night ride. Despite whether her father would be proud, she was proud of her skill to control the horse. She patted his shoulder as she walked beside him.

A gentle breeze carried the soft strains of music. Beautiful tones, something like a lute but different. Evelyne tied the destrier's reins to a nearby tree and tentatively walked into the woods, following the sound. She lost her footing and caught her dress in the tangle of undergrowth but pushed forward, intent on discovering the source of the alluring music.

The twilight played tricks on her eyes. Trees looked like giants and ruffians, devils, and other scary characters from fairy tales. The music became louder as she approached a giant oak tree as big around as an oxcart. Evelyne didn't believe in fairies, but what could make a tree play music? And such wondrous music. The evening's discomfort almost forgotten, she touched the tree bark and slowly walked around the girth until she saw the hollow in the center and a person inside it.

Evelyne could barely see the girl, no older than herself, dressed in a simple shift over leggings, holding a stringed instrument Evelyne had never seen before. She listened to the music for a few moments, appreciating the ethereal quality of the tune, drawn by its somewhat melancholy phrasing. The song ended abruptly. The girl in the tree gasped, no doubt finally noticing Evelyne. She dropped the instrument and reached for something on her belt.

"Maiden's blessing to you." Evelyne held her empty hands out in front of herself.

"Oh. You scared me, m'lady." The girl's voice was as melodic as the instrument she played. Soft and warm and somehow soothing. She brushed off her tunic as she stood. "Maiden's blessing. How may I serve you?"

"You know who I am?"

The girl nodded. "Yes, m'lady. You're a lady of the manor."

"May I ask who you are?" Evelyne swept some loose hair from her eyes. "I was beginning to believe in wood fairies for a few moments. I thought one was drawing me to my end."

"Annika. I tend your fowl, m'lady."

"I did not know I was so foul as to need tending." Evelyne chuckled but heard only silence from Annika. "A play on words. Fowl with a W is a bird. Foul with a U is to be noxious and unpleasant."

Annika nodded again. Evelyne realized her joke was not received as intended. She placed her hands on her hips as she had seen her father do many times when he spoke with the people of their demesne.

She tried to bring confidence and sincerity to her words. "You make the birds plump for our dinner table. They have been quite spectacular this season." Yes, that would be something her father would say.

"Thank you, m'lady, but it's my father who keeps the fowl. I am only his vassal." Annika kept her head in a lowered position.

"Well, your father has taught you well indeed." Evelyne tried to reassure with her words. "Brave of you to be out in the dark alone. Won't your father worry?"

"He's taught me to protect myself from wolves and such."

Evelyne noticed her touch her belt again as she spoke. This time, Evelyne saw the knife hanging there. Maybe coming upon people in the woods at twilight wasn't the smartest thing she had done of recent. Had Annika not recognized her, she might have been stabbed.

Evelyne placed a hand on her side and looked down, wondering what the strike of the blade would have felt like. "I was thinking of men, not wolves," she replied. Her brothers were as dangerous as any wolf to a servant girl.

"Bandits would never come this close to the castle," Annika said incredulously. "At least, I don't think they would."

Evelyne laughed. "No, they wouldn't dare. My father would have none of that." She shivered, thinking of the arms and legs hanging from the gates of Tarburg. Best not mention those.

Annika fidgeted with the length of her belt and looked about the woods but not at Evelyne. She wasn't surprised. Her presence made people nervous. No one dared talk to her or treat her like a peer unless they were a peer, which was limited to nobility and royalty.

She fidgeted too. She wasn't sure why she was nervous. She tried to remember if she had seen Annika's face in passing. At night, the forest washed all the color from the world, cloaking her features in shadow. Only the outline of a long thick braid to the side of her head was clear. She was thin, like most of the peasants and servants, and she was several inches shorter than Evelyne, but she was tall for a girl, and Evelyne felt a kindred spirit in her.

"Aren't...aren't you afraid?" Annika asked.

Was she afraid? She didn't feel like it. Maybe she should have been. Not everyone liked her father. A rival lord, a money deal gone bad, a tenant farmer who lost his lease, there could be so many people who could use her as profit.

"I'll tell you a secret." Evelyne leaned closer. Was she going to do this? Tell a total stranger. "I know how to fight a little myself."

Saying it out loud was satisfying. She might not be as practiced as her brothers or the other squires and knights, but she had trained in secret for many years. Watching the others fight, carefully memorizing moves and strategies. Someday, she hoped to prove to her father that she was as ready to wear the house colors and play a part in the long tradition of her house to defend the realm.

Annika interrupted her thoughts. "I should get home before my father worries." She picked her instrument off the ground and brushed it gently.

"Where do you live?"

"Pardon, m'lady?"

"Do you live nearby?"

"Yes, m'lady." Annika pointed. "We live a little before the village, next to the lake."

"Why not in the village?"

"You've not been around geese much, have you?" Annika asked, her voice slightly amused.

"In actuality...I have not," Evelyne admitted.

"Any little thing will send them honking. Every trip to empty a chamber pot would wake the entire village."

Evelyne chuckled at the thought of her mother being chased by a goose on her way to the garderobe. "Would you be averse to showing me your home?"

"Be *what*?"

"Would you be so kind as to invite me to your home?"

"Um...my father would be honored, m'lady." Annika's voice trembled slightly. She said honored, but she hesitated.

Evelyne realized with unease that Annika couldn't refuse her request. "I know it is a strange question, but I would like to see the instrument you carry in firelight rather than this dimness." Speaking to anyone about anything other than marriage and babies seemed like a wonderful distraction, and the last thing she wanted was to return to the great hall and confront Samuel's drunken father once again.

Annika visibly relaxed. "It is a gittern, m'lady." She held it reverently, the same way Miriam held her child. "It belonged to my mother. She died when I was young."

Several questions came to mind in rapid succession. What had caused her death? When did she die? How did it feel? In the end, she chose one that felt less intimate. "How did she come by such a fine instrument?"

"She was not from here."

"Was she from Tarburg?"

"She was from the north." The answer was vague. Perhaps Annika didn't know the name of her mother's village. She'd said her mother had died when she was young.

Evelyne retraced her steps to retrieve her courser and walked beside him with her hands around the reins below his chin. Annika led the way back toward the mill, and within a few minutes, they were on the well-groomed path between the mill and the village.

"We don't have much to offer you, m'lady. Unless you like mead."

"Please, call me Evelyne." Now that they had emerged from the small woods, the sky was brighter, though the sun was below the horizon. She could see Annika look over her shoulder but couldn't clearly see her features.

"The cottage is not a fit place for someone like you." She gestured to Evelyne's gown. "You might ruin your fine garment."

Evelyne looked at her own silk tunic, the belt links of gold. Was Annika embarrassed about her home, or was she more concerned about Evelyne's garb? "Damn the gown." She lifted the hem and dropped it again with aggravation. "If I should never wear another one, I would be happier than you would ever know."

Annika giggled. Still mostly in darkness, Evelyne couldn't get a good look at her, but she saw the outline of the instrument she carried. A stringed instrument with a straight neck rather than the bent one of a lute.

"How did your mother arrive in the village?"

"My father met her while he was fighting for your father...I mean, Lord Cederic."

This subject piqued her interest. "Did he fight in a war or local skirmishes?"

"He fought in a war near my mother's village."

"A northern campaign?" Evelyne's heart rate increased. This was exciting news indeed. She was incessantly curious about war, but Berin and Master Jacob never had time to answer her questions.

"Yes m'la...yes. He's a foot soldier, a pikeman. But he can fight with sword, ax, and knives as well." Evelyne could hear the pride in her voice. Annika's pace quickened, and they turned off the main path and along a smaller offshoot, almost invisible in the darkness. Evelyne paused and tied her horse to a nearby tree before following Annika down the path. The trail sloped downward and flattened out near the dim outline of a single-story building.

Drawing closer, Evelyne could see silhouettes of rough fencing, a low-slung lean-to, and wattle mounds for keeping birds and a building she assumed was their home. She also heard the slow burbling of the river in the distance and the rustling of what must have been hundreds of birds nearby.

For the sheer number of bird noises, the smell wasn't overwhelming. Just a musty odor with a whiff of something tangy. Annika opened the door to the home, silhouetting her against the light from a central firepit. Why had Evelyne never noticed this place or Annika before?

A mounted man shouting, "Evelyne!" rode into view on the higher path while carrying a flaming torch. She sighed and watched Annika pause and turn, giving Evelyne a glimpse of her face before the door shut.

Evelyne turned to the man on the path. Timothy. She was glad it was him and not the constable. "I'm here," she called. A cacophony of honking erupted beside her.

The geese.

"Maiden's eyes! What noise." Timothy leapt from his horse and came toward her. "I saw you leave. I was worried about you."

She smiled. His father had sent Timothy to their manor when he was six years old to be a page. Now a squire awaiting his turn in combat, hoping for knighthood someday. They had become close over the years. He was dearer to her than her own brothers. And he kept her confidences in all things. "I'm fine, Timothy. I merely wanted to take a ride."

"In the dark?" He looked at the horses. "A courser, Evelyne? That horse could have killed you."

She sighed heavily. "Of course, I can't ride a horse on my own."

"You know I wouldn't imply such a thing."

"It wasn't dark when I left. I wished to take a ride and reflect on my newfound destiny."

He nodded. "I've been expecting your betrothal for a while." He glanced at her and at his boots. "You will make someone a wonderful wife."

"Besides…" She pivoted the uncomfortable conversation. "Can I not ride on my own land?"

"Not at night without a torch or lantern. Not without an escort," he replied in a pleading, loud tone.

Was he implying an unsuspecting peasant girl might stab her or that rumor could besmirch her reputation? "I had an escort." She turned to the cottage doorway, but the door was shut. Dim light showed through a cloth hung in a small window opening. Annika was gone for now.

"The horse or the birds?" Timothy remarked, looking at the honking mass of geese.

"Yes. The geese," Evelyne replied sullenly.

"Let's get back to the castle before you are missed."

He assisted her onto his palfrey, and he mounted the courser. She had no choice. If she argued, he would have an answer. One that would make sense about proper appearances.

Evelyne stared back at the retreating cottage and the din of honking. She'd return. If not tomorrow, then someday soon. She wanted to see Annika's face. She did not know why it was important to her. She felt a longing she couldn't place or define. Like why she enjoyed riding. She just did.

Chapter Five

Annika tried to focus on her tasks. She shook out the straw mattress and laid it in the sunshine. The cottage was small, but she kept it as clean as she could. She still needed to milk the cow, and she needed to get rennet from a slaughtered calf so she could make cheese. Once the village calves were weaned, cheese would have to wait until next season. It added a treat to their daily bread and mead. She never wanted for more, but every now and again, when she saw the tarts displayed in the kitchen at the castle, her mouth watered.

Her father worked the bird pens, pushing them around, searching for something. He leaned down, grabbed a swan, and carried the bird to a smaller pen. He waded back into the flock, looking for another bird. They had not spoken about the other night. Annika had stopped him from taking his pike and skewering Lady Evelyne by accident after the geese had woken him. His answer? She was never again to go into the woods alone at night. No more.

Lady Evelyne had frightened her. Not because she had arrived unexpectedly in the one place Annika usually felt safe but because she was a noble. And as nobility, Evelyne would surely be in league with the temple when it came to a rogue Talent. Wouldn't she?

Annika was confused. She was afraid of Evelyne, but Evelyne was warm and kind. Not dismissive of her or ignoring her as others might.

A man on the path caught her eye. Her heart rate soared, and she froze. But it was only a carpenter on his way to the mill. She let out a long breath. She'd felt like this since they'd returned from Byetown. Every new person, each unexpected movement, and her body became overwhelmed with fright.

"You all right?" Her father must have noticed her unease.

She nodded.

He was a good man, her father. Protective. Loving. But in a way, he was like the nobles, only ignoring her gift rather than her person. He didn't talk about it. He pretended she was normal, like all the other village girls, but they both knew she wasn't. She had visions. She'd always had them. For as long as she could remember.

Sight was an unusual gift. Usually, Talents were healers, at least all the ones she'd encountered. She'd had the waking dreams since she could talk. She could see where a lost bird was hiding. She could find wild berries by the road to collect. Sometimes, she could see people arriving in the valley and other times, someone's death in the night. She dreaded those visions the most. The sorrow. The crying.

Her mother had been the first to tell her she was a Talent. She'd held her hand as they'd walked along the banks of the river and had explained how Annika was special, that she had a gift from the gods, and one day, she would know why she'd been blessed.

Not long after that, her parents had argued in harsh whispers. Annika knew they had been talking about her, but she didn't ask questions. She'd learned to stay quiet, especially around the village children. They didn't know she was a Talent, but they knew she was different, and they clustered around her, teasing and tormenting her. So she stayed away from them.

After her mother died and she was old enough to understand the rules of the temple, she'd realized she was a rogue Talent. She should have been given over to serve. Why they had kept her home, she didn't know. And now, more than ever, she wanted to understand, especially after she'd seen what they did to rogues instead of only hearing about it through village gossip and temple sermons.

"Da. What about the girl?" Annika called but kept her eyes on her work, scrubbing a water bucket with salt.

"The girl?" he called back.

"The one in Byetown." She had wanted to ask him for days, but each time, she'd thought she was brave enough, she'd waited. The fear was burning her from the inside, much like the fire had burned the girl from the outside. What an awful way to die. Slowly, painfully. She felt sick to her stomach every time she remembered it. "Will her hunters come for me too?" Her voice trembled. It was out.

Her father grabbed a swan more violently than necessary. He moved through the gate and placed the bird in the smaller pen before limping to where she stood. She rose at his approach, threw the cloth in the salt bowl, and wiped the excess on her apron.

He shook his head. "There's no reason to worry." He lifted several wooden tools and moved them under an overhang. "That girl must have told someone."

She imagined being close enough to someone to tell them. Her mother had tried to help Annika make friends, but it was difficult. Her fear of them finding out she was a Talent and their fear of her mother, the Weyan woman, got in the way.

"Why didn't they take her to the temple? Why...burn her?" She shut her eyes tight. Saying the words brought memories of the smell and taste of burning flesh. She reached for her belt and worried the fabric.

"I don't know, Annika."

She felt his hand on her shoulder and opened her eyes.

"Put the event out of your mind. Nothing anyone can do for that girl now. 'Cept pray for her soul."

Who should she pray to? If the gods required that rogue Talents burn, should she pray to the Maiden to protect her in the afterlife? But if that girl was in the place of nothingness and the Maiden refused her spirit, to whom should Annika pray? Her mother had never believed in the unending nothingness. She'd believed they were part of the life force which created everything, and when they died, no matter the circumstances, they returned to the earth to become one with everything.

"But what if they come for me?" Her heartbeat rose again. Now that she had spoken the words out loud, she couldn't take them back.

"No one is coming for you. No one knows but you and me."

"What about the man who...ordered her set alight?" Her voice rose with the panic building in her core. Saying the words made her nauseated. She shivered, her mind reliving the vision of the girl in the village as the executioner extended the torch and set her on fire. "He was a Talent. I could see him...see his power surrounding him. What if he saw me too?"

Her father grabbed her more firmly and leaned closer. "Listen to me, Annika. He's not coming for you. He's the king's Paladin. A fightin' man. He fights for the temple. He won't bother with the likes of us. A cripple and a peasant girl."

She hung her head at the description. Two nobodies at the bottom of society. Was that what Lady Evelyne saw? What did it matter? It wasn't like they would be friends. As if he could hear her thoughts, her father met her eyes.

"You need to stay away from the noblewoman." He released his grip and strode back to the bird pens.

"I couldn't tell her no, Da." She couldn't tell him she wanted Evelyne to come back. Confusing as it all was. She'd seemed different somehow.

"Stay away. She'll forget soon enough." He stooped and gathered some twine and ran it around a loose part of the wattle fence. "We don't want attention. Do our work. They leave us alone."

"What about the beggar woman, Zuri? She was a Talent too. She said she knew mother. Why wasn't she—"

"Enough!" He rarely raised his voice to her.

She bit her lip to stay quiet. She always did everything he told her to without complaint, even if she protested in her head. Right now, she wanted to ask so many things.

"Forget about Zuri. Forget the Paladin. Forget it all," he yelled.

A few moments passed. She didn't dare say anything else. Maybe he was as scared as she was, but she would have to wait for a better time to question him. How could she forget any of it? A girl burning to death in front of her. A girl like her. A man ready to kill her slowly for the sake of the temple and a strange woman who said she knew her mother. She wanted to yell at her father and tell him it was too much to ask. She balled her hands into fists instead.

"Take these swans to the kitchens." He pointed at the birds in the smaller pen.

She nodded.

"Annika."

She turned to face him.

"Stay away from them nobles." He grabbed a stick near the fence line and opened the gate to the larger pen. He drove some of the younger geese out. They waddled at an unseemly, awkward gait as he drove them toward the fallow common fields.

Annika stepped into the small pen with the swans chosen to be part of tonight's meal at the great hall. When she was younger, she'd named birds, a habit she'd stopped when each Mary, Sally, and Ugg met his or her end. As she moved around them, the swans took no notice. They were used to her and probably sensed nothing out of the ordinary. They shuffled about and picked at chaff on the ground. She approached the first one carefully. They hated their beautifully curved necks to be touched and would bite or flap if she did this wrong.

She grabbed over the back of the head where the head met the neck. The feathers were soft while the shafts were stiff, and she could feel the bird's muscles underneath. She wrapped her other hand around the neck and cocked the head sharply to the side while lifting the neck straight up. The weight of the bird snapped the neck cleanly, and it collapsed in a limp pile.

She stared at the bird's warm, dead body. Death was all around her. The sweating sickness that had struck the village last winter, the waterwheel that had crushed the miller's son, untold stillbirths, and the men who'd never came back from the king's service. The Maiden had a plan, the temple elders proclaimed. Her mother had told her the gods were fickle creatures who ended lives for spite. She gazed at the swan, beautiful even in death. She turned her hands over and stared at her palms and fingers. They'd killed the bird. She'd killed the bird. And she felt the hot tears flow down her cheeks.

The other swans continued to walk about, unaware of the demise of their companion. Annika broke their necks quickly, crying the entire time.

Once they all lay still and unmoving, she wiped her cheeks with her sleeves. She tied the birds by their feet with a thin hemp rope, hung them over her neck, and started her walk to the castle on the hill.

CHAPTER SIX

S mack.

Evelyne dropped the wooden practice sword in the dirt. The stinging on the back of her hand matched the welt on her palm she'd gotten from Master Berin a few days ago. She bent and retrieved the sword.

Timothy gave her a sheepish look and a small shrug. She pulled her courage together and took a stance, putting the sword in front of her. "Are you ready to be finished now?" he asked. "Sixth time you've tried and been unsuccessful."

A touch of anger rose in her. "You try this in a lady's tunic and see how well you do." She pulled the fabric off the ground to prove her point.

Dodd, one of her father's guards, snickered. He sat on a barrel nearby, keeping watch. Evelyne paid him plenty of coin to do it.

They had picked this spot to practice because it sat between the closed end of the stable and the servants' gate on the outer wall. A row of wagons sat in stages of repair, along with a pile of wagon wheels, axles, and tools. When they fought behind the wagons, the only way to be seen was from above on the wall, and since no one regularly paced the walls, the location was as good as being in the woods.

"A right Queen Neera she wants to be." Dodd paused in cutting his nails with his knife to comment. His lisp was more pronounced with all his front teeth missing. He looked simpleminded, but he wasn't. He was one of the best of her father's guards and a brutal fighter.

"What would you know about Queen Neera, Dodd?" Timothy spoke to him with something different in his voice from how he spoke to Evelyne. As the son of a lord, Timothy ranked higher than Dodd, even though Timothy was no older than Evelyne. Nonetheless, he was the son of a minor lord, nobility.

"I listen to your lessons with Master Jacob." Dodd knelt in the dirt. He started drawing lines across from each other. "Placed her forces here in a narrow pass and forced her foes to attack four abreast. Defeated a horde thrice as large as hers." He dreamily looked at the drawing. "I'd like to have been there."

The idea of Queen Neera leading men into battle mesmerized Evelyne. She stared at the lines in the dirt, trying to imagine the encounter. Battle raging, men fighting, the eventual surrender, Neera's satisfaction.

Timothy's shoe swept the drawing away. "Queen Neera had competent advisors and experienced leaders at her side."

Evelyne respected him, but sometimes, she wished he understood her better. If he did, he would never discount the ability of a woman fighter. "Do you not believe she could recognize and plan something herself? Maybe she was familiar with the terrain the way I am with our manor."

"No offense to you, Evelyne," Timothy began, "but women are not known for strategy. Certainly not in the art of war."

"Neither are you," Dodd replied with a smirk.

"Someday, I'll be lord of a manor," Timothy replied coolly.

Evelyne smiled at her conspirator in Dodd. Neither of them was in the same social hierarchy as Timothy.

"Mayhap, it is time to quit playing at fighting, Evelyne." Timothy didn't look her in the eye when he spoke.

Quit fighting? They had sparred since he'd arrived. He'd been eager to help her as a child. He knew how much these sessions meant to her. She loved it. She felt alive when they fought. All the aggravation of her day was released as soon as she blocked or parried or thrust or grabbed at him.

He seemed to notice her disappointment. "I only say this because it's unseemly for a lady to act like a man. Besides, you will be busy in the coming months with wedding plans and whatever lessons you must take part in to ready you for your responsibilities."

"Like how to play with Simon's yard," Dodd added with a chuckle. Timothy smacked him on the side of the head. His eyes burned hot, but he didn't move. He could crush Timothy without effort. "Beggin' your pardon, m'lady." Dodd lowered his head in her direction.

Evelyne heard plenty of talk of yards around her brother, Witt, and his cohorts. She wasn't offended, but she knew she should act offended for Timothy's sake. He was defending her honor. She didn't want to think about Simon's *yard* or any other part of him just yet. "Again," she called and took her stance.

Two strikes and she was looking at the sky. She groaned as she sat up.

Timothy walked backward, swinging his sword loosely in his hand. "Are we done now?"

Evelyne shook her head. She rose and brushed the dust from her backside. The move shouldn't be this hard. She'd watched Dodd do it a hundred times. Yet every time she tried to fend off Timothy with the same moves she'd seen Dodd use, she was unsuccessful.

"Again." She stared Timothy down and readied herself.

He drew his lips in a thin line. "We're done for now, Evelyne. Your hand is bruising."

She glanced at her sword hand. A purple bruise filled it from side to side. "No worse than others. Come now. I'm certain I will succeed this time."

He shrugged and made his approach. Evelyne blocked his strike with her forearm to his, stepped in close, and grasped his sword arm under her arm. She held his bicep tightly against her chest so he couldn't strike again. His expression slackened and...was he staring at her breasts? She took advantage of the moment, sliding her sword against his side to indicate running him through. When she released his arm, he pulled away as if it had hurt him. He rubbed the spot where Evelyne's breast had touched him and paced.

Something had been different between them since the announcement of her betrothal. He was moody and darker. His sense of humor lacking. Now he even wanted her to quit sparing. Whatever was wrong with him, she wished he'd return to his normal self.

"Someone's coming," Dodd warned.

Evelyne threw her practice sword to Timothy, and they both huddled close to the wagon nearest them.

Evelyne felt her heartbeat in her ears. She was nervous every time Dodd noticed someone nearby. The last time they'd found her fighting, not only had Timothy been punished, but she had been thrashed and confined to the castle. The thrashing she could live with, but the limiting of her freedom had crippled her. To hunt, to ride, to be outside the walls was how she kept herself from drowning in darkness. She understood her role as a woman, but when she felt the weight of it, her mood soured, her anger simmered, and she paced like a caged animal.

"The goose girl."

Timothy visibly relaxed and let out a loud sigh. But Dodd's comment didn't slow Evelyne's heartbeat. Her hand trembled slightly. She peered around the wagon bed, pressing her cheek close to the wood, so close she could smell the tar sealing the planks.

There she was, a young woman in a simple brown tunic, a blond braid on her shoulder, carrying several limp swans toward the kitchens. The shape of her body, the sway of her hips; Evelyne was certain she was the young woman from the other night. This was her chance. She pulled a small coin from her purse and handed it to Dodd. He hopped from the barrel, smiled in his toothless way, and left.

She hurried in the castle's direction and spoke over her shoulder to Timothy as she walked. "I am indebted to you."

He opened his mouth to speak and grumbled, "Yes, yes."

Evelyne slipped through the inner gate, past the well, through the small apple orchard and the kitchen garden where wattle fences—to keep out unwanted animals—bordered the path.

Annika moved at a brisk pace, but she walked outside the gardens, whereas Evelyne walked inside on a parallel path, trying to glimpse her face. She knew what Annika sounded like, but had yet to see more than her back and her straw-colored braid.

When Annika disappeared through the kitchen doorway, Evelyne stopped at the fence edge, staring at the dark entrance. She placed herself behind a piece of crumbling stone wall, a leftover from when the inner walls had been the outer walls. So many versions of the castle had sat atop this hill, so it wasn't unusual to find steps to nowhere and piles of ancient rubble to hide in. She crouched and waited.

An eternity passed before Annika reappeared and walked back the way she had come, no longer encumbered by the birds. From this distance, it was hard to see much more than a general outline of her face and nose. Evelyne followed again at a crouching walk, still inside the garden. She was close enough to hear Annika humming a familiar tune, the one from the woods the night they had met.

Evelyne's legs began cramping. She was the daughter of the manor lord. She didn't need to skulk in the bushes. If she wanted to talk to Annika, to see her face, all she need do was stand and call out.

Instead, Evelyne gathered the lower part of her tunic, raising it to a scandalous height, took a running start, and leapt the wattle fence.

When she thought she had cleared it, she felt her foot catch on the top, breaking several of the branches, and she sprawled on the ground on her face. The fall knocked the breath from her, and she let out a loud "oof." Embarrassment seeped through her.

"Are you all right, m'lady?" a melodious voice above her asked.

Evelyne pulled herself to a seated position and brushed the dust from her dress. When she felt more presentable, she met Annika's gaze.

Annika bowed slightly. She looked at Evelyne directly before demurring her gaze once again to the ground, but not before Evelyne had seen her eyes. The color of ice on the lake in winter or the blue of a pale sapphire. Warmth filled the pit of her stomach, her breath shortened, and she felt shaky. Annika's plain clothing did nothing to hide the foreign beauty of her pale skin and blond hair. Not the dark hair and dark complexion of Evelyne's family. Evelyne felt certain this was what it was like to look upon the harvest goddess herself. What the poets wrote about, the spiritual epiphany. The overwhelming beauty of the arts. The feeling the sculptors claimed they felt as they created the statues of the goddess and her many siblings.

"Is there something I can do for you?" Annika inquired curiously and with growing concern. She glanced at Evelyne while keeping her head bowed.

Evelyne shook her head and scrambled to her feet. "No, no. I'm fine." She looked back at the now damaged fence. "I was eager to speak to you, and I took a shortcut."

Why had she admitted that?

She gathered a few of the longer sticks and tried to press them back into the cradle of the fence posts. Some stayed, but most were now too short and fell to the ground.

"I'll fix it, m'lady." Annika headed to the orchard gate.

Evelyne shoved another piece in place and rushed after her. "It was my fault. I should fix it myself."

Annika gave her a startled look over one shoulder. "Repairing the fence is not something you should do, m'lady. I'll take care of it."

Even Annika knew what she was supposed to do and not do. The rules were clearly communicated at all levels. Evelyne drew alongside her but a step behind, near enough to watch her gait and look at her gently swaying hair. At the first tree, Annika picked the branches closest to dead or those needing pruning and broke them at the base nearest the main branch. She chose several long pieces, not too thick.

Evelyne watched her hands while she worked. Her fingers were long and slender, and they would be delicate if she was noble.

"Let me carry those." Evelyne reached for the growing stack, gently brushing Annika's stomach as she did. Her hands tingled where they had touched her.

Annika stepped back. "The branches might tear your dress."

"I've torn it before." Evelyne smiled.

They returned to the fence, and Annika began the repairs. After all the excitement of catching her, Evelyne couldn't think of anything to say. She kept thinking of the look of Annika's eyes. Annika expertly weaved the branches in the cradle.

"You are good at this," Evelyne finally uttered. She rolled her eyes. Of course Annika knew what she was doing. She worked every day, unlike Evelyne, who sat stitching embroidery and poorly at that.

"Thank you, m'lady," Annika acknowledged and continued to make quick work of the fence repair.

Seen but not heard, Evelyne thought to herself. The mantra of all the serving folk at the manor. Seen as little as possible and heard even less. Though her father and the other lords might encourage this behavior, Evelyne wished Annika would talk more without prompting.

"Have we met before?" Evelyne asked. "I mean, before the other night."

Annika answered without looking up. "Yes, m'lady."

"Do you remember when? I seem to have forgotten."

"You stole some tarts and knocked me over outside the kitchen." She pushed on the fence, checking if it would hold.

"I think I remember that. Nan chased me with a wooden spoon. Although Nan chases me with that spoon a lot. Not so much now that she's getting older."

Evelyne could see Annika's lips curve into a small smile.

"Did Nan ever chase you with a kitchen implement?" Evelyne inquired.

"Implement? A spoon? No, m'lady." Annika replied, the smile now firmly in place. "There. All fixed." Annika nodded and looked pleased with her handiwork. Evelyne pretended to examine it and nodded her approval, though she didn't know if the fence repair was done right or not.

"And we never met other than that?" Evelyne knew her line of inquiry was redundant, but she truly felt as if they had known each other longer. Or perhaps, she only wished so.

"I see you often, m'lady. At the harvest celebrations and when your father calls the villagers for a public spectacle."

"By public spectacle, you mean punishment." Evelyne shivered at the thought. She hated them but wasn't sure what could replace them. Sometimes, people did horrible things.

"I don't watch, but we are all required to attend." Annika kept her gaze downward as she spoke. "I also see you when you are riding."

"I've noticed the geese in the fields sometimes. I'm sorry I never stopped to notice you." Once Evelyne uttered the words, she felt the heat of a blush. Her mother told her never to apologize to her people, especially the servants.

"You have no reason to notice me, m'lady."

"Evelyne. My name is Evelyne."

Annika nodded.

"Do the birds get loose often?" Evelyne inquired, trying to extend their time together.

"Not often. The fencing keeps out the foxes more than it keeps in the birds."

"Ah, like the manor walls resist invaders but rarely confine me," Evelyne replied thoughtfully.

"Your chemise." Annika pointed to her blouse.

Evelyne's cuff had come undone, the strings hanging down. Annika reached out and took them in hand. As she laced, Evelyne was aware of how close they stood. She stared at Annika's long neck, her delicate ear. The tiny wisps of hair on her neckline blowing in the breeze. She didn't pay this much attention to the girls who dressed her in the morning. Annika was different. More interesting.

When she finished, Annika smiled in a self-satisfied way.

Evelyne watched her brush a stray strand of hair behind one ear. Impulsively, she reached out and grabbed the hand. Her fingers tingled where they touched Annika's, and a rush of heat filled her. Annika's hands were rough but not unpleasantly so. Wouldn't the Harvest Maiden herself have worked the fields and had these same powerful hands? Annika turned her gaze upward. Those ice-blue eyes. Somehow hypnotic. Evelyne froze in her gaze. Annika's face…was concerned? Uncomfortable? She felt like her own face mirrored the same confusion. What was she feeling?

"Thank you."

A blush crept across Annika's cheeks.

Evelyne reluctantly and slowly released her grip on their hands.

"Making friends of the serving wenches now?" her eldest brother Witt called from behind her, startling her. He moved between them and grabbed Annika's face by the chin, pulling her head upward to look at her. "This one is quite pretty."

Evelyne felt her anger building. How dare he touch her?

"Maybe I'll have her attend me in my chambers one night."

Evelyne knocked his hand away. "She's not a plaything. She tends the fowl." She kept her eyes on Witt but directed her next statement to Annika. "Thank you for your help with the fence. You can go."

She heard footfalls move away. She didn't look back to see if Annika felt the dismissal as harshly as it sounded.

"Doesn't matter what she does on the manor. As lord heir, I can have anything I want." Witt leered, elbowing Daniel, the son of a minor lord who served as his page.

"Don't touch her," Evelyne replied angrily, pushing her open hand against his upper chest. His raised eyebrow came as a warning. She was overstepping her boundaries. They weren't children anymore. She changed her tactic. "Father would love to hear that you've sired a bastard at the manor."

"It wouldn't be the first," Witt replied dryly. The young men with him laughed.

Frustrated by the response, she felt the urge to stomp her foot and plead with him, but pleading would make him more interested in Annika to spite her.

"I heard her betrothed is a man-at-arms." Timothy stood behind them, leaning on a longsword. "A brutal one. He might pay the death price if someone despoiled his betrothed."

Witt looked less interested after hearing that. "Ah, a brute for a wench. Here's hoping she gets what's coming to her." He smiled and slapped Daniel's shoulder. Daniel smiled as if Witt had let him in on a secret only the two of them were privy to.

The young men, except for Timothy, walked away, heading for the practice fields. Evelyne's shoulders relaxed. She was ready to fight her own brother to protect Annika. She looked through the inner gate, but Annika was no longer in view.

"Is she betrothed to a man-at-arms?" she asked Timothy.

"I don't know who she is, Evelyne," he replied. "I saw your tension and heard Witt's coarse language."

Relief set upon her. She grasped his upper arm. "Thank you, Timothy. You are a good man."

"If only you could see the truth." He twirled his heavy sword, this one steel, not wooden, laid it on his shoulder, and followed Witt and the others to the practice field.

Evelyne watched them walk away, then looked to the servants' gate. If she could split herself in two, she'd go in both directions at once, but neither path was truly open to her.

CHAPTER SEVEN

Evelyne knelt beneath the half dozen tall, narrow windows of colored leaded glass on the southern-facing side of the manor's chapel, each panel depicting a different story in the Enlightened Book. Green, red, and brown sunlight fell on the floor and across the stone columns. The flame of the central fire flickered and danced across the cornucopia at the feet of the twenty-foot-tall statue of the Maiden. Fruits, vegetables, and a dead chicken spilled out, all placed to pray for something: rain, crops, weather, health. Love.

Evelyne's gaze traveled up the statue. Her breasts were full. In one hand, she held the scythe. In the other, sheaves of wheat. Tight braids coiled around her head, and when Evelyne gazed at the face, something about the tilt of the chin and the slight smile made her think of Annika.

What was this feeling? Evelyne couldn't stop thinking about her. She could still sense Annika's hand in hers. She rubbed her fingertips at the memory.

The head priest stood in a pulpit overlooking the congregation. The passage he read was familiar and boring, about the objectives of grace and goodwill, told in a parable. He spoke in traditional High Valmoran. Evelyne understood most of it, but she much preferred the common tongue, and her thoughts drifted away from the lessons. Her family knelt in a semicircle around the central fire, her mother and sisters to the left and the men of the family on the right.

She wiped her eyes. They burned from the smoke of the fires. Then she shifted, her knees uncomfortable on the stone floor, and bunched the skirt of her tunic under her as padding. She glanced at her mother. She hadn't moved at all since they'd arrived, and Evelyne wondered if she'd surreptitiously sewed stuffing into her shift for kneeling. How did she possibly stay so still, as pregnant as she was?

Evelyne looked at her father, brothers, and her father's men-at-arms, all dressed in their surcoats with bold patterns of red and gold. The uniform of comradery, marking them as special. Special for their prowess and fighting skills. She glanced at her solid yellow tunic and felt a rush of jealousy. She wanted to wear the same tunic as them. She wanted to feel a part of something bigger than herself. To protect and defend the realm. The pride she would feel if she put on the colors of the manor or Maiden bless her, the king's colors.

She pulled her shoulders back and lifted her head. Dodd's tale of Queen Neera meant that in the past, a woman had led an army. Maybe she could be a part of something too someday. Strength. Duty. Honor.

"And the Maiden gave us the first of many harvests..." The priest's voice drew her back to him. His vestments and the robes of the innocents were uniforms of their commitment to the temple, but nothing about the religious symbolism tugged at her as the colors of the manor. No matter how much she wished it. In her heart, she knew her father would never let her ride at his side in a warrior's tunic.

Rustling and scraping around her ended her contemplation.

"Maiden bless you," the priest chanted.

"Maiden bless you," Evelyne and the rest responded as they stood and left the chapel. A firm hand stopped Evelyne before she passed the door.

"Elder Theobald will have words with you." Her father released his grip.

What had she done now? She caught the sympathetic looks from Winifred and Birgitta as they left. Obviously, they also thought she was in trouble.

She waited while two young male innocents removed Theobald's heavy ornate robe and his round padded cap, draped with several lengths of fabric. They scurried away behind a screen, and the priest approached, dressed only in a plain brown tunic, a tan linen belt, and a simple skullcap.

"Do you know why I asked you to stay?"

Evelyne shook her head. Better not to admit guilt for something before he pointed it out, since she could be guilty of several sins, she was certain.

"Your lord father has tasked me with your preparations for marriage."

Evelyne let out a relieved breath, although now a new sort of dread filled her.

He grasped her hands, his fingers cold and moist. "I was here for your presentation to the Maiden after your birth. I'm delighted to prepare you for your marriage duties."

Evelyne felt the grimace on her face. She didn't mean to show her discomfort, but the whole idea of this marriage was unsettling. She still wasn't warming to the idea of marrying a man she had never met and knew nothing about.

"Come." He led her to a window well and gestured for her to sit. An innocent appeared and placed a thin, leather-bound book next to her and moved away as quickly as he had arrived. "I'm sure you are aware the temple has specific rules for how a wife should behave. The most important being, you must obey your husband in all things."

"Has that always been the way?" Her question tumbled out before she could stop herself.

"For a thousand years."

"What of before that?"

Elder Theobald frowned and tugged the sleeve of his tunic. "There is no before. The pantheon of old gods was wiped from the earth before that."

"But others still worship the old gods."

"Yes, and they are doomed to eternity in the nothingness of death." His voice became louder, as if he was proselytizing to the full congregation.

"What about the Maiden?" Evelyne glanced at the statue over Elder Theobald's shoulder. "She never took a husband."

Theobald followed her eyeline with his own. His expression softened as he gazed upon the sculpture. "She represents the perfection that is woman. She is the symbol of creation and harvest. She is pure, and her purity brings us prosperity."

"There are stories I've heard…" she said. *More like bawdy songs.* "Where the Maiden has other women around her. Maidservants or companions. Ones who were intimate with her. What does the Book say about intimacy between women?"

Theobald looked flustered. He strode a pace away and looked at the floor. "My Lady, these are things you really shouldn't repeat."

"You've heard them too, yes?"

He looked at the door then back to her and said gravely, "Special friendships between women are allowed…if…they are practice for marriage. You must keep your virginity intact for your husband only."

"Was that what the Maiden had? Special friendships?"

He turned a bright red. "The Maiden was pure, as you should be. If you wish to be like her, you should—"

Evelyne interrupted him. "Enter the temple as an innocent. Yes, I'm aware." She cringed. She didn't mean to be flippant with him. He believed in the rules. Her frustration came from those rules being different for her than her brothers. If her behavior perturbed the elder, he didn't show it.

He continued, "Besides, the Maiden too is beholden to her father, the sky, for his continued guidance in all things that give us the cycle of creation and death."

Evelyne glanced at the ceiling. Painted across its entirety in silver and gold were the constellations of the night sky, dulled now with soot. Here and there, a particular star or a meridian line marker still shone brightly. Their harvests depended on constellation maps and the lunar calendar. Fortunately, this one was to awe the people, not to direct them. Plenty of parchment maps existed in temples, manors, and libraries across the kingdom.

"What if I want to help my husband run his manor?"

"Some partnerships may have variances from time to time. If your husband is called to fight, if, Maiden forbid, your husband should die before you or fall ill, you will be called upon to do things in his stead, but only for a short period. But there are consequences for abusing that freedom."

"What consequences?"

He sighed as if tired of her questions. "Punishment by the temple. Sometimes, a public spectacle, readings, supplicating oneself in the eyes of the Maiden, and in extreme cases…the shunning."

The shunning. Your neighbors no longer spoke to you. No one could buy products from you. If you left your home, your name was sent to every temple in Valmora, and you were refused entry to guilds, schools, and temples. You were refused work. You could literally starve to death. And for what? Because you wanted to help your own people to succeed or wanted to defend them from their enemies? Evelyne couldn't imagine leaving everyone and everything she'd ever known, and yet, that was what they were asking her to do by marrying Samuel.

Elder Theobald pointed at the book. "You will stay here each morning after first prayers and read from the Tenets of Marriage. I will quiz you on what you have learned before you start each new reading, and we will continue for a fortnight until you have read them all."

Half a month? This was torture, not teaching. With anyone else, she would have grumbled, but with the Maiden staring down at her, she felt compelled to behave.

"Today, you will start with the first Tenet. You will memorize it and the story that accompanies it. No reading aloud. I have things to take care of." He touched the small version of the Maiden that hung at his neck, the same gesture her mother made when she needed comfort. He was nervous about something, but what? Her parents would not blame him for her poor performance; he had nothing to worry about. "Do you have any *more* questions?"

She shook her head.

He nodded and strode to an alcove on the opposite wall and sat at a heavy wooden desk.

She touched the cover of the Tenets. The book had undergone several repairs. Heavy patches of mismatched colors overlay the soft, dark, original leather. A musty odor greeted her as she opened to the first page. The parchment was stiff and discolored along the edges. Beautiful script letters spelling words in High Valmoran greeted her. In the margins, decorative drawings of animals and strands of ivy filled what should have been empty. The first passage stared back at her.

A husband is in all ways the authority in marriage. His word is the word of the temple made flesh. A wife must defer to his decisions without question. In return, a husband will provide for and protect his family.

What if the wife wanted to protect her family? Was that even allowed? She scanned through the pages of the book: purity, procreation, gentility, quiet, patient, submit, the weaker vessel, created for his pleasure, silence, your children are your legacy. Was this what the Maiden wanted for her? She looked at the statue that now reminded her of Annika. Was Annika to be wed soon too? Who would her father choose for her?

What about Elder Theobald? Didn't he want a wife and children? Had he been able to make a choice, or was he told this was his destiny by his family? She could see his face illuminated by pillar candles. He glanced repeatedly at the door, all the while touching the Maiden around his neck. She looked at the open entryway. All she saw was a beautiful day outside that she was missing sitting in this chapel.

CHAPTER EIGHT

H ow come you're so pale?" a childish voice called out.
Annika carried two buckets of feed from the grain stores through the village. She ignored the boy and kept her pace brisk. The barefoot boy, his face smudged with dirt, no older than ten harvests, jogged along next to her.

"Do Weyans believe in the Maiden?"

"I don't know, Mertius," Annika replied. "I'm Valmoran. Like you." She tried to keep her tone friendly.

"My da says your mother was a Weyan bitch."

She wanted to reply with, "My da thinks your da is a bastard," but she held her tongue.

"He says Weyans have tails. Do you have a tail?"

Annika wished she could outpace him, but the buckets were weighty, and her feet moved heavily.

"Is it a long tail like a lion's or short like a sheep?"

"Mertius, I don't have a tail." Frustration crept into Annika's tone.

"But my da says Weyans have—"

"Off with you." Hilfa stepped in Mertius's path and waved him away. With her blacksmith's hammer in hand, she was a formidable sight, her leather apron singed, and her face and arms covered in soot from the charcoal forge. Mertius walked away, a scowl on his face.

Hilfa's assistant, Jack, pulled the bellows chord rhythmically up and down, the smell of charred wood and the metallic tang of burning iron ore blowing in the air with each pull.

Annika dropped the buckets and caught her breath. "Thanks."

Hilfa smiled. "He's a little shit." She waved her hammer toward his retreating form. "His father was the same way when he was a boy. Curious but trying to get a rise out of you."

"I try not to care, but sometimes…"

Hilfa wrapped an enormous, muscular arm around her. She was warm and smelled of charcoal and sweat, but the hug was welcome. "It's all right. You keep your head up." She released her grip. "Where's Steffen? Tell him he needs to come see me. I'd like his thoughts on a new arrowhead."

"I'll tell him."

"I know he misses your mum something fierce." Hilfa looked at her with sympathy. "And you looking so much like her." She pivoted. "Maiden's hands! That iron will burn." She grabbed a set of tongs and pulled the glowing hot metal from the forge, laid it on the anvil, and began swinging her hammer with a loud clang.

Once outside the village, Annika noticed that Mertius had returned with a small band of village children along the path. They fell in behind her as she headed to her cottage. She trudged along without looking back at them.

"My da says Weyans are traitors and heretics." If Mertius was trying to make her take his bait, he was doing a good job of it. She clenched her jaw tightly shut.

"Does she really have a tail?" a small voice asked.

"Annika doesn't have a tail," another exclaimed.

"Are you sure?" asked Mertius. "Let's find out."

Annika felt little hands grasping at her tunic. She dropped the buckets and pulled the fabric down against their insistent yanking. They laughed as she swatted at them.

Mertius, his eyes squinting, stood back from the others. "The priest says you'll go to the underworld when you die."

Annika sighed. She'd heard it all before, but still, it was tiring. She'd lived in this village her whole life. Flayed and threshed grain. Helped when the villagers called. And yet, she was still the other. Never truly a part of village life.

"What does it matter where I go when I die?" she asked in frustration. "You'll be snug in the Maiden's lap when your body has turned to dust. Go home, Mertius. Leave me be."

She grasped the rope handles of the buckets. She lifted the heavy load and walked away when she felt the first pain in her back. Then another. Pebbles. They were throwing stones at her. She ignored them. What good did it do to yell and curse or try to explain the way of things to them? They were children. Barely old enough to know what they were doing. Something cold and soft hit her with less power. She could smell the dung a moment after she felt it.

"You, there. Stop."

Annika heard the familiar voice. She stopped, not knowing if Evelyne was yelling at her or the boys. She placed the buckets on the ground and turned to find Evelyne and her sisters, Winifred and Birgitta, on horseback. Servants followed with several hooded falcons and a collection of dead rabbits on a carrying rack.

Evelyne swung off her horse quickly, with no sense of modesty or delicacy her social position should encourage. On her hip, she wore a quiver of arrows, and a bow was slung across her shoulder, the string still taut, as if she planned to shoot her prey from horseback. Her leather falconry gloves were tucked neatly over her belt.

At one glance, she was beautiful. Her long dark hair pulled into a single braid wrapped intricately around her head. At another glance, she was handsome and strong. She was like the Two-Faced God of Annika's mother's religion. Neither man nor woman. Both and yet none.

She strode purposefully toward the boys. Her unusual height meant that she towered over the cowering children. Mertius and the rest huddled together, their little shoulders drooped, and their heads bowed in fear. Relief flooded Annika. Evelyne wasn't addressing her. "What business do you have with this girl?" Evelyne asked, her voiced raised. She pointed directly at Annika and bent her face toward the group.

This girl? Was that who she was to Evelyne, this girl? Had Evelyne forgotten her name so quickly? Her face warmed, embarrassed by the reference as well as the fact she smelled like shite.

"We didn't mean no harm, m'lady," Mertius mumbled.

"No harm?" Evelyne stepped closer. "You wretched little whelps."

Mertius clenched his fists as if the insult emboldened him. He pointed at Annika. His voice trembled, but anger filled his eyes. "She's a Weyan."

Evelyne stiffened. Annika waited for the repercussions.

After a few painfully slow moments, Evelyne replied, "I don't care if she's the Maiden herself. I'll take you over my knee and make you rue the day you harangued our fowl keeper."

Annika stepped forward quickly and placed a hand on Evelyne's arm. Evelyne froze under her touch. Annika moved without thinking. No one touched nobles without permission. She swallowed and pulled her hand away. "Please," Annika whispered. "You'll only make it worse for me."

Evelyne stared with those deep brown eyes. She went from a frown to a softer expression. Annika was not sure if Evelyne was waiting for her to explain in more detail, but she stayed silent. Evelyne's shoulders rose and fell with a deep breath, then she stood tall and addressed the boys again. This time with more haughtiness and less anger. "Your friend has requested that I show leniency to you," she said, emphasizing the word *friend*. She paused and looked at each boy. "I will ignore your behavior for now, but should I find you have insulted her again, you will feel my wrath." She raised her voice on the word wrath. "Now, go. Out of my sight."

The boys didn't wait for further instructions. They scampered away as fast as they could, tripping and stumbling as they ran.

Evelyne laughed as she watched them leave.

"Father would be proud of your display," said Birgitta.

Evelyne turned and smiled at her sister. "That was quite invigorating."

Annika, smelling the dung on her tunic, blushed and stepped back. "I need to get the feed to my father. M'lady." She nodded to Evelyne. "M'ladies." She nodded to Winifred and Birgitta and hustled away.

❖

"What was that about?" Winifred stroked her steed's neck. The horse pranced slightly, perhaps knowing home and a bucket of food was not far away.

Evelyne watched Annika struggle with the heavy loads. When she had seen Annika's distinctive blond braids and watched the village urchins throwing missiles at her, anger had overtaken her so quickly, she couldn't stop herself from acting. Her father and mother would have taken no notice at all, but she felt the overwhelming urge to protect Annika. "Would you mind riding back without me?"

Winifred gave Evelyne a questioning look but didn't press the issue in front of Birgitta or the servants. "We'll talk later, yes?" Winifred, always wanting the latest gossip. "Mother won't like this."

Evelyne handed her bow and quiver to a servant. "Let's not mention it to Mother. Yes?"

As soon as her retinue trotted past Annika, Evelyne increased her pace, overtaking her and reaching for one of the bucket handles. Their hands touched. She felt a tingle or a chill or…something. Annika jumped.

Evelyne felt awkward. "Please, let me help." She took the bucket in two hands, surprised by its weight. Annika was stronger than she appeared.

"It's not right, m'lady."

"Evelyne…remember?"

"Yes, Lady Evelyne. I remember."

Was that bitterness in Annika's retort? Evelyne had protected her from the village urchins, and now she was angry with her?

"You should stand away from me," Annika said.

Evelyne's confusion must have shown on her face.

Annika gestured with her free hand to her back. "Covered in shite."

"Shite? That's what they were throwing at you?" She growled. "Why, those little buggers—" Evelyne stepped aside a pace. She didn't notice the smell, but she obeyed anyway. Perhaps Annika was embarrassed and not angry. "Can I ask why they were throwing shite at you?"

Annika sighed. "You heard them. My mother was Weyan. I'm a demon."

She certainly didn't look like a demon. She looked more like the Maiden herself. Skin like cream. Unblemished. No pox marks. And eyes the color of the sky, their rarity in Valmora unusual. "You said she died when you were little. Were you born in the village?"

Annika nodded.

Evelyne took a few more silent plodding steps with her heavy load. "You are Valmoran. And more so, you are a member of our manor lands."

"Once a Weyan, always a Weyan," came Annika's resigned reply.

Was that true? Her own mother was born in the Concordant Kingdoms, but no one would dare call her anything but Valmoran. She glanced at Annika. Her beauty was far from the sinister entity the village boys feared. "I don't understand why you frighten those boys." Her words came out stilted. The weight of the bucket winded her.

"More likely, I scare their parents." Annika made an aggressive face. "Afraid my tail will come out, and I'll eat their children."

Evelyne swallowed. She knew demonizing others was a tactic Valmora used against her enemies. She had surreptitiously overheard

Master Jacob explain the process to her brothers during one of her "embroidery" sessions near their lessons. The Great Horde had an even fiercer reputation. If one of them arrived in the village, the folk would greet them with clubs and spades.

"The villagers don't actually believe you have a tail, do they?"

"What they believe doesn't matter. When they see me, they see everything they don't know and don't understand."

The rope handle was hurting her hands. Evelyne placed the bucket on the ground and massaged her palms. Annika grabbed the bucket with her free hand and kept walking. Evelyne reached for the handle. "I can carry it." Evelyne winced at the sound of her own voice. Whining was not commanding.

Annika stopped, and Evelyne stared back at her, both with a grip on the handle. "You've helped enough, m'lady." Annika's features were serious, her expression resigned.

Evelyne hoisted her end of the bucket. "Together, then."

They walked the rest of the way in silence, except for the occasional grunt that escaped Evelyne's lips without her permission. What would her mother think if she saw her? Sometimes, Evelyne wondered what her mother's childhood had been like. Her accent was posh, but every now and again, she'd slip to a coarse accent, especially when she was happy. When she held Miriam's first surviving child and cooed at her, Evelyne could hear the difference. Evelyne couldn't imagine her mother carrying a bucket of feed...ever. Except maybe if her father commanded it.

Evelyne glanced at Annika's profile. Annika hadn't asked her for help. She wanted to do it. She wanted to impress Annika. Show that she was as capable as anyone on the manor. At the same time, she was like a puppy, curious and excited, following Annika to see what she'd do next. Maiden help her, this was not what was expected of her.

CHAPTER NINE

The cottage was a few hundred yards from the village, but the distance seemed infinite to Evelyne. They dumped the buckets in a wooden box against the side wall of the cottage, under an overhang of the thatched roof. Evelyne rolled her shoulder. It burned. She was sore after her sword fighting sessions with Timothy, but not like this. Her hands and her elbows ached, and her feet had the heaviness of stone shoes.

She looked about the cottage grounds. An ax lay near a pile of split logs, and a small food garden grew outside the bird yard. Wattle fences, earthen mounds, and multiple lean-tos that had every kind of edible bird she had ever seen filled every bit of space around the home. The smell was stronger in the heat of day. A ladder led up to the roof with a bundle of extra thatch lying nearby.

Annika had not mentioned siblings nor any other fowl handlers, meaning she and her father did all this work and more by themselves. Evelyne didn't even dress herself. A chambermaid named Peg sewed her into her tunic each morning. Nor did she prepare any of the food she ate. She didn't even empty her own chamber pot. So many things she took for granted. Suddenly, her life at the manor seemed easy.

She valued strength. She had always wanted to fight, to be a protector. Watching Annika made her realize that strength came in many forms. The hierarchy of the manor might be random and unfair, but the world was created that way...wasn't it? When she looked at Annika's gentle smile and sad eyes, none of what she understood made sense anymore.

"Is your father here?" Evelyne asked.

"Yes, inside, taking first sleep." Annika walked to a small gate and carefully opened and closed it as she slipped from the yard. "He is not idle," she added quickly.

"I'm here as a friend. As anyone else who might attend you," Evelyne reassured her.

No matter what she might say, Evelyne knew Annika would treat this visit as an official inspection, even though Evelyne had little to no sway in the affairs of the estate. Were they even allowed to be friends? Her mother might have something to say about it.

Evelyne followed Annika through the cottage door, bending her head to clear the short door frame. The warmth of the room hit her first, then the smell of the earthen floor under a thick layer of rushes and the whitewashed straw and mud walls. A large pot hung over a firepit. A grain ark, two wooden stools, and a rough-hewn wooden table sat to one side. Cups and bowls and small utensils sat on a shelf above the table. Around the walls were edible dried plants and other foodstuffs, hung high enough for the hazy smoke from the fire to keep away the flies. Opposite, a bolt of cloth hung from the ceiling, creating a division. Next to the front door, tools of their trade—a spade, a hoe, a rake, and a pitchfork—hung on pegs. Part of a wooden trunk was visible behind the fabric divider.

Annika walked to the cloth and pulled back a corner. "Father, we have a guest."

Evelyne could hear a grunt and the sound of boots being pulled on. Obviously not used to a guest of her station, the man pulled back the curtain the rest of the way while still lacing his trousers.

His eyes widened when he looked up. "Your ladyship!" He bowed stiffly and waited. He was taller than Evelyne. Built as she would suspect as a man who'd spent his life as a warrior and a peasant. Broad-shouldered with muscular arms.

Evelyne noticed Annika's gittern on the wall behind him. Slightly smaller than a lute, the body was pear-shaped with a rounded back. Five pairs of gut strings reached up the fingerboard to the ten pegs at the top of the head. The headstock was carved in the shape of a goat's, his horns bent backward in a delicate curve. What should have been a rosette carving for a sound hole was another goat's head with detailed, twisting horns.

The instrument was as beautiful to look at as it had sounded in the woods. She looked at Annika again. Her beauty was a match to the instrument. They were meant to be together.

Annika's father shifted uncomfortably in his bow and glanced up at her, uncertainty showing on his face. Evelyne realized staring at Annika for so long had left her father in the unacknowledged bow, and she should have released him by now. She cleared her throat.

"Please stand, sir. What shall I call you?"

"Steffen, m'lady." He gestured toward the stool closest to him. "My home is your home." He grabbed the end of his shirttail and swept the seat with it. He motioned again for her to sit. Evelyne obliged him. "Would you like a cup of mead? Or I can send Annika to the village for an ale."

"I'm fine, Steffen, thank you." Evelyne shifted on the stool, realizing how inappropriate her outfit must seem to them. She glanced around casually, realizing they had nothing more than what she could see. Nothing was without necessity. A roof that did not leak. A bed. A stool for each of them. A way to prepare a meal. Nothing frivolous. Nothing unnecessary. In contrast, Evelyne's whole life was full of the unnecessary.

Steffen and Annika waited patiently as she sat on their stool. She became angry with herself for imposing on them. Why was she here? What had she wanted to know? Even she wasn't sure. Initially, the music had called to her. Then, she'd wanted to see Annika's face. Now, she waited for the answer to a question she hadn't asked.

Annika interrupted the silence. "You wanted to see mother's gittern."

"Yes." Evelyne turned toward the instrument, glad to have something to talk about.

"Ah." Steffen nodded knowingly. "A beautiful sound it makes. I was drawn to her mother when I heard her play."

Evelyne understood the sentiment. "Your wife was a Weyan?"

A look flitted between Steffen and Annika. Evelyne wasn't sure of its meaning, but concern or even distrust seemed the watchword between them.

Steffen looked down, his eyes unfocused as he spoke. "Yes. Hair the color of gold, like my Annika. I was a young man. Came home from war with a wife. Sometimes, I wonder if I should have left her where she was. Maybe she would still be alive."

Evelyne tried not to look when Annika changed her tunic behind the curtain, removing the offending muck the children had thrown on her back, but she took quick sideways glances. When Annika reached for the gittern, pulling it from the wall, Evelyne noticed the shape of her hips outlined against the fresh tunic.

"But you wouldn't have such a lovely daughter." Evelyne wasn't sure what made her say that. She sounded like her scoundrel of an older brother, Witt. She felt the heat rise on her cheeks.

"Indeed, m'lady." Steffen reached his hand out to take Annika's. "She has taken good care of me. I am a lucky man."

Annika smiled lovingly at her father. Evelyne felt a pang of jealousy. Her father never touched her and certainly said nothing nice about her. She observed their intertwined hands. Annika unlaced their hands and stepped toward Evelyne, handing the gittern to her reverently.

Honored to hold it, Evelyne touched it gently, caressing the wood with her fingertips. "May I?" Evelyne gestured to the gittern.

"Of course." Annika stepped back behind her father.

Evelyne could play a lute, but this was different. She tried a few chords, but the dissonance struck her immediately. She made a face and held it toward Annika. "I believe this is meant for you alone to play." Annika's gaze caught hers as she returned the gittern. For those few moments, Steffen didn't exist. She shook herself. "Would you play something?"

The moment Annika strummed the first chord, the music mesmerized Evelyne, the sound so different from her own disastrous attempt. She felt all the tension leave her body, and she drew softer, slower breaths. She could see her calmness reflected in Steffen's face. He closed his eyes and swayed gently where he stood, and she wondered if he pictured his wife while he listened.

When she turned her gaze back to Annika, she could do nothing but watch her fingers lie across the neck in dexterous shapes and watch her right hand delicately pluck the strings, the music she produced so lovely.

The sound stopped too soon, and for a moment, the silence froze Evelyne in place, leaving her staring at Annika's soft lips and sad eyes. How could she be sad after playing so wonderfully? Annika was the first to break the gaze, looking away and putting the gittern back in its place on the wall.

Evelyne's hands came together in spontaneous applause. "Beautiful...so beautiful." And Evelyne meant both the music and Annika. This feeling was odd. She knew she shouldn't feel attracted to

Annika, for many reasons, but each time she was around her, she noticed something new, something that drew her in like delicious sweets.

Her thoughts wandered to the stained-glass windows in the castle at Tarburg depicting the lovers Guedelon and Gennifer, fated to be together in life and death. The paired windows faced one another, the lovers staring at each other forever in a longing gaze. The tale was a favorite of Birgitta's. Evelyne had listened to it many times. Each trip she made to Tarburg, she stared at the effigies in glass and wondered what love was.

Nothing tangible described it. Most stories made some vague references to intuition and sacrifice. None of her siblings, nor she, would marry for love. And yet, her sisters tittered and murmured and sighed over young men more and more with each passing harvest, and she felt nothing. Until she looked at Annika, and her stomach tumbled. Her thoughts were chaotic, and she didn't want their time together to end. Was this what her sisters felt when they gazed on the knights?

She hoped Steffen couldn't see the uncomfortable desire coursing through her veins. If Witt were to call on Annika, Steffen would have no choice but to allow his courting, but she wasn't Witt, and whatever she felt, she knew it wasn't the way things were done. Dusty, ancient poetry referred to the sisterly love between women. Nothing in them reflected the idea of carnality. Did it? Because her thoughts were not sisterly.

Uncomfortable and self-conscious, Evelyne forced herself to look elsewhere in the small room. Her gaze fell on the far wall. Almost imperceptible in the dark gloom of the far corner was a pike. She stood and walked over to take a closer look.

"May I?" she asked as she gestured at the weapon.

"Of course, m'lady. What is ours is yours," Steffen said with a nod.

Evelyne hefted it and felt the weight. She easily found the balance, running her hands along the well-worn dark wood. She touched her thumb to the tip and felt the sharp prick. Blood pooled on her skin. Sharp as any at the manor. Steffen took great care to keep it ready for use. The pike was a simple design, much like the rest of their home, functional and without excess.

"Annika tells me you served my father as a man-at-arms." She carefully set the pike back in its place, glad to have something to distract her from her confusing thoughts about Annika.

He shook his head. "No man-at-arms. I'm no knight. A foot

soldier. I've answered your father's call for men more than once. Thank the Maiden, the kingdom's been quiet since the treaty with Iola."

Maybe she followed Annika for a reason after all. Maybe Annika was a muse placed in her path with music and beauty to bring her to the thing she wanted most. Steffen was a man of experience but not one of her father's castle men. Perhaps he would help her learn more.

"Steffen." Evelyne said his name slowly as she rounded back to face him. "I believe the Goddess of the Harvest has brought me to you herself."

Steffen and Annika looked at each other in confused surprise. He moved Annika partially behind him. Evelyne admired him for the good sense to protect his daughter before himself. She did sound a little crazy.

"I wish to learn the ways of personal warcraft from you." Evelyne moved back to the stool and sat to make him feel more at ease. "I have trained on horseback. I can fly a falcon. Shoot a bow. I've tried my hand at swordplay with one of my father's squires, but he is not an experienced fighter. I want to learn to fight."

He rubbed his chin. "Annika, fetch me a mug of mead." He drew up the other stool and sat. "Does your lord father approve of this, m'lady?"

"Please, call me Evelyne. My lord father does not approve of me at all," she replied emphatically. "He wishes my brother Erik to be a knight, but Erik wishes to be a scholar. I wish to be a knight, but my mother and father have arranged my marriage. Once I leave, I may never learn how, and I feel the need to learn. You could teach me moves I could memorize and practice later."

She did not know what lay ahead for her when she arrived at her married life, but until then, she wanted to pursue as much knowledge about fighting as she could. Next year at harvest, she might find herself confined to her new home, as Miriam had been. Some ridiculous tradition of not disturbing the chances of her first childbirth. Why hadn't she been born a man?

Annika handed her father his mead and gently laid a hand on his shoulder and stood at his side. Evelyne stared at the hand. At the fingers and their gentle curves. Did Annika ever want more from her life? She looked at Annika's face. Their eyes met, and Annika held her gaze. This time, Evelyne was the one to look away.

She looked at Steffen. "I will not take you away from your work. I'll help you while I am here. And I swear on the Book of Enlightenment,

I will do as you say without regard to my status." She leaned toward him. "I beseech you, teach me what you know."

He shook his head.

She dug in her purse, pulling out a gold crown. She put it on the table. "I can pay you."

His face grew stern. "The life of a fighting man is not what you see at the manor on the practice field. Battle is full of blood, with no regard for station or status. There is no chivalry on the field. Only survival in any way a man can survive."

"I understand."

"You do not understand," he replied firmly. "Begging your pardon, miss. You will not understand until the day you take the life of a boy no bigger than ten harvests. You will not understand until you watch your mates take their spoils in the form of the enemy's women, or until you see a man ripped apart by the blow from a mace by a knight on horseback. Not until you shit yourself from fear. Only then will you understand."

She winced. His descriptions didn't sound like the stories her father told of returning triumphant from battle. Head held high on horseback as the villagers cheered from the roadsides. All her life, she'd dreamed of being like her brothers, certain it was what she was meant to do. She felt the call of battle in her blood. She'd felt the strength pulse through her as she swung at a quintain and every time she'd thrust a sword into a straw dummy. Although those times were far and few between, she'd felt enthralled by them. How to make that clear to Steffen or her father or her husband-to-be, she did not know.

Why was everything she wanted controlled by men?

"I am certain I have been called to protect the realm. Since my first memories, I have always known I was destined for it."

"Very few women are warriors," Steffen continued. "A brutal and immoral work 'tis."

"But there have been some, yes?" Evelyne asked, trying to keep her eagerness at bay. She shifted, placing her elbows on the table. "Queen Neera."

Steffen waved a dismissive hand. "A tale. I've seen women warriors. In the North. They fight as fiercely and cruelly as their men. But they have no choice. We come with siege weapons, better armor, crossbows, and warhorses. They're shepherds, fishermen, traders. They don't have a system of squires and knights. Everyone fights. And they fight for their lives. They don't parley."

Evelyne tried to imagine what he had seen. She had some misgivings, but the battles still sounded glorious to her. One day, they might immortalize her deeds in books of learning. "I am stronger than my brothers." She gestured at her silk tunic and surcoat. "I know this outfit makes me look weak and frivolous, but I want to fight for my people, Steffen. I want to fight for the Maiden."

"The Maiden has nothing to do with it." He shook his head and took a drink of mead. "Men bring war. Greedy, jealous, angry men." He spit in the firepit. "Your father would have my head if I taught you to fight. I cannot risk his ire. I'm sorry, but I'll not train you."

Evelyne's head fell forward. She had been certain her plea would work. Now she was the one who was sad.

Steffen took his cup and hers and threw the contents on the fire and dipped them in a bucket of sand, rubbing the sand around the inside to clean them. "What I will do is tell you how to be better prepared if you ever fight."

Excitement coursed through her. Had she heard him correctly? She looked at Annika, who gave a half-smile and a subtle nod. She leapt from the stool. "Thank you, Steffen."

He put up a hand to stop her. "Hold now." He shook his head. "You won't like what I tell you. You're tall, yes, but you're not as strong as your brothers. You need to build your shoulders, and the best way is to apprentice to the village blacksmith, Hilfa. She's stubborn, but she'll tell you true."

"The blacksmith is a woman?"

Steffen and Annika looked at each other again. Their unspoken words made her think she'd said something foolish.

"Yes. And if anyone can get you stronger…'tis her." He walked to the door and held it open, obviously waiting for her to understand it was time for her to leave.

"Thank you, Steffen." She turned to Annika. "I would like to hear you play again sometime." She wanted to reach out, take her hand, and bow to her as if she was a noble lady. It was hard to keep her arms at her sides. How silly she'd look if she did it, but she couldn't help thinking about it.

Annika nodded curtly but said nothing.

Steffen spoke as Evelyne stepped into the yard. "I ask that you not share this visit with anyone, m'lady."

What a curious request. So many people would want to boast about a visit from a noble. If keeping his confidence was what she must trade for the tutelage of a proper warrior, she would do it a hundred times over.

❖

When Annika was sure Evelyne was gone, she sat on the stool across from her father. She retrieved the gold coin and turned it over, staring at the unfamiliar etchings on either side. She'd never seen one before. It weighed more than a copper coin. "Can't you teach her a few things? Like what you've taught me?" she asked.

"Bad enough she's still hanging around here. She brings too much attention."

Annika understood the risk, and yet, she wanted to see Evelyne again. She held the coin toward her father. "More coin than I've ever held before."

He snatched it from her palm, stood, and placed it in a drying herb bag hanging on the wall. "Coin can't buy you everything," he replied.

She stared at the coarse linen pouch. Coin bought Evelyne the best cloth, the rights to come and go as she pleased, and a life without fear of starvation. Maybe it could buy her and her father a small bit of freedom.

Chapter Ten

Stealing one of Witt's unused outfits was easier than expected. Not even a single servant was in the room when Evelyne snuck in. She chose hunting garb buried deep in one of his chests, a simple short tunic and a pair of leggings. He had almost as many tunics as her father, and her father had an entire room for his clothes. The outfit smelled faintly of long-unattended sweat. On her way through the bailey, she swiped a wide-brimmed straw hat from the stables and tucked her hair underneath. By the time she slipped through the servant's gate, she hoped she looked little like herself.

She found the blacksmith easily. She'd passed the forge every time she'd ridden through the village, but she had taken no notice of the blacksmith herself. The forge sat at the north end of the sparse buildings. A roof but no walls covered a large stone forge. Dozens of tools hung from every available post and beam. A woman nearly as tall as Evelyne, with broad shoulders and massive arms, rapidly struck a glowing red slab of metal, sparks flying. Each strike was like the tolling of a dull bell. It was fascinating.

"Instead of standing there, be useful and bring me the heavy hammer." The woman pointed vaguely with her free hand.

Evelyne moved forward and looked at the table. Several hammers of different sizes lay on the wood. She turned back to the blacksmith. "If you can describe which one is the heavy one, I'm sure I can accommodate you."

The woman's head snapped around. "M'lady." She stopped hammering and bowed her head. "I didn't recognize you."

"I'm Evelyne. Steffen said you could help me." Now that Evelyne moved closer, she felt the heat pulsing from the burning coals in the forge.

The blacksmith took the bar of iron, placed it back in the forge, and laid her tools on the anvil. She wiped her hands on her leather apron, leaving wide wet streaks across it. "Hilfa, m'lady." She bowed. "Maiden's blessing to you. What is it you need made?"

Evelyne moved closer, keeping her voice low so they wouldn't be overheard. "I am in need of training. I...I wish to become stronger. Like you." She looked at the bulging muscles in Hilfa's shoulders. She had to be as strong as any of Evelyne's father's fighting men.

"Steffen sent you to me, did he? That bugger." She crossed her arms. "He's gone soft. Doesn't want your father giving him what for."

"Can you help me?"

"Who am I to stop a lady?" replied Hilfa with a grin and a flourish of her hand.

"What will I be doing?" Evelyne hoped she could strike the hot iron bar.

Hilfa smiled and strode back to the forge. "Jack here will explain what needs to be done. You'll be doing his job today."

Jack was young, thin, and obviously uncomfortable around women...or nobles. Evelyne looked at her tunic. Even as plain as it was, it didn't hide her educated diction. He showed her how to pull the bellows, and she took over from him.

"Jack, fine knife you have." She pointed to the one on his belt. "Did Hilfa make it?"

He smiled. "Made it myself," he replied.

"May I see it?"

He unsheathed it and handed it to her. She examined the hilt. The leather handle was worn and thin, with a cross guard of bronze. The blade itself was shining steel, only slightly wavy from heavy sharpening. She checked the edge with her fingernail.

"Very sharp. Well done." She handed it back.

He stood a little taller and thrust his chin in the air at her compliment.

"You going to keep that fire going, or are you here for a chat?" Hilfa asked.

Evelyne pulled the cord tied to the far end of the bellows lever. Air blew into the forge, and the coals burned hotter. At first, her pace was too brisk, causing Hilfa to make her slow down. Then her pace was too slow, making Hilfa bark at her about not getting the metal hot enough.

Hilfa and Jack worked in silence, seemingly able to understand what the other needed without communicating. Jack would hand her exactly the tools she needed. Occasionally, they worked the metal together, the forge ringing with the dueling hammers.

Sometimes, Hilfa worked alone, bending the softly heated metal around the point of the anvil or punching a hole through the reddest part for a lanyard. Most of the finished products were spoons, knives, and ladles. Not the great helms, longswords, and pike heads made by the castle's blacksmith. These were daily items. Mostly iron. Some were simple, some with twisted handles and small twirls at the top.

The actual surprise was how fast Hilfa and Jack created them. Heat, pound, heat, pound, repeat, then cool and heat and cool and eventually, the quench, the liquid hissing from the heat.

"You can stop now, m'lady."

"Evelyne," she replied as she collapsed in a heap on the stone floor, drenched in sweat.

"You ready to go back to the castle now?" Hilfa ran a long, thin piece of steel along a grinding wheel, taking off the excess. Was that a smile on her face?

"I finish what I start," Evelyne replied stubbornly, but her hands betrayed her. They shook, and she could barely raise her arms.

"Tell me. Why do you want to get stronger?" Hilfa asked.

Evelyne eyed Jack and decided he wouldn't tell anyone. "I want to be a fighter."

Jack stopped pouring water over his head and peered at her. Hilfa paused her grinding, letting the wheel spin to a stop. "You want to be a knight?"

Did she? "I don't care if I'm a knight or a mercenary or a pikeman. I want to fight." Evelyne stared at the finished knife and ax blades lying on the table nearby.

Hilfa waved to Jack. "Go get yourself an ale."

He nodded and quietly left.

Hilfa stooped, got a cup of water, and handed it to Evelyne. Then she grabbed a stool and sat close to her.

Evelyne took the cup clumsily. "I'm not going to quit if Steffen will help me learn to fight."

Hilfa cocked her head and crossed her massive arms across her chest. "Maybe none of my business, but why do you want to fight?"

Evelyne pointed to several of her father's men riding through the village. She lowered her head as they drew closer but not before drinking in everything about them. The tunics in the house colors. Their heads held high. The way people gave way as they came by. "That is why."

Hilfa nodded, seemingly understanding without needing to hear the specifics.

When the men had passed, Evelyne relaxed. She took another sip of her water. "Why did you want to be a blacksmith?" she asked. "Not a woman's job, either."

"All my brothers died when they were young. My da had no choice but to teach me to forge. We'd have starved otherwise."

"Do you like it?"

Hilfa smiled and pointed at her. "I see what you did there. Yes, I do. I wouldn't do anything else."

"We both know I'm never going to be a knight. I'm to be married and set in a gilded house to embroider my way to heaven. But I can dream." Everything would be easier if she had been born a boy.

Hilfa nodded knowingly.

"Um, is it normal not to be able to feel my fingers?" Evelyne asked sheepishly.

"May I?" Hilfa reached for her hand. She nodded. Hilfa took her left hand and rubbed. She worked her way to the other arm and Evelyne's shoulders before she finished. "Make sure to keep moving them later, or you won't be able to move them at all on the morrow."

Tomorrow? At the moment, she was too tired to think beyond the long walk uphill to her bed. Was she really going to be able to do this each day?

❖

"You smell like you stood in a firepit." Winifred made a face and walked around her in a circle. "What have you been doing?"

Evelyne sniffed her clothes. She had changed in the small wood, tucking Witt's stolen tunic in her bag before returning to the castle. But the forge smell was well and truly deep in her skin. "I was hunting," she lied.

"Where? In the kitchen?" Winifred teased. "Looking for those tarts you love so much?"

Evelyne ignored her and changed clothes for dinner.

Winifred sat on the edge of their bed and watched her. "While we're alone, are you going to tell me about the girl in the village?"

Evelyne froze.

"The one you threw yourself off your horse to rescue from a gaggle of little urchins. Remember?"

"I remember." Evelyne tried to fasten the top of her tunic, but her fingers were stiff, and her arms shook.

Winifred stood and helped her, taking hold of the fastenings and doing them for her. "And?"

"She's the daughter of the bird keeper."

Winifred didn't seem satisfied by the answer.

"I didn't want them to hurt her."

Winifred worked on Evelyne's sleeves. She was rougher about it than Annika had been. She turned Evelyne on the spot and checked her appearance. "I don't know what you are up to, Evelyne, but promise me you won't get the rest of us in trouble."

Evelyne smirked. "I promise."

She felt bad not talking to Winifred, someone who had never betrayed her secrets, but somehow, this felt different. She didn't want Winifred to know about her conversations with Annika or Steffen or Hilfa. She selfishly wanted to keep her training, and Annika, to herself.

Chapter Eleven

"Move, you blasted ratter." Annika stumbled; the bucket of water she carried sloshed over its rim. Their house cat, appropriately named Underfoot, slinked around her ankles, keeping her from getting to the cottage door. The sound of voices drifted through the window.

"Zuri? In Byetown?" That was Hilfa's voice.

Annika tiptoed closer to the wall to listen.

"She spoke to Annika," said her father.

"Why would she be so close to the castle? If the bailiff catches her, he'll drag her back in chains. Maiden knows what they might do to her then. Ow."

"I don't know why she's back, but I don't want her anywhere near Annika. Filling her head with nonsense."

"Gah!"

"Stay still."

"Those thick fingers of yours weren't meant for this kind of work."

Annika peered through the opening. Hilfa sat at the table. A long gash, raw and bleeding, ran the length of her forearm. Blood pooled on the table and covered her father's fingers as he worked a needle and thread.

"I've stitched up many a man on the battlefield. They'll work for you."

Annika rushed into the cottage. Hilfa and her father looked startled by her arrival. She dipped her hands in the bucket of water and wiped them on her tunic. "Let me do that, Da." She pushed her father aside and grasped the thread and needle from him.

"Yes, please. He's trying to kill me." Hilfa pointed at her father.

The wound was clean and deep. Muscle and skin flared outward like with a sliced pig. She could see the bone. "Da, she needs a healer." She looked up at him, worried.

Hilfa waved the comment away. "I don't have coin for the temple healer. And I'm not going to that hack of a woman who calls herself a healer in the village. Better you and your da tend me than her and her smelly concoctions."

Annika continued to stitch, sinking the needle as deep as she dared, trying to make the skin meet and stop the bleeding. "We have the coin. Da, take the crown Lady Evelyne gave us and fetch the healer."

"Lady Evelyne? Well, la-di-da," Hilfa mocked.

Her father limped to a small bag of dried herbs hanging on the wall and dumped out the coin. "I was hoping this would give us the beginning of what we need to buy our release from the lord, but you're too damned important, you sodding idiot. Cutting yourself with your own blade."

Hilfa smiled. "You try making knives for a living sometime, you big oaf."

Annika stuck her with the needle, and she grimaced. The blood covered Annika's hands, slick and warm, making it hard to hold the wound closed.

"Keep your coin, Steffen. You'll need it. A pilgrim came through the village yesterday. Said he'd been at the temple across the valley. Had a story about the Paladin traveling nearby."

Annika went cold. She could still see the Paladin in Byetown, his blue clothing draped around him, and she could smell the burning girl. Her hands shook. She paused and closed her eyes, taking deep breaths to calm herself. If he was across the valley, how long before he might be here in Marsendale? What would she do if he came? Would he be looking for her?

The familiar feeling overtook her. The energy that filled her before a vision. Warmth, light, and sounds falling away. She knew the vision would come soon.

"What the…" Hilfa's voice drew Annika back to her surroundings.

When she opened her eyes, her hands were aglow. White hot. And where they touched, Hilfa's wound sealed itself. Startled, she pulled away, but Hilfa grabbed her and pushed her hands on the bloodied wetness of her forearm. Annika watched, her mouth agape, as the cut sealed. She stared at the space that had been raw and bloody only moments ago. Though still covered in blood, Hilfa's arm was now completely healed.

Annika brought her hands to her lap. She looked into her da's eyes. He was clearly shocked. He moved to the window and looked outside before turning back to the table and grasping her by the shoulders.

"How long have you been able to heal?" he asked in a harsh whisper.

"Never. I…I don't know what happened." She'd displayed no other gift than her visions. Certainly nothing as complex as healing.

Hilfa was examining her arm, flexing her hand. "How did you do that?" Other than the drying blood, there was no hint of the wound itself.

"I don't know," Annika said quickly. "You mentioned the Paladin. I felt scared, and suddenly, you were healing."

Her father asked angrily, "Did something happen recently? Anything at all?"

She shook her head. Nothing she could remember. Then she felt the irritation, as if she had scratched her arm unknowingly. She pulled up the sleeve of her tunic and shift. There, on her forearm, was the inking her mother had given her when she was a little girl. The dark lines were red around the edges, as if the inking had been done yesterday and not a dozen years ago.

"Zuri," Annika whispered. "She touched me in the square. In Byetown. My arm burned and tingled."

Her father grasped her wrist and pulled her arm forward to look at the mark. What was he looking for? The shape was the same as always. The only difference was the irritated skin surrounding it. He turned to Hilfa. "Can we burn it off?"

Annika yanked her arm away. "What? No."

"Steffen, be sane, man." Hilfa stood and gently pushed him back. "We don't know it has anything to do with what happened. Mayhap, it's fate. You've known she was a Talent. Maybe if she'd gone to the temple when she was supposed to, they would have taught her to use her powers. She's had to learn on her own, so it took her longer."

"Who is Zuri?" Annika demanded. She was tired of secrets. Her father and Hilfa exchanged glances.

"Zuri—" Hilfa began.

"Stop," her father bellowed. "The less she knows, the less she has to lie."

"She needs to know the truth, Steffen." Hilfa laid a hand on his taut forearm and then turned to Annika. "Zuri lived here for several harvests. She was a close friend of your mother's. They had a bond. I never understood it, really. They shared a belief. Something older and less well-known than the Enlightened Book."

"Heresy is what they shared," said her father. "Mumblings about ancient rites and royalty. Nonsense."

"Was Zuri from Weya too?" asked Annika.

Hilfa shook her head. "No. She's from a place where the sun stays high in the sky."

"Did you know she was a Talent?"

Her father looked away. "Yes. Which is why she ran away. I had hoped she'd made it somewhere safe, but now…" His voice drifted off.

"They'll flay her if they catch her," Hilfa added. "You mustn't tell anyone. About you…or Zuri."

She nodded, but she didn't understand any of it. Not telling anyone was easy. She'd done that her whole life. Living in silence. Feeling alone.

Her father retrieved the gold crown from the bloodied tabletop and placed the coin in the pouch on his waist. "We'll need more of these if we're going to leave."

"Leave?" Annika asked.

"You're not safe here anymore. Not with the Paladin and Zuri wandering the valley. We'll pay for the right to leave from Lord Cederic and head for Weya as soon as possible."

Annika felt the pain as she dug her fingernails into her palms. She wanted to ask her father why he'd put her in this situation. Why hadn't he given her to the temple when she'd first showed her skills? Now that she had seen the girl die in Byetown, she was certain she would live the rest of her life in fear. All because he hadn't done his duty. But she said nothing. Just stood mutely and nodded. She knew they were right. She'd seen what could happen. But why now? Why did Zuri show up now? How could Annika do something she'd never been trained to do? And would she be able to do it again?

Hilfa moved to the door. "I'd best get back to the forge. No telling what trouble Jack is causing." She flexed her arm. "Thank you for this, Annika."

"I'll walk with you," her father said. "I need you to tell the Lady Evelyne that I will train her."

"Of course. I'll get the message to her." Hilfa admired her arm. "Your mother would be proud," she called back to Annika.

"She would not." Her father pushed Hilfa through the door.

She knew they had to leave. Marsendale was no longer safe for them, but it was all she'd ever known. And...she'd only just met Evelyne. That shouldn't matter. Evelyne was a noble, and she was a peasant. Worse than that, she was a rogue Talent. Apparently, one who didn't know her own powers.

CHAPTER TWELVE

E velyne walked back from the forge along the path through the small woods. She felt light and happy. Hilfa had told her to see Steffen on the morrow. He'd agreed to train her…for coin. She'd pay whatever he asked for the chance to learn from a true fighter. A man who had been in battle and survived.

It wasn't long before she heard the familiar sounds of Annika's gittern. She stepped off the path and worked her way through the undergrowth, ducking under branches and stepping over roots. The old tree was even more impressive in daylight. Thick and gnarled, with a heavy canopy of leaves towering over her, the tree blocked out the sunlight and created a clearing around itself. She ran her hand along the trunk, as she had done the first night she'd found this place, feeling the deep ridges of bark against her fingertips. Her heart beat faster when she came around face-to-face with Annika.

"I thought I might find you here." She kept her tone light. She could feel the grin on her face from one side to the other.

Annika stopped playing. She laid the gittern carefully at her side and looked up. "M'lady," she said with a nod.

"Please, just Evelyne." Her smile was still firmly in place. She motioned around them. "There is no one here to see us. I could scarcely find it myself."

Annika smiled in return.

Evelyne brushed some twigs and stones from the ground and stretched out next to her, propped on one elbow. "Please, play me a tune."

Annika nodded and took up the gittern. She played an even and relaxing melody. The instrument was rich and bright and the song hypnotic.

Evelyne listened without taking her eyes off Annika's movements. She didn't miss a note, and the rhythm was perfect throughout. She was masterful. Evelyne wondered if the music reflected how she felt. Was she sad when she played sad music? Or happy when she played a light and airy tune? When the song ended, Annika once again put the gittern aside.

A dove cooed as if in response to the music. The bird picked its way across the ground in front of them, approaching slowly, cocking one eye at the instrument. "I hope he doesn't plan to try to eat it," said Evelyne.

"Bit big for him," Annika replied with a smile.

"You're really magnificent with that instrument. How did you learn to play so well?"

Annika shrugged. "My mother taught me when I was young. After she…after that, I listened to others play, especially traveling bards on feast days, and tried to remember the tunes. I'd come here and play for hours to get them to sound the way they should."

"You'll get plenty of inspiration at the harvest burn. My father has requested musicians from each village within the manor borders to come this year. He's expecting a full crop with the way things are going. Much to celebrate. Maybe you could play as well?"

Annika blushed. "No, I don't enjoy playing for others. The music is for me."

Evelyne looked down and pulled at a clover. "Is that because of the way the village children treat you?" She peeked at Annika's face to see her reaction.

Annika turned away before answering. She ran her fingers over the strings of her gittern gently. "Perhaps a little."

"Well, you have nothing to worry about while I'm around," Evelyne said boldly. "I'll protect you from those little twats."

Annika laughed. "I'm sure you'll keep me safe." Her expression became serious. "The gittern is special to me. I hear my mother every time I play it. I suppose I don't want to make new memories with it." She shook her head. "That makes no sense."

Evelyne scooted to sitting and moved closer. She touched Annika's forearm. "You don't have to do anything you don't want to. I'm sorry if I implied you did."

Annika laughed again. This one seemed incredulous rather than amused. "Do you know how that sounds?"

Evelyne withdrew her hand and frowned. "I meant it."

"You could make me play any time you wished. I live to serve the manor."

Evelyne leaned against the tree. Was that what she wanted to do? Make Annika play for her? "I don't want to make you play, but I would be honored if you ever felt like playing for me again. Maybe you could make fresh memories including me?" Her heart jumped a bit at that admission.

Annika reached for the gittern and smiled at Evelyne before playing another tune. When she finished, they stayed motionless, listening to the sounds of the woods, feeling the gentle breeze, watching the sunlight change through the moving leaves.

"Why did your father change his mind?" asked Evelyne. "About training me?"

Annika shifted and brushed the front of her tunic. "You'll have to ask him."

"He seemed definitive about it when last we spoke." She picked at another clover. "I wondered if maybe you had something to do with it."

Annika stilled. Had Evelyne gone too far?

"I only mean that I like you, your company, so I thought maybe you liked my company as well."

Annika let out a small sigh. "Yes. I like you as well. Da thinks we could use the extra coin." She paused. Her eyes shifted away from Evelyne's gaze. "Buy another cow, perhaps."

Evelyne frowned. "A cow?"

"Yes, a cow," Annika repeated.

"A cow." Well, her coin would go to a good thing, then.

Annika grabbed her gittern and stood. "I must get back." She bowed to Evelyne. "Maiden bless you."

Evelyne stood as well. She nodded and watched as Annika made her way through the woods to the path. She wanted to follow her. It was as if Annika was fire in midwinter, and all she wanted was to stand in her light and warmth.

CHAPTER THIRTEEN

Evelyne prepared before dawn, her bow and quiver in hand. She'd always been the best hunter of her sisters. It was the one pursuit her father and mother allowed her. So under the guise of going hunting each morning, she started for the door.

She felt a tug on her tunic. Matilde stood in her loose night shift and bare feet, looking up at her. She rubbed a sleepy eye before reaching for Evelyne's hand. "Can I come with you?"

Evelyne smiled and knelt. "Not today, Tildie. To catch my prey, I need to move quickly."

"I'm swift." Her sister stuck out her lower lip. "I beat Gregor in a footrace just yesterday."

Gregor was five, not a difficult feat, but Evelyne knew how it felt to want to beat her brothers at anything. "You did?" She acted surprised and touched Matilde's nose. "You are too swift for me. You'll run right past me and my prey."

"Please. I don't want to sit in the solar all day. I want to go with you."

A pang of sympathy rushed through her. She understood how it felt to be cooped up in the solar all day. "Not now, Tildie. After the harvest burn, I promise, you and I will spend a whole day in the Great Woods together. I'll let you use my falcon."

This seemed to placate her. She nodded and ran back to the bed she shared with Birgitta, slipping under the covers. Evelyne might not want to bear children, but she felt warm inside when she spent time with Matilde. They were alike in so many ways, though Matilde would be beautiful in a feminine way she was not.

She slipped through the kitchens, grabbing a loaf of bread and a piece of cheese and slipping them in her bag. She left on foot. A horse would draw attention to both herself and the cottage. By sunrise, she arrived, excited and ready for the day.

Steffen spent some time making sure she knew a dagger from a short sword and explained a few exercises she could use to test her reflexes. He was curt, though polite, and their first session was over too soon. Evelyne could continue all day if he'd let her. As she made to leave, she couldn't help noticing Annika lurking about the edges of the yard.

Annika appeared to be chasing something in the small cottage garden, but the willow branch fencing blocked Evelyne's view. As she drew closer, she saw a chicken had gotten in the garden, and Annika was running about, shooing the bird toward the gate. Evelyne stopped at the fence and rested her elbows atop a cross post.

"Come now." Annika stalked closer as the bird stopped to inspect an insect. "Be a good girl." She fluttered her tunic hem and stomped a bit to move the bird in the desired direction. Instead, the hen hopped, fluttered, turned, and ran in the opposite direction.

Evelyne laughed.

Annika looked up at her with a smile. "Think it's funny, do you?" She walked to where Evelyne stood. She wiped her hands on her tunic and tucked a loose hair back in place.

Evelyne put her hands up. "I'm not a specialist in this sort of thing, but she seems to be giving you a bit of trouble."

Annika tilted her head and gestured with one hand. "Would you like to give it a go?"

Evelyne stood to her full height. She'd come down to fight today and had spent the whole time with Steffen, testing her knowledge of arms instead of testing her strength. Chasing this chicken might be what she needed to burn off the extra excitement coursing through her muscles. Displaying her prowess for Annika wouldn't hurt, either.

"How hard can it be?" She walked to the open gate and stepped inside. Annika swept by her with a gentle smile. She stood outside the fence line and held the gate, ready to close it.

Evelyne looked back at the bird now pecking the ground in the far corner near some cabbage. How difficult could this be?

She approached with confidence, certain a few well-placed shoos and a stomp or two would have the desired effect. The bird moved. First, it ran across the garden; then it ran back the other way. It maneuvered through a patch of leeks, winding through the aboveground greens. Several times, Evelyne attempted this approach, and each time, the chicken clucked, hopped, ran, and fluttered its way into different locations, none of which were near the gate.

Winded, Evelyne stopped and placed her hands on her knees. When she stood, she caught Annika's eye. Annika leaned against the fence, her chin resting on one hand. Her eyes twinkled with mischief.

"Don't get too comfortable," said Evelyne. "She will be through the gate at any moment."

Annika murmured, "Mmm," and waited in the same relaxed position.

Soon took longer than Evelyne suspected. Sweat dripped from her forehead as she rushed side to side, hollering at the bird and waving her arms. The spectacle succeeded only in making Annika giggle and winding Evelyne once more.

"Underworld spawn," said Evelyne to the bird. "I'll best you yet."

This time, she approached with stealth, creeping up on the chicken, slowly closing the distance between them. When she was within an arm's length, she dove without thought to how she looked to tackle the bird, succeeding only in landing facedown in a fresh patch of carrots.

Annika laughed. The sound was charming to her ear.

Evelyne sat up. "Seems I have landed on my face around you once again."

"Not as easy as it looks, is it?" Annika teased.

Evelyne watched as the hen strutted through the gate on her own. She shook her head and stood. She leaned across the fence near Annika. "Care to try to get me out of the garden now?"

Annika's cheeks flushed. She turned away. "I have much to do."

"Afraid you might have to catch me?" Evelyne teased.

"Good day to you, m'lady," Annika threw back over her shoulder in a light tone.

Evelyne watched her walk away before opening the gate, stepping out and closing it behind her. The hen pecked about at her feet. "Next time, might you do me a favor and let me look better in front of the girl?" she whispered to the bird. She smiled to herself. Maybe learning to fight wasn't all she enjoyed in life.

❖

For the next few weeks, at Steffen's behest, Evelyne started her day at the forge at dawn and then went to the cottage, and each midday, she went hunting to cover her activities. She was too tired to put much effort into the pursuit, so she'd returned with a squirrel the first time. Old Nan had tutted and taken the scrawny little thing by the tail. Evelyne was certain it was destined for the servant's pottage, but at least nothing would go to waste.

The time went by quickly, and now Steffen was letting her use a practice sword. Evelyne thrust her wooden sword from behind a small round shield. Steffen easily deflected the blow. Quick short bursts of thrusts, parries, and slices, each fight lasting only moments. Sometimes, she won, but most times, she lost.

Steffen ignored Evelyne's curses. "I'm bigger than you. I have a longer reach. You must find a weakness and use it."

She waited for his counter against her shield before moving in close to try to take him off his feet. He didn't budge. He laughed. She stomped on his toes. He wailed and stumbled back. She took her buckler and leapt at him with the flat front. He recovered, blocked her shield with his, and used the blunt side of his sword to knock the wind out of her.

She fell to the ground, gasping and trying to catch her breath. She glanced to where Annika sat weaving a basket. Annika didn't meet her eye, but she could see the smile on her face. Evelyne was once again on the ground.

"A good try," said Steffen.

Though she could barely catch her breath, the praise exhilarated her. This was the first approval he had given her.

"Feet, throat, nose. They're all sensitive. Even someone my size reacts to pain without thinking. Gives you a moment to strike. Remember, you can use a buckler for more than defense." He helped her up and handed her the buckler. "You can hit with it like a pike or knife." He pulled the edge of the shield toward his nose, his neck, and finally his knee. "Or a man's rod and balls. Beggin' your pardon, m'lady."

Her cheeks warmed. Hearing it from Witt and Dodd differed from Annika's father. She didn't enjoy thinking about what hid under men's tunics. She'd seen them, but it made her queasy to think one day Samuel would mount her. And what if he was shorter than her?

"Remember. In battle, you'll have one chance to kill your enemy before he or she kills you. You won't be parrying and toying with each other like the squires at the manor." He rushed her unexpectedly. She parried his first strike. He swept his foot under hers, bringing her to the ground, and he motioned a thrust to her chest as she lay undefended. "That is a fight, m'lady."

He reached out and pulled Evelyne to her feet. She nodded, understanding.

"Time for you to leave."

"Can't we go again?"

He turned away and placed his practice sword against the cottage. "You agreed, m'lady," he said. "I have work to do."

At moments like this, she wished she was her father. Wished she could order him to keep training her. Do what she said. Until she caught sight of Annika watching from the edge of the yard, gathering carrots in her apron. What would Annika think of her acting petty and petulant? She thought back to how quickly Matilde had accepted that Evelyne would take her hunting in a few weeks. If her sibling, ten harvests her junior, could accept what she could not control, so could Evelyne.

She wandered to where Annika sat weeding in the garden. "The hen isn't in here, is she?" asked Evelyne, looking around as if wary of the bird.

Annika smiled. "Afraid of a chicken? I'd think a noble lady like yourself would need not worry about a tiny thing like her."

Evelyne leaned against the wattle fence. "Not worry as much as awaiting a rematch." She strolled to the gate and came in. "I was wondering if you might teach me how to play the gittern?"

Annika stopped pulling weeds and wiped her forehead. She frowned. "I doubt I'm a good teacher."

"Maybe just a few lessons?" She knelt beside Annika and took the weeds from her hands, placing them on a pile with others. "A few chords. Save me from having to spend the rest of my day listening to my sisters prattle on about hairstyles and embroidery and handsome knights."

Annika eyed her suspiciously. "Don't take to handsome knights?"

Evelyne felt the blush creep up her neck. She smiled and tried to sound confident. "I prefer musicians."

Now it was Annika who blushed. "All right." She stood. "Come, then. But I'll warn you, the chickens like the sound of the gittern. You may have an admirer before long."

Evelyne wished the admirer was Annika, not a chicken.

During the first few lessons, Evelyne found her fingers played familiar chords from her lute. The instruments looked so similar, but the sounds were so different. Annika would laugh and take her fingers and place them in the right spots. Evelyne would sigh and spend more time staring at Annika's profile than at the chord shapes.

As the days went on, she found Steffen's fights to be more and more challenging, but she spent more time thinking about being close to Annika. After one particularly tough music lesson, her frustration boiled over, and she handed the instrument back to Annika.

"I don't understand why it is so hard to learn to play. You make it sound so beautiful. If you were to play at a celebration, everyone would be enraptured." She pointed at the gittern. "I play it, and it sounds like a horse braying."

"You're frustrated because you aren't good at it right away," Annika said knowingly.

Evelyne frowned.

"True, isn't it?" said Annika. "You've always been good at everything, haven't you? Well, everything that requires strength, speed, and accuracy."

"Your point?"

"The gittern asks that you play it with your heart, not your head."

Evelyne drew her shoulders back and strutted to the other side of the room. "Are you implying I have no heart?"

Annika gave her a knowing smirk. "I'm saying you like to be the best at everything."

"Have you ever danced?"

"What? Of course. Well, a few times at the celebrations."

"I mean a courtly dance, you and a partner."

Annika played with the end of her belt. "No. When would I have been at court?"

Evelyne pointed at her. "Good argument. I think we shall have a few dance lessons. If I'm not taking too much of your time."

Annika stood and opened the door. "I will think about it. M'lady, my chores await." She gave an exaggerated bow. Evelyne returned it.

She stood tall and bounced as she walked to the castle. She didn't even bother to hunt. Every squirrel along the way seemed to take note of their freedom, running across her path in packs. She felt light and happy, perhaps happier than she had ever been.

❖

Steffen gave her a thrashing one day. He made her fight with no weapon while he swung at her with a sword. He told her that one day, she would lose her weapon and need to stay alive long enough to find another. She jumped and ducked and weaved, and most of the time, he hit her. Hard.

"Dead," he'd say each time.

Now she limped inside the cottage. "Maiden's blessing on you," she said to Annika. She wiped her dirty hands on her tunic. "I haven't seen you these past few days."

Annika stirred a pottage over the firepit. "I've been quite busy."

"I think you're avoiding our dance lesson." Evelyne sat on the floor and stretched her legs. They were already seizing from the fighting.

Annika poured an ale from a stoppered jug to a wooden mug and offered it to her.

She took a drink. "Your father is an excellent teacher."

"He is that, yes. And you once again, you sprawled on the ground for me," Annika teased.

Evelyne smiled and stared at the golden liquid in her cup. A few fermented bubbles popped along the sides. She sipped the ale. It tasted and smelled like warm bread.

Annika moved to the window and looked out, her face concerned. Evelyne could hear indistinct voices become louder and then softer once again. Annika reached for her Maiden necklace, rubbing it the way Evelyne's mother did when she felt concerned.

"You seem nervous."

"Yes. I mean, no." Annika appeared flustered. "Villagers on their way to the mill. Should they see you here and your father was to find out, they'd punish my da."

Evelyne hadn't thought of Steffen's welfare when she'd asked him to teach her. She knew she could get in trouble, but she was used to being in trouble. She hadn't thought through what might happen to him. She patted the floor beside her. "Please, sit."

Annika poured herself a drink and sat cross-legged on the floor next to her.

"I'll deny he ever did more than tell me what each weapon is called and the purpose of each. That should keep him safe." She watched Annika continue to rub her necklace. "Does she bring you comfort?"

Annika dropped her hand. "Sometimes." She took a drink of ale. "I try to feel her presence, but she's never appeared to me or spoken to me the way the elders say she should."

Evelyne waved a hand. "I'm the worst adherent to the Book of anyone in my family. I can barely stay awake in temple. Unless there's a battle. Doesn't help that we worship the Maiden, but only old balding men get to tell her story."

Annika looked as if she was concentrating or deciding about something. "In Weya, they worship female and male gods. Gods that are both and gods that are neither. Anyone can choose to lead a worship service. They don't even have to know the language of the gods."

Evelyne sat her mug on the floor and lay on her back. She stared at the crossbeams of the roof and the dark thatch. A glimpse of blue sky shone through the hole in the center. Neither nor both. Some days, she felt that way about herself. She turned her head to look at Annika. "Did your mother teach you those things?"

Annika nodded. "She told me stories in bed to help me fall asleep. Fairy tales, they were. Odd names, strange gods, peculiar places. Craggy mountains full of great horned beasts. She said the mountain she was born under was as tall as the sky." Her voice became louder with amazement. "Is that even possible?"

Evelyne thought about it. "I've never seen the Dragon's Back. But they say they are much taller than the mount across the valley."

"I've forgotten the names now she isn't here to repeat them."

Evelyne pushed up on one elbow. "I'm sure Master Jacob has some books on Weya at the castle. I could bring you one."

Annika turned her head away, looking at the ground. "You needn't do that."

"I'll talk to him next time I'm in the library. He loves to push dusty books around and lecture me on things I do not know. If I show the slightest interest in Weya, I'll be up to my knees in parchment."

Annika frowned. "I...I cannot read." Her embarrassment was obvious.

"Not at all? Your father?" she asked softly.

Annika shook her head. "No one in the village reads. Books cost coin. People would prefer to eat."

Shame flooded Evelyne. How did she not know this? All her siblings, all the knights and the trainees, the elders, they could all read. She thought of Old Nan in the kitchen. Could she read? When would she have time to do so? "Would you like to see Weya someday?" she asked.

Annika frowned and shook her head slightly. "I don't know. I've only ever known this valley. Weya seems so...very far away."

It was farther than Evelyne had traveled. A full cycle of the moon or more. The entire length of Northern Valmora. She could only imagine what the great heights, snows, and cold of the dark north would be like. And yet, she thought she might go if Annika asked her. "You miss your mother a lot."

"I think of her every day." Annika hung her head. "I would trade anything to have her here with us again."

Evelyne reached out and took Annika's hand. She squeezed gently. As much as she complained about her lot in life, her mother was sitting in her chamber right now, available to hug and play cards and argue with. Annika didn't pull her hand away, and when she looked up, her eyes wet with tears, Evelyne sat up and pulled her into a hug.

Annika felt good against her. The hug was to give comfort, but she melted into the embrace as well. She stroked Annika's hair, turning her head closer until loose tendrils tickled her face. She inhaled an arousing, heady scent and couldn't stop herself from reaching with her free hand to touch Annika's back where it curved slightly inward.

She did not know how long they held each other. The moment kept her from thinking about anything but the warmth and comfort of their fit.

Annika broke the hug when she stood abruptly. "I must get back to my tasks."

Evelyne frowned. She wanted to stay here on the floor, wrapped in Annika's arms for a while longer. Reluctantly, she rose and brushed off the loose reeds. "Thank you for the ale." She handed over her mug. "See you on the morrow?"

Annika nodded. "On the morrow."

Outside, Evelyne retrieved her bow and quiver from their hiding place and headed home. Though her body was tired from the training, she floated in a fog of satisfaction. Her progress wasn't the only thing pleasing her. There was something about Annika, a feeling that they were becoming friends. But the farther she walked from the cottage, the more the distance brought her destiny back in clarity. Before long, she would live at the home of Samuel, minor lord of a minor manor on the edge of nowhere. If only she could somehow take Annika and Steffen with her.

Lost in thought, she nearly stumbled into a familiar face sitting on the stone wall before her, a bow leaning against the stones. *Maiden's eyes, why now?*

"Timothy." She nodded at him.

He hopped from the wall and retrieved the bow before falling in step with her. "I thought we spoke of this, Evelyne."

"Of what?" If he was going to berate her for something, he'd have to say it clearly.

"Fighting."

She stopped. "So you followed me?"

"Matilde told me you'd gone hunting. I thought I'd join you. Wasn't hard to find you. The miller saw you come this way, and I heard the practice swords from the top of the hill."

"So why wait? Why not barge in and embarrass us all?"

He looked hurt. "Because we're friends, and I care about you. I thought you understood why you shouldn't fight anymore. I never thought you'd ask a peasant to spar with you instead."

"Steffen is a pikeman. He was a foot soldier for Father. A good one, from what I can tell. His leg is injured, and nevertheless, he beats me nine out of ten rounds."

"Of course he does. He's a man."

Evelyne's face burned at the comment. She shook her head. "And when I beat you? Am I thus a man?"

He sputtered. "You know what I meant."

"I don't, actually. Is it because he is larger than me? He is heavier and has longer arms but is no taller. More experienced? Yes. Or do you mean it's because he has bits dangling between his legs I don't have?"

"Evelyne, you shouldn't talk so."

She increased her pace. "Because it isn't ladylike? Or because you don't want to think about my marriage to Samuel any more than I do?"

He stopped.

She stopped and turned to him. "Let's not talk about this anymore. What I want to know is, are you going to tell anyone about Steffen?"

"I should tell your father." He crossed his arms and huffed.

"And get Steffen in trouble for my selfishness? Do you hate me so much?"

He looked aghast. "Hate you? I don't hate you, Evelyne. I…I care about you…deeply."

She pressed her forefinger to his chest. "If you care about me, keep this a secret. He's only agreed to teach me a few moves, a few days at most." She pulled her hand back and softened her tone. "Please, Timothy. Let me have a few more days before Mother has me readying for my wedding."

He looked as if the request was warring in his head. "All right, but if he hurts you in any way, I will tell your father."

Good thing he couldn't see under her tunic. She was certain that the bruises stretched from shoulder to hip.

"In return, the least you can do is take me hunting." He pointed to the pack on his back. "Nan packed enough food for the both of us. I'm starving from sitting around all morning waiting for you."

She was glad to change the subject. And though she loved hunting almost as much as fighting, something made her want to turn and run back to the cottage as fast as she could.

CHAPTER FOURTEEN

Moonlight filtered through the window, drawing Evelyne's attention to the delicate vines and flowers painted on the white walls of her chamber. In winter, the drapes covering her canopy bed blocked her view of the room, but summer meant she could see the decorative paintwork, though sans color.

This was the fourth night in a row that slumber had eluded her. The room was quiet, considering three of her sisters and two servant girls were together in the chamber. None of them seemed to have any trouble sleeping. Just her.

Her thoughts drifted from the excitement of learning to fight from Steffen to the songs Annika played on the gittern. The way she moved through her chores. The color of her hair. What was she doing right now? Was she asleep, or was she lying with her eyes on the thatch roof and rough beams of the cottage ceiling?

When morning began, the rain was relentless. Evelyne meandered through the castle, periodically stopping and looking outside. She wanted to be at the cottage, but she had no excuse to go out in the rain.

She was restless. Now that she was learning how a real soldier fought, she wanted to use the training. Instead, she was confined to the castle, trying to remember all the things Steffen had showed her. She mindlessly wandered to the armory at the bottom of the great tower, strolling from rack to rack, fingering the gambesons, stroking the spear shafts, and following the intricate chain mail weaves with her fingertips.

A poster hung above the racks of swords. Someone had scrawled a crude drawing of a person wiping a sword and placing it in its scabbard. Of course, every knight knew that if they didn't clean their sword before putting it away, it would rust or become pitted. This drawing must have been a reminder to the pages and squires.

And with that, an idea blossomed.

Evelyne took the spiral staircase two steps at a time in her hurry to the library. She came to an abrupt stop and searched the large room. "Master Jacob?" she called.

The elderly scholar stuck his head around a full shelf. He was wearing two odd circles on his face made of wood and glass. He pulled the contraption off and moved in her direction. "Lady Evelyne." He dropped a heavy tome on the nearby table, sending dust in the air and filling the space with the dreary smell of mildew. "What can I do for you today? More books on strategy? Or are you ready for a challenging read? I have a new book of philosophy from Iola. So many interesting ideas."

She drew a circle in the dust on the table between them. "Actually, I would like to write a book."

"I see." His eyebrows raised slightly. "And Maiden tell me, what do you intend to write?"

"Draw, actually. I want to make some drawings." She made gestures as if drawing in the air. "I was hoping you might have some parchment I could have."

"Patterns for embroidery?" He chuckled.

Because of course, that was all women would want to draw. He knew her better than that. She realized he was teasing her. "Something like that, yes. I need several sheets. I'd like to cut them down to about so." She held her hands apart to show the width and height.

"Hmm." He laid the wood and glass apparatus on the book and headed to the back of the room. "I might have something."

While he made shuffling noises, Evelyne took the item on the book and held it to her face as he had done. It instantly gave her a headache. The glass made everything look odd and distorted. What in the world did he use this for? She put it down on his return.

"A merchant from the Concordant Kingdoms was in Byetown on the last market day. He gave me this to try." Master Jacob carried a stack of white parchment tied in a bundle. He put it on the table between them. "He called it paper. Made from rags, apparently. I've not found a use for it yet."

Evelyne touched the top piece. It was stiff like parchment but felt like felted wool.

"I don't believe this will replace parchment. Too flimsy." He pushed it toward her along with several dark sticks. "The merchant said you can use these to write with." He held up one stick. "Have as much as you like."

Evelyne was overjoyed. This would do well. "Master Jacob." She bit her lip and ran a finger over the stack of paper. "Do you have any books on Weya?"

He cocked his head as if he was thinking about it before he answered. "I might have something." He moved to the stacks. "The Weyan language is obscure. Very few people speak it. And there is little written by them, but we might have something." She could hear him shifting something heavy. "They don't have great cities like us or any culture to speak of." He came back with a small stack of parchment without a cover and gave it to her. He waggled a finger, accompanied by a smile. "Make sure you bring it back intact."

Without a cover, discoloration mottled the first page, and the edges frayed like dried meat. The book was loose parchment stitched together; eight pages long, written in a delicate, wavy script, hard even for her to read.

She thanked him and walked back down the stairs toward the armory. She heard the clinking of swordplay before she turned the corner. In the corridor, her brothers and the other young men were lined up to challenge one another, swords in hand. She tucked herself in an alcove meant for a bowman and watched. This was a great opportunity to think about what Steffen told her. She pulled a sheet of paper and tested the writing implement. It left a dark gray line behind. Convenient not to have a pot of ink to carry around.

Erik and another boy fought nearest to her. She watched their swings, footwork, and feints. Her brother was using too much energy. His strikes too wide. Too much flourish. When he lost to his opponent, she spoke. "You could win in three strikes if you made your movements smaller."

"You think it's so easy? You do it," he spat back.

There were snickers from some of the other young men.

She hopped off the window, setting the paper down and tucking the little book underneath, and strode over to his opponent. She took his sword and readied herself. When she clasped her hand around the hilt, it felt like an extension of her arm. Even dull and rounded, the sword was steel, and it would sing when she struck her first blow.

This was the moment she had waited for. A few weeks with Steffen had changed this moment from wishful to meaningful. She would win this fight. She was certain.

"Evelyne," her mother's voice rang out. "To me."

It wasn't a request.

Her bravado crumbled. She handed over the sword while the others bowed to her mother. She felt the loss of the weight as soon as the sword left her hand.

Under his breath, Erik muttered, "Saved from a bollocking, cunt."

The insult burned. She flexed her hands. It took all the energy she had not to round on him and knock him to the ground. After gathering her paper, she fell in beside her mother. The chatelaine and a servant trailed them as they walked away.

When they were no longer in sight of the fighters, her mother stopped and turned to her. "What were you thinking?"

"I was going to show him a better way to beat his opponent," she replied honestly.

Her mother rolled her eyes. "You don't seriously think you can beat any of your brothers at swordplay, do you? You must train for years to become proficient. Your archery is magnificent, as well it should be, but swords are a great deal different."

"I've been training." As soon as the words slipped out, Evelyne knew she'd made a mistake. "I have been training in my mind for as long as I can remember. I've watched them. Examined the moves. Memorized them."

"No matter. We have so many more important things to accomplish." Her mother walked again.

With the sword in her hand facing her brother, she'd stood tall, wanting to prove herself. Now, she hunched, falling into the pattern of making herself smaller around her mother, trying not to be the unusual daughter. "You don't believe I can do it."

"What?"

"You don't believe I could fight them."

Conflict crossed her mother's face before she finally answered. "I know you can fight them, Evelyne. And I know you want to, but you mustn't." She glanced back at the women trailing them. In a lower voice, she said, "This isn't about how accomplished you are or how strong you are. What do you think would happen if you defeated Erik in combat in front of the others? He already doesn't wish to be a knight. You would have shamed him. The others would beat and taunt him mercilessly. You haven't seen the bruises. I have. He was twelve when I had to tell him not to come to me crying."

Evelyne didn't want to hear about how he felt. "So not only do I have to consider my reputation but his as well?"

"Do you hear yourself?" her mother asked incredulously. "When you are the lady of your own manor, you'll be thinking of your husband, your children, your servants, the people on your lands, your reputation for trade and allies. You'll be thinking of everyone else."

Was this what lay ahead for her?

"When you're married," her mother continued, "perhaps you'll have more freedom to do as you please. Maiden willing, Samuel will get to know you and understand your desire for independence."

"And perhaps he won't." She heard the bitterness in her own voice.

Her mother's eyes narrowed. "You won't know until you meet him."

They walked in silence for a few steps. She was certain her mother was letting the words sit upon her before saying anything else. Evelyne felt bad for Erik, but she felt bad for herself as well.

"I want to embroider your wedding coverlet. You've spent much too much time hunting these past few weeks."

Something about the way she said *hunting* made Evelyne uncomfortable. Her mother seemed to have a sense of Evelyne's doings. Was she aware of all her activities?

"There are things you need to know about your wedding night."

"Mother." Evelyne felt the blush fill her cheeks. She knew about what happened on the wedding night. She'd watched enough animals and listened to Witt and the other young men talk about their conquests, the advantage of secretly observing boys her whole life.

"I will help you with this discussion myself. I don't believe Elder Theobald knows enough to explain things properly."

Was that a bit of humor? Evelyne eyed her mother carefully, but she gave nothing away.

Evelyne nodded appropriately as her mother continued to discuss wedding needs, but her thoughts were on fighting. The stack of paper Master Jacob had given her felt soft against her palm. If she could capture what she had learned from Steffen, she could practice the moves repeatedly, even if only with a straw dummy or a tree in the forest. She couldn't wait to get somewhere and begin. She would prove her mother wrong. She would prove them all wrong.

CHAPTER FIFTEEN

Evelyne held the staff of the pike with both hands. The sharp metal tip gleamed in the sunlight. She trembled slightly at the thought of using the weapon against Steffen. One wrong move and she could kill him.

"Don't worry," he said, as if he had read her mind. "I want you to practice with a real weapon. Feel the weight. Know the balance point. I'll call out a swing for you to parry and counter. We'll go at a slow pace."

She understood; nevertheless, the fear was there. They started slowly, a blow and a counterblow. Then the pace quickened. Overhand. Counter. Slice. Counter. Thrust. Counter. Over and over and over. Low thrust, high thrust, reverse-hand thrust. Evelyne parried Steffen's move and repeated his action as her counter. Sweat dripped in her eyes, the muscles cramped in her arms, and her toes dragged as her feet came forward. Finally, Steffen stopped the practice, and Evelyne rested the pike carefully against a pile of hay. She retrieved a bucket of water, pouring half of it on her head, and drank from the bucket itself, not bothering with a ladle.

When she had a few moments to catch her breath, Steffen approached with a wooden replica of the pike, a perfectly shaped point and crescent beak on its top. "Time to give it a better try."

Evelyne grasped the wooden pike the same way she had held the metal-tipped one. Steffen called out the first few blows with his practice sword, giving her time to adjust to the differences in weight and balance. He swung without warning. The first couple caught her off guard, and the welts from his touches stung.

She readied again, this time with the point in front of her. Steffen thrusted, and she spun the handle of the pike upward to parry the blow.

On her counter, she thrust the pike's beak behind Steffen's knee and pulled as hard as she could. He lost his balance, crashing to the ground on his back. Evelyne mimed a killing blow to the chest, stopping an inch from the fabric of his gambeson. She threw the weapon down and squatted next to him.

"I'm sorry, Steffen. Are you hurt?" She'd intentionally gone for his good leg, knowing his stiff leg might not hold his weight. Now she felt guilty for the choice.

"Well done, Evie," he cried as she helped him to his feet. He seemed genuinely happy, and that made her happy as well.

When they restarted with more blows from his sword, something changed for her. She envisioned the twitches, the slight movements, the way Steffen set his feet and his fingers. Things she had never seen when working with Timothy in their furtive, quick fights. When half the day had passed, she had won seven of every ten attacks.

Steffen sat against the outside wall of the cottage. "I'm proud of you."

She sat next to him and fished out bread and cheese from the bag Nan had packed for her. She broke off several pieces and handed them to him. She didn't bother to wash her hands. She was becoming used to the black fingernails and open blisters. "You're a wonderful teacher," she replied. "Better than Master Berin, I suspect. I only wish my father would see fit to assign the squires to you."

"Oh no." He wiped the sweat from his face with the tail of his rough woolen shirt. "I've not been deemed a knight with a sword on my shoulder." His words betrayed sarcasm. "Besides, who of your brothers would have a bird keeper best them in a fight?"

"I know this is the way of things, Steffen, but I wish they were different." She paused. "For you...and for Annika."

"We're all here to do our part for the king and Valmora." He shrugged off the compliment. "There are worse places to live. I've seen them."

"Tell me about your fighting in the North," she said.

"What do you wish to know?"

"Your wife was Weyan. Did you go to Weya?"

"I did. We were fighting the Mons. They came across the plains, along the Dragon's Back to our northern border, raiding farms near Weya. We fought them right along the foothills of the Weyan Mountains. The Weyans wouldn't fight with either army, but they supplied us with food when they could. They have no love for the Mons, but Weyans only fight when they must. They can hide in those mountains for years if they want, and you'd never see a one of them."

Evelyne shoved the last of her bread in her mouth. She wished she had brought more. "How did you meet your wife?" she asked.

"The minute I laid eyes on her, I knew she was the one for me."

He didn't answer her question, but she didn't push. She hesitated to ask the next. "Steffen...why didn't you ever take another betrothed? With a young daughter to care for, most men would have found a nice young woman...to help."

He stood and shuffled about, scraping dirt off the pike. "I wasn't planning on taking a wife the first time. I thought I would live the life of a wandering foot soldier. Going from one fight to another. Or that I'd be dead at a young age." He stared into the distance. "When I met Hella, I was full of myself, cocksure and arrogant." He leaned on the pike. "She calmed me with her smile. No one could ever fill her place in my heart. I decided it wouldn't be fair to marry a young woman. Better she married a young man who would love her the way I loved my Hella."

Did her father love her mother in that way? "You believe in love. Not duty?"

"I believe in both," he replied. He collected the weapons and handed them to her. "Put these in the cottage, would you? And you'd best be on your way. Don't want the watch looking for you."

"Damn the watch and damn my father."

"Please, m'lady." He looked around nervously. "You never know who might hear."

"I don't care who listens," she replied. "He hates me anyway. He wants me married as soon as possible. If I had the choice between love and duty, I know which one I would choose." She'd choose to stay here and learn more. "He's not my father. He's my keeper," she said, her tone sullen.

He moved forward and laid a gentle hand on her shoulder. "I know I was not welcoming at first, but I've grown fond of you, as has Annika." He pulled his hand back.

"I too." Evelyne smiled. "On the morrow?"

He nodded.

In the cottage, Annika worked a needle and thread, repairing hose. "Maiden bless you."

"Annika. Good day."

Why was she nervous? Her hand shook slightly, but maybe that was from wielding the pike all morning. She dropped her tunic and bag on the floor and walked the weapons to the corner, placing them carefully against the wall. She moved to her things and pulled her tunic over her head, extending her arms fully, and wriggled to get the garment on. The fabric rubbed across her nose as she shimmied, but it wouldn't fall into place.

Annika's hands on her sides startled her. She'd been dressed her whole life, but it never felt like this. Everywhere Annika touched, she felt nothing else. Her breathing was shallow, and she had an odd, pleasant feeling in her stomach. As the fabric cleared her face, Annika stood in front of her, so close Evelyne could hear her breathing. She tugged the sleeves and reached under the hem and pulled the shift down so it wouldn't bunch. All the while, Evelyne stood stock-still. Lastly, she took the belt from the pile and reached around Evelyne's waist, bringing it forward and looping it through itself.

Being this close was intoxicating. Everything inside Evelyne was screaming to reach out and pull Annika into an embrace. To kiss her and tell her secrets. To whisper thoughts she wasn't supposed to say to anyone but her future husband. And yet her arms felt too heavy to lift, as if the weight of moving forward was too much. What had Steffen said? He wouldn't take another young wife because she deserved to marry a man who could truly love her. Annika deserved someone who could give her all those things and more. And Evelyne was neither available to marry, nor could they marry even if she was.

She reached out and tucked a lock of Annika's hair behind her ear. In return, she was greeted with a gentle blush and a tender smile.

The door flew open. Evelyne quickly withdrew her hand.

Steffen hung several tools on a hook. "Still here, I see."

"I am leaving momentarily." She and Annika gave each other amused smiles.

Steffen lay on his hay mattress. "Good...good." And with that, he was snoring loudly.

"He hasn't worked this hard in many years," Annika whispered.

Evelyne looked at his sleeping face. "No need to whisper. He's visiting the dream keeper already. I have something to show you." She pulled up a stool to the table and retrieved a thin parchment book from her satchel. "This was the only item Master Jacob had in the library."

Annika sat next to her and moved close. Their knees touched, setting off another round of flip-flopping in Evelyne's stomach. She cleared her throat and forced herself to focus.

"This is the account of Warembaldus, a master assigned to

the retinue of King Gregor the Emboldened. This is a first-person account of something he called 'the great war.' I've never heard of it, so I thought it must not have been actually great, but once I read it, I changed my mind. Seems a foe, called the Horde, came from the southeast and overran Iola, Valmora, and the lands we know as the Concordant Kingdoms. All of them together were fighting this Horde."

She turned several pages. "Mostly, he notes battle locations, who attended, and results, but the reason this was shelved near the books on Weya is because of this." She pointed at a passage and read it aloud.

While she read, her knee brushed Annika's. When it did, her breathing became shallow, and she dared not move. Her heart beat hard, and she felt a pulsing between her thighs. She was distracted to where she didn't hear what Annika asked. She felt the contact of their knees and watched the movement of Annika's delicate lips.

"What does it mean that Elder Eberwulf *touched* the enemy?" Annika asked. She pointed to the illustration.

"What?"

"You said, Elder Eberwulf *touched* the enemy."

Evelyne blushed. She looked at the words and the tiny illustration that accompanied it. A robed figure stood on a hilltop, and an inset illustration showed an army covering their ears and falling in agony to their knees. "The army was pushed to Weya, their rear to the Dragon's Back. They had nowhere else to go. He says Elder Eberwulf performed a miracle. I don't think Eberwulf was a real Elder, not the way we think of one. She was Weyan. In the description, he says, she reached across the great plain and struck down the enemy with the vision of the gods."

"Vision of the gods?"

"I think he means a seer. She was a seer."

"You think a seer struck down an entire army?"

Evelyne studied the illustration. "I suppose he might exaggerate somewhat, but it makes a thrilling story, yes?"

Annika looked enthralled. She fairly shook with excitement. Evelyne wondered if the story brought her closer to her mother in some way. Evelyne looked at Steffen, still sleeping, snoring loudly. She turned back to Annika, leaned close, and kissed her on the cheek. When Annika didn't pull away, she lingered for a moment. Even through the competing smells of geese, earth, and straw, the delicate and enticing smell of Annika herself came through. A thrill coursed through Evelyne's body. She wondered if Annika could feel it too.

When she pulled away, a blush filled Annika's cheeks. She

wouldn't meet Evelyne's eyes. She placed her hands in her lap, and a half-smile played on her lips.

Should Evelyne apologize for taking advantage of the moment? "There is something else." She let the kiss be. She turned the crisp page and removed a folded sheet, unattached to the rest. She unfurled it on the tabletop. "I thought maybe you might know something about these symbols."

Annika's eyes went wide. She leaned over the table, taking a closer look. "I can't read the words, but I know these symbols. I've forgotten their proper names, but this one"—she pointed to the bottom—"is the God of the Underworld, and his opposite"—she pointed to a symbol at the top—"the Goddess of the Sky."

Evelyne studied the symbols. They were swirls and dots and circles and curves, triangles, boxes, and lines. They meant nothing to her.

"The row on the bottom is the minor gods. Here's the Maiden." She pointed at a symbol vaguely reminiscent of a woman holding wheat.

Weyans believed in the Maiden? If so, why did the Book say they were heathens?

"This one is the Goddess of the Hunt, and that's the River of Life, and here is the Cave of Beginnings."

"And these?" Evelyne pointed to the center of the page at the largest of the symbols.

"The left one is the Two-Faced God. Both woman and man, and this…" She trailed off, looking pensive while she pointed at the right one, a semicircle with a zig-zag pattern curved over top. She slowly pulled her tunic sleeve up to her elbow. There was an inking on her forearm.

Evelyne had only seen them on visiting merchants from Iola. Now she realized what she was looking at. "Your mark and the one on the page…they're the same." She gently traced the inking with her fingertip.

Annika shivered beneath her touch. "My mother inked me right after I…turned six harvests." She pulled the tunic back in place. "I don't know what it means."

"Could it be the sun?"

Annika shook her head and reached to touch the written version of the symbol. "I don't know. I don't think Weyans worship a sun god. I wish my mother was here to tell us."

When Evelyne looked back at Annika, she was glowing. Everywhere.

"Maiden's eyes!" she exclaimed and stumbled off the stool, falling to the floor. "You're—"

But now there was no glow. Annika's golden hair was backlit by sunlight, and tiny dust motes floated on either side of her head.

"You were..." Evelyne closed her eyes, shook her head, and opened her eyes again. Nothing looked amiss. She turned the stool upright and sat. "I must be tired. I'm seeing things." She rubbed her eyes and blinked a few times. "I need to go." She grabbed for her satchel.

"May I...keep this...for a while?" Annika pointed at the page of symbols. Her hand shook slightly.

Evelyne folded it and left it where it sat. She stuffed the thin book in her pack and slung it over her shoulder. "Keep it as long as you like. No one will miss it." She stood to leave.

"On the morrow."

As she walked back to the castle, she wondered about what she had seen. Annika had been glowing. She wasn't certain of it. Maybe the sunlight had played tricks on her. And yet, something in the pit of her stomach told her she had seen something unusual.

CHAPTER SIXTEEN

Rain drummed on the forge roof and plunked in puddles on the ground.

"She saw something?" Hilfa asked. "You're sure of this?" She pulled Annika behind the forge where Jack wouldn't hear them. They stood close to the stones, trying to stay out of the heavy rain.

"Yes." Annika pulled on her wet braid, nervous. "I glowed, Hilfa. Just as I did when I healed you." She glanced at the strong, muscled arm, unblemished now. Even old scars from hot coals and sharp blades had been healed.

"Did she say anything?"

Annika tried to remember what they'd said. She'd been so scared; she didn't remember much from the exchange. "She was tired. She said she'd return in a few days, but she hasn't come back."

Hilfa took her by the hand. "Don't worry. She's not likely to tell anyone. She has secrets as well. And...I don't know, but I trust her."

"I can't help worrying. Why hasn't she returned?"

"Maiden knows. What gift did you manifest?"

"A vision." She couldn't bring herself to tell Hilfa what she'd seen. She felt her cheeks heat.

"Did it have to do with her?"

Of course it had. There was the sunrise, the grasses heavy with grain, and Evelyne smiling at her...from below her. How could she explain that?

Hilfa smiled. "We all have those who make us feel warm and safe."

Annika laid her head in her hands. "Why a noble?"

Hilfa scratched her own neck. "I can't claim to know the ways of the Maiden. What did your father say about it?"

"He doesn't know."

Hilfa's eyes grew wide. "He needs to know if you're in danger, Anni."

Anni. She hadn't heard that name since her mother had died. "He wouldn't understand."

"He's seen much in life. You'd be surprised what he might understand."

Annika gazed up at Hilfa. "Please, don't tell him. Not yet."

Hilfa didn't look convinced. "For now, let Lady Evelyne spend her coin learning to fight. She's not paying for your company."

Annika nodded.

"And for Maiden's sake, don't touch anyone." Hilfa smiled and cuffed her on the shoulder. Hilfa retreated to the fires of the forge, leaving Annika beneath the roof edge.

She watched the rain pelting the leaves of the bushes and splashing in puddles. For three days, the rains had come. Already, the storms put the harvest at risk. Too much rain and the grain would rot. If they lost the crops, the entire village would suffer this winter. Would she and her da even be here this winter? If they got enough coin, they might head north in the worst of the storm season.

She drew the hood of her mantle over her head and struck out across the wet ground. The rain ran off the oiled mantle fabric but soaked the bottom of her tunic. Hilfa didn't say anything she hadn't already thought about. Yet she wished Evelyne would return so that she would know for certain. The waiting kept her fearful.

She'd spent too much of her life fearful.

At the cottage, she fed the pigs midday leftovers and climbed into the loft of the livestock quarters and sprinkled fresh hay for the cow. Done, she sat and turned her hands over. What made her gifts happen? There was no rhythm or reason for her visions, and Hilfa's healing had seemed almost an accident.

Hidden away with no opportunity for someone to see her, she closed her eyes and willed herself to have a vision. When nothing happened, she rolled the damp sleeve of her shift to her elbow and stared at the marks on her arm. Her mother could explain it all, were she still alive. Annika was certain of that. She touched the inking. Still nothing. Maybe the paper had something to do with it.

She climbed down and found the document tucked behind an earthenware bottle where she'd left it. She took it back to the loft and unfurled it. What about these odd marks and shapes had made her vision occur? As she touched the symbol, she braced herself for the result. She waited. She slowly opened her eyes. Nothing had happened. No vision. No glow.

If it wasn't the document and it wasn't something she could call upon, then what made her gifts work? She remembered Zuri in Byetown telling Annika she could change her appearance if she wished. Annika couldn't even raise a vision at will. How would she ever be able to hide herself in plain sight as Zuri had done?

She closed her eyes and tried again. She thought about Zuri. About what she had said. If Annika needed her, she need only think about her, and Zuri would find her. She tried to remember her features. The hand on her wrist. Her ebony skin. She felt a pull. A forward motion. As if she was being pulled toward the memory. Then the smell struck her. The smell of burning flesh. She recoiled from the memory.

"Takin' a nap?"

She leapt to her feet, grabbing her pitchfork and holding it out in front of her.

"Good to see you've remembered what I've taught you." Only her father's head and shoulders appeared at the top of the ladder.

She pointed the pitchfork downward. "I was feeding Sturdy and the piglets."

He nodded and disappeared down the ladder.

She sat back down. She had been so close. This time, she had felt the pull of the memory. Felt the pull toward Zuri. Later, she'd try again. Her da didn't want to talk about Zuri, but someday, Annika would force him to help find her. She had too many unanswered questions.

And there was Evelyne.

She touched her cheek, remembering the kiss Evelyne had placed there. So many things to think about. None of them made any sense. How could she possibly stay away from Evelyne when she wanted to do exactly the opposite?

CHAPTER SEVENTEEN

D inner was a somber, quiet affair. Everyone, even Evelyne's sisters, seemed unusually silent. Up in the gallery, Elder Theobald looked as if he was going to fall asleep on the lectern. The Book of Enlightenment lay open in front of him. He read the evening's passages with little enthusiasm. Or maybe this was the way things always were, and Evelyne only noticed now.

Before she'd met Steffen and Annika, all she had ever wanted was to learn to fight. To be like her father and brothers. Now all she could think about was spending more time with Annika. She'd even considered offering to help with chores instead of training. She'd be paying to do someone else's household responsibilities, but it would mean spending more time with Annika.

And Annika was becoming all she thought about. She had put the paper and writing sticks to good use in the afternoon, doodling a small drawing of Annika in the margins instead of drawing her fighting stick figures.

She noticed she wasn't the only one distracted. Matilde was ignoring her food and playing with a tiny model of a trebuchet. The same one Evelyne had played with many times. Sending little pebbles across the floor in imitation of a siege, Matilde hit one of her father's hunting dogs. The wolfhound lifted his head and looked around before lying back down. Though he kept one eye open.

Was life always so complicated? She couldn't fool herself. Of course it had been, ever since she'd realized there was something different between her and her brothers. Apparently, the difference wasn't the desire to serve or the desire for women.

A serving girl brought a platter of goose to the table, placing it in front of Evelyne. She was young and pretty, her braided hair wrapped around her head in the same style Annika wore hers. The girl caught Evelyne looking. She winked and smiled. Evelyne felt the blush fill her cheeks. She lowered her eyes to the bird. Had her thoughts been so obvious?

Evelyne stared at the goose, knowing full well where the bird had come from. Knowing that recently, Annika had tended the bird. This one and every other fowl being eaten. Evelyne looked over the room at them all. Annika's handiwork surrounded her.

Evelyne angrily grabbed a handful of meat from the goose. Everything came back to Annika. She even dreamed about her. A few evenings before, her younger sister, Birgitta, woke her, worried when she'd heard Evelyne moaning and had thought she might be sick. Evelyne had coughed and turned away quickly, realizing she had been dreaming. The moaning had resulted from a dream in which she was sitting in a field watching Annika smile. The sun on her golden hair. Biting on a ripe strawberry that had left her lips a ruby red.

Evelyne shifted uncomfortably in her seat.

Winifred tittered. "Mother says I received plenty of offers for courtship over the past few days."

"Did she?" Evelyne asked insincerely.

"I overheard her talking to Father. He said as soon as you and Samuel are married, I'll be allowed to do so. And Mother replied that arrangements were already being made." She smiled happily, oblivious to the sour mood her words brought to Evelyne. "I hope my husband is handsome and strong."

"I hope he is gentle and kind, for your sake," Evelyne replied. The thought of Samuel and her future life left her cold. She wasn't sure if it was the unknown personality of her betrothed or the thought of being tethered to any man or place that was giving her a sense of dread.

The young serving maid at the end of their table caught her gaze and smiled at her again. If only she was Annika. Evelyne pushed the trestle table away, moving it several inches, knocking over a mug of ale, and startling her siblings. She stood and stepped up and over the table and left the room by the servants' passageway. She vaguely heard her mother's admonishment as she left the hall. She ran up the tight spiral staircase to the upper floor and collapsed on a stone window ledge, lowering her head to her hands.

She knew of attraction between girls. Even Elder Theobald

had explained that experimentation between women was allowed as practice for marriage. But nothing about her attraction to Annika felt like practice. It felt like everything.

"Are you feeling well, Evelyne?" Timothy asked.

She raised her head and appraised him. He was no longer the boy she'd always known but a man. He was tall and strong and handsome. She admired his new tunic, given to him as a gift. The gold embroidery shone along the edges all the way to the bottom below his knees. A new, more ornamental belt hung at his waist, made up of connecting metal squares, each square decorated with a scene from the Enlightened Book. Though he wasn't wearing it now, she had seen his ceremonial helm at his table during the meal. Wrapped in red and gold cloth with giant peacock feathers reaching a foot above the rim. He had a strong jawline decorated with the shadow of a beard. His dark eyes made it hard to distinguish between pupil and iris, able to pull a gaze in like a whirlpool.

Evelyne understood so much more now than she had ever before. Timothy was attracted to her. More than the youthful friends they had always been. The way his eyes followed her. His concern. His constant attention. She'd never noticed before because she was never attracted to anyone before.

She stood and pushed him backward against the opposite wall. His lips met hers. She felt the prickly stubble on his upper lip. The roughness of his tongue. She ran her hands along his well-muscled sides. And she waited. Waited for something special. Waited for the tingling, the feeling between her thighs, the desire she had felt when Annika was beside her. She felt none of these things. Timothy didn't even smell good to her. He smelled of sweat and musk and ale.

She pulled her lips from his and lowered her head. He was breathing heavily, and she could feel the swelling of his privy member against her thigh. She was searching for a substitute for Annika, but there was no replacement. Even Timothy, whose counsel she had taken since they were children, couldn't replace the maid with the golden hair. She cried.

He looked at her with concern. "What's the matter, Evelyne?"

She wiped the tears from her cheeks and regained her composure. What would it be like without Timothy, without her siblings, without Annika? "What was it like when you left your family?" she asked him.

He smiled at her tenderly. "Is that what this is about? You're worried about leaving Marsendale for your wedding?"

She nodded. It was, and it wasn't.

He slid down the wall and sat on the floor. She sat beside him. "I don't remember much of my life before I came here. I was young. I remember the trip. I was excited at first, to be traveling so far from home. New villages, new people. And the first time I saw the castle, I was in awe. Our home was a great hall surrounded by a half-timber, half-stone fortification. Nothing like Marsendale."

He paused, perhaps taking a moment to remember. "Then, when I started my training, I missed my siblings...and my mother." He rubbed his eyes with his fingertips. "But Witt and the other boys made sure I knew that was folly. If they caught me being maudlin, they'd strip me naked and lock me out of the page's rooms."

Evelyne shook her head. "He's a bastard."

Timothy nodded. "He is that. He's also a good leader. All the younger men are loyal to him. Only a matter of time before he and they become the best of the best."

"What about you?"

"I'll do what they ask of me. Go where your father tells me," he said.

"Will you miss it here if he tells you to go away?"

He took a moment to reply. "I'll miss you."

She looked away. He was treading on feelings she didn't have for him. "Do you wish you could go home?"

He laughed. "This is my home. My father wouldn't know me if I stood in front of him and said my name. I don't think there is any going home for me. Wherever I am, that's my home."

She wondered if that would be how she felt when she arrived in Dungewall. She knew for certain that Lord Tomas would never replace her father. "I apologize for earlier, Timothy. I wasn't myself."

He took her hand and squeezed. "There is nothing to forgive." He helped her to her feet.

She let go of his hand and looked longingly through the arrow slit near them. Because of the darkness, she couldn't see the meadows, the forest, or the mountains in the distance, but she knew they were there. The same as she knew Annika was out there, even if she couldn't see her.

CHAPTER EIGHTEEN

Evelyne's mother created another task for her the next morning, once again keeping her from leaving the castle to continue training. She sat with her sisters around a large trestle table in her mother's solar, embroidering. The room was well lit, with windows on three sides, each filled with leaded glass, sunlight streaming in and falling on the large bedspread covering the table.

Her wedding coverlet, the one she and her husband-to-be, Samuel, would sleep under…for the rest of her life.

While Birgitta embroidered a delicate scroll of vines and Winifred worked on the petals of a tulip, Evelyne embroidered two men-at-arms fighting, one whose hand was separated from his wrist. Bloodred thread sprayed in all directions. Matilde leaned over Evelyne's shoulder and giggled. She wasn't allowed to work on the blanket, only observe and practice her stitches with an exemplar.

Her mother noted the giggle and paused her thread. "Evelyne."

This started a cascade of head turns and tittering, and everyone, including the serving girl, stood and bent over the table to get a look at Evelyne's handiwork.

"What?" Evelyne felt the awkwardness of all eyes being on her.

"You can't have that on your wedding blanket," her mother replied. "You'll need to pull the thread and start over."

But she wanted warriors on it. She started undoing everything, but she did so at a slow and meticulous pace. Mother could make her do it, but she wouldn't do it with any enthusiasm. And there was the other reason she was eager to get to the village. As much as she wanted to learn to fight, her mind replayed the moments she'd spent with Annika. The way her fingers deftly played the gittern. The beauty of her eyes.

How they drew her in. And the few times she saw Annika smile, subtle and timid but seductive.

Seductive? Where had that thought come from? She glanced up at her mother, worried she could hear her thoughts, but her mother only held her belly with her hand and fanned herself, seemingly unconcerned with Evelyne's thoughts. People couldn't hear her thoughts, Evelyne reassured herself. Not even Talents, though she'd only ever known the few healers from the temple.

The bells pealed, breaking her thoughts and signaling the arrival of outsiders to the castle. Evelyne leapt from her chair and pushed open one of the smaller windows. Several men rushed in the outer wall's direction, clearly not knowing if the visitors were friend or foe, the precaution a requirement of her father's long experience in war. A young man ran in the opposite direction toward the great hall.

Evelyne yelled to him, "Who comes?"

"King's men, m'lady," he yelled back without stopping.

King's men? This far from Tarburg without a royal messenger to precede them? Evelyne's curiosity grew. "I'm going to see the arrivals." She hurried from the room before her mother could respond. Exhilarated to be free of the company of her siblings and the tedium of the embroidery work, she dashed through the yard along the inner wall and came to a stop at the gateway. She stood partially hidden behind the stone archway and peeked into the outer bailey as the king's men entered through the gatehouse.

Twenty men, all in bright and clean king's colors. The exception being a single man leading the group wearing indigo from head to toe. Evelyne drew a sharp breath. The Paladin of the Harvest Maid. The most powerful Talent in the kingdom. The defender of the faith. His hair fell to his shoulders in curling, dark waves, and his face was clean shaven. Head erect and shoulders back, he dismounted, handing his gloves and horse's reins to a groom.

This was him, the man chosen at six years old to be the Paladin. Few men had gifts, and those who did were healers, but this man had a more powerful and useful gift than healing for his duties. The king had tasked him with finding Talents across the kingdom. Rumor said he could convince anyone to help him.

Evelyne didn't trust rumors. She thought back to when *she* was six. The main gatehouse behind the Paladin reminded her of the time she'd thrown horse chestnuts, still in their spiky outer shells, on her brothers through the murder hole. She was pretending to defend the castle; she'd rained the pointy ammunition down until she'd hit Master Berin on his balding head. Her siege defense had ended with her father's seneschal grabbing her and dragging her to her mother's solar, where a handmaiden had paddled her so hard, she couldn't sit for a day.

She rubbed her backside at the memory. Not as auspicious a start as the man before her. His life was as preordained for him as it was for her, but at least his was an interesting role to play for the kingdom. Hers was to marry and have babies. Make more aristocratic Valmorans to rule and have a say in how to run things. Of course, that assumed she had male heirs. She would be stuck in the solar, embroidering to her heart's content, if she survived the birthings. Being the temple's one and only warrior priest seemed much more adventurous in her mind.

Where others would pace or become agitated waiting for her father's invitation to enter the inner bailey, the Paladin stood motionless, his expression calm and placid while he waited for the official recognition. She understood now why women, and some men, whispered of his beauty. His features were chiseled, symmetrical, and smooth, as if he was carved from marble. Even his eyes were a dark gray like stone, unusual for Valmorans.

A groom brushed by Evelyne. "M'lady." He bowed as he moved past her.

The interaction seemed to catch the Paladin's attention. His eyes fell on Evelyne, and he squinted slightly. Under his gaze, Evelyne felt exposed. She shifted uncomfortably, still partially hidden behind the archway.

"Come here, my child." The Paladin gestured to her.

She bristled at being called a child. He was barely older than she.

"What is your name?" he asked, his voice melodious and even.

"Evelyne."

"Lady Evelyne." He rolled the name around. "Are you my welcome?" he asked with amusement.

She blushed under his scrutiny. "My father, Lord Cederic, will attend you momentarily. I should not be here at all. I will be in trouble for it, no doubt." She wasn't sure why she told him that.

"I see you are unmarried. Do you have plans to enter into service for the Maiden?"

She touched her uncovered head at the mention. "I am to be married in the spring."

"That is a pity." He shook his head. "Someone as brave and curious as you would do well in the ranks of our beloved elders."

She stood a little taller at the compliment. He continued to speak, but she didn't hear the words. A dreamy gauze filled her vision. The sound of his voice was all she heard, though she knew a dozen men and horses surrounded them. Service in the temple now seemed like a wonderful idea. Perhaps she should mention it to her father.

The Paladin broke his gaze and looked at something behind her. The world snapped back into full view for her. The neighing of the horses, the smell of wet leather, the sounds of clanking chain mail and shuffling boots behind her. What had happened?

"Your Eminence." Evelyne's father drew up next to her and gave a curt nod to the Paladin. "The Maiden's blessings on you."

"And with you," the Paladin replied but gave no bow to her father.

"I see you have met one of my daughters." His pained voice told Evelyne she was in an unwelcome situation.

"She was a lovely companion while I waited."

"What brings you? Is there trouble?"

One of the king's men approached. He was middle-aged with gray hair. A sizeable chunk of his ear was missing, and a giant scar ran on either side of it. His overtunic had the two colors of Valmora and the stacked crest of the king. "We should discuss these matters in private," he said.

"I'll have some rooms prepared." Her father motioned to his chatelaine, who sent a page running ahead to the keep. "How long will you be with us?"

"Until the king sees fit to recall us," replied the man.

Her father gave Evelyne a look and gestured with his head toward the solar. She understood the meaning. "Your Eminence." She bowed to the Paladin.

"Lothaire," he replied.

She smiled and quickly retreated through the archway to the inner bailey, glad to be free of the odd feelings she had. Now away from the Paladin, she realized she had no desire to join the temple. Not even in the slightest. She dreaded every morning visit memorizing the Tenets of Marriage.

Back in the solar, she found her sisters pressed to the windows in a group. Winifred turned to her as she entered. "Who is it?"

"The Paladin."

A collective gasp filled the room. The prospect of the most powerful man in the temple being at their home excited everyone else.

"The Paladin, here?" her mother's brow furrowed. "Did he say why?"

"I don't know. The king sent them." Evelyne sat at the table and fingered the fabric where she'd erased her fighting men.

"Stay away from him. All of you," her mother said.

"Why?" Winifred whined.

Her mother looked concerned. She shifted in her seat and looked at the door and then back at Winifred. "He does things for the temple that are indelicate. Not for women's ears or eyes."

Indelicate? Wasn't everything men did, which women weren't allowed to do, indelicate? His presence felt warm and calming, so indelicate didn't fit Evelyne's memory. She wanted to tell her mother about the odd conversation with him. She tried to remember what was said, but it seemed hazy, as if she was already forgetting. Perhaps the rumors about him were true. He could control minds somehow.

"Is he here to find wayward Talents?" Birgitta asked.

An unease overcame Evelyne when she heard the words. The moment in the cottage with Annika flashed in her mind. Rogue Talents were a danger to the kingdom. Everyone was aware of why. Without the temple's guidance, they couldn't control their gifts. They were called rogues since thieves and con men used them for misdeeds. Was it possible Annika was a rogue here at Marsendale?

"That is his trade," her mother replied. She began stitching again. "Let's not talk of this."

"Why don't their parents turn them in to the temple?" asked Winifred. She moved from the window and took the seat next to Evelyne. "The priest says to give Talents up in the service of the temple as soon as they show their gifts. Why hide them?"

Evelyne eyed her mother.

She shifted in her seat, grasped her necklace, and fanned herself faster. "One day, when you have children, you'll understand these things are more complicated than they might appear."

"Would you have given one of us to the temple if we were Talents?" Evelyne asked.

Her mother's piercing gaze returned her own. Evelyne knew she was challenging her. She shouldn't have done it, but it was done now. Her mother looked away before answering. "I do the Maiden's bidding in all things."

Was it so easy to send your child away? Evelyne guessed it wasn't much different for her mother than sending her brother, Edmund, to apprentice with Lord Meygroot's estate as a page. He had been six when he'd left the castle.

Still, something didn't feel right. Death was a harsh punishment for a rogue. Then she put the two things together. If Annika was a Talent, and the Paladin was here to discover them, Annika would be in terrible danger. She shook her head. No. Annika couldn't be a Talent. Or could she?

She threaded her needle. The sooner she finished this blanket, the sooner she could get back to the cottage.

CHAPTER NINETEEN

Annika shooed the chicken out of the lean-to while her father dug a small pit in the floor. A small wooden box sat at her feet, hiding the coins Evelyne had given them for her lessons. When the hole was deep enough, her da placed the box in the ground and covered it with dirt. To make it look undisturbed, Annika spread fresh reeds.

Her father said thieves always found a box buried in a home, but even they disliked the smell of bird droppings. "That should do."

"How much longer before we'll have enough coin?" she asked.

He walked past her and laid the shovel against the side of the cottage. He drank from the ladle in the water bucket nearby, rinsing his mouth and spitting it out. "A while yet. They make the cost high so it's hard for freemen like us to move around. The lord likes to keep good workers."

Freemen. What about freewomen? The women of the village, Hilfa notwithstanding, didn't own anything. Their husbands owned it all, including themselves. The tools, the ovens, the animals, the leases on the land. She should be angry at the system that kept them this way, but king's law and temple law said it was so, and she had no rebuttal to that.

All these thoughts were new.

"Until we leave, I want you to stay away from Lady Evelyne." Her father eyed her, waiting for her to respond. When she didn't, he continued, "Hilfa told me Lady Evelyne saw you while you were... using your gift." He looked uncomfortable talking about it.

She should say, yes, Da, and leave it at that, but that wasn't what she wanted. She wanted to be around Evelyne. She wanted to know more about Weya. More about herself. Evelyne was the first person to tell her anything since her mother had died. "Hilfa trusts her."

"Hilfa always sees the good in people," he replied quietly.

Annika wanted to see the good in others. Wanted to believe the Maiden had a plan for them. Believe this world was merely a test for the glory of the next life. Her mother's death and her father's stoicism made it difficult for her to believe in anything beyond this small patch of ground upon which she stood.

"She looks at you the way I looked at your mother."

Annika felt her face bloom with heat. She touched her cheek, tracing where Evelyne had kissed her. She turned her other hand over and stared at it. She could still feel the tingling from Evelyne's touch. Her cheek burned.

"Don't worry, lass. I've seen men in battle love each other as they loved their wives. I've seen tribes of shield-maidens take women to their beds as spoils of war, as men do. I've seen men bugger men, men bugger women, and men bugger sheep. I've seen much more."

She stood rigid and burned hotly with embarrassment.

"I'll only warn you once, when we have enough coin, we leave." He placed a hand on her shoulder. "Evelyne is a lady of the manor. Enjoy your youthful friendship, but it will come to an end soon. We are not them. Once you give yourself away, they have power over you."

Annika nodded. Afraid if she spoke, emotions she could not name would spill out of her unchecked.

"At least I don't have to worry about bawling brats about the place," he said with a shrug and headed into the cottage.

Annika opened the garden gate and knelt to select vegetables for the evening meal. She hummed a tune. The music was always in her head, but now she felt the need to release it. Even her father thought Evelyne cared for her, and she was happy.

Funny thing about happiness, it didn't ever seem to last long for her. As if to echo her thoughts, darkness drew across the sky. She felt a chill, and a clap of thunder filled the air. Several large drops of rain fell, and a blackbird plummeted to its death in front of her. It lay on its side. Its head was at an awkward angle, its claws clasped tightly, as if it had fought its death.

She stared into the lifeless eyes and grasped her necklace. She stroked the Maiden's likeness. A dead bird in the garden. A bad omen. Was the Maiden warning her of her behavior? Or was the warning about her gifts?

She scooped the bird up and took it outside the garden and gently placed it in the rubbish pit. "Maiden, take this gentle soul to your breast. Forgive us our violations."

As quickly as the darkness had arrived, the sun once again shined. She shivered nonetheless. Something was in the air filling her with dread. Maiden help her, she hoped she was wrong.

Chapter Twenty

With everyone at the castle involved in planning an impromptu tournament in honor of the Paladin's unexplained arrival, Evelyne slipped away in her brother's clothes and made her way to the cottage. There was no sign of either Annika or Steffen. She was disappointed, but she needed to excise her nervous energy.

Hilfa gladly put her to work, and now Evelyne and Jack trundled along next to a small cart, a powerful pony leading them along a rutted path through the grainfields and into the forest beyond. They passed by the wood yard where a dozen men worked felling and cutting lumber and deeper into the forest on a recently created path, until the first signs of smoke hung between the branches. Evelyne wasn't certain where they were until they moved into the open clearing and saw the five large mounds covered in sod. A charcoal burners' camp.

The smell of the burned wood filled the air. Next to the large mounds, several men poked holes in the sides to release smoke and allow more air, while another filled holes to allow less air in a pile. It seemed a long and tedious process. These men never left the camp. They lived here night and day, tending these great burns. She tried to imagine the boredom of doing the same thing every day.

A giant pile of charcoal sat at the edge of the clearing, uncovered and black as night. As the mound loomed ever larger, Evelyne's stomach roiled a bit. She might have asked for more than she was expecting. Jack stopped the wagon near the heap and pulled two shovels from the cart. Evelyne took the shovel he pressed into her hands. Without a word, he began scooping charcoal and flinging it into the cart's bay.

First, she adjusted her hands on the shovel and leaned over, digging in and raising the load. She lost half the scoop before she placed it on the cart. She dug again and again until she could handle a full shovel. On the next try, she felt a tap on her shoulder.

"You...you'll be laid up for a fortnight like that," Jack stammered. After all these weeks, he still couldn't meet her gaze. He took his shovel, bent his knees, and drew in charcoal nearer to the middle of the pile. He swung around at his hips and dumped it cleanly in the cart.

Evelyne mimicked his movements, and the action came easier, but the cloud of dust became greater. A few minutes of this and her eyes watered, and her vision blurred. A charred taste filled her mouth, and the smell overwhelmed everything else. She stopped and coughed.

"How long have you apprenticed to Hilfa?" she asked Jack during the pause.

He grunted and shoveled more, still not looking her in the eye. "Long while."

Conversation wasn't going to be easy. She sighed and dug the shovel edge into the coal, the charred wood grating on the iron. After a while, the sound became hypnotic. They worked on one shovelful at a time, periodically taking a brief break, during which Evelyne would watch the surrounding activity. No one seemed to have taken notice of her. That was good.

When Jack raised his shovel, she raised hers and started again. Her hands screamed in pain this time. She turned her palm over and saw the open blisters. Blood and dust mixed to form a black paste across the pads at the base of her fingers.

"You can stop, m'lady," Jack said, his voice shaky. "I'll do the rest."

She would not give up. She'd never been that person. When her brothers had held her down in the mud and paddled her, saying they would stop if she would admit they were the best hunters in the world, she'd said nothing. They'd continued until her skin was red and raw, and tears had run down her face, and yet she would never give in to them. Never.

"Thank you, Jack." How few times had she ever said thank you to anyone? She dug hard into the pile. "I'm fine." She pushed herself to finish. The choking dust, the raw hands, the pain in her arms and back. She tried to think of anything else.

Her mind wandered to the one thing distracting her every day: Annika. The heavens only knew why she was so obsessed. No, she knew. Everything about Annika was beautiful, from her golden hair to smooth skin. Evelyne felt shame creep into her body. She remembered the kiss with Timothy. Though she felt nothing for him, he was a noble, an appropriate status for her attention. Annika was not noble. Would it be acceptable if she had a crush on another noble girl instead of a peasant girl?

Peasant. The word felt wrong as a description of Annika. More like a curse or a swear word. And they weren't girls. They were women. In her case, a marriageable woman committed to a man she didn't know who lived in another part of the realm. Damn being a woman. She might have growled a little at the thought because Jack flinched.

Witt boasted constantly about his trysts with young women in Byetown and Tarburg. Certainly, they weren't noblewomen, or he'd have reluctantly marched to the temple for a wedding long before now. If he and Erik—and maybe Timothy—could have paramours, what was the harm in her pursuing someone herself? She looked at the sky through the gray haze. The Tenets of Marriage replayed in her mind. *A wife was created for her husband's pleasure.* Well, she wasn't a wife yet.

She grunted again in frustration. She wasn't her brothers. She wouldn't take advantage of someone who couldn't refuse her advances. She heard the clinking of bits and padding of horse's hooves and the sounds of a wagon near them. She didn't move but inspected the shovelful of charcoal carefully and waited.

"M'lady, Maiden's blessing," someone called.

Dread filled Evelyne. Was he speaking to her? She turned her head just enough to peek at the arrivals. She recognized the forester as he walked toward a fire tender, who had pulled down the cloth covering his face, and behind him walked Evelyne's mother. Shite. Her hands shook so hard, she had trouble gripping the shovel. She wouldn't see the light of day for a month if they caught here her.

She looked at Jack. What would they do to him? She hadn't thought of that, but she rarely thought about anyone who worked outside the castle. Damn it all. She could handle punishment, but Jack hadn't done anything. She motioned to him, subtly waving, gesturing for him to come closer. She laid down the shovel and reached under her tunic and pulled out the bottom of her long shift.

"Give me your knife."

He paused but handed over the small blade he wore at his hip without question. Not large, but well cared for and honed. The tip made quick work of the fabric. She ripped a sizeable piece from the garment and handed the blade back with a nod. She tied the fabric square around her nose and mouth.

She glanced back at her mother. She was as regal as any woman could be without being a queen, and the men in the camp responded as if she was their queen. A pregnant queen. What was she doing out of the castle? Out of her solar? The tenders stopped their work and bowed. Evelyne's heart raced the nearer they came to where she and Jack worked. She could do nothing more. She hoped the mask hid her well enough.

"We've sold several tons to the smiths in Byetown. They should arrive any day now to transport," said the forester as they got closer.

Evelyne tried not to look at her mother, but each time she lifted the shovel to the cart, she was in her line of sight.

"How much will that bring us?" her mother asked.

"Eight hundred crowns."

"Good."

What was her mother doing? She'd never spoken of any of this. And her accent seemed more pronounced as she spoke with the forester. Rougher, like her uncles from her mother's family.

"We'll need a few tons at the castle for the tournament. Make sure someone delivers it today. We need several carpenters and enough lumber to build the stands as well."

"Yes, m'lady."

They drew closer. Evelyne's breath was shallow.

"Make sure not to take down too many trees in the area around the old growth."

How did her mother know any of this?

"You, there. Hold." The forester addressed her and Jack.

She halted her work and tilted her head down, trying to behave like Annika would. Nothing about it felt comfortable, staring at her filthy shoes and the ground strewn with charcoal bits.

"Sorry for the dust, m'lady," he said to her mother. She could hear his footfalls drawing nearer. "Show some respect boy, take off that hat."

Jack pulled his hat and cap off and placed them against his chest.

If she took off her hat and the cap beneath, her hair would fall out. If her hair fell out, they'd know she was a girl. If they knew she was a girl, they'd make her take off the mask. If she took off the mask… Evelyne drew a shaky hand toward the hat. She had no choice.

"Don't bother the boy," said her mother. "Let them keep working. Let's move on to the logging camp. I need to get back to the castle."

Evelyne closed her eyes and thanked every god—old and new—for whatever assistance they provided. She looked at Jack. He looked relieved. Was he worried about being punished too? He had to be. She watched the forester help her mother into the wagon. Her belly swollen and her face red with exertion, she had come all the way out here to the forest. When her mother's carriage had driven away, Evelyne let out a long breath.

By the time they finished, dust covered her from head to toe. Her clothes were dirty, her hands were filthy, and if her face looked like Jack's, her mother might not have even recognized her without the mask. With the cart full, they climbed aboard and started the trip back to the village. Evelyne's back ached, and her hands were blistered, her palms full of raw spots and ripped skin.

If it was possible to fall asleep while walking, Evelyne would have done so on the way back to the forge. Even the chance that they might run into her mother again didn't stop the exhaustion. Back at Hilfa's forge, she grabbed her shovel and got to work unloading the cart. It went quickly. Good thing because Evelyne felt dizzy.

This hadn't been what she'd had in mind when she'd asked Hilfa for work. She had hoped to be striking the red-hot iron with her for once, but Hilfa still seemed reserved and wary around her.

She thanked them both and began her walk to the castle.

Her mother was involved with the forest. Wasn't that the seneschal or her father's work? Did she do this often? Why hadn't she ever mentioned it? And knowing that her mother was riding about somewhere on the lands meant sneaking back into the castle without being seen, covered in char dust, in Witt's clothes, would be difficult.

CHAPTER TWENTY-ONE

Annika cleaved a wood round and laid the two halves in a pile with the others. She reached for another and glanced up, catching sight of a young man heading toward her, a charcoal burner by the looks of him. Her da had said to stay away from them. She knew the old tales, but she didn't believe they communed with the undergods. She shifted her ax. Since the trip to Byetown, anyone she didn't know gave her pause.

But the young man looked familiar somehow. The way he walked. A few more steps and she realized it was Lady Evelyne. What in the world had she been doing? Annika froze. She was excited to see Evelyne, and part of her wanted to run to her, but her father and Hilfa's warnings swam in her mind.

Evelyne leaned against a fence post, using it to help her sit. She wrenched off her hat and dropped it on the ground. An obvious line separated the dirty half of her face from the clean half on top.

Annika laid down her ax. Her feet moved her forward before she could resist. She leaned down to her. "Are you hurt?"

Evelyne shook her head. "No." Frustration filled her voice. "Just tired. And…I missed you." She broke into tears.

Annika could see open blisters on her hands. "Maiden's eyes. What have you been doing?"

"I collected charcoal for the forge." She wiped her eyes on her sleeve, pushing the dirt around.

Annika reached out and carefully took her hand to examine it closer. When their fingers touched, she had a vision. More a glimmer than a vision, the two of them together, closer than they were now. So close they—

She dropped Evelyne's hand, flustered by the image coursing through her mind. Her cheeks felt warm. She felt the urge to flee and jumped to her feet. "Have you eaten?"

Evelyne shook her head.

"Let me get you something." She headed to the cottage, unsure what her vision meant, but she needed a few moments to collect herself. To understand what it meant to see herself in a vision.

Visions were always of others. Never of herself. They were premonitions of now or the immediate future. Now she had seen herself in two. What did it mean for her to see Evelyne's face so close to her own in a vision? A vision of the future?

She retrieved a mug and a thick slice of brown bread and butter. She looked at the four-day-old, coarse bread. Hard and stiff. It wouldn't be easy to chew, but it was all she had. She took a few deep breaths before she returned to Evelyne.

Between sniffles, Evelyne ate and drank so fast, Annika brought more. She stood beside her until Evelyne finally stopped crying, waiting for what might come next. Should she excuse herself and return to her work?

"I can't go back like this." Evelyne gestured at her clothes and splayed her damaged hands. "My mother will never let me leave the grounds again."

Covered in coal dust, her eyes puffy from crying, Evelyne's vulnerability was endearing. Annika hadn't seen this side of her before. She'd only seen the capable, commanding noble. "Wait here." She went in the cottage to her mother's chest. She ran her hand along the intricately carved symbols, so foreign to her and yet familiar. Inside, she removed her best tunic and shift, the one she wore to religious services on high holy days. It would be short but should fit Evelyne well enough. She grabbed a piece of clean linen and a sliver of black soap.

Back outside, she tentatively held her hand out to assist Evelyne to her feet. She prepared for the possibility of another vision and steeled herself. "Come. I know a spot where you can bathe…at the fishpond. The reeds are high enough. No one will see us."

Evelyne wiped her hands on her tunic but grimaced in obvious pain as she smeared the dust rather than removing it. Annika nodded to reassure her and took Evelyne's hand gently, pulling her to her feet, relieved when no vision occurred.

She led the way down a path behind her home. With their hands intertwined, she noticed the warmth of Evelyne's. She glanced over her shoulder. Evelyne followed, her eyelids drooping and feet shuffling, but she smiled when Annika looked at her, setting Annika's heart beating faster.

As they got farther from the cottage, the familiar scents of geese gave way to the clean smells of pastureland and wildflowers. Reeds grew tall along the water's edge. She walked in a small, tight circle, tamping down the reeds and made a clearing for them to sit. Seated on the ground, she could barely see anything but the pond. She removed her shoes and stockings and stripped off her tunic.

When it came time to take off her shift, she hesitated. She was rarely around others naked, mostly because she had few friends in the village. She wasn't embarrassed by her body, even if the priest read stories from the Enlightened Book meant to shame her, stories of temptation of the female form and its effect on men. But Evelyne wasn't a man, so it didn't matter, did it?

She stood, dropped her shift, and ran for the water. "Come join me," she yelled when she was in up to her neck. The water was warm from the sun beating on it all day.

Evelyne stripped off her shoes, tunic, and trousers but left her undershirt on.

"Are you coming? Or are you afraid?" Annika teased, trying to lighten Evelyne's low mood. She smiled, but when Evelyne pulled the hem of her shift up over her muscled thighs, Annika looked away and dipped under the water. She swam a few feet and rolled over on her back, watching the wisps of clouds pass overhead against the blue sky.

The crisp crunch of feet on the flattened reeds and gentle splashes signified Evelyne's entry into the pond. Annika looked back, hoping she had given Evelyne enough time to be fully immersed. Why was she afraid to look upon her naked body? There was no sin in that.

She swam the few strokes back to where Evelyne squatted in the shallows. Evelyne tried to wipe the dirt from her arms and face. Annika scampered up the bank and grabbed the soap and linen she'd brought and rushed back under the water before Evelyne could look at her. How silly she was being. She approached her from behind and tentatively rubbed the soap on the linen. It smelled of animal fat and char, not of lavender like Evelyne would be used to, but it would get the job done. She removed the dirt from the back of Evelyne's neck and swiped across her broad shoulders. She wanted to run her bare fingertips across the skin without the barrier of the linen cloth.

Annika moved around in front of Evelyne and took one of her hands. She scrubbed the raw palm, careful not to rub too hard on the open blisters. She moved to the fingers, wrapping each one and carefully pulling the linen down, the charcoal dust falling and floating on the water like oil before being drawn down and disappearing. She rinsed the cloth and worked on the other hand, then her wrists. Evelyne's forearms flexed at her touch, the muscles tight under her skin.

The only sounds were the soft rustling of the wind on the reeds, birdsong in the trees, and the soft hum of insects. She moved on to Evelyne's face, wiping her forehead and down her nose, eyes, and cheeks. When she reached her lips, Annika hesitated. She wiped gently across them, spending more time than necessary. She averted her eyes, embarrassed by the thought of kissing those lips, and wrung the linen in the water.

When she leaned forward again, Evelyne was watching her. Before, her eyes had been closed, perhaps because of the exhaustion of hard work, but now, she appeared revived. Annika glimpsed Evelyne's breasts below the water, and with that, a sensitivity to the pond grew between her legs. Longing swelled in her, startling her. She knew what it meant. She'd been around enough of the villagers, their encounters in barns and behind hedgerows, but she had never felt desire. And now that she felt it, she could never forget it.

This was what the vision meant. This was the moment she'd seen. Rather than sinking lower to hide her nakedness, she rose out enough to make her own breasts visible. She leaned in closer and slipped the linen cloth around Evelyne's shoulders. They were cheek to cheek, so close she could hear Evelyne's ragged breathing. Annika gave in to her impulses and ran a hand along the muscles on the top of Evelyne's shoulder. The thrill of Evelyne's skin made her burst with desire.

Evelyne turned her head and Annika turned to meet her. She hesitated. Evelyne's lips called to her as if they were all she could see. Her heart pounded. She shook faintly. She leaned closer. Closer to those lips. And as she was within a hair's breadth, she stopped. Evelyne's lips parted, and a slight smile formed. Annika returned it.

Evelyne reached around her head and gently pulled her forward. Once she did this, their relationship would never be the same.

A chance she would take. She pressed her lips against Evelyne's gently and then harder as desire overwhelmed her. She closed her eyes as they explored each other with lips and tongues and teeth. She felt so many unfamiliar feelings, all of them wondrous.

She leaned into Evelyne, starting a whole new fire burning between her thighs, as well as a surge of power, making her feel as if she could lift the world. A bright light lit up the back of her eyelids, and she felt the familiar feeling of a vision coming.

He was here.

Annika pressed a hand against Evelyne's chest and pushed her back. Panic welled in her. This vision was not in the future. She only had a few moments to decide what to do. Evelyne stared with a hurt look on her face, perhaps confusion as well. If Annika told her about the vision, Evelyne would know she was a Talent. Would she turn her in?

Annika could leave her here alone. Feign needing to be somewhere else, maybe meeting her father. She ran her hands through her wet hair and pulled slightly in frustration. What should she do? "Someone is coming." As soon as the words spilled out, she realized she had put her life in Evelyne's hands.

"I don't hear anything." Evelyne's brow furrowed. "If this is about what happened—"

"Trust me." She rushed from the water, no longer shy about her nakedness. "Someone is coming. We must go."

Annika pulled on her clothes. Evelyne followed her but with less urgency as she dressed in Annika's nicest outfit. Annika wanted to yell at her to hurry, but she couldn't. She couldn't shout at her lord's daughter. She could tell her what she had seen, try to give her a sense of urgency, but that would require more of an explanation.

One she wasn't willing to give yet.

Dressed, she hurried from the reeds onto the path toward the cottage, flushed and confused about what she felt and what might lie before her, with Evelyne's footsteps close behind. Her heart raced. She wanted to break into a run, to get as far from the coming storm as possible. And the Paladin was a storm. A tempest of death.

"Lady Evelyne. Is that you?"

Annika recognized the priest's voice. If Evelyne stopped, she would have to stop as well and show her respect. "Elder Theobald," Evelyne said. "Lothaire."

Annika's blood ran cold at the sound of the second name. She turned, her head bowed. The man hadn't spoken yet, and she hadn't seen his face, but she was certain it was him, the man in blue. She'd seen him in her vision, and her visions never lied. She raised her gaze along the hem of his tunic to the gilded pommel of the sword at his side, to the circle of the constellations around his neck. Until they locked eyes.

Nothing prepared her for the shock of seeing him so close. The man who burned young women like her. She heard Evelyne continuing to speak to the priest, but a rushing noise and the pounding of her heartbeat in her ears drowned their conversation. He held her gaze, and Annika saw the faintest light emanating from him, surrounding him. Could the others see it?

The surrounding reeds and tall grasses morphed and turned into a hallway of stone. Blocking the sunlight, the hall was decrepit, with broken stones on the ground. Moss grew from the cracks, and the only light emanated from the Paladin himself. His expression changed from stoic to sad, and he reached toward her, but they were at opposite ends of the hall.

"What is your name?" She heard his voice clearly.

"Annika."

"Who are you, Annika?"

"I am no one, m'lord."

"And I am no lord."

The hallway crumbled away in a wisp of fog, leaving sunlight and reeds in their rightful place. Evelyne now stood in her eyeline, blocking the view of the Paladin. Annika took the bundle of dirty clothes Evelyne held out to her. Their hands were touching. How long had they been standing like this? Unsure of what had been said, she could tell Evelyne had dismissed her and was cutting her eyes to the side with a grimace. Annika took this as a sign to bow and scurry away.

Had Lothaire spoken to her, or was it all a vision?

Evelyne watched Annika rush away. She wasn't sure what had occurred. Annika had looked frozen with fear when Lothaire and Elder Theobald had approached. Granted, Evelyne didn't enjoy Elder Theobald's company, but his balding pate didn't inspire fear in her.

"What brings you to the millpond, elder?" she said, trying to sound light and unfazed by Annika's bizarre behavior.

"I was showing Lothaire the workings of the village so he will be able to do his diligence."

Evelyne focused on Lothaire, but he was preoccupied with looking after Annika.

"Might I help you with this task?" Evelyne asked.

Lothaire didn't respond. Theobald cleared his throat, most likely not wanting to answer for the Paladin.

Evelyne was certain Theobald felt as uncomfortable as she did. She tugged on the sleeves of Annika's tunic, trying to make them longer. She wondered how soon Theobald might notice she was wearing a tunic that obviously didn't fit. Maybe elders didn't notice such things. In the silence, she noticed something more obvious and more dangerous.

Her hands. She turned them over several times. They were pristine. Not a blister or cut or spot of redness remained. How had this happened? She closed her fists and stared at Theobald. He was not using his Talent to heal. He'd have to be much closer to her.

Annika. Could it be?

She turned to the empty path beyond. She hadn't been seeing things in the cottage before. Annika had glowed. She was a Talent. Evelyne returned her gaze to Lothaire. He hunted rogue Talents. She needed to get him away from the cottage. "Why don't we return to the castle?" she said. "I can show you the armory."

"Yes. Yes. Let's do that," agreed Theobald.

Lothaire didn't look at either of them. He turned away from where Annika had gone, sweeping his cloak behind him, and stalked away without them.

What should she do? Confront Annika? Ask Theobald?

She turned toward the cottage, but Theobald interrupted her. "Why don't we take advantage of the time and discuss your learnings from the Book?" He directed his hand out in front of the path, expecting her to follow.

Talking to Annika would have to wait.

CHAPTER TWENTY-TWO

A nnika rushed into the cottage and shut the door. She looked out the open window, making sure no one had followed her. She was certain she would see the man coming for her, walking down the path from the village. All she saw were chickens pecking insects in a patch of sweet violet. The color reminded her of the man's clothing. So much fear in such a beautiful color.

After a while, when no one arrived, she threw the bundle of clothes on the ground in a heap. She didn't know whether she should be angry at Evelyne or grateful. Had Evelyne dismissed her to help keep the Paladin's attention away from her, or had she done it to put Annika in her place while the elder and Paladin were around?

She paced and worried her belt. What would she tell her father? She couldn't tell him she'd kissed Evelyne or that she'd bathed with her. The thought was too intimate. He wouldn't understand at all. She touched her lips. They tingled, and she remembered how it had felt when Evelyne kissed her. A glorious and thrilling moment, only to be replaced with terror when she'd envisioned the man who burned people to death. Who would burn her.

She dropped to her knees and placed her hands on either side of her head. What should she do? Would they kill her? Would Evelyne realize that Annika was a Talent? Would she tell the Paladin? Would he force her to tell him? She became dizzy and realized she was panting. Overwhelmed. Confused. She finally released all her frustration in a bloodcurdling scream.

The door flew open. She grabbed her dagger. At the sight of her da, relief flooded her as well as tears.

"What's wrong?" He moved to her, bent, and held her shoulders to look at her.

"He's here."

"Who's here?"

"The man from Byetown," she replied between sobs. "The one who sacrificed the wealthy girl."

He wrapped his arms around her and held her tight. His coarse tunic scratched her cheek. "Are you sure? Might it have been someone who looks like him?"

Annika shook her head. "I saw him…in a vision. He arrived whilst I was at the pond with Lady Evelyne." She shuddered. "All in blue he was."

Steffen released her. "Did he see you?"

"Yes."

"Did he say anything to you?"

"Yes, and he stared at me. As intently as anyone has ever looked at me."

"I've heard rumors. He can make you confess things. You need to stay away from him."

She knew the man would come for her now that she had spoken of him aloud.

Her father stood and shut the door. She watched him peer through the window before returning to her side. He helped her up and sat her on the straw mattress. "We haven't enough coin to buy the rights to move. If we run, they'll come for us." Resignation tinted his voice.

She put her hand on the wooden chest beside her. She ran her fingers over the carvings of people she didn't know. Were they Weyan gods? Her mother had died before she could ask. Now she used them to ground her, keeping her mind still and helping to bring her emotions under control. After a while, she turned to face her father. "I could turn myself over to the temple. I could go before the Paladin finds me."

His eyebrows rose. "The temple gives no mercy to a rogue Talent."

"What if I said I didn't know my visions were a gift? I can claim I never told you. I thought they were fantasies. Like the village madwoman who lived in the cave below the castle. Maybe…maybe they'll believe me." They had to believe her.

"You'll do no such thing. We'll wait. The Paladin might leave and never know you existed." He paced, making her nervous.

She mindlessly rubbed the chest. Her father reached for an earthenware bottle. He uncorked it and took a long swig. He sat at the table and tipped the bottle again. She noticed his knuckles turning white as he made fists.

"When I lost your mother, I lost more than a wife. She was my soulmate." He waved a hand. "I didn't care for no nonsense about this god or that goddess. I knew the moment I saw her that she would be my wife." His voice broke, and he swiped the back of his sleeve across his face. "I swore I wouldn't let them take you." He looked at her and pleaded, "You're all I have left of her. They can't take you...I'd be broken." He hung his head, and she heard his quiet sob. "Now look what I've done. If I'd done right by you...you'd be safe in the temple."

She rushed to his side and draped her arms around his neck. "I'm glad we're together. I don't want to go to the temple. I want to stay with you, Da."

"You're so like your mother." He sobbed again.

She pulled him tighter against her. She felt the same as he did. She couldn't imagine being without him. They had little, but they had each other, and she enjoyed tending the birds. Sometimes, the villagers treated her harshly, but why would she expect anything different from the temple? Cruelty didn't stop at the temple doors.

She rubbed her fingers in the cooled ashes on the edge of the fire and stepped to the door. She ran her finger in a semicircle, retrieved more ash, and drew another curved line below the first one.

"What are you doing?" her father asked on her third trip to the firepit.

She created a circle in between the two lines, smudging the ash to blacken the center. "Mother used to draw the eye when we were sick. Remember?" She smiled at the memory. "Maybe it will ward off the Paladin as well."

Her father stood, pulling his sleeve, and seemed about to wipe off the pagan symbol.

She reached out and stopped him. "Please. Leave it for a day or two. If only for the memory of Mother."

He nodded. "For your mother."

She could do nothing about the Paladin, but she could try to soothe her father's broken heart and her own. Whatever had happened between her and Evelyne, it wouldn't happen again. Annika had too much to lose. She released her grip on her da and pulled down her gittern, plucking the strings and testing the tune. She played a soulful melody her mother had taught her, a story in music about a girl who found herself at the edge of the ocean and thought she had entered the afterlife.

Her father sat and swigged his mead, and though his head and shoulders hung low, Annika hoped the music eased his tension as it was relieving her own.

He raised his eyes. "I won't let them hurt you. I promise if it comes to that…your death will be quick."

Her fingers slipped on the strings and made a strangled sound.

CHAPTER TWENTY-THREE

Evelyne's sisters giggled. They rushed about, fixing their hair in long loops and adjusting each other's silken gowns. The tournament was beginning soon. Ten days of fighting, drawing knights and squires from several of the manors bordering theirs. For a man who rarely bowed to anyone but the king, her father seemed to go out of his way to impress the Paladin, and that meant Evelyne had no opportunity to return to Annika's cottage.

Her parents expected her to host each meal, piously attend every prayer service, and observe the tournament. Under normal circumstances, Evelyne would have been in the yard by dawn, watching every preparation and practice. Examining every new sword, flail, and lance. This time was different.

"Are you coming?" Winifred looked back while holding the door open as the sisters filed through to leave.

"I'll follow shortly."

With the others gone, the silence swallowed her. She stared at a spiderweb woven in the corner of the bed frame supporting the drapes. Several insects were stuck, cocooned and unmoving. She felt that way. She hadn't seen Annika since the afternoon at the mill pond. Since the kiss.

Evelyne touched her lips. That kiss had been glorious. Nothing like the one with Timothy. Towering over most of the young pages as a child meant she had little experience with kissing. Her sisters, other than Matilde, were well versed in secret kisses, but not Evelyne. She smiled. Now she was. And yet, she was confused. What did it mean?

She slipped off the bed and opened her wooden chest. Annika's tunic lay under her own clothes, hidden so no one would ask questions. The delicate embroidery filled the cuffs and the neck. Much better needlework than she'd ever do. She'd been so distracted at the time that she hadn't noticed the work at all. She touched the front of the garment, thinking about the way Annika had touched her at the pond. It was all she had thought about for days. She lifted the cloth to her face and took a deep breath. It smelled of the cottage. Subtly of woodsmoke and a bit of soap. She wished it smelled like Annika.

The door creaked. Evelyne threw the tunic back in the chest and slammed the lid shut.

"M'lady." A young servant bowed to her. She laid a bundle of clothing on the end of the bed and withdrew with another nod.

Evelyne was angry at herself for letting a piece of cloth make her weak in the knees. She turned to look at the bundle of clothes that had been delivered. Her male disguise, Witt's old tunic, lay there freshly laundered and tied together with a long piece of linen.

Annika was here.

Evelyne dashed out of the room and looked both ways in the hall, trying to find the servant who'd brought the clothing. When she saw no one, she ran down to the staircase nearest the kitchen and took the stairs two at a time. Rounding the corner on the final landing, she ran into a man painting the walls with a fresh coat of limewash, knocking him into his bucket and sloshing white paint all over the floors. He cursed at her until he saw her. His face went pale, and he bowed deeply.

"My fault, sir. I will tell my mother so."

She rushed past him and into the hall, past the buttery and pantry, to the kitchen. She found Nan tending her cooking. Two boys turned spits of meat in front of the grand fireplace. Several women worked flour for breads and pies. She ran through and out the kitchen doors to the inner bailey courtyard. She looked around wildly but saw neither Annika nor the servant girl who had brought the clothes.

She returned to the kitchen. "Nan, was Annika here? The girl who brings the birds."

Nan chopped leeks on the table, making quick work of them. She bowed to Evelyne but didn't stop cutting. "I know who she is. I've known her as long as I've known you. I've not seen her for several days."

"A girl brought some clothing to me. Do you know who brought it to the castle?"

Nan kept up the chopping, grabbing another leek. "A laundress from the village brought it. Said it was for you. I sent Prue up with it. Was it not properly cleaned? I can send it back."

Evelyne shook her head. "No. Very fine work." Evelyne felt the heat from the fireplace forming sweat on her forehead. She ran her fingers along the end of the table, trying not to look odd. "Who's bringing the birds for the table if not Annika?"

Nan stopped this time, holding the knife's pointed end in her direction. "Why are you so interested in the birds? Has your mother said something to you about them? If so, you tell me."

Evelyne waved in front of herself. "No, Nan. Nothing like that. Mother is pleased, as always, with your delicacies. I...I recently met Annika and her father." She tried to come up with a believable answer. "They've...been showing me the birds. The feed. The pens. The processes. I'm simply curious if she's healthy and hale." Evelyne turned away and examined a rack of tarts, hoping Nan wouldn't see the white lie she was sure was crawling across her face.

Nan's chopping sounds restarted. "Steffen brought them up himself the last few mornings. I'll ask after Annika for you when he comes next."

Evelyne nodded. She reached out toward a particularly attractive tart.

Thwack. The knife hit the table loudly, and she pulled her hand back. "Don't you even think about it," Nan admonished. "I'm running this kitchen all day and into the night to feed all these extra people. I'll not have you stealing the wares. Your mother would still let me put you over my knee. Right until you marry."

Nan had long since passed the time when she could bend Evelyne over her knee. Her fingers were curled and crooked. Her back hunched. And though she had a heavy stomach, she was spindly and thin elsewhere.

"I'm sure she would, Nan." And Evelyne would submit to any punishment from Nan purely out of love for her.

She sighed and looked through the open doorway to the orchard beyond, the fence visible where she had tripped and looked into Annika's eyes for the first time. They needed to talk. She had so many questions about things she probably shouldn't ask, but she needed to know.

Was Annika a Talent?

CHAPTER TWENTY-FOUR

Nightfall meant darkness filled the cottage. A single weak rushlight on the table cast odd shadows across the three of them. Annika's father shuffled the coins they had saved on the table with his fingertips, counting them.

"We haven't enough yet to buy a release from the lord," he said.

"I can make butter and cheese to sell at the tournament," Annika offered. "Would that help?"

Steffen covered her hand and gave a slight squeeze. "It will."

Hilfa leaned in. Deep shadows crossed her face. "I know someone who could help. Wilkin, the boatman down river in Blackhedge. He knows some smugglers."

"No." Her father shook his head. "It's too dangerous. If we're caught, we'd have no chance."

Hilfa turned away, obviously frustrated with his answer. "How much more dangerous than if the Paladin discovers you?"

"Smugglers have no honor," he said. "They'd as soon sell us back to the Paladin as take our money and leave us with nothing." He looked at Annika. "And if they found out she's a rogue Talent…" He shook his head. "They'd sell her to the highest bidder."

"I could try to contact to Zuri. She told me—"

"No." He cut her off with a palm to the table. "I'll not have that woman around you."

"But, Da, Zuri's the only other Talent I know. She knew Mother. She said I only needed to reach out. If she's been on her own all this time, she must know how we could escape."

"You'll get her flayed," Hilfa said. "She's a runaway slave." She glanced at Annika's father. "As was your mother."

A slave? Annika was confused. Her mother had married her father in Weya. Was she a slave before she came to Marsendale? "I don't understand."

Her father stood and paced. He put his hands on his hips and kept his eyes cast downward. "Your mother didn't want you to think badly of me."

"Why would I think badly of you?"

"She was a spoil of war. We rounded her up with all the women in her village. They were tied together in a long line. Crying. Spitting. Some quiet. Some yelling like banshees. When I saw her, your mother was standing on the rocky ground in a dirty shift, her hair matted with dried blood. Still, the most beautiful woman I'd ever seen."

He limped to the back wall by the bed. He touched the ribbon that hung there, the ribbon her mother had worn every day in her long braid. "I went to the quartermaster and traded all I had and all my future pay and bought her. I should have asked her if she wanted me to do it." He turned away from the ribbon and returned to the table. "She made only one request of me. To find her gittern. Took me three days of threatening every one of our men until I found it."

Annika looked at the instrument. How had her mother played such beautiful music? She must have been devasted. Ripped from her home and brought to a place where she was never truly accepted. She hadn't known the language or the religion. How had she done it? Annika wondered if she could make the strings sing again knowing what she knew now.

"Annika," Hilfa said softly. "Hella was content here. She told me many times. You were everything to her."

"If Zuri and Mother were both slaves and shared a bond, why not let her help?"

His face darkened.

It was Hilfa who continued to speak: "Your mother had a big heart. Zuri was a rogue, as you know. She would never be safe in Valmora. So your mother helped her escape. Smugglers were engaged to take her south. When she disappeared, one of the other girls told the bailiff that Hella had been involved. The girl had only guessed, but your mother was disliked by some for her pagan ways. He whipped her on the village post until she couldn't stand."

Annika cringed at the thought. She'd seen the results often. "Why didn't you stop them, Da?"

"I wasn't here. I was in Byetown." He looked ashamed. "Believe me. I wanted to rip him limb from limb, but your mother begged me not to. She reminded me you would have no one if something happened to us both. Was the infection took her several days later."

"She was sick. I remember. But whipped? No. I don't believe it."

"You were so young, Anni," said Hilfa.

She remembered the day her mother died as if it was yesterday. The bad blood had brought the fevers. Her feet and hands were swollen. Her eyes blood red. Annika had fought back tears while she and her da had taken turns fetching cool water to keep her comfortable and clean the filth from her. She couldn't rise, nor could she eat at the end.

Annika had prayed nonstop all night. She'd prayed to the Maiden, but she'd also tried her mother's gods. When she'd realized none of them were listening, she'd cursed them. Every god, everywhere in the world.

Her father had fetched the herbalist from the village. She'd taken one look at her mother, shaken her head, and patted her father's hands. She'd given him a tincture of opium and another satchel. They'd whispered where Annika couldn't hear them, but the grave look on her father's face had told her the herbs weren't to help her mother.

Annika had run all the way to the castle chapel, crying so hard that she could barely see one step in front of the other. She'd fallen more than once. She'd thrown herself at the elder's feet and had begged him to come save her mother. He was a healer, after all. Elder Theobald had denied her request. He'd explained he could not because her mother was a pagan. Stunned, Annika had wept. Perhaps in sympathy for her, he'd replied that he would say a prayer for her mother and sent Annika away.

She'd returned to the cottage dejected. She'd found her father asleep, sitting against the far wall, the satchel still in his hand. She couldn't sleep no matter how tired she was. She'd curled on the floor, her head on the edge of the mattress, and had watched her mother through the night.

Right before dawn, her mother's breathing had come in heavy, uneven spurts, punctuated with wheezing. With a great gasp, she'd turned to Annika and with complete clarity, spoken to her. "The Sky Goddess is coming for me." Her expression had been elated, her eyes wide.

"Is she coming to save you? I've prayed all night," Annika asked through tears.

"She's here to take me home," her mother replied. "I'm sorry I won't see you become a woman."

Annika had taken her hand and kissed it. "Please, don't leave me. Tell her to save you. I prayed to her. To all of them."

"She heard you, Annika." Her mother had smiled. "You will save more than me someday. I love you." And she was gone.

The reeve had refused to allow them the wood to build a pyre, the custom of her mother's people. They'd buried her in the village temple's graveyard with only a small rock to mark the spot. Annika hadn't been since. Her mother wasn't there, anyway. She was with the Sky Goddess, sitting at the top of the world.

Her mother had died on a beautiful spring day, daffodils and bluebells in bloom everywhere. The sunlight. The color. None of it had matched Annika's dark and broken heart.

Now she viewed that day with more confusion and anger. How could the temple have denied her mother care because she was Weyan? At the edges of her memory was a glimpse of Zuri.

"Why can I not reach for Zuri? She's knowledgeable, Da. We need help. I need help."

"She was my soulmate. That's why," he said angrily.

Now she realized. "You blame Zuri for Mother's death?"

"I blame them all. I will as long as I live." He shook his head. "We will find a way ourselves."

Annika said nothing more. What was there to say? She looked at her father. Watched him drink his ale. He was forever different to her now. He had rescued her mother from what? Her home? Her family? Perhaps her family was dead. So many men worse than her father could have bought her and never freed her. And Annika didn't know how she felt about any of this.

CHAPTER TWENTY-FIVE

A covered viewing platform was constructed next to the outer wall by the practice field. Evelyne sat on a stool in the canopy's shade. Several melees were occurring at the same time in different squares in front of her. Usually, she watched with rapt attention, but today, she watched the servants' gate in the far distance. She scrutinized every face coming from that direction. None of them were Annika.

She was brooding. She knew she was. All over a kiss. A kiss. A single kiss. One that might have been given in sympathy. She was overwhelmed. Exhausted by the work. Maybe it had meant nothing to Annika. Perhaps she had kissed her to calm her crying.

A familiar yell drew her attention back to the fighting. Timothy must have won his bout. Witt was patting him on the back, and Timothy's smile was brighter than a night star. He slipped under the rope and approached Evelyne. He rested his arm on the floor of the platform. "Did you see the takedown?"

"I did," she lied.

"I'm glad you were here for my fight."

She felt a twinge of guilt for missing the move.

A young man with smooth skin, full lips, and long, flowing brown locks approached. He slung an arm over Timothy's shoulders. "I'll beat you next time."

"Evelyne, this is Finn. He'll be accompanying you to Dungewall. Part of your marriage retinue."

She could see Timothy's discomfort when he said the word *marriage*. She nodded toward Finn. "Well met, Squire."

"M'lady." He dipped into an overly dramatic bow.

"Don't let our contest fool you," said Timothy. "Finn is a good fighter. He'll serve you well."

"Come on, then," Finn said to Timothy, "I need practice at drinking ale."

Timothy bowed to Evelyne and followed Finn, but he cast a backward glance as he went.

"He likes you." Winifred's teasing voice drifted over her shoulder.

"Finn? I've just met him."

"Not Finn," Winifred replied. Then she whispered, "Timothy."

Evelyne frowned, annoyed at Winifred's constant interest in romance and boys. "He's my friend."

"That's not what Erik says. He says Timothy is all moony for you."

"He is a little late."

"Never too late for a bit of a snog," Winifred whispered with a giggle.

Evelyne swatted her away. The mention of a kiss only confused her. She thought of the kiss she'd shared with Timothy, one that had felt perfunctory. Then she thought of the kiss she'd shared with Annika, and her heart skipped a beat. She turned her gaze back to the servants' gate once more.

"You seem distracted."

Evelyne stiffened. Lothaire's voice was close to her ear. Very close. So close, she felt his breath move her hair. She turned her head, brought her eyes around to the fighters, and nodded to him.

He sat back. "I would have thought you pleased to have a tournament," he continued, his voice low. "I heard whispers. You have some experience with a sword yourself."

She swung her head around. He sat still and watched the fights and not her. Was he trying to see how she'd react? She looked past him at her father, who sat on his right, but he had taken no notice of the conversation.

Lothaire covered his mouth with a hand and leaned closer. "Don't worry. I have no reason to dissuade you from doing harmless exercise."

She felt her cheeks flush. She didn't like anyone having knowledge they could hold over her. Especially this. Her gaze wandered to the servants' gate once more. She couldn't help it.

"Are you looking for someone in particular?" he asked.

She intended to answer, "No one." But when she turned back toward him, their eyes met. An odd sensation of soothing liquid ran through her. The gray eyes and colorless face that should have been cold were not. She felt comfortable and safe. "I'm looking for a friend."

His gaze held her still. "The one from the other day?" he asked gently.

"Yes. Annika."

"Annika." He seemed to think hard about her name.

She hadn't forgotten the terrified look on Annika's face when the Paladin and Elder Theobald had approached them on the path, but Evelyne hadn't been comfortable with the situation, either. Still, something had passed between Annika and Lothaire. They had stared at each other but had said nothing. Fearing Lothaire might wheedle the truth out of them about their rendezvous, Evelyne had sent Annika home with the wet clothing.

"Tell me more."

"Her father, Steffen, tends the demesne's fowl. My father's flock. Not freemen's birds." The words tumbled out.

"Was she born here in Marsendale?" he asked. His voice was like a lute, playing sweetly in the distance.

"Yes. Born in the village, but her mother was from Weya."

His eyes widened a little. Was he surprised? He turned away and looked out at the fights on the practice grounds, his face placid once again. Like their first meeting, Evelyne noticed the clashing of metal, the grunts, and the cheers around her with more clarity when he looked away.

She snuck another look at him. He could sit so still, he looked inhuman, but now his fingers worked across his knees as if he was ready to leap to his feet at any moment. Why the change? What had she given away? Annika's mother being Weyan wasn't a secret, and it shouldn't matter to anyone from outside the castle, especially the Paladin.

Her sister Winifred leaned in close from behind her. "What did he say to you?" Excitement sounded in her voice.

Evelyne shrugged. "Pleasantries," she replied.

"He's so handsome. If he speaks to me, I'll die."

Evelyne rolled her eyes. He was handsome and tall. She didn't look down on him the way she did most others. And he exuded a warmth she didn't feel from her father or many other men around her. But the way Annika had reacted to him stuck in her mind. And if Annika was a Talent, she was in grave danger. Whatever Lothaire did to make her talk, she was glad she hadn't mentioned anything about her suspicions.

Or her feelings.

Her brother Erik appeared in front of the Paladin. He looked as if he wanted to say something serious, but he smiled gently, and his eyes were glassy. Out of character for him. Usually, he was surly and aggravating, though not physically, like Witt. He was too slight and short.

"Lord Erik. What do you wish to accomplish with your life?" Lothaire asked.

"I want to be the most learned elder in all Valmora. To be like Master Jacob. Only, I want to be master to the king."

"You'll do nothing of the sort," Evelyne's father's voice boomed. "You'll be a knight if I have to break you to do it."

"I once put raw egg in Master Jacob's hooded cape. He pulled it over his head, and it spilled all down his forehead."

Evelyne was surprised and amused by her brother's candor and unsure why he was providing such a detailed confession.

Lothaire smiled. "Is this the worst thing you've ever done?"

Erik's face turned the color of a radish. He shook his head. "No, Your Excellency. I have done worse." Tripping over his tongue, he added an undeserved honorific. "I cut Birgitta's hair while she slept."

Evelyne glanced back at her sisters; anger coursed across Birgitta's face. She had blamed Matilde for the deed.

"Revenge for when she hid my *Book of Constellations of the Valmoran Sky in Winter*. I know girls' hair shouldn't be shorn. Will the Maiden forgive me my transgression?"

Lothaire laughed and leaned forward. "I'm sure the Maiden will forgive you." His smile was reassuring. He seemed to like this game, and a game it was. Evelyne was beginning to understand. Lothaire's gift was tied to his eyes somehow.

"Get back in your place with the other squires," her father directed. "Show the Paladin what you're made of, boy."

Lothaire turned toward her father, and Evelyne saw an odd look cross Erik's face, probably the same one that had crossed her own face when she realized she had spoken things she had not intended.

"You're the most feared man in Valmora, and yet you speak to my children as if they were your own," Evelyne's father said to Lothaire.

Nothing made her suspect that Lothaire's gift was at work when he and her father looked at each other. Maybe that wasn't the key to his gift, or maybe he could control who he influenced?

"Maybe I am the most misunderstood man in Valmora."

Her father smiled and took a swig of ale from his mug. Lothaire smiled too, but it didn't reach his eyes.

A great crash drew Evelyne's attention to the fight directly in front of the platform. A knight stood with his hands high, pumping a blunted bludgeon in the air. His opponent sprawled in the dirt in front of him. Other knights cheered, slapping the winning knight on his padded shoulders.

A familiar excitement thrummed through her, the desire to fight alongside these knights, to show off for the men and women gathered. Even with a man down and possibly dead, she still felt the familiar call. To hold the bludgeon in her own hand. To swing it and take down a man across from her. To celebrate in front of her father and mother and receive a tribute for her deeds. In her mind, the tribute came from Annika. Smiling and sweet. Lifting her hands to present a crown of flowers to Evelyne.

Armorer's assistants rushed to the downed man. The bludgeon, though wooden, had hit a weak spot on his helm, creating a great dent and breaking the hinge on the jaw guard. Blood spilled out as they worked the broken helm from his head. He might be dead. All so her father could impress the Paladin, a man who didn't seem to care. The knight knew the risks. He could die at any moment. The only thing that kept any of the knights from fearing death was the knowledge that the Maiden would take them to her bosom when they died. They would see their loved ones who'd preceded them in death. All living in the constellations forever.

Evelyne watched as others yelled and gestured for a healer until one, standing with other religious men in the shade of an outbuilding, heeded the call. The healer held his headdress with one hand, its fabric rolls wound around the rim, and the tail flapping behind him as he ran. He dropped to his knees, turned his head to the sky, and began an incantation. Evelyne couldn't hear the words, but she could see his mouth moving and the telltale glow of light beginning under his hands.

"*Ah!*"

The cry wasn't from the man under the care of the healer. It was her mother's voice wailing. She staggered to her feet, holding her belly. "It is time."

Attendants took her arms and helped her from the platform. A page ran for a sedan chair, which returned quickly with two men on each end of the rails. Her mother looked pale as they placed her in the seat and carried her toward the inner bailey.

As she watched her mother being carried away, Evelyne thought how strong she must be to ignore the recommended months of bed rest and attend a tournament. Stronger even than that when she'd gone riding in the forest to oversee the demesne needs. Neither the temple nor the king took notice of the strength of women. And neither had she.

Her sisters all stood and filed from the platform. All were expected to sit in attendance at the birth. Evelyne reluctantly stood to join them. She took one last look at the fights. The injured man was sitting, still covered in blood but alive thanks to the healer in attendance. In battle, he might not have been so lucky. The other competitions continued as if nothing had happened.

"We will talk again."

Evelyne glanced at Lothaire only long enough to nod and turned away from his inquisitive gaze. As she trailed the others across the yard, she cast her eyes over the villagers and travelers coming to watch the tourney, but no one with flaxen hair was among them.

CHAPTER TWENTY-SIX

Annika stood at a community table, her last cheese round carefully displayed in its wrapping. Lord Cederic had allowed the villagers to hold a market during the tournament. With the festivities ended, a steady stream of travelers, lords, knights, and their retinues passed by on the village paths on their way to their home manors. Everyone in the village had taken in lodgers during the past ten days, except for her and her father. He had said lodgers were too risky.

What was worth the risk was the sale of milk, butter, and cheese. Annika had churned more butter, strained more milk, and sold more rounds of cheese in the past week than in her entire life. The visitors had bought it all, and all of it in coin that might allow them to buy Lord Cederic's permission to move.

Now, with the cow and the goats milked dry, she had a single round left.

"A half round," a serving man requested. He served someone wealthy from the look of him. His tunic was simple and bright yellow, and his hat was clean and stiff. There had been many like him in the past few days.

"Half a sheaf," Annika said.

He nodded and handed over the copper coin.

Annika cleanly sliced the round in two. She handed one to the man and placed the other back on the wrapping cloth, covering it partially to keep off the flies.

"Goose girl." Lord Witt stumbled toward her, several young men in tow. He slapped his hands on the table heavily and leaned toward her. "My sister's not guarding you today?"

She could smell the ale on his breath as he leered at her.

"Come on, Witt." His friends tugged on him. They were all drunk. Stumbling about and laughing.

Annika could see Evelyne's similar features on him. The long lashes. The sharp chin. The full lips. But he was as different to Evelyne as summer was to winter. He took the last of her cheese as his friends pulled him away, breaking it apart and sharing it with his fellows.

Half a sheaf she'd lost, but there was nothing she could do. He turned back toward her and grinned before stumbling farther along the street.

She folded the wrapping cloth and tucked it in her now empty canvas sack. She closed her eyes and turned her face to the sunlight and listened to the sound of horse carts and laughter. Everyone seemed to have lightened their spirits. The tourney was good for the village. Even so, a chill ran through her. The visitors were here to impress the Paladin, and once they were gone, he would turn his attention to his true calling.

Her heart fluttered as she heard someone who sounded like Evelyne. Her eyes snapped open, and she scanned the exodus. It wasn't Evelyne, but the thought excited and surprised her. How could she have such different emotions at the same time? Fear and happiness. The desire to run and hide and the desire to sprint to the castle and wait in the kitchen gardens for Evelyne to appear. Several days ago, the castle steward had announced the birth of a baby boy to Lady Wilhema and Lord Cederic, so she imagined Evelyne was attending her mother.

She headed for the cottage. Most of the travelers were heading through the village to the King's Road. They did not need to walk down the path ending at the mill, so the sounds faded away as she walked home. The weight of her purse felt reassuring against her hip. As tired as she was from the extra chores, the knowledge this money might soon be her savior lifted her mood. Before long, she and her father would be on the road to Weya. A frightening prospect but better than death by fire.

She didn't notice Witt until he'd pulled her off the path into the chest-high grainfield. "Goose girl."

She struggled against him. "Please, m'lord."

"Yes, please me," he slurred. "Give us a kiss, girl." He leaned toward her even as she stiffened her arms to keep him away. He changed the position of his hands, trying to get a better grip.

She looked around for anyone who might help but saw no one.

Screaming might draw attention, but it was Lord Witt. Who would believe her side of the story? "M'lord. My father awaits my return. Please. I cannot be late."

He paused for a moment, perhaps thinking, then a wicked smile crossed his face. "A kiss won't take long. Just one kiss." He pulled her toward him again.

Anger welled in her. All she had to do was pull her knife and cut him to make him let go. But if she did, all their plans to escape the temple would come to nothing. They'd clap her in irons and try her for assault. His face drew nearer. She closed her eyes and willed him away. Away from her.

He yelped in pain and dropped his grip. When she looked at him, he swayed slightly and stared at his hands. "What witchcraft is this?" he asked. His eyes narrowed, and his drunken smile fell away. He reached out to grab her again.

She readied her hand on her blade. She would use it this time if need be.

A hand spun Witt and forced him to his knees. The Paladin stood before them. His long hair fell across his face, blowing slightly in the wind. His expression was sympathetic. "Lord Witt," he said, "I believe you have taken a wrong turn this day."

"Let me go, you clodpate. Do you know who I am?" Witt said.

The Paladin leaned down. "I believe you've had too much to drink. Do you know who I am?"

Witt tried to focus on the face in front of him, only to look surprised. "Your Eminence. I apologize. I didn't recognize you."

The Paladin helped him to his feet. "Your day is done, Lord Witt." He encouraged Witt to move toward the mill path. "We'll not talk of this again."

Witt looked over his shoulder and yelled to Annika, "I'll be back, goose girl."

The Paladin grabbed him by the opening to his tunic and put his face close to Witt's. "Listen to me. You will never touch this girl again. If you do, I will bring all the force of the king's justice against you. Do you understand?"

"But—"

The Paladin lifted him until Witt was standing on his tiptoes. "Do you understand?"

Witt's expression turned fearful. He swallowed and nodded. The

Paladin shoved him. He stumbled and fell in the dirt. Wobbling to stand, he turned for the village.

Annika watched until Witt was no longer in sight. Then Lothaire brought his attention to her. He came close but not too close. She felt no relief from Witt's expulsion as she had now gone from the attention of a barking dog to a snarling wolf.

Had he seen Witt's reaction to touching her and overheard his accusation of sorcery?

"Are you well?" His question seemed sympathetic.

She nodded but kept her hand on the hilt of her knife.

He glanced at it. "You're safe now."

She slowly released her hand and instead grasped her belt.

"A beautiful day, is it not?"

She nodded. The day was cool for summer, and nary a cloud was in the sky.

"I'm Lothaire. And you are Annika, yes?"

She nodded slowly. He knew her name. He'd asked her when they met before. Or had that all been a vision? Was it possible it was only a vision?

"We didn't get to speak last time we met," he replied as if he'd read her mind. "Lady Evelyne sent you away on an errand."

Annika took a quick glance at her feet, trying to hide the emotion Evelyne's name brought to the surface.

"Let me walk you home."

Home? What would her father do? He might try to fight Lothaire. Or Lothaire might somehow know she was a Talent and be testing her. "Sir, I am fine now. I don't wish you to take time from your proceedings. I think you have scared Lord Witt away."

"I insist." His tone implied the discussion was over.

She led the way. He followed at a respectful distance.

"I hear you are a bird keep. Must be wonderful to spend so much time alone. Gives you plenty of time to think and dream."

Dream yes. Of being found and impaled.

"I haven't been alone since I was a boy. Such is my life since the Maiden called me to her house."

She heard his footsteps in the dirt behind her.

He went on, though she hadn't asked a single question. "From the time I was born, I thought the world smelled of tanning hides. My father was a tanner. The animal skins hung all about our house and in the drying shed, each in a different stage of preparation. My earliest memories are of working the leather, scraping and scraping and scraping off the flesh and fat. It's an awful smell, really. Urine, shite, lime, rotting flesh."

Annika flinched at the description but said nothing.

"When the faithful came to take me away, it surprised me to find the world had so many beautiful smells. Perfumes, flowers, breads. But sometimes, I miss that uncomplicated life amidst the bitter stench of my home."

They walked on in silence. Was this what it was like for the girl who'd burned in Byetown? Had she walked at his side to the pyre in a terrified calm, readying herself for the inevitable?

"Do you ever dream of being somewhere else? Someplace without birds?"

She looked at him warily. Was this a trick?

He twisted a ring on his finger over and over. "They tell me you are an accomplished musician."

"Pardon?" She panicked. Had Evelyne told him? If so, what else had she said?

His laugh was soft. "My job is the seeker of knowledge. I know many things. My burden is to sift through the gossip and lies to find the truth."

She tripped and righted herself. "You have found someone in a lie, then," she said. "I can play an instrument, but I am not accomplished at anything."

"I beg to differ." He gazed at her. "You are an accomplished beauty."

Her cheeks flamed. She hurried on.

"Lady Evelyne tells me you are Weyan."

Annika stiffened. Was this it, then? Had Evelyne turned over her secret too? With his powers, could Evelyne resist him even if she wanted to? Annika nodded eventually.

"And yet, you believe in the Maiden?" He moved next to her so she could see his face.

She stared at him. He was a handsome man for someone who killed children. She brushed away an insect. They buzzed around the Paladin as well, but he didn't seem bothered. "Of course."

"Do you favor your mother?" he asked. "She is Weyan, is she not?" This time, she noticed a halo of light glowing slightly around him. He must be using a gift, but what he was doing, she didn't know. She felt nothing and saw nothing odd other than the glow.

"My mother is dead." The words came out clipped and bitter. She didn't want him knowing anything about her mother. Not one thing. This cat-and-mouse game was tiresome. If he wanted to know if she was a Talent, he should ask, and she would lie. See if he was as powerful as everyone claimed.

She wanted to tell him to go sod himself. Kiss her arse. She rarely let slip her aggravation. All these years of making sure she did and said all the right things. Always pleasing everyone. Never saying no.

The Paladin's glow dimmed, and his shoulders slumped slightly.

What would they find together at the cottage?

CHAPTER TWENTY-SEVEN

Finally, Evelyne slipped away from the confines of her mother's chambers. She'd been cooped up in that room for the past four days. The birth had been everything she'd feared: hours of her mother wailing in pain, linens full of blood, the smell of piss and shite, the heat of so many people in the room together, and the inability to escape. The midwife had tied an eagle stone talisman to her mother's thigh to make the birth easier, but it didn't seem to work.

The babe was breached, little skinny legs turned the wrong way. The midwife had worked for hours to turn the child in the right direction. All while her mother howled. A boy had emerged from the mess and anguish. Another brother to be a hearty, fighting man for the family. At least he was alive, as was her mother. The blood had frightened Evelyne at first, but the midwife had sewed a tear with silk thread, stopping the bleeding.

The child was swaddled and passed from woman to woman to receive each one's acknowledgment and requested blessing. When the midwife had handed the child to Evelyne, she'd stared at his tiny hands with their tiny fingernails and imagined him holding his first sword, but at present, he was as fragile and vulnerable as he would ever be. And for all the stress and anxiety of his birth, Evelyne had missed the rest of the tournament.

As soon as she was through the gatehouse and outside the castle walls, she breathed easier. She pushed her way between carts and people as they made their way down the switchback path outside the main gates of the castle toward the village. They gave her odd looks, not because of her nobility, but because she towered over most of them. She took advantage of her height this time to move people out of her way.

She couldn't wait another hour to see Annika. She'd thought of little else, even while listening to the constant fretting and gossip and prayer of the past several days. She'd never felt this way about anyone or anything. Her obsession with learning to fight was as close as she could get.

It wasn't long before she saw Annika and...Lothaire. She slowed and stayed at a distance as she followed them. They weren't speaking, only walking together, Lothaire following a few steps behind. Evelyne's heart pounded in her ears. Would Annika tell him about their kiss? Would it even matter to him? It wasn't unusual for young women to dally, but she knew this wasn't a dalliance. Something stronger was at work for her. She didn't know if Annika felt it, but she wanted to find out.

What was she thinking worrying about herself? Annika was a Talent. A rogue. Evelyne was sure of it. She looked at her hands again. If Lothaire could make Annika admit her secret as he had been able to make Erik admit his transgressions... She shuddered at the thought.

When they reached the cottage, Evelyne leapt a stone wall separating the path from the fallow field beyond and squatted on the other side where she could watch from cover. The dry stalks of last harvest's grain and the new grass growth crackled beneath her feet. Annika led Lothaire to the cottage door and disappeared inside. Evelyne pressed closer against the cool stones. After a few minutes, she sat on the ground to wait.

❖

Annika's father sat in front of the fire mending a shirt when she entered the cottage. When he looked up to see Lothaire, his eyes went wide, and he jumped to his feet. He placed the mending on the stool next to him but never took his eyes off the Paladin.

"Da. This is Lothaire. He's the temple Paladin."

Her father's discomfort showed in the squeezing of his right hand and the shifting of his weight. "Welcome, sir. I am Steffen Garethson," he said with a stiff bow.

"Maiden's blessing." Lothaire replied. He made a gentle scan of the cottage as Evelyne had done. His gaze stopped on the pike and the other practice weapons Steffen had gathered for his training with Evelyne. He walked a few steps closer. "Expecting an invasion?"

"I try to stay in shape. Though my leg is no longer agile," Annika's father replied. While Lothaire's attention was on the weapons, her father gave her a confused look. She shrugged in reply. Her father looked past her at the door, and his eyes went wide again. He stared at her intently, gently nodding toward the door.

She stepped back, thinking he wanted her to leave, but when she looked over her shoulder, she saw the all-seeing eye on the door. The symbol was heresy in Valmora. She looked around for a way to cover it without drawing attention to herself.

Lothaire strolled closer to a shelf with plates and cups and examined them casually before turning back to her father.

"Please. Sit." Her father grabbed the only other stool and placed it across from his own, keeping Lothaire's back to the door. Lothaire took the seat offered. "Bring the Paladin a drink, girl."

She did as she was told. Her hand shook as she offered the cup to the Paladin. Lothaire seemed to notice and glanced up. His unblemished face and cool eyes made him appear unyielding. She pulled away.

He turned his attention to her father. "Do you believe our lives are preordained?" After a moment, he waved his hand. "No, of course you don't. I see it in your eyes. You've seen too many things to believe in destiny."

Her father tensed.

"Don't worry. I'm not using my gifts. They don't work on men like you and me. Our minds are like steel. No more pliable than a slab of marble. Your mind is closed to me." He swung his gaze toward her. "And your daughter's mind is as closed to me as yours."

Annika rubbed the hanging length of her belt.

"Which tells me she has seen much hardship, or the Maiden has made her in her image."

Annika's heart skipped a beat. He knew. He must know.

"I think it is the latter," he said.

Annika shook her head.

"You are someone special, Annika. Who—or what—I am not sure." He took a drink, leaving Annika as tense as her father, waiting for what would come next. "Have you ever considered giving Annika to the temple?"

He wanted her in the temple. He couldn't know about her.

"I'd let Annika decide for herself," her father replied.

Lothaire turned to look at her. She moved to get her father a cup of ale, trying to keep Lothaire's eyes on her and not on the door. She handed the cup to her father.

"Innocents are dedicated to the betterment of our society. It truly is a blessing to become one of them." Lothaire hunched over and leaned his arms on his knees. "My parents gave me to the order when I was very young. Honored to have a child called from our family. Proud to hand me over."

Something in the tone contradicted his words. Bitterness? Sadness? She wouldn't feel sorry for him. Not when she knew what he was capable of.

Her father twisted his cup in his hands. "Yes, yes, of course. It's only…since her mother died, I depend on her. I don't get around well, you see." He touched his stiff leg.

"You should find yourself a young bride," Lothaire offered casually as he straightened.

Annika could see her father grip the cup tighter.

"Yes, you're right. I should."

Lothaire turned his attention to Annika again. She could see him glowing slightly. Why bother to try again if he'd admitted his gifts didn't work on her? "What about you, Annika? Do you want to join the temple?"

She had no idea what the correct answer should be. "I would be honored to take the calling of an innocent." She turned to look at her father. "After my father is properly cared for." She hoped the answer would satisfy him.

He squinted at her as if in thought. He no longer glowed.

Her father put a hand on her forearm. "She's a good girl."

"Much like her mother, I suspect," replied Lothaire, watching her closely.

She grabbed for her belt and rubbed it with her thumb. She wanted him to leave. To leave them alone. To never come back.

Lothaire gestured to the wall above the bed. "Is that your instrument?"

"Yes."

His gaze moved from the gittern to her and back. He handed his cup to her and stood, the stool scraping gently in the rushes. "I've taken enough of your time."

Her father stood with him. "It is an honor to have the Paladin of Valmora in our home."

Lothaire cut his eyes to the corner and the pike. His hand went to the pommel of his sword. "I believe we have much in common, Steffen, son of Gareth. I was born in a village smaller than Marsendale. Until the Maiden called me to serve."

"I pray my fighting days are over."

Lothaire nodded and went to turn toward the door. Annika's father grabbed his arm and pulled him around. Annika tensed, waiting for Lothaire to be angry. He did nothing. Only looked patiently at him. Her father dropped his grip.

"Would you bless our house before you leave?"

Lothaire looked pleased. "Of course." He nodded and lifted his hand.

The words he spoke were in High Valoran. She recognized one or two—Maiden, bless—but the rest sounded like the tune of a songbird. She wanted him to leave. As pretty as his words, as beautiful and handsome as his face, he was still the man who'd set the Byetown girl on fire, and she was sure it wasn't his first, nor would it be his last.

While he was distracted, Annika threw open the door, keeping the symbol toward the wall.

Lothaire stepped outside the cottage and turned back to her. "We will talk again." He gave a gentle bow.

It felt odd for a Paladin to bow to her. She was no one. She bowed in return.

When he was well away from the house, she closed the door. Her father barred it with a length of wood. She leaned over and placed her hands on her knees, breathing out in short gasps. Her head spun. They had survived. Somehow, they had survived. She grabbed a rag, dipped it into the remainder of ale in a cup, and rubbed the black eye from the door with ferocity.

"How could I have been so stupid?" She sobbed and pressed her forehead to the door.

Her father took the rag from her and finished the job. "It's fine. We'll be fine. He doesn't know. If he did…"

She nodded.

"Be glad. Maybe that eye worked better than you thought."

She wished it was true. That her mother was somewhere watching over her, protecting her.

CHAPTER TWENTY-EIGHT

Evelyne dug her fingers into the dirt and grabbed a handful of pebbles. She threw them out in the grass in front of her. Periodically, she rolled to her knees and peeked over the top of the wall at the cottage before sitting back down. The uneven stones dug into her ribs. Speckled sunlight peeked out from behind clouds moving overhead. What were they talking about?

Why was Lothaire interested in Annika? Did he suspect something was unusual about her, as did she?

She crawled up on her knees and took another look over the wall. He was coming up the small hill from the cottage. She ducked back down. In that quick glimpse, he was smiling. Not a polite smile. A broad smile. As he passed, she stayed still. She could hear his footsteps on the dirt. She wasn't sure why she didn't want him to know she was here. She felt it. Whatever Annika was, Talent or not, Evelyne wanted to protect her, and she knew the Paladin was a dangerous man.

Irritation flooded her as he moved up the path to the village. She grabbed hold of a stone, smooth in her hand, and watched his back, watching his springy steps. She wanted to throw it at him. Hit him in the head with it. Make him bleed. Make him stay away from Annika.

When he was out of sight, she scrambled to her feet and dashed up the wooded path toward the castle.

She hustled through the kitchen and up the servants' stairs to the second floor. By now, Old Nan and the rest were immune to her comings and goings in her hunting outfit. She crept toward the men's quarters and paused at the corner nearest Lothaire's rooms and waited. She didn't have long to wait before he arrived. She ducked back behind the corner, hoping he hadn't noticed her.

When she heard the door close, she crept closer. She heard several voices, but the thickness of the door made the words unclear. With no one around, she dropped to the floor and put her ear to the gap under the door.

"Should I send word to the temple in Sevenshadows?" She recognized the voice. The king's man with the scarred face.

"Not yet," said Lothaire. "I'm not sure there is anything amiss. Just a feeling I have."

Amiss about what? About Annika? She saw their shadows moving on the other side of the door.

"We can't stay on a feeling, Lothaire. The last communication mentioned a potential rogue in Welford. A three-day ride."

The voices faded as they moved farther from the door.

"Have you lost something, Evelyne?"

She bolted upright.

Her youngest brother, Gregor, stood behind her. In his hands, he held a mewing kitten. His adorable eyes were so sweet. She wished he could stay this way forever. Sweet and kind. Unlike Witt and Erik.

She put a finger to her lips and whispered, "Yes. I lost a brooch somewhere between here and the kitchens. Will you look for it on the stairs?" She eased him in that direction.

He nodded, put down the kitten, and began crawling on all fours, mimicking her until he turned the corner. Relieved when he moved out of sight, she turned back to listen more. The door opened as she did so. She jumped up and turned away.

"You there, boy," said the scarred man.

She knew he was talking to her. Thank the Maiden, he thought she was a young man. She stopped and dropped her head.

"Bring some food."

She dropped her voice as low as she could. "Maiden's blessing. Right away." She hesitated, waiting to be sure he had nothing else to say. When he reentered the room, she slipped away to the women's quarters on the other side of the castle.

Maybe Lothaire's feeling had to do with Annika, and maybe it didn't. But one of them—Lothaire, Theobald, or Annika—had healed her hands at the pond, and she was certain about which one. She worried Lothaire knew as well.

Chapter Twenty-nine

Annika sat on the fieldstone wall while the geese waddled about the fallow field, eating residual grains and weeds. They would be good and plump come mid-autumn and grace the trenchers in the castle by the holy days of winter.

She had counted the coins saved from the tournament and added them to the ones Evelyne had given her father. A few were fake. Her father had spotted them and thrown them in the rubbish pit behind the cottage. All those nobles and their wealth, and still, some of them had cheated her of her due.

Soon, they would have enough money to begin their journey. Annika was both relieved and saddened. In the small, controlled world of Marsendale, she knew what to do and when to do it. Once they left, what would she experience? How would they live, and what would they eat?

The north, with its long, dark nights and weeks of snow, would be a challenge she had never experienced. She'd be leaving everyone she had ever known behind. Including Evelyne.

As if summoned, Evelyne approached.

Dressed in her own clothes, a long flowing tunic with intricate gold embroidery, her hair twisted in looping braids, there was still a towering strength to her. More so since Evelyne had been fighting with her father. As she approached, she wore a soft smile rather than her normal, self-assured grin. She held out a bundle. "I meant to return your tunic sooner."

Annika took the bundle and placed it on the wall next to her. "You needn't have worried."

"Well, I did worry. What would you wear to the summer burn if I had your best dress?"

The burn. How had she forgotten the highest holy day of the year was fast approaching?

"Do you not like the burn?" asked Evelyne.

Annika reached for her necklace. She never enjoyed being on display. The stares from the folks who came from Byetown and the villages around Lord Cederic's holdings. They all attended. Whether they stared at her because she looked different, she felt different, and that made her uncomfortable in their presence. In the past, she'd prayed for an early chill so that she could hide beneath a hooded mantle.

Maybe because the tournament drew folks from farther away, she hadn't felt as odd. But the burn was for the people she had known her whole life. Somehow, it was different.

Annika shrugged.

A silence dropped over them.

Annika picked up a broken branch from the ground and was mindlessly pulling smaller branches from it. She finally cracked the branch in half and threw it away. Evelyne made her way to some honeysuckle creeping over the wall and broke off several flowers, bringing them back and settling down again slightly closer to Annika than before. She broke off a flower and pulled the stem through until a small ball of nectar sat at the end, then offered it to Annika.

She shouldn't encourage Evelyne. She should refuse the offer. But something deep inside her wanted it, wanted her.

She took the nectar on her tongue. So sweet.

Evelyne appeared frozen in place. She still held the flower in front of her. There was desire in her eyes. Before she knew it, Evelyne leaned in and hesitated inches from Annika's lips. Annika could see the request for permission in her eyes. She leaned forward, and their lips met.

This kiss was tender and luxurious. Evelyne's hands went to the sides of her face and held her softly.

Annika knew she should be afraid. She was everything their religion told her was sinful and dangerous. She was a rogue Talent in their midst. What would Evelyne do if she knew? Should she tell her now before she and her father fled Valmora?

But the kiss was holding her in its grasp. How many people could see them kissing on this wall from the castle or from the path? Would they care? Did she care?

When they separated, Evelyne offered her the rest of the sweet-smelling honeysuckle. She took the blossoms and tucked them behind her ear. Evelyne sat next to her and placed a hand on top of hers.

She wasn't certain how long they stayed like that. Almost as if neither one of them wanted to do the things they should. But the truth couldn't hide from them forever. Annika needed to tell Evelyne about her. Otherwise, the secret would hang between them like a portcullis, ready to slam shut at the first sign of movement.

"I need to tell you something."

She felt Evelyne take a sharp breath. "You healed me," she whispered.

Annika's heart raced, and she stiffened underneath Evelyne's grasp.

She knew.

Evelyne pulled away and displayed her hands. "Not a scratch, a scar, a blister." She pointed at the middle finger on her right hand. "I had a scar from the top of my finger to the base, where I caught my ring on a branch and ripped it open. I didn't even know scars could be healed. Elder Theobald can't heal scars."

Annika took the outstretched hand, gently touching the place where the scar had been. She turned Evelyne's hand over, admiring the unblemished skin. She felt the touches in her core.

"How long have you been a healer?" Evelyne seemed excited rather than fearful. "Does your father know?"

She dropped Evelyne's hand. She had thought letting Evelyne know about her gifts would remove the weight of her secret. Instead, she felt trapped. "We shouldn't speak of this." She hopped from the wall and began corralling the geese.

She heard Evelyne's footfalls behind her. "Trust me, Annika. I could have turned you in to the temple, but I haven't."

"You still might." She knew the comment stung.

Evelyne took hold of her shoulder and turned her so they were facing. "Can you not tell how I feel about you?" she pleaded.

Annika didn't want to think about how Evelyne felt. She knew how she felt about Evelyne, though. She couldn't run from it. What could she say that would make any difference? She and her father were trying to leave Marsendale. Evelyne was herself leaving for her betrothed's lands. No matter how they felt about each other, what difference would it make in the scheme of things?

And there was Lothaire.

"You're special, and I'm not afraid of you."

"I'm no one. I want to stay no one. Now, I'm beholden to you to keep my secret."

"I will keep your truth, Annika. You can trust me with your burden."

She looked at Evelyne's earnest expression. If only it were as easy as Evelyne believed. "The Paladin has powers. Great powers to find the truth. Have you forgotten?"

Evelyne straightened. She looked down for a moment as if thinking about something. "I overheard him speaking to a king's man. I didn't hear everything, but I think he might already suspect something about you."

Annika wasn't surprised. He'd alluded to as much at the cottage. The real question was, could she and her father leave before Lothaire acted against her?

"How did you know the Paladin was coming when we were at the millpond?" asked Evelyne. "I've thought about it over and over. They were much too far in the distance for anyone, save a dog, perhaps, to have heard them coming."

Annika turned her head but was sure Evelyne could see the tears trickling down her cheeks. "I have waking dreams." Her voice was small.

"Waking dreams?"

"I see things. I see where the geese are when they get lost. I see where a tool is lying. Or I'll see someone coming from the village before they arrive."

"You have the vision of the gods?" Evelyne's eyes widened, and her mouth fell slightly agape. "I thought you were a healer?"

"I don't know what I am." Annika swept the geese toward the cottage path. "I don't know how to control myself. The visions come as they please. The healing was a surprise."

"A surprise? How does one have multiple gifts and not know it? Have you been this way all your life?"

"I've had the visions since I was little. The healing happened only recently."

"You're a seer." Evelyne spoke the words as if she was talking to herself. "Lothaire can't find out. I'm uncertain if there is another seer in all Valmora. Did you not know how rare your gift is?"

"If Lothaire finds out, he'll burn me, just like he burned the girl in Byetown."

"When was this?" asked Evelyne.

"No matter."

The geese waddled awkwardly as Annika pushed them more quickly from the field.

Evelyne kept pace with them. "What can I do?" she asked.

Annika shook her head. "Nothing. There's nothing you can do, save keeping me at arm's length until the Paladin is gone. Please, I beg you. Forget me."

"You know that is impossible." Evelyne reached for her hand. "I know you're afraid, but I will find a way to help you."

Evelyne's bravery couldn't sweep away Annika's sadness, but the fact that she was trying made Annika's heart soar.

Annika reached for her and pulled her into an embrace. Their lips met, a searching kiss. Searing. Frantic. Not at all the gentleness of the earlier one. When they broke apart, Annika left her palm on Evelyne's chest. She looked up into Evelyne's eyes.

"I will not forget your kindness." She turned and pushed the geese onto the path.

CHAPTER THIRTY

Evelyne had to help Annika. She couldn't ask her father to make the Paladin leave, and she couldn't throw Annika on a horse and ride away. But perhaps, somewhere in the castle's dusty books, she might find something helpful.

She looked at every scrap of writing she could find on Talents. In particular, ecclesiastical trials and rogue Talents. Master Jacob brought her tome after tome, each one heavier and dustier than the last.

She rubbed her eyes. She'd been at it for hours. The candle near her was but a nub, sputtering in the little liquid wax left at the bottom. She got up and retrieved a fresh one from the box next to the door and glanced over to where Master Jacob sat. His head was canted to one side, his mouth open, and his eyes closed.

She gently roused him. "Master, you should go to bed." She helped him to his feet. "I'll put out the candles when I'm through."

He looked disoriented but nodded. "Yes, don't leave any burning. You must promise."

She guided him to the door. "I promise. Good night, sir."

She stretched and sat back down. She stared at the *Council of Sevenshadows in the 20th Year of King Grandon's Rule*. The book stank of mildew. The pages were wavy and stuck together as she tried to turn them. The scribe's letters ran one on the other, and she had to blink to clear her vision.

Rules about how the faith should be preached. Rules about returning temple livestock in disputed territory. Rules about handling innocents who had relations with an elder. Rules about what time of the day to eat and what to eat and on which high holy days not to eat.

Near the end, she found the court cases, one of which involved a rogue Talent. A girl of twelve was accused of healing a cow. A village neighbor claimed to have seen the act. The cow fell on its side and wouldn't stand. The animal stayed this way for several hours. Eventually, the owner was resigned to putting the animal out of its misery, but the daughter—the accused—in tears, fell upon the animal and performed a healing ritual. The cow stood, to the surprise of all, and lived.

The case was referred to the local temple, but when the elders arrived to take the girl, the manor lord called his right to act as jurist since the girl lived upon his lands. Evelyne read with renewed interest, hopeful that the lord's intercession was successful. To her disappointment, the outcome was the same. The girl died on the pyre.

Evelyne closed her eyes and laid her head on her outstretched arm. She'd read a dozen of these cases. Every one ended the same way. There must be some way to change the outcome if the Paladin found out about Annika. She merely needed to keep searching. She opened her eyes and lifted her head, only to let out a sharp gasp.

Timothy stood above her in the shadowy gloom beyond the candlelight's edge.

"You scared me."

He drew closer, looking at the book before her. She slammed it shut. Dust motes flew in all directions, a few floated slowly into the flame. Dying in the fire. "Why, Evelyne?" he asked.

She was confused. "Why read?"

"Why do you humiliate me so?"

"You're talking in riddles. How does my edification humiliate you?"

She'd never seen him look so angry. His eyes narrowed, and his brow furrowed. He clenched his fists as if he was about to fight her. She moved her chair away from the table, giving herself some distance from him.

"It's late, and I'm tired. If you wish to be angry with me, then tell me what I've done this time."

"I saw you with the goose girl today."

She waited for more. Did he know she was a Talent?

"I saw you, Evelyne. Why would you give your affection to her and not me?"

Affection? He wasn't talking about Annika's gifts. He saw the kiss. She stood. Now eye to eye with him, she felt more in control. "Timothy, I'm sorry if this hurts you, but you mustn't tell anyone."

"Why would I wish to tell anyone about your unnatural affair?"

The response stung. "You can't mean that."

"Which part?" he asked. "I won't tell anyone, or that you are unnatural?"

"There is nothing unnatural about love." Once the words fled her lips, she knew she couldn't take them back.

He looked surprised. "You love her?"

She was glad of the low candlelight. She could feel the flush growing on her cheeks.

"All these years, did you not know how I felt about you?"

She played with a frayed spot on the hem of her sleeve. She had known he cared about her but not how much. She didn't answer his question.

He threw his hands in the air. "How could you not know that I love you, Evelyne?"

Now that he said it, she couldn't ignore it anymore. She had been selfish and had thought only of herself. That was becoming quite clear to her. Had he done so much for her over the years because of how he felt about her? "I never meant to hurt you," she said.

"Ha." He shook his head. "The worst part? A peasant girl, Evelyne?" He pointed in the general direction of the village. "I'd expect this from Witt but not from you."

"If we lived in the Concordant Kingdoms, this would be nothing. There is no disgrace in love between those of different status."

"Not if you were a man." Timothy leaned in closer. "Do you trust her to keep your confidence? Your reputation is already suspect. One word of this and your marriage might be in jeopardy."

"A marriage I didn't ask for," she exclaimed, thumping her fist on the table.

A noise came from the hallway beyond the doorway. They both turned to look. One of her father's beloved sight hounds wandered aimlessly down the hall, casting a dark shadow in the faint light from a wall torch. No one else appeared. Evelyne realized she had been holding her breath and sighed.

"What's keeping the girl from making demands of you? Threatening to sully your reputation in hope of financial gain?" Timothy said, his voice lower.

"I trust her with my life." She knew this in her bones.

Timothy ran his hand through his hair, seeming frustrated by the conversation. "She could go to the temple and claim you turned her to your ways without her consent."

She knew this would never happen, either. "She won't betray me."

"How could you possibly know? What hold does she have over you?"

She could tell him the truth. Tell him that Annika was a Talent, hidden amongst them in plain sight. Tell him that Annika was the one who needed their protection. Would he be her friend in this, or would he turn Annika over to the temple?

No. She couldn't take the risk, even if it hurt him to think she didn't love him.

"You must trust me on this, Timothy," she said. "She won't betray me." She met his gaze. "I pray you won't, either."

"You're making a mistake, Evelyne."

He faded into the gloom of the shadows once more and left her alone.

She laid her head in her hands.

Now she had more worries.

CHAPTER THIRTY-ONE

Annika sat in the shade of the thatch overhang. She worked strips of flattened, dried reeds, weaving them over and through each other. Making a wicker basket was mindless work. She could do it while dreaming about anything. Her father was on the roof, repairing a section of thatch that had come loose. She could see his shadow on the ground.

She wished she had been harsher with Evelyne the other day. Pushed her away before they could have had the conversation that had confirmed Evelyne's suspicions. And yet, Evelyne hadn't turned away when she'd discovered the truth. In fact, it felt as if they were closer than before.

Rather than being afraid, Annika hoped to see her again soon. And at the same time, Evelyne was dangerous. She brought unwanted attention, following her around the village, kissing her in open fields. Where Evelyne brought attention, the gossipmongers would begin their chatter. And those whispers could get to the Paladin. He'd already taken more interest in her than she wanted.

But she was happy it was Evelyne following in the fields the other day and not Witt or a king's man come to take her away. She thought of Evelyne's big brown eyes—always so happy to see her—and wished she could stop thinking about the Paladin long enough to enjoy Evelyne's company. When she had licked the honeysuckle from Evelyne's hand, a sensation had torn through her core. Everything in her had felt like it might burst. She would have kissed Evelyne if Evelyne hadn't done so first.

The reed she pulled snapped.

She hung her head. How could she be so preoccupied with Evelyne when so many other more important things swirled in her surroundings?

She reached for another length when she heard footsteps. A young boy in an unremarkable tunic, one stocking down around his shoes, shoes a few sizes too large for his feet, approached from the castle. He held out a rolled parchment.

"For you, miss."

She held it as he turned away. "Wait," she called after him. "Do you know what it says? I cannot read."

He shook his head.

"Who is it from?"

"The Paladin, miss."

She held it as if it would burn her. Balancing it with only her fingertips, she called up to her father, "I'll be back in a few minutes. I need to speak to Hilfa."

"Don't be long," he replied, tucking a line of thatch under another.

She ran the entire way to the center of the village, holding her tunic off the ground in one hand with the scroll of parchment in the other. What could it say? Why had he sent her something he had to know she couldn't read? Arriving at the forge, she pulled herself up against the nearest wood pillar and caught her breath. When Hilfa saw her, she nodded to Jack, who didn't need an explanation. He walked away, and Hilfa wiped her hands as she approached.

Annika held out the document, the seal visible on the edge, the mark of the Maiden deep in the wax.

"What's this?" asked Hilfa.

"I don't know." She handed it over. "Please, can you read it?"

Hilfa broke the seal and opened the page. She was the only person besides the village reeve who could read, a product of Hilfa's father's need for her to understand numbers, orders, and transactions. Her face grew ashen as she read to herself. She rolled it up and handed it back. "You are to dress appropriately and arrive at the hour of evensong at the castle with your gittern."

"Why?"

"The Paladin made the request."

Her hand shook as she stared at the red wax seal and its intricate details. "Should I go?" Her voice trembled.

"You should ask your father, but I don't believe you have a choice," Hilfa said sympathetically.

Annika thanked her and headed back to the cottage. More slowly this time.

❖

Annika stood in the entryway to the castle, not the servants' entrance by the kitchens. She'd never been in this hallway before. The thick walls were covered in vines and flowers painted in umber and red ochre. Several towering tapestries hung on either side of the doors to the great hall: Two mirrored fight scenes. Horses rearing. Men on foot with pikes. Snarling dogs. She looked more closely at the pikemen. One of them could be her father, even though she knew these tapestries were much older than him.

She adjusted the gittern on her shoulder. Would Lothaire ask her to the castle with her instrument if he meant to arrest her? Her father had assured her he would not. The wait made her nervous. She paced back and forth, unable to stay still. The man who'd met her was not someone she recognized. He had told her to wait, and she waited. And waited.

Finally, the man returned and bid her follow. He led her to the great hall, opened the doors, and stepped aside to allow her to enter. The room was taller than any she had been in, lit by a dozen chandeliers full of thick beeswax candles. The expense. The coin spent on each one could have fed her and her father for a month.

Alone at the far end of the room, the Paladin rested on the edge of a heavy trestle table, leaning against it, a candle in hand as he examined an enormous book. He slammed it shut, put it on the table, and stood tall as she entered. She walked forward, taking in the giant tapestry behind him that was filled with words she couldn't read, but its meaning was clear with the images of lords and ladies in pairs. Was Evelyne on there somewhere?

As she drew closer, her stomach grumbled. The magnificent oaken table, long enough to seat a dozen people, was set with a feast. Roast duck, salted eel, roast sparrows, small rounds of white bread, tarts, spiced boiled eggs. She'd only ever seen these things being prepared in the castle kitchens. Never displayed and presented.

Lothaire gave a small bow as she arrived at the table. She returned it with a nod. He'd asked her here for a reason. He wouldn't kill her for not bowing, and she was tired of being the lowest of the low in Valmora.

He gestured to the bench nearest her. "Please sit."

She did as she was told, but every muscle was tense and ready; she felt like a hare watching a fox.

"The feast is for you." He moved to the opposite of the table and sat across from her. "Eat."

She sat with her hands in her lap and stared at him. The dishes were magnificent. So many things she had never tasted, but she was too nervous to eat.

He nodded and tore off a piece of duck. The grease on his fingers reflected the candlelight. He placed the meat in his mouth, careful to block her view while he ate.

"You eat like them," she said, surprised at her own daring.

"Like whom?" he asked.

"Nobles. Merchants. The reeves and the village wives who want to pretend they are mightier than others."

He looked thoughtful and took another bite. "The duck is delicious. You should try it."

She worried he was fattening her for the kill, just as she would a goose. She kept her hands in place on her lap.

He shrugged. "The food really is delicious."

"Where is everyone?"

The household should have filled the room at this hour. With Evelyne.

"I made a special request. They won't disturb us." He ripped a piece of bread and dipped it in drippings.

The thought of interrupting the noble household discomforted her, knowing she was the reason for this inconvenience.

Lothaire took a drink of red wine out of a glass as clear as air. The bevels flickered as he tilted it away from his mouth. His lips were as smooth and as perfectly shaped as the rest of his unblemished face. No wonder the village women tittered as he passed by. He was nearly flawless to look at. And yet, all that beauty held no sway for her. Fear was all she felt as she looked at him.

He wiped his mouth on his sleeve. "So, Annika, daughter of Steffen, tell me about your mother."

Spiced wine. She could smell the flavors as he spoke. "She was Weyan," she said tentatively, uncertain what he wanted from her.

He gestured in a circle. "Yes, yes. Tell me about her. Her name. Where she was from in Weya. How she came to be in Valmora."

Was she here to defend her rights as a Valmoran? What should she tell him? That her mother had been a slave bought on the open market?

Humiliating for herself and her father. She wasn't ready to share that with anyone. Besides, if he was all-knowing, he'd already know how she came to be here. Perhaps this was a test of her loyalties? "Her name was Hella. Her home was called Vlamdal. My father married her in Lord Cederic's service, fighting in the north."

"Did she have a surname?"

Annika knew her mother's surname, but she tested Lothaire's abilities. She shook her head. "Hella of Vlamdal," she replied.

He seemed satisfied with the answer. He took a boiled egg and bit into it. "You really should eat. The kitchen staff worked very hard to prepare this meal. You wouldn't want to insult them, would you?"

Even without using his gifts, he was convincing. She imagined the many young women he had persuaded to turn over their friends and family members to the stake. Taken by his beauty and his attention. She reached for the one thing she had always wanted to try: a candied fig.

Figs didn't grow in Valmora. They came from the south, dried or candied. Her fingers stuck to the dark brown, wrinkled skin. She closed her eyes as she raised the fig to her mouth. The first bite was unexpectedly sweet and slightly tart. Upon opening her eyes, she found Lothaire watching with a satisfied smile. The fig felt heavy in her stomach. She laid the rest on the trencher in front of her and placed her hands in her lap.

"You could have this and more if you choose to join the temple."

Was that what this was about? He still wanted her to become an innocent? She doubted they would feed her candied figs at the temple.

"Your instrument is quite beautiful." He gestured at the gittern still hanging on her shoulder.

She wiped her hand on her tunic and reached for the instrument on instinct.

"Play for me."

She held the gittern closer. She'd never played for anyone other than her father...and now Evelyne. The music was for her. To soothe her. To bring her peace when there was none to be found. As well as to remind her of her mother.

"Please, I'd so love to hear you play." There was his soothing voice, the one he must have polished over the years. "Lady Evelyne was quite taken by your playing."

She snapped her head up at the mention of Evelyne. Did he know what they meant to each other?

A ratter moved between her feet. His purr was loud in their silence.

The cat moved on to Lothaire, and he tore off a piece of duck and threw it on the floor. His face softened. "I'm trying to help you, Annika. I understand how you feel." He broke a small round of white bread and looked at it rather than at her. "I told you, I was taken from my family… well, taken isn't the right word. My father was terrified of me. After the first time I forced my siblings to tell their secrets, he couldn't wait to get rid of me. Afraid I'd get him to tell all the horrible, rotten things he'd done to me, my brothers…my mother." He blinked and swallowed hard. "He didn't understand how my gift worked." He dipped his bread in a bowl of perfectly whipped butter and took a bite.

Annika's stomach growled traitorously.

"Even when people understand, they are still afraid of me." He looked at his hand holding the bread. "So afraid, they confess wrongdoings with no use of my powers at all. Most of them can't be forced. My gift is for the young. Sometimes, an adult mind is so childlike, I can persuade them to tell me the truth, but it feels wrong."

He threw the rest of the bread on the table and raised his eyes to hers. In the candlelight, his skin looked golden, taking the stone feeling away from his chiseled face. She could see the little boy he had once been somewhere behind his façade.

"When I arrived in service of the temple, I thought they would have me solve mysteries, make men admit their crimes, maybe sit by the king someday and help with trade negotiations. I never imagined what they had in store for me. When the previous Paladin told me I was to one day take his place as the defender of the faith, I laughed."

She couldn't see young Lothaire laughing. She wished she could laugh.

"He hit me so hard, they had to bring a healer to my bedside. I suffered headaches for months." He took a drink from his sparkling glass. "And here I am." He raised his arms to his sides. "The most powerful theologian in Valmora, and I can't even get a peasant girl to play me a tune."

Annika looked at the gittern. She could make her life easier if she would do what he wanted. Play him a tune. Eat his food. Listen to his story. Her hands went to the starting point on the instrument, her fingertips on the gut strings. One tune. Maybe something somber and dreary like she felt.

She closed her eyes and played. The music coming from her fingers was stronger and more spirited than she intended. She followed the music. The instrument had made this choice, not her. At least, it felt that way. So play she did. With her eyes closed, she was no longer in the great hall of Marsendale; she was in the open fields of grain, sun on her face, wind in her hair, casting about in the beauty of the natural world. In the music's circle, the rest of the world was a dream. A dream on the edges of her awareness.

When she finished, she found Lothaire looking at her the same way Evelyne had when she'd played for her in the cottage. Maiden, what now? She held on tight to the gittern for strength. A silence hung in the air.

"I've heard nothing like it," he said. "How is it you have kept this gift to yourself all these years?"

At the word *gift*, Annika stiffened. Had he used it on purpose? She crossed her feet and tightened herself around the instrument.

"Play another." He reached for his wine and sat back.

She couldn't. She placed the gittern carefully beside her on the bench. "I'm sorry, but I'm quite tired. May I be excused?"

"You haven't eaten a thing." He leaned forward, buttered a pristine white roll, and offered it to her.

She took it tentatively and held it in her lap.

"You're certain your mother had no surname?"

She was startled by the repeated question. She nodded.

"I would have thought a girl as talented as you would have come from a significant lineage in Weya."

Again, his choice of words chilled her. "I don't know anything about Weyans."

"Did your mother ever show any abilities around you? Feats of amazement, perhaps. Magical sayings or things that were Weyan and not familiar to you?"

Of course she had told her things. The pantheon of gods. Thirty words for snow, though she could only remember a few of them now. Stories of her sisters and brothers. She shook her head.

He held out a piece of duck. "Try it." He nodded.

She took the dark meat, slippery with fat, and ate it. Lothaire was correct. The bird was delicious. Like nothing she'd ever tasted.

"The recipe is my own. They prepared the bird in wine from the vineyards of the temple of Trevasa in the far south, near the border with Iola."

At the mention of Iola, she thought of Zuri. Worried Lothaire might sense her thoughts, she finished the duck and tried to quiet her mind.

"I wasn't born to this." He speared an eel with his knife. "But look what the Maiden has provided for me." He threw his arms wide, the eel dangling over the table. "She could provide for you too, if you let her."

She lifted her courage. "Why do you wish me to join the temple?" She was tired of sitting and waiting her turn to be sacrificed like the animals on the table.

He eyed her while he ate a chunk of eel from the knife point.

She took several deep breaths while she waited. Her ears rang, and she reached for her belt, rubbing the fabric with familiarity.

"I believe you are special," he said. "I'm not sure why the Maiden has led me to you, but I have learned not to ignore her guidance." He stared at her again with that look, the one that made her uneasy. An emotion she didn't want to see from him.

She leaned forward and instinctually put her hand over the knife next to her trencher. Under his gaze, she felt trapped. She wanted to run. "How do you know it's the Maiden? Does she speak to you?" she asked.

He reached between them and placed his hand over hers. He smiled. "You are a smart girl. I do not hear voices. I'm not a mystic. Rather, when something is in my path, I believe the Maiden has her hand in the act."

She slipped her hand out from underneath his and laid it in her lap. "I do not believe the Maiden knows who I am."

He sat back and crossed his arms. "Even if she does not, I do."

She shivered.

"Think about what I've said, Annika. I believe you and I were meant to cross paths. I could help you on your journey in the temple." He pounded the table, startling her. A serving man entered from behind the dais. "Please see that my guest is escorted to her home safely."

She fairly leapt to her feet, ready to escape the room as quickly as possible.

"Annika."

She turned back toward him.

"May the Maiden bless you."

She could see the aura surrounding him. She bowed and rushed out of the room. The serving man refused to allow her to journey on her own, insisting she wait in the entrance for an escort. He walked away, and she considered fleeing, but she thought better of it when the family approached from the left.

Annika caught Evelyne's eye as she stood taller than her siblings and mother. She wanted to smile at her or run to her or call out to her, but she knew none of those things was appropriate. Instead, she bowed as they passed. She saw Evelyne's fingers raise slightly, the only recognition allowed before a young man approached and led her from the building.

CHAPTER THIRTY-TWO

Evelyne prowled her mother's solar like a trapped animal. Old Nan was the one who'd told her Annika needed to speak to her. She knew it had something to do with the meal with Lothaire. Each time she looked through the window, she could hear the rain hitting the glass. The drumming she heard matched the one she could feel in her chest.

"Sit, Evelyne," said her mother. "You're making us all fret. The rain will stop soon enough." Her new, unnamed baby lay wrapped in a sling around her breasts. She alternated between stroking his head, kissing his forehead, and working her needle on the cloth before her. The rest of her sisters worked on their own projects.

"Why did the Paladin ask the village girl to the great hall the other day?" Birgitta asked their mother. "Is she in trouble?"

Evelyne stopped pacing and listened intently.

Her mother seemed to notice her interest. "I don't pretend to know the Paladin's mind."

Birgitta continued, "Well, I think it was rude to leave us waiting for evening meal for so long."

Her mother put down her work with a loud sigh. "We are all servants of the Maiden. If her protector of the faith says we wait for our food, we wait for our food. If need be, we would fast for a week."

"Even Father?" Birgitta asked.

"Yes, even him."

Birgitta looked at Evelyne. "You know the girl. I've seen you together. In the village."

Evelyne stiffened and turned to the window.

"Do you think she knows something sinister the Paladin is searching for?" Birgitta's voice fairly trembled with excitement.

Evelyne's jaw clenched. She wanted nothing more than to melt into the rain. What could she say that would satisfy Birgitta's curiosity?

"I know her too," said Winifred. When Evelyne turned, Winifred gave her a quick glance before continuing. "She's very devout. I'm sure he is rewarding faithful peasants with a special meal."

Her mother nodded. "Birgitta, not everything is like a story from the Enlightened Book. Now pay attention to the details in your embroidery."

Winifred didn't know Annika from Peg or Daniela, but she had helped to change the subject. She was more observant than Evelyne realized. All this talk of Annika made the closeness of the solar worse. "I'll be back." She strode through the door. Her mother called out, but she didn't stop. She rushed through the baileys to the covered main gatehouse. The flagstones were slippery, and a wall of water rushed in front of the portcullis. A bright flash of lightning and a crack of thunder greeted her.

"Here, m'lady," said one guard on duty. "You shouldn't be out in this."

Water dripped down her face. "I'm already wet. What difference will it make?" She rushed into the downpour, intent on getting to the cottage. Annika had asked for her. She would come.

As she approached the cottage, she saw Annika, dressed in a hooded cloak, hefting a bag of barley chaff. Drawing near the outbuildings, she saw Annika throw feed inside for the birds. The rain brought with it the first chill of the season. Evelyne should have worn a cloak. She hunched her shoulders to stay warm and approached. The rain streamed off the edges of Annika's hood.

Evelyne didn't know what made her do it.

She grasped Annika by the shoulders, turned her, and backed her against the walls of the lean-to. The kiss was glorious. She pulled back slightly so she could look at Annika's face. Then, she took her into a tight embrace. "I was worried about you. When I heard the Paladin had asked for you, I thought the worst."

The rain was falling harder now. Annika tightened her grip on Evelyne's back. "I'm sure he knows."

Evelyne pressed her forehead to Annika's. "What does your father say?"

Annika turned her head away. Was that rain or tears on her cheek? "He says we must leave." Her voice was small.

More rain fell between them like a curtain. Evelyne felt like she'd been punched in the gut. "Leave? Where will you go? How will you survive?"

Annika shook her head. "You know I cannot tell you. If the Paladin asked, you could not lie." A pained expression crossed her face. She touched the middle of Evelyne's chest. "I don't want to leave you."

"No. You can't go. We'll find another way." Evelyne wiped the wetness from her eyes. Tears not rain, she knew. "You can come with me. Both of you. To Dungewall. Steffen can be part of my personal guard, and you..." She could see the disappointment on Annika's face.

"I can't go with you. I need to leave Valmora. You know why."

"I haven't thought it through." She leaned against Annika, her hands on Annika's hips, her face close. "I can't lose you now I've found you."

"Annika." Steffen's voice cut through the rain.

Evelyne released her, wiped the rain out of her eyes, and backed away unsteadily on her feet. And then she ran. She slowed as she passed Steffen. She wanted to say something to him. To tell him how important he was to her. How much she had learned. Instead, she bowed to him but didn't stop. She kept moving. With each step, she realized Annika was about to be a shadow of a dream.

CHAPTER THIRTY-THREE

Hilfa helped Steffen with his backpack. "You want me to come with you?" she asked.

"No. If someone came looking, it wouldn't do for you to be missing as well."

Annika finished tying her sack to the pack frame. Hers contained food and a change of shift, socks, and a sewing kit. Her father carried items for hunting and fishing, a few bits of clothing, a blanket, a leather cover, and more food.

Hilfa moved to Annika and took her in a hug. She smelled like the forge and sweat, familiar and soothing. Annika clung tightly to her. She'd miss her. Hilfa was like an older sister, and parting from her felt like a death.

"You help your da," Hilfa said as she leaned away and wiped a tear from her cheek.

Annika wanted to cry too, but she was afraid she would collapse, overwhelmed by emotion. She swallowed the urge and nodded. Then she looked around the room once more. They were leaving almost everything behind. At least if someone entered the cottage tomorrow, they'd not know Annika and her father would be gone for several days. She noticed her father's pike in the corner, gleaming in the candlelight. She hoped it would find its way to Evelyne. She'd worked hard to learn to use it. The weapon should rightly be hers.

What of her mother's gittern? She stared at it on the wall. It served no purpose on the road except to entertain them. And yet, she knew she couldn't leave it behind. She took it down and tied it to her pack frame.

"You can't take that," her father said. "Only what you must."

She kept tying. "I'll not leave it."

He could make her, but he said nothing more. He and Hilfa nodded and shuffled and gave each other a slap on the shoulder. No hugging for those two.

Hilfa's last words were "Maiden protect you both," and she left without looking back.

Her father made Annika tie her purse to a second belt under her tunic, less of a target for a cutpurse. She felt the few coins left inside. The smugglers had demanded payment before they would risk the trip. Now she and her father had only a few days' coin for food and drink and perhaps a shared common room in an inn along the way. So many worries yet to come on their journey, and they hadn't even left the cottage yet.

While they waited for evening, she was too restless to sit. She paced and ran her fingers across all the things they were leaving behind. The carved chest. The dried herbs. The small earthenware and wood utensils. Underfoot appeared and rubbed her legs as if the cat knew she was leaving.

Her thoughts replayed the last time she had spoken to Evelyne. How hurt Evelyne had looked as she'd run away. Inside, Annika felt the same. When Evelyne had grabbed her and embraced her, she had held on to her muscled back and hadn't wanted to let go.

Once darkness fell, Annika and her father headed toward the mill. They needed to avoid the King's Road, and to do so, they crossed the river, walking in ankle-deep water overtopping the stone dam by the mill. On the opposite side, they followed the river to the northwest.

They walked several hours through the old growth forest by starlight alone. The smugglers picked the night of the new moon to meet, making their journey more difficult. The trek was extra tough for her father. He stumbled on the uneven ground, his stiff leg dragging. Annika knew they were following the river, though she couldn't see it; she could hear the trickling of water against the banks. Mostly, she heard the crunching of her footsteps on the leaves and branches littering the ground.

The trees towered eerily over them. Thick and tall, these trees had watched over this part of Valmora for hundreds of years. Under the canopy, the air was cool.

She did not know what landmark let her father know they had reached their destination. But when they did, he took her hand and moved toward the riverbank. They crouched at the edge of the tree line and waited. Annika didn't know what they were waiting for. She could see little on the water, but occasionally, starlight reflected off the smooth surface. She sat back against a nearby tree and drew her cloak around her.

Soon, they would be on their way down the River Lewes as it flowed to the Hava Sea. With luck, they'd go past Tarburg and on to the crossroad to the Concordant Kingdoms. And there, they would turn north and walk to Weya. How many weeks would their journey take? She shivered. Winter would meet them before they arrived. She trusted her father would guide them safely.

She looked at his profile in the darkness. His heavy fist clenched tightly around the hilt of his knife. On his back, he wore enough supplies for a few days but not enough to get them all the way to Weya. They would have to find food along the road. Most pilgrims could stop at temples, each a day's walk from any other, and receive food and lodging for the night. She and her father would have to stay off the road in fields and woods, foraging for their food. He'd already warned her it would be hard and long.

What choice did they have?

He silently tapped her knee. She stood. He'd seen something. She peered across the gently flowing water, looking for whatever he'd spotted.

A small light approached, swaying back and forth. A signal.

"Be ready," her father whispered.

The boatman ran the shallow boat upon the shore, holding it in place with a pole, while a companion leapt ashore, rope in hand, and pulled it farther on to solid ground.

This was it. Annika looked at the familiar stars. She'd never see the same sky again. Never see Evelyne or Hilfa or Jack. Never be somewhere she knew intimately. What would her life be like?

They had no choice now. Lothaire was too close. She could almost feel his presence, hanging around her like a cloying fragrance. The boatman swung the lantern again. Time to go.

Before she could take the first step, she heard the clink of chain mail and heavy footfalls coming from the north. Her father pulled her deeper into cover. Even in the darkness, she saw the mass of king's men overrun the boatman's crew. A few carried torches. A fight ensued, but it was over quickly.

Her father yanked her back and began stumbling deeper into the forest. She followed unsteadily, her feet catching on unseen obstacles. She heard the crack of branches. Were the sounds from her stumbles, or were the king's men behind them? She turned her head, but her father pulled her to him. He cut the gittern from her pack and threw it to the ground with an off-key twang and a hollow thud.

"Run as fast as you can," he said.

"No!" She gathered the gittern in her arms.

"Leave it. Run. Hurry."

She didn't care if she was caught. She wouldn't leave the gittern here. This was the one thing of her mother's that still spoke to her. Spoke in musical notes but spoke, nonetheless. Rather than a carved container or an embroidered dress, the gittern was both physical and spiritual to her. "I'll not leave it behind," she said. She slipped her pack off and left it where it landed, but she held the gittern tightly.

She couldn't see her father's expression in the darkness, but she hoped he understood.

Someone called out, and she heard movement.

"Run and don't stop. Run until you can't run anymore." Her father pushed her ahead of him.

"What of you?"

"Go."

She did as he told her. Willing herself not to fall, she ran and ran and ran. Ran until her lungs burned, and her legs felt heavy. She stumbled and fell to her knees. She clung to the gittern with one hand, the other dug into the ground to keep her from crushing it.

She slumped against a tree to catch her breath and waited for her father. She waited, and though she was silent, the forest wasn't quiet at all. She heard a fox squeal in the distance. Something small shuffled in the undergrowth near her. An owl hooted. Each sound brought dread.

The longer she waited, the more worried she became. What would she do if her father was injured or captured by king's men? Or Maiden preserve her, what if he was dead? What would she do? How could she get to Weya alone?

The animal noises faded as she heard the familiar sounds of a person approaching. She held her breath and pushed as close to the tree behind her as she could, trying to make herself a part of the surrounding landscape. The sounds drew closer. She pulled her knife and waited. Fear filled her.

"Annika?" came the harsh whisper.

Relief flooded her. "I'm here, Da."

He crouched beside her. She threw her arms around his shoulders. "There. There," he said. "No one is following us. Let's go."

She stood and brushed off the debris on her tunic. "Where will we go now?" she asked.

"Home."

"Home? But the Paladin?" She was confused.

"We have no more coin." He shouldered his pack and took her hand. They began the walk back to Marsendale. "Without the smugglers, we've no chance. We'll have to find someone else or some other way."

Start over. Say good-bye to Evelyne and Hilfa again. Feel the dread of Lothaire. Stare at their home and leave once more. She clutched the neck of the gittern tightly and trudged onward.

CHAPTER THIRTY-FOUR

The sun was low on the horizon. A whisper of wind rustled the stalks of wheat against one another. Their heads curved toward the ground, full of grain and ready for the reaping. A line of villagers stood several paces apart at the edge of the field. The strongest among them had scythes in hand, while the youngest and oldest waited behind them to gather and bundle the cuttings.

An elderly woman called out a chant to the Maiden, and as she finished, the villagers began their swings. Full measures of wheat fell with each one. The harvest began, and with it, Annika took her first swings.

Having something mindless and physical was good to keep her from worrying about her situation. The coin was gone. They couldn't get it back. All that work she'd done during the tournament had been for nothing. Her father had considered selling their personal animals to other villagers, but the risk was great. Someone would suspect their actions.

And there was her gittern.

She knew it was valuable. She also knew selling it would be like carving her heart from her chest. But if it came to it, she'd do what needed to be done. For herself and for her father. A pang of anger struck her. Her father had bought her mother as his bride. She'd had no choice in the matter. When Annika looked at him, the man who had been so good and so important to her, she couldn't see the man who had taken her mother from her home. Someday, they would need to reconcile the deed, but now was a time for them to be of one mind. To survive.

At the end of the first row, the chantress stopped singing. Everyone paused to rest. Annika held the scythe upright, allowing it to support her weight, and lay her head on her arm. Her breathing was still labored. The little girl following her sat on a bundle of cut wheat, waiting. Annika smiled at her. She smiled in return, her front baby teeth missing.

The break was too short. The song began again, and so too did the cutting.

Three passes in, someone touched her back and reached across her hand for the handle of the scythe. Evelyne. "Let me." She took the tool in hand, trying to find the balance.

On her first pass, a few stalks fell, but more stood than lay on the ground. She tried again, already falling behind the others as they made a straight line toward the far end of the field. A few more stalks fell this time, but still not a full clearing.

Annika heard the youngster behind her sigh. The girl was in for a long morning. A few more attempts, and Annika approached her. "I can do this, Evelyne."

Evelyne shook her head. Her eyes pleaded. "I want to do this."

Annika nodded, then stood on her tiptoes and whispered in Evelyne's ear, "Listen to the rhythm of the others." She felt Evelyne shudder against her.

Evelyne closed her eyes. When she opened them, she took her swing at the same time as the others, cleanly cutting everything in front of her. She stepped forward and swung again and stepped and swung and stepped and smiled. Annika smiled with her and began gathering the felled stalks.

Every stroke was in time with the others, all three dozen of them. Even the footfalls as they moved forward were as a single entity. An army of workers, felling for the survival of the realm. Gathering the fruits of their labor.

How many times in the village temple had Annika listened while the temple elder had droned on from the Enlightened Book about how the harvest was the gift of the Maiden? The Maiden wasn't here cutting the wheat. She wouldn't bundle it, thresh it, winnow it, or turn it into lifesaving bread.

By the time the old woman sang her next chant, it was midmorning. Annika and Evelyne followed as the rest of the villagers set down their scythes and moved to the center of the cleared field. Annika was used to field work, but sweat soaked Evelyne's tunic. The tunic was so ornate, she stood out like a beacon of wealth against the villagers. They wore rough homespun without decoration, covered by the occasional cotton apron. Most of the men had started the morning in tunics, but now they were bare-chested and stripped to their underclothes, which they bunched around their hips.

Evelyne grimaced in pain when she sat on the ground.

Annika sat beside her and pulled her hands to her lap. Even though calluses bloomed on Evelyne's hands from the summer work with her father, new blisters were forming, peeling, and bleeding. As if reading her mind, Evelyne gave her a sharp look Annika took to mean not to heal her. As if she could. She did not know how it worked.

A pretty girl approached carrying a basket and set it beside them. Inside was bread, a wedge of cheese, strawberry jam, and a small clay bottle.

Annika removed the stopper from the bottle and took a sip. Goat's milk.

Laughter rose to her ears. A man in a circle of youths near them moved his upper chest muscles in a sort of dance. His naked torso glistened in the sun. The girls surrounding him giggled and hid their blushes behind their hands. When they noticed Evelyne was watching too, they quieted, giving her nervous glances. No one from a noble family ever worked the fields, and never would a noblewoman do it. No wonder they all felt unsure around her.

Even if Evelyne tried to understand the villagers' world—working beside them, eating with them—she would never be one of them. At least, not in this village on her family's land. She would have to go beyond the manor. Evelyne would leave within weeks for her future husband's lands, but Annika wondered if it would be any different there.

"How are you feeling?" Hilfa approached and sat. Jack followed. He smiled. Not a welcoming one, a more sympathetic smile.

Evelyne showed her hands. Palms up. "I don't think I'll be able to hide this from Mother."

Hilfa pulled a clean cloth from the inner pocket of her tunic. She poured some mead on it, ripped it in half, and wrapped Evelyne's hands.

"Keep it on while we eat. Might help some." Hilfa tore at her bread and handed a chunk to Jack. She looked from Annika to Evelyne and spoke in a hushed tone. "I saw the Paladin ride away yesterday. Has he returned?"

Annika stiffened. His name brought a queasy feeling to her stomach. She felt Evelyne's hand cover hers.

"I think we all know his presence is a problem." Evelyne drank some milk, no doubt to hide the discomfort building in her voice. "No one knows when he will return."

Hilfa handed her the mead. Evelyne toasted with the flask and drank. "I've never had so much mead as these past few months."

"We'll make a peasant of you yet," Annika joked.

Evelyne gestured to the surrounding workers. "They only see me as one of the ladies of the manor."

"Why would you want to work if you could sit on your bum and diddle all day?" Jack asked. "That's what they're thinking."

Evelyne frowned. "Do you really think I diddle all day?"

Jack shrugged. Hilfa stared at her loaf of bread.

"I'll admit, I've never worked as hard since I met Annika and Steffen." She smiled shyly at Annika.

Hilfa tapped her leg. "Come on. Can't have you diddling, can we?" She stood and helped Jack to his feet. "We've got more wheat to cut, bless the Maiden."

Evelyne stood and reached to Annika and pulled her up. She leaned in close, so close Annika could smell the sweat and mead. "We need to speak. Meet me at the edge of the village on the north path to the hunting grounds."

"But…" Annika barely let out a retort before Evelyne walked away. Annika looked about her. The others were already returning to their work. Hilfa caught her eye but only nodded. What should she do? She looked at Evelyne's retreating form and once again at the field.

Maiden take them all. She'd go. She had nothing to lose. What did it matter if anyone saw her? What could they do? Gossip? Punish her?

She lowered her head and moved quietly toward the village. She found Evelyne near the carved stone that acted as a mile marker, a small brown mare beside her. She brushed the animals' hindquarters and cooed.

"This is Willow. She's a jennet." She stroked the horse's neck. "Not as fast or strong as my father's horses, but she's steady and gentle." Evelyne took the reins and swung onto the saddle. She reached a hand down.

Annika's eyes widened. She had never ridden a horse. Had almost never touched one except for the draft horses that pulled the ploughs.

"Come," Evelyne encouraged her.

Annika looked back at the village. She should stay and work with the rest of them. She should not be seen with Evelyne on a horse.

Maiden's bones. She would do what she wanted. She took Evelyne's hand, and Evelyne lifted her effortlessly to the animal's back.

"Hold tight."

Annika wrapped her arms around Evelyne's waist. As the horse moved forward, she pressed herself against Evelyne's back.

"Maybe not that tight," Evelyne said and laughed.

A woman with two small children, a dog, and bundles of sticks, stopped and bowed to Evelyne as they passed. Her eyes narrowed at Annika. Annika turned her head away from the gaze. She knew word would spread quickly. She didn't know how much longer she would be in the village or how much time she had with Evelyne. While she could, she would enjoy it.

Looking down on them had felt uncomfortable. This must have been what power felt like. She felt it even though she knew the deference wasn't for her. And a small part of her liked the feeling. *What must it be like to have others appreciate you, come to you for advice, and to be able to ask for what you wanted?* She moved her right hand from Evelyne's stomach to her shoulder and pulled her closer.

Several miles from the castle, Annika saw the cliffs of the gap, the odd, flat-topped mountain whose bluffs bordered the River Lewes. A waterfall flowed from the cliff top down the face and into the river below. Evelyne dismounted at the water's edge under a massive stone bridge—a bridge for a giant. She'd heard about it but had never seen it before. Parts of it appeared to have collapsed into the river and onto the surrounding ground.

Evelyne helped her off the horse, lifting her by the waist and bringing her so close, they touched each other. "I thought the worst when Lothaire left the castle," said Evelyne.

Annika gazed up at her earnest face. Confusingly handsome and beautiful at once. If only she could memorize these moments for when she was far away. She stepped back. She wanted to tell her everything. "We tried to leave," was all she said.

"Come with me." Evelyne led her up the side of the nearest hill, climbing past the pillars of the structure above. Built into the hill itself, the pillars were longer at the bottom and others shorter near the top, but the bridge itself stayed level along the whole path. When they reached the hilltop, Annika could see across the entire valley. Far in the distance to the east, the local temple monastery sat on the small hills, the tower visible on the horizon. Farther north, she could see the roofs and fence lines of the other villages marking Lord Cederic's holdings. In the distance were more pieces of the bridge, crossing the entire valley to the other side. Annika leaned her head back to look at the structure above.

"I come here when I want to be alone," said Evelyne. "Truly alone."

"Where does this bridge lead?"

Evelyne smiled. "I know the villagers call it the Giant's Bridge, but it isn't a bridge at all." She ran her hands over the stone. "It is called an aqueduct. A thousand years ago, it carried water over the hills to the valley beyond."

"Who built it?"

Evelyne shook her head. "The ones who came before the Maiden's time. The ancients. Giants. Whoever they were, this is an amazing feat. The Eastern Valley is too dry for a good harvest now. Father uses it for cattle." She put her arm around Annika's shoulder and pointed into the distance. Her hand felt warm through Annika's tunic. "If you follow the ruins across, you'll see the cut they made in the hills on the other side."

"Have you ever traveled far from Marsendale?" Annika asked.

Evelyne stepped back and looked proud. "As far as Tarburg."

"Have you ever been gone for a long time?"

She shook her head. "A few weeks at the most." Her expression became somber. "There must be something we can do. Hide you and your father until the Paladin is gone?"

"Evelyne," Annika said it as a warning. She was tired of explaining.

Evelyne turned away, obviously frustrated.

Annika's stomach felt leaden.

"I know we have no obligation to each other. But maybe I can convince your father to come with me. Both of you. To Dungewall." She paced while she spoke. "He can be a bird keeper there. Or I'll make him part of my personal guard." Her voice became excited. "And you, you can be a household attendant. They don't know you there. I can convince them you have the proper pedigree."

Disappointment weighed on Annika. "But I'm not, am I? I'm a peasant. Born to a Weyan. And you'd have me pretend my da is not my father."

"Around the manor." Evelyne strode back and forth. "At first, but as things settle, you'll get used it." She grasped Annika's hands. "I only know I want to be close to you."

Annika's conflicting emotions left her confused. What was she to do with this knowledge? She needed to get away from the castle, as far away as she could from the temple's reach. To Iola or even Weya. Not to the far end of Lord Cederic's lands, still under the watchful eye of the elders and the Maiden. Even if they went with her, lies still lay in wait, with more lies upon lies, building. Annika moved away, pulling her hands from Evelyne's. "You will be married. You think so little of me as to make me your whore?"

Evelyne looked shocked and shook her head. "No, I never meant to imply such. I don't love him. I don't even know him."

"But your life is to be his wife, and mine is someplace else."

"I never meant to impugn your honor in such a way."

"I can't stay in Valmora." Time to make her own decisions. "I must go, and you need to let me."

Evelyne turned her head away.

"I will leave as soon as we have enough coin to buy your father's leave. Or we find someone to take us."

Evelyne didn't look at her.

"I must get back to the village." She began to climb down the hill. After a moment, she heard Evelyne following.

Upon the horse once again, Annika glanced back at the trail of ruins across the fields of golden grain, a reminder of how change came regardless of how she wanted things to stay the same.

❖

The little sheet of parchment Evelyne had brought was perched on the shelf, tucked behind the salt box. There it sat. Staring at Annika. Her fingers trembled as she reached for it. She looked around, afraid someone would see, though no one was here. She spread it on the tabletop, careful not to touch the symbols, and stared.

When Evelyne had showed her the page, Annika had reached for the symbol she knew as well as the inking on her wrist. This time, her hand hovered over the page. She closed her eyes and let her hand fall where it wanted. The vision was abrupt and startling: Evelyne stood in front of her, wielding a sword. It glimmered in dim light. All around her were the crumbling walls she had seen in the vision when she'd met the Paladin. A blow struck Evelyne; from what, Annika couldn't see. She crumpled to the ground and held a wound in her side. She turned to Annika and held out a bloodied hand.

Annika ripped her fingers from the parchment. The vision dropped away, but it was obvious which symbol she had touched. The symbol of the Two-Faced God dimmed slowly. Was this the future or a fear?

A knock on the door made her jump. She hastened to fold the sheet and placed it back on the shelf before answering the door. A page stood outside. A boy of eleven or twelve. He was sweating as if he had hurried. "Nan requests you bring two swans and six ducks to the castle."

"Eight birds?"

The boy was already hustling back the way he came. "Paladin has returned," he replied over his shoulder.

Now, as she was on the cusp of being the woman her mother would never see, she had found a light. Evelyne made her heart flutter every time she looked at her. Even the sounds of her gittern were lighter, happier. And yet, like the day her mother had died, the color had matched the darkness. And his name was Lothaire.

Chapter Thirty-five

Six giant bonfires lit the twilight sky in a circle on a barren field outside the manor village. Evelyne gazed around at the attendees. Castle servants, men-at-arms, villagers from the entire valley, religious initiates, innocents and elders from the local temple, and merchants of Byetown. All taking part in the festivities. The harvest burn was one of the most important celebrations of the year. Unlike the midwinter burn, where everyone's fate hung in the balance at the end of winter, and they asked for the Maiden's blessing to thaw the frozen ground and bring the rains that would lead to a plentiful harvest, the summer burn was a tribute to the Maiden for her bountiful harvests already gathered.

Trussed up in silken finery with her best silver belt glimmering in the firelight, Evelyne sat on her mother's left with the rest of her sisters, under the tent set for their family and honored guests.

She eyed Lothaire at the right of her father. He had returned earlier in the week with an older woman, Elder Braga. She was serious and frail, and her face hung heavy with wrinkles. She could have been anyone from a servant to a grandmother, except for her immaculate religious garments. Crisply pressed. Black as night. And her dual-coned wimple reaching high above her head. Castle whispers had quickly spread the word that she was from a temple outside of Tarburg: Sevenshadows, the great learning center of the kingdom. What she wanted here, Evelyne was unsure of, but the elder watched the crowds like a falcon on a hunt.

Evelyne reassured herself that the document she had forged was waiting, hidden in her trunk in her chamber. Once it was in Annika's hands, her concerns would wane. Getting her father's seal had been easy. A few days ago, he and his retinue had ridden off to take stock of one of his other properties. While he was gone, his stamp sat in the lockbox in his chamber. The seneschal always kept a copy of the key on his person, and her father had a second key hidden inside his Book of Enlightenment. She'd found it when she was still a precocious girl, reading his correspondences with the king and dreaming that someday, the letters would be addressed to her.

She'd heated and poured the wax and stamped a blank sheet of her paper. The document didn't have to be sealed shut since it wasn't addressed to a specific person. A happy fortune. In the dark library, late enough for Master Jacob to have shuffled to his own chambers, yawning, she'd written the words she hoped would grant safe passage for Annika to start her new life.

She stared at the bonfire in front of her, watching the flames burn high into the sky, the embers like stars rising to the heavens. Having the letter was both relieving and sad. Once she gave it to Annika, she would leave. Most likely forever. The thought made her angry. She was being selfish. Annika's life was at stake. Even if they weren't together, Annika would be safe.

Raucous laughter floated from the tent to her left. Witt, playing up his role as lord heir, stood surrounded by rowdy young knights and squires, each trying to outdrink the other. She glanced at the tent in direct opposition to the raucousness, the elders and masters of the valley, somber and sober, huddled in small groups discussing Maiden knew what, but their glances at Elder Braga said that fear of her was a consistent emotion.

Her stomach growled as she caught a whiff of the boar cooking on the spit in front of the tent, a show of her family's wealth. She stood.

"Where do you think you're going?" her mother asked.

Evelyne pointed at the boar. "I'm hungry."

Her mother gestured to a servant, requesting drink and meat be brought.

Evelyne sank back in her seat. She smiled at the serving girl and acknowledged the food. She made a pact with herself. She would no longer ignore her servants as if they were furniture. Getting to know Annika, Steffen, Hilfa, and the others meant she'd not take servants for granted again.

She swung her gaze around the field. Open fires blazed, tripod cauldrons hung above, and long benches and trestle tables bore minor lords and knights grouped together. Pots full of root vegetable stews and fish sizzled on the flames. And farther from the bonfires was a small army of tents where the merchants of Byetown, careful not to upstage their gracious noble hosts, were holding their own small courts. And somewhere in the darkness, the servants and peasants congregated, Annika among them.

Evelyne watched the young people of the villages join hands in circles around each bonfire. Groups of minstrels played religious and uplifting dance tunes, the competing melodies floating on the night air. Several large vats of ale, transported from the keep, sat in various spots around the field. Queues of men and women holding wooden mugs and bowls eagerly awaited a free drink, courtesy of her father.

"I have something for you." Evelyne's mother held out a small envelope. "It arrived by messenger today."

The red wax seal, a hare and stag in a fight, was already broken. The symbol of Lord Tomas, the repulsive father of her betrothed. She peeled open the parchment. Under the standard greetings was the line, "We request Lady Evelyne arrive for the wedding on the Feast Day of St. Olette." Only a month away.

"What does this mean?"

Her mother watched the festivities with a smile, glancing momentarily at her. "It means Samuel has completed his manor, and your wedding is eminent. We'll accompany you. Your father and Lord Tomas will discuss the dowry and sign the legal documents which will transfer your care to your husband, and you'll be wed."

"So exciting." Winifred leaned in and took the note from Evelyne's loose hand. She and Birgitta giggled and mooned over it.

Evelyne felt dead inside. "Can we not wait until spring? Tell him I wish to spend one more winter here with you and my newest brother?" Maybe using the baby would convince her. When she looked back at the wet nurse, she got an unsympathetic look. Even she knew Evelyne disliked babies.

Her mother turned, her expression serious. "The time has come, Evelyne. There can be no more delays."

"What if I go during Sol Invictus?" She heard the desperation in her voice. "That's only three months. Surely, he can wait until then."

"I understand you are afraid, but—"

"I am not afraid."

"Does it matter what day you go? Whether you leave in six weeks or six months, the result is the same. You will marry." She touched the Maiden around her neck. "I blame myself for your reticence."

"Are you sad?" asked Matilde. "Maybe she's sad like me. I'll miss her." She stuck out her bottom lip and crossed her arms.

Evelyne couldn't help but smile. "Yes, I am sad. Sad to leave you all." She was. Had she known this was happening? Yes. Was she ready for it to happen? No. And what about Annika? They hadn't spoken of it since the ride to the aqueduct, but they both knew this would transpire.

She needed to see her. Speak to her.

She leapt to her feet and jumped down off the front of the dais rather than taking the stairs.

"Where are you going?"

"To dance, Mother." She raised her hands above her head. "To celebrate all the Maiden provided for us." If her mother heard the bitterness in her voice, she didn't show it. She turned and ran into the crowd. She heard Tildie asking Birgitta to take her dancing too. *Ah, Tildie. May the Maiden bless you with a better future.*

Annika stood close to her father. He was getting drunk with Hilfa, Jack, and several of the castle guards who had fought with him at one time or another. The heaviest of the men looked in the distance at nothing, his eyes unfocused. His left hand was heavily scarred, twisted, and angry.

Ever since Lothaire had invited her to eat with him, the villagers had split into two camps: those who wanted to become close to her, thinking the Paladin had taken a shine to her, and those who were certain she was someone to be feared. The older villagers ignored her or eyed her warily. Mertius had stared at her in a combination of awe and fear, but his father had shooed him away.

Her afternoon ride with Evelyne hadn't helped. The gossips were claiming she was trying to climb beyond her status. No matter. All this would be over as soon as she left the valley. What did she care about the gossips anymore?

A young woman with a long brown braid, several silver bracelets on her arms, and a warm, inviting smile grabbed Annika's hand and dragged her toward a dance circle. She glanced back at her father, a little afraid to be far from the comfort of the group. The woman wasn't from Marsendale, or she wouldn't have been so eager to encourage Annika to join her. Annika followed reluctantly, drawn by the woman's warmth and the uplifting sounds of the music.

She skipped, following the circle of others around the bonfire, hand in hand with the girls on either side of her. She concentrated on the dances, trying to ignore the many faces, both familiar and foreign, surrounding her. Surprisingly, she enjoyed the dancing, and she felt uplifted. Happy, even?

Periodically, the dancers stopped and ceremoniously clapped, then reached to recapture the hands of their fellow dancers, only to swing them up over their heads and down again. During one of these pauses and claps, Annika felt the hand to her right change, and as she raised her arms up and down again, she felt a thumb run along her hand in a familiar way. A tingle followed, going up her arm and throughout her whole body. Her chest tightened, and she hesitated to look. She kept dancing for a few moments, her eyes on the bonfire. The hand tugged on her fingers slightly, and she knew the owner was signaling her.

The song ended with everyone smiling and taking great gulping breaths from the exertion. Though Annika dropped the hand to her left, the one to her right held fast, forcing her to turn and acknowledge the holder. She drew a sharp breath upon seeing Evelyne. Her hair was in decorative, looping braids, and she wore a beautifully embroidered, vivid red tunic and surcoat of silk with long draping sleeves. Annika's mind ran through a million responses as she watched the firelight dance like amber in Evelyne's brown eyes.

Evelyne pulled her out of the circle, away from the curious looks of the other dancers, and led her through the thick crowds, past the groups singing and drinking by smaller fires, out into the darkness on the edge of the fields. Other figures moved in the dark, mostly young people, she suspected, sneaking kisses with their sweethearts away from the gazes of their parents.

Once they were far enough away, Evelyne stopped and turned. "I have a letter of release for you."

Could it be? Could she and her father merely walk away?

"A forgery, but my father's seal is real. You'll have no trouble traveling. Though I don't have it with me. My sisters wouldn't leave me alone at all while we prepared. But it is ready, and I need only meet you tomorrow at the cottage, and you'll have it."

Annika stammered. "I…I don't know what to say. Thank you, m'lady."

Evelyne took both her hands. "I had hoped we were beyond titles now."

Annika stared at Evelyne's face in the dim light. Were they truly beyond their status? No matter what Evelyne thought, could Annika truly be beyond their differences? She wasn't sure. So much about their situations felt unequal, and she couldn't ignore it, but regardless, she wanted this relationship.

She stroked Evelyne's cheek. "I won't forget what you've done."

Evelyne brushed a hair from Annika's forehead. "You must promise me you will let me know when you arrive safely and tell me your destination. Somehow, someway, I will find you again." She swept Annika into an embrace.

Annika clung to her. She felt safe in Evelyne's arms. Safer than any place else she'd ever been. She buried her face in the soft silk of Evelyne's gown and listened to Evelyne's heart beat loudly in her chest. She thought her own heart was beating in the same tempo, as if they were one. If only she could stay here in this moment forever.

A scream cut through the dull sounds of the festival. A terrible scream, a girl's scream. Other screams, less intense but still shrill, filled the air, followed by shouting and silhouetted movement against the fires.

"Hurry." Evelyne took off in a run, dragging Annika forward. She stumbled in the darkness, and Evelyne helped her up and kept them moving. As they approached the crowd, they heard more shouting. Calls for a healer.

"She fell into the fire," one man told another.

Evelyne pushed people aside and forced her way through until they stood in the clearing at the center of the throng. "Tildie!" she shouted, dropping Annika's hand and rushing forward, throwing herself to the ground next to a burned body lying still in the grass. Birgitta was kneeling next to Tildie, crying and screaming.

Annika wanted to turn away, but she felt as if roots had sprouted from the ground and held her in place. Nausea overcame her. The smell. The sight of burned skin. The burned clothes. The moment in Byetown rushed back to her. She was watching the young merchant girl burn all over again. The revulsion. The terror.

But that was Evelyne on the ground, crying, begging someone to do something.

Lord Cederic burst through the crowd, Elder Theobald in tow, followed by others. "Do something," he yelled at the elder.

Theobald shook his head. "I cannot heal her. There is too much damage."

Lord Cederic grabbed him by the collar and threw him to the ground next to his daughter. "Heal her," he demanded.

"Lord, I cannot." He cowered, waiting for a blow. He began praying. His hands glowed, and he held them over Tildie's listless body.

Annika took another look at Evelyne's distressed face. All her physical strength, and she was helpless to do anything. Annika felt the vision coming, the familiar tingle, the slight roar in her ears. But a vision didn't come. Instead, her hands lit up as if she carried two torches. She heard the people around her gasp. The light blinded her, but she moved forward.

She dropped to her knees beside Evelyne and reached out to touch Matilde's burned flesh. The light grew, covering her arms until it encased her, surrounding her and the girl. She felt the trickle of energy leaving her body like ants crawling down her arms, marching to their destination. Annika wasn't sure if she was in control of them or they of her. And then, the energy was gone, and the glow died slowly to darkness. When her vision returned, Matilde was whole and unscathed, blinking up at her.

"A miracle," Elder Theobald whispered.

Evelyne scooped Matilde in a hug. Still crying, she reached out with an arm and drew Annika to her. "Thank you." She kissed her cheek. "Thank you. Thank the Maiden."

"What's the fuss?" Matilde asked, looking around at all the people. "Did I fall?"

Evelyne smiled through her tears. "Yes, you scared me, but you're fine now."

Birgitta stared at Annika, and she knew that look. Fear. Fear of the other.

Elder Theobald seemed so overwhelmed by the act itself, he wasn't even looking at her. He shook his head, mumbling to himself, "I could never have repaired so much damage. Stop the pain, mayhap, but heal the scars? Never. Never."

A large hand grabbed Annika by the upper arm and yanked her to her feet. The man wore the king's colors. A sword hung at his side.

"Is this the one?" A woman's voice, pinched but clear. She stood with the Paladin, wearing the robes of the temple.

"Yes," he replied.

The woman pulled off a long leather glove and reached out and grabbed Annika's face. The nails dug into her skin. A halo glowed, partially obscured by the ornate headdress. "She appears nothing more than a blank slate. She's been hiding in plain sight?"

Lady Wilhema arrived and gathered Matilde to her. Evelyne was telling her something and gesturing at Annika. Evelyne; she knew the truth. Now was too late to save herself, but might they punish Evelyne as well?

"Eh, what are you doing to my daughter?" Annika's father limped into the small opening. The ale caused him to wobble a bit. He held a stool in his hand, waving it threateningly.

"No, Da. Stay back!"

Lothaire moved swiftly. Her father had no chance to react as Lothaire broke the stool in three pieces and took her father to his knees, his hands behind his back, before he could say anything else. A king's guard took him in hand.

"The father?" The elder woman moved to him and leaned over. "You'll wish you had given her to the temple, as is the law." She turned to another king's guard. "Prepare a proper pyre. Let's get this over with quickly."

Lothaire stood close and whispered to Annika, "I knew there was something special about you. You should have told me. I could have helped."

"No!" This time, it was Evelyne who yelled. "She saved my sister. Mother, please. Annika saved her."

"Cederic, the girl saved our daughter," said Lady Wilhema. "She can't burn tonight. Not during such a sacred occasion as this."

His posture shifted, the same way Annika's father's did when he was ready to fight, but he reined himself in. "Hold, Elder Braga," he exclaimed. He stepped close to the Paladin. "My man, my land. I call right to trial."

Elder Braga looked perplexed. "There is no precedent for a trial. Rogue Talents are the purview of the temple. The Paladin is judge and jury."

"Paladin?" Lord Cederic was playing his only card in this game.

Annika understood. She was going to die tonight or tomorrow. Either way, she would die. She looked at Evelyne, whose expression of fear mirrored her own. She turned her gaze to Lothaire. She found his expression to be sympathetic, a sadness behind his eyes.

"A trial it is," he agreed.

Elder Braga's lips pressed together in a thin line, but she nodded to the Paladin. She was the older of the two, probably with decades of experience in these matters, and yet, the Paladin, young and male, seemed to have more authority. Annika didn't want to die, but she couldn't help seeing the inequality.

Lord Cederic's men took her and her father, marching them toward the Castle.

Her father limped along beside her. "The lord is a good man. He'll see fit to help us."

Annika breathed a long sigh. She looked at her hands. She wondered, when they set her alight on the pyre, could she heal her own burns before she died?

CHAPTER THIRTY-SIX

Murmurs spread throughout the great hall. Some of the festival participants from the night before, merchants, their wives, and lesser lords, filled the room. Smells of stale ale filled Evelyne's senses. Her father sat in the middle of the dais, alone, waiting. She sat with her mother and siblings to the side. She chewed her fingernails as she waited. Her mother grabbed her hand and eased it to her lap. She couldn't help but be nervous.

Annika was a rogue Talent. A powerful one.

Evelyne knew she should be afraid of her. Afraid of the power and the possibility of what she could do to others without the guidance she would have gotten from the temple. She also knew what was supposed to happen to Annika. A rogue, used by the wrong people, was dangerous to the kingdom. So dangerous that the temple sent Lothaire to find them with the king's blessing. Or perhaps, the king had no other options.

She stared across the room at Lothaire. His beautiful, sculpted face and his commanding gaze didn't sway her now. He would pass sentence. She should be angry at herself for not doing more to help Annika find freedom, but she was angrier at Lothaire for being here in time to take her away. She should have convinced her father to let Annika and Steffen disappear. Give them new names and send them with her to Dungewall. Anything but this.

The bailiff struck the floor three times with his staff. Silence fell over the room. Steffen limped through the crowd, guards on either side of him. Then Annika appeared, her unbound hair falling around her shoulders. She kept her eyes on the floor as she stumbled forward. Dodd held her arm and left her a few feet from her father. Several king's men stood nearby, swords drawn. Evelyne wanted to leap to her feet and yell at the soldiers, tell them they were afraid of the wrong person. They should fear Evelyne. Her anger seethed. She grasped the loose cloth of her tunic so tightly, her knuckles turned white.

Elder Braga swept in and stood next to Lothaire. Evelyne caught his eye. She willed him to feel her anger, but he looked away.

"Annika Garethson, you've been accused of heresy. Do you deny the charges?" Her father spoke loud and clear so everyone could hear him.

"No, m'lord." Her head hung low.

"Steffen Garethson," her father stated tiredly, "your daughter displayed the ability to heal last evening, and yet, you never brought her to the temple. Do you agree with this?"

"Yes, Your Lordship." Steffen nodded.

He had known. They'd both known. No wonder they hadn't wanted Evelyne at the cottage. Her presence might have given fodder to the gossips. Brought Lothaire's attention to them.

"You are aware of the tenets of the faith requiring you to bring her to the temple when she first showed her gifts?"

"Yes, Your Lordship."

"Why, man?" Exasperation filled his voice.

"She didn't show any gifts before. She had a knack for finding lost geese. Sometimes, she'd know when a storm was coming. I wasn't sure she was a Talent, but her mother...she knew."

Evelyne noticed Braga and Lothaire both looked shocked. What had he said to draw their concern?

"Do you have anything to say in your defense?"

"No, Your Lordship. I was selfish." Steffen turned to Annika. "I loved her too much to let her go. You're a father. You understand these things."

Evelyne's father sighed. He bent over and rubbed his forehead. This was the one time Evelyne didn't envy his position and power. If she sat on that chair, she wouldn't follow the law. She would release them and fight anyone who dared defy her orders. She'd curse and spit and damn them all. As he sat back in his chair, she edged forward in her own, her knee moving up and down.

"Steffen, I know you as a man of integrity. You served honorably in my service." He drummed his fingers on his chair. "I believe you and your daughter did not do this with malice."

A disappointed murmur ran through the room, as if the crowd believed there would be no death today until another voice spoke up. "I beg to differ." Braga stepped forward. Above her head, she held a folded piece of parchment. "I found this in their home." She unfurled the edges, displaying the symbols. "They are not mere honest, working folk who didn't want to be separated. They were engaged in Weyan magic and religious rituals."

Steffen shook his head. "I know nothing of this, m'lord. I can't read. Neither can my Annika."

Evelyne went cold. She grabbed her mother's arm. "I gave Annika the parchment." Evelyne insisted, "You must tell Father they knew nothing about it."

"What are you saying?" her mother replied.

"I wanted Annika to know more about Weya." She spoke quickly. "I brought the parchment with me to their cottage and left it there."

"Evelyne, how could you?"

"We're friends."

"I warned you of such things. No matter what you think, you'll only disrupt their lives."

"Yes, but I did make friends with her." She grasped her mother's forearm. "Please, I beg of you. Tell Father what I've done."

"The parchment is mine." Annika's melodic voice broke through Evelyne's panic. "The symbols are the gods of the religion of my mother." Her eyes sought Evelyne's. She was giving herself up. She wasn't going to tell them that the parchment wasn't hers.

Why? She'd end up on the pyre. Evelyne felt tears coursing down her cheeks.

"She believed in them. They were her comfort. Why should you punish us for something that brings us peace at the end of our miserable lives?"

Braga waved an arm around the room. "You see? Not only a heretic. An unrepentant one. Sent here to sow chaos in our midst." Nods of agreement met her raised voice.

Annika interrupted. "But my father knew nothing of this. He is a good man. A kind man. If I must burn, so be it."

Braga made the symbol of the Maiden on her forehead and waved the parchment high in the air. "Liar! Serpent of the underworld. Your lust for knowledge was your path to deceit. You've cast a pall on your father's life as well. She must die, now."

"No!" Evelyne jumped to her feet. Her mother pulled her back. "They've done nothing wrong."

"Quiet," her father bellowed. He clasped his hands together, running one over the other several times. "Paladin, what say you?"

Lothaire looked up and blinked as if he had been asleep or in a daze. He looked at Annika, Steffen, and then at Evelyne. "The laws are clear." His voice cracked as he spoke. "Guilt has been admitted. Punishment must be meted out."

The crowd murmured. They would get their pound of flesh after all.

"I gave her the parchment. It was me!" Evelyne moved from her chair toward her father. "Please, Father. Don't let them do this."

He motioned for someone to remove her. A firm grip took her by the arms. She shrugged off the first pull and continued to move forward. The second grasp was familiar. "Stop struggling. You do her no favor by being punished with her," Timothy whispered in her ear. "Annika knows how you feel."

Startled that he knew Annika's name, Evelyne stopped struggling and let him lead her away. She looked over her shoulder. Annika stared back at her. Evelyne moved her gaze to Lothaire. She hoped he could feel the hatred emanating off her. If he hadn't come to their manor, none of this would have happened. If she had the power to make others tell the truth, she'd hunt him down. She'd make him want for the place of nothingness.

❖

Annika watched a squire drag Evelyne from the proceedings. She could see the hurt in Evelyne's eyes. Did she feel betrayed? Annika had claimed the symbols as her own, making sure not to drag the house of Marsendale down with her. Evelyne's outburst was unexpected but reassuring. She'd risked herself.

Lord Cederic looked defeated, his head in his hands. "Lothaire. Braga. To me, please," he commanded. "Steffen is still my man, and by king's law, I pass judgment."

"Your house is already implicated in this affair," said Braga. "Your daughter made that clear from her outburst. Why make this more difficult? We'll take care of the man."

"My daughter's punishment has already begun." Lord Cederic stood. "I believe she will carry the burden of her role far longer than any of us will." He looked out over the room of onlookers. "Steffen Garethson, I sentence you to banishment from Valmora. You may never return."

Annika released her breath. With her father safe, she was calm and at peace with the prospect of her eminent death. She was tired of being a field mouse waiting for falcons. Tired of hiding. Tired of being hated for who she was. If they wanted to hate her, then she would give them something to hate. She would be what they wanted. She would be true to herself.

The bailiff struck his staff to the floor, signifying that the court was closed.

A tear glistened on her father's cheek. "Please, take me in her stead."

"I have decided," replied Lord Cederic. "I'm sorry, Steffen."

"I'm sorry, my pretty girl."

"You've done all you could, Da." She gave him a reassuring smile.

His eyes held sadness, but she knew hers did not. She was proud. For the first time in her life, she was proud to be herself. A Talent. A Weyan. A feared woman.

Her only regret…Evelyne.

Braga reached for her arm. Annika didn't know how it happened, but when they touched, she felt the tingle of power and a surge against Braga's hands. The woman yelped in pain and rubbed her hand with its opposite. Was that fear in her eyes? "Take her." Braga pointed at her and commanded a guard.

He seemed wary, using the pommel of his sword to push her forward.

The entire village waited in the outer bailey near the practice yard. The crime and sentence must have spread like wildfire through the village and castle. A murmur began in the crowd as they arrived from the fields and homes to view the punishment.

Following on Annika's heels were the minor lords, the manor servants, and the lord and his family. Even Evelyne's five-year-old brother had to watch her execution, his hand wrapped in his mother's.

The manor guards stopped her and her father in front of a hastily constructed post above a pile of kindling and dry wood. Other guards pushed back the spectators who crowded the event. The guard spun her and placed her back against the post. He tightened a rope around her wrists, the roughness scratching her skin. Her fingers, stiff and swollen, became hard to move.

She scanned the crowd. So many of them were unrecognizable. But there were others, the baker and his wife, his stare intent, his eyes burning with rage. Theobald and his innocents all dressed in their religious finery, looking smug in their righteousness. Mertius and several other children acting as if this was another game. A few village women she knew whispered to each other. Someone yelled, "Heretic," from the back.

She spotted Hilfa standing tall, her arms crossed. Her apprentice Jack stood next to her, his expression somber. Hilfa's clenched jaw and twitching arm muscles signaled she was ready to use her hammers on anyone who got in her way. She was a good friend to Annika's family. Any act on her part to stop this punishment would be futile. Hilfa would die with her. *Don't do it.*

One face was missing: Evelyne's.

She'd been dragged away after her exclamations in the great hall. Annika turned to look at the keep. Its towers peeked over the inner curtain wall. She was somewhere in there, and though Annika would have liked to see her one last time, she was glad Evelyne wouldn't see her burn and smell her flesh on fire.

The executioner lit a torch in a bowl of burning pitch. A black hood covered his face, only his dull eyes visible. As he drew nearer, she could see the bloodshot whites and the drooping eyelids. He smelled of stale ale and unwashed linen. She could only be thankful he wasn't contracted to chop off her head today.

Lothaire began a Maiden's prayer in High Valmoran. Annika didn't hear or understand a word of it. She stared at her father, and he at her.

"I love you," he yelled.

"I love you, Da."

The executioner brought the torch closer. She could feel the heat from it now. Her heart leapt, and her breathing became shallow. She remembered the screams, the stench, the curling agony of the girl in Byetown. She took a deep breath to calm herself. She would be all right. She would soon be in someone's hands. The old gods? The Maiden?

She smelled the burning wood and the crackling of the fire as it took hold of the kindling beneath her feet. The smoke choked her eyes, and the heat built. So this was it. This was how she was going to die. A smoldering pile of ash on a bonfire built in the Maiden's name, someone she had worshipped her whole life. She looked at the blue sky. *Why? What did I do to you? Each week, I went to worship. I toiled at my work every day. I gave what I could to others. I tried to be humble. I respected my elders. Now they are literally burning me in your name.*

The faces in front of her blurred from the smoke and heat. She heard her father cry out. A strangled sound. Half sob, half cry. He had promised her a swift death. *How he must be hurting.*

She smiled to herself. If her life was about to end, at least she had known what it meant to feel love. She thought of Evelyne, her beautiful and handsome face. Her powerful hands. Her expressive, deep brown eyes.

She closed her eyes and waited for the pain, the smell, but instead, she felt the tingle and the surge of her gift. What vision awaited her this time? Perhaps heaven? Silence. No crackle, no smells, no pain, only a collective gasp.

She opened her eyes. Everyone around her looked on in stunned silence. Her vision was no longer blocked by waves of heat and smoke. The fire was out. Not even a smoldering ember left, only partially burned logs. They must have put it out, but there was no sand covering the remains. How had they done it?

"Amazing." Lothaire drew closer. He bent and examined the unburned wood.

Elder Braga joined him. "Was the wood wet?"

"She must have multiple gifts," he replied.

"Multiple…" Braga looked shaken. "That's not possible."

The crowd became restless. With Lothaire and Braga concerned, the crowd murmured their own fears. Annika could almost feel it.

"Maiden, save us."

"What evil is this?"

"She is more than I imagined." Lothaire studied her before turning to her father, motioning for his men to bring him closer. "Steffen, son of Gareth, did you mean what you said before? Would you sacrifice yourself for her?"

Braga looked startled. "What? If we spare her, we invite chaos to the realm. We must adhere to the strict tenets of our faith."

Lothaire held up his hand to her.

"I would give my own life," her father replied.

"No." Annika struggled against her restraints.

He looked at her and nodded. "I will gladly take her place."

Lothaire's face showed relief. "So be it." He commanded the executioner to untie Annika and replace her with Steffen. As soon as her bindings were cut, her hands throbbed.

"Take her. Prepare to leave immediately," Lothaire said to one of his men. "I don't want her to see this." He leaned closer to her. "We will say a prayer for your father's soul when we reach the temple."

"Your concern for her is unwarranted, Lothaire," said Braga.

A guard grabbed Annika's upper arm. She pulled against his grip and looked at her father. His eyes told her what she needed to know. She could get away from the guard, but where would she go? She stopped struggling. The guard dragged her through the crowd. She remembered this feeling well from the day in Byetown. The angry, confused faces. The spitting. Only now it was her neighbors making the sign of evil and the Maiden. All because she differed from them.

Annika shuffled her feet, turning her head to try to see her father's face one more time. If only she could see him, know that he was still with her, even if only for a few more moments.

From outside the walls, she heard the roar of the spectators.

She felt as if she would collapse on the ground, her legs shaky and unstable. Pain flooded her shoulder as the guard pulled her forward with strong jerks.

Her tears followed quickly in great, gasping sobs.

CHAPTER THIRTY-SEVEN

Evelyne watched from a crenulation gap up on the south curtain wall of the keep as Steffen burned. She beat her fist on the cold hard stone until her hand bled. The Paladin mounted his horse and looked back at the castle. The horse stamped and turned in a circle. Was he looking for her? He prodded his mount and rode out the gatehouse. She paced along the wall, staring out at the tournament grounds, watching the villagers leave. They'd trickled away as soon as Steffen had stopped thrashing. Only two figures stood watch over him. Hilfa and Jack. She was sure of it.

Evelyne had prayed to the Maiden, asking her to do something, anything to help Annika. Until she'd realized with horror that Steffen was taking Annika's place. Evelyne had waited and watched, hoping another miracle would occur, starting yesterday over so she could...do what? Spirit them away to somewhere safe? Fight the Paladin?

She wasn't sure who she was angrier at, herself, Steffen, the Paladin, her own father, or the Maiden. Maybe they all deserved to be hated. Each one had created this swirl of deception and confusion. Annika had lied to her, but she'd also asked Annika and Timothy to lie for her. The Paladin was doing the temple's work, but what shameful and dirty work. And where was the Maiden? If sinners should pay, Evelyne was paying the price. Steffen was dead, and Annika was on her way to who-knew-what because Evelyne had been selfish and unaware. Sin. She was sinful. This might have been a test she'd failed. If she couldn't protect Annika and Steffen, how could she protect the people of Valmora the way she desired?

She paced her way onto the covered wooden parapet walk surrounding the top of the great tower. She kicked at a board on the railing and kicked again and again and again until she heard the unmistakable crack of wood. A piece broke loose and fell several stories to the ground. She didn't care if she kicked through and fell off the tower herself.

Several hours passed before the fire died out. Two men arrived with a handcart. They shoveled Steffen's cremated remains from the tournament grounds. He wasn't even getting a decent burial. Those were pitmen, not temple innocents. They would toss him in the quarry with the castle's offal and shite instead of burying him near the village shrine.

At least Annika wasn't here to see this desecration. Cold comfort. She had been wary of Evelyne from the beginning, and yet, she had risked her safety to do as Evelyne asked, to play for her, be her friend, tend her wounds, help her train. That day in the village, when Annika had been angry with her, made sense. Annika had feared for her life all this time. What must it have been like for her? Always looking over her shoulder, knowing she would be dust before her time if anyone knew.

Exhausted, Evelyne sat with her back to the stone tower and pulled her legs to her chest, the wind the only sound. She cried until she had no more tears to shed. As night fell, a wisp of a night guard, no older than herself, made his rounds. She growled at him, forcing him to back away. He did not return.

She rested her head against the cooling stone and closed her eyes. Finally, the grayness of oblivion found her.

When she awoke, she was in her own bed, disoriented by the change of location. She threw back the linens and rose to use the piss pot.

"Ah, finally." Winifred put down her needlework. "How are you feeling?"

Evelyne stumbled to the screen and squatted over the bowl. "How long have I been asleep?" she asked.

"Most of yesterday and today," Winifred replied. "Timothy carried you here. He's been outside the door ever since. You fretted most of the night as if in a fever, so I told Mother I would attend you until you awoke."

"Has anything changed?" She came out from behind the screen, stripped, and wiped her arms and legs with a clean linen cloth.

Winifred looked at her warily. "I'm sorry about your friend, Evelyne. I had no idea you knew each other...so well."

"I gave her the parchment," Evelyne admitted. "She doesn't even know how to read." The tears threatened to fall once again.

Winifred wrapped her arms around her shoulders and rested her head on Evelyne's arm. Evelyne took little comfort in the gesture. "Mother wants you to come to her solar as soon as you are able. I'll tell her you are awake. I'll send someone to dress you." She turned at the door. "I am sorry."

Evelyne nodded in acknowledgment. She didn't wait. She dressed herself in Witt's castoffs once again. Outside the room, she found Timothy seated on the floor, twirling his dagger in the wood planks.

He leapt to his feet. "Are you well?"

She nodded. "I have to go. Excuse me." And she moved past him toward the stairs to the kitchens, the ones she always used to avoid the rest of her family. She heard his footsteps behind her. "Go away, Timothy."

"I'm coming with you."

"I don't need a spy to tell them my movements."

"I'm coming with you," he responded resolutely.

She held a hand along the wall of the spiral staircase. She'd been in bed so long, she felt unsteady. She tried to remember the last time she'd eaten. Two days now? As she swung through the kitchen, she grabbed a round of bread and a bottle of mead, and cut herself a wedge of cheese. No one stopped her. Old Nan tutted, gave her a sympathetic look, and went back to work.

Timothy stayed with her like a shadow while she strode through the gardens and out of the walls toward the village. He stayed a few steps behind her. She was thankful for that. She was in no mood to have him telling her what she should or shouldn't do. Her anger was boiling, and no amount of talking was going to change that.

She could smell the smoke before they were even close to the cottage. By the time they crested the hill, she knew what she would find. The cottage was nothing but smoldering remnants. Nothing left of the thatched roof but a few darkened, heavy timbers. Several of the walls had collapsed outward, and the reeds that had covered the floor were piles of char.

Evelyne dropped to her knees.

"The king's men must have burned it," Timothy said. He walked carefully around the perimeter.

"It wasn't theirs to burn," she yelled angrily.

"In their eyes, she was a heretic. Dangerous. Would eat their children and all the rubbish stories they tell us to scare us. They wanted to cleanse the site with fire."

"She's a girl." Evelyne hung her head. "A girl."

Timothy returned to her side. "I know you think thus, but she was a Talent. We all saw it. The Paladin granted her a reprieve from death for now. Be glad of that."

"And what of Steffen?" She looked Timothy in the eye, but he turned away.

"We all know the price of wickedness."

"His sin was protecting his daughter." Evelyne drew herself up and stepped inside the ruins of the cottage. She trod carefully through the warm remains, lifting larger pieces to look underneath. It had to be here somewhere. She grabbed a blackened tool handle and began digging under the debris.

Timothy joined her. "What are you looking for?"

"What does it matter to you?"

He rubbed the back of his neck. "I wasn't trying to stop you from coming here. I worry when you insist on doing things you know will get you in trouble."

She threw the handle across the rubble. "What does that even mean? Trouble. Trouble with whom?"

"Your father. The temple. Your betrothed," he said, bitterness creeping in his voice. "Everyone talks behind your back, Evelyne. The same things Erik has said for years. Your height, your mannerisms, your strength. You are not a delicate flower to be picked by a worthy husband. Even Elder Theobald discussed this with your parents. They've purposely kept Samuel away until the marriage is complete."

Shame flooded her. "How do you know this?"

"They talk in front of me as if I do not exist." Timothy, son of a lesser lord, a level above a hedge knight. Friend of an aberration.

"I wanted to find her gittern."

"Her what?"

Evelyne shuffled her shoes, kicking up dust. "I was looking for a musical instrument of Annika's. She played it the night I met her. I was hoping to find it and return it to her."

"It must have burned."

The tears she'd held back flowed. She stepped forward and melted into the hug from Timothy.

❖

Annika sat quietly in the back of the two-wheeled cart as it bumped across the rutted path to their destination. A light rain had begun halfway through the journey. Now her hair was matted to her forehead, and her tunic had grown sodden. Neither the king's guards nor Braga nor the Paladin had spoken to her since leaving the manor. All the bravado she'd gained when she'd thought she was about to die had crumbled when her father had taken her place on the pyre. Now all her fight had left her. She cared not what happened to her. She followed their orders without question.

The temple sat on a hill overlooking the fields of the valley. She could see Marsendales's manor keep in the distance, as well as the River Lewes that wound its way through the valley. The temple was surrounded by a low stone wall. Not one that would repel enemies, like a castle's fortifications, but designed to keep unwanted animals away from the gardens. A young peasant boy ran out to open the gate as the cart came to a stop.

Annika's legs were stiff from the miles of journey. She jumped from the cart, landing in a large puddle, and soaked her shoes. She faced the stone temple, its steeped roof held aloft by a series of six columns carved as maidens. Intricately detailed scenes of peasants hard at work creating the food they needed to sustain life were carved into the massive wooden entry doors.

A guard pushed her forward toward the temple. Inside, torches and candles burned along the walls, and a giant fire burned in the center of the main hall, the smoke lazily drifting upward to a hole high in the roof rafters. A giant stone statue of the harvest Maiden loomed over the interior, thrice the size of the one in the manor chapel, with food and offerings spilling from a marble cornucopia at her feet. Her hair was literally golden, not only in color, but covered in gold so that it gleamed in the firelight.

An older woman approached, her robes delicately embroidered with golden threaded sheaves of wheat. A likeness of the Maiden swung on a thick gold chain around her neck, the face worn from years of touching and rubbing. Several temple innocents followed in her wake. "Paladin." She nodded to Lothaire. "Elder Braga. Maiden bless you."

"Confessa Celestria." Braga nodded.

A temple servant, a portly man, pale and wearing a threadbare linen tunic, rushed forward with a stool for Elder Braga on which she sat while he pulled the muddy boots from her feet.

"What brings you to our humble temple?" asked the Confessa.

"We have need of solitude." She motioned the servant away as her own servant provided her with fresh shoes. "You'll provide us with quarters and somewhere we can be undisturbed. Away from any common areas."

"Of course," replied the Confessa. "And your men?" She directed the question to the Paladin. She seemed uncomfortable.

"They will stay outside," said Lothaire. "Your convent is safe. I will put to death anyone who dares challenge this."

Annika saw several of the guards stiffen. She was sure they would be as far away from Lothaire and the temple occupants as possible.

The Confessa whispered to the portly servant. He nodded and gestured for Lothaire to follow him. Lothaire glanced back at Annika. His expression was soft and concerned. How could he try to be caring to her when he'd had her father burned to death just yesterday? Once he left, Braga and Celestia brought their attention to each other.

"We weren't expecting you, Braga," said Celestia. "If you had sent word ahead, we could have prepared appropriate quarters for you."

"Yours will do nicely," said Braga from her seat.

A flash of irritation crossed Celestia's face. "And who are you, my dear?" she asked Annika sweetly.

"No one of concern." Braga stood. "Prepare her and place her in a cell near my quarters." She turned her attention to Annika. "She is not to leave her room unless I request it. Is that understood?"

Celestia nodded. "As you wish."

Braga leaned close to Annika and said, "Don't think of escaping. Should you try, things will be much worse for you. You might douse fire, but I doubt even you could put yourself back together after being drawn and quartered. And Lothaire will have no choice in the matter."

Annika swallowed hard.

Celestia and the three women behind her all bowed as a servant led Braga to her quarters. Another servant, as pale as the first, stripped the muddy shoes from Annika's feet. The Confessa gestured for Annika to follow. They walked along a side corridor of the temple, through a doorway that separated the public space from a private one. The private areas lacked glass windows, having only small slits near the tops of walls dark with the soot of candles and stone floors as cold as ice, even in summer. Annika didn't care that no one spoke to her. She didn't want to talk to any of them, either.

They took her to a common bath, where female servants stripped her clothing and placed her in heated water. She watched the servant take her clothes away and wondered if she would ever see them again. Naked, nothing was left of her world from before. No tangible possessions to say she existed in the village, in the cottage, in her life before this moment. She thought about her carved trunk containing her mother's tunic, a lock of hair, the tiny carved goat, her mother's necklace, her father's shirts, the smell of him. The music she played each day now silenced.

A servant bathed her with scented soap and brushed the tangles from her hair. She felt guilty allowing the bath to feel good, but it did, and she couldn't help but sink into the warm water. Done, the servant dried her with a long roll of soft cloth, softer than linen. Another servant dressed her in the gray woolen tunic of an innocent and gave her a pair of leather shoes with woolen strips to wrap her feet.

The Confessa examined her last. "Those who enter these halls take their commitment seriously." She motioned to another woman. "Innocent Helena, I leave her in your hands." With that, the Confessa swept from the room without another word.

Annika could no longer hold in the anguish of the day. She folded in on herself and sobbed.

Helena, dressed in less ornate robes than the Confessa, approached. "There, there." The girl placed an arm around her shoulders. Pox had scarred the side of her face. Her right eye was cloudy white and blinded. "It's not all bad. You'll get used to it. A lot of the girls are homesick at first, but you'll make friends here."

Annika wanted to scream out that her father was dead, she had been stolen from her home, and ripped from her best friend and love. But part of her remembered her father's words: *Trust no one. Keep quiet. Learn about strangers before you speak to them.* She was certain of one thing, she would never let his, or her mother's, memories fade.

Helena led her to a small stone room no bigger than the straw mattress that filled it. Raised several inches above the floor on a wooden frame, the legs were sitting in dishes filled with oil. Tiny insects floated on top, drowned while trying to climb to the warmth of the hay. The smell told Annika not to put her candles too close; the fear of fire followed her like darkness followed day. They'd left her two rough, homespun blankets, a basin of water, and a brass pot for relieving herself. Pegs on the wall stood ready to hold clothes. Several combs and items for minimal self-care, including a basket of cloth strips for monthly bleeding, sat in the corner. Above it all hung a wooden effigy of the Maiden.

"Are you hungry? I'll get you a little something to eat. Take the homesickness away quicker." Helena gave her a soft smile. "Maiden bless you."

Annika heard the iron bolt lock from the outside when the door closed. There was no escaping this room. Annika leaned her forehead against the heavy oak door, running her fingers along the iron hinges. Without her father, without Evelyne, the temple was a prison. Or perhaps a grave. She curled on the bed and tucked herself into a ball.

CHAPTER THIRTY-EIGHT

Evelyne could barely see her opponent through the slit in her helm. She'd picked an older style of helmet with a full face shield so no one would recognize her. The padded gloves and heavy gambeson slowed her. She'd fended off several blows from her opponent, but now he backed her against the wood railing of the practice ring. Nothing she had learned from either Timothy or Steffen had prepared her for this fight.

The squire was heavier than her but several inches shorter, which was the only thing saving her from utter humiliation.

Finally, in his overconfidence, he made a mistake. He gave telltale signs of a slashing blow with his long, hand-and-a-half sword, giving her the moment she needed to move in close, grab the sword with a gloved hand and pull it close to her side. He pulled his sword backward, but she used her short sword, twisting it around and striking a heavy blow to his face with the hand wrapped around the grip. The heavier man collapsed in a heap, leaving her holding both swords. She laid her opponent's sword on his chest as squires scurried to his side to tend him.

Evelyne pulled the helm from her head, wiping the hair from her face. Quiet fell over the space. Whether from the fact it was her, a woman, or the fact she had cut her hair, she didn't know. She couldn't fit her long hair inside the helmet, and had she worn her braid down, they would have known she was a woman before she'd gotten a chance to spar. So she had taken shears and cut it off at her shoulders. The lightness of her head still felt odd.

A page half her height ran to take her sword from her, but she refused. Steffen told her to care for her own weapons, and she intended to do so. Several of the other young men waiting their turn at armed combat murmured amongst themselves. She could feel the stares, the unease, and the sense that she was unwelcome.

Someone patted her shoulder.

"A fine fight, Lady Evelyne." Good old Dodd. He'd get another gold crown for this.

Master Berin was yelling at several men who had stopped grappling on the ground until he saw what they were looking at. Her. He charged at her. "What in the Maiden's name are you doing?"

She pointed at her opponent. "Winning against one of your best squires." They held the man upright in a seated position, his head lolling on his shoulders.

"When your father finds out about this, he'll send us both to the borderlands. What were you thinking?"

"How to beat a man with more experience and a longer sword than me," she replied.

Dodd snickered. Witt and Erik wandered over and were examining their fellow swordsman. "My sister knocked you on your arse?" Witt asked with a laugh.

Erik cut his eyes toward her. "I told you, she's not normal. Maybe she's like her friend, a Talent."

Evelyne feigned a step toward him, sword up. He scurried behind Witt's bulk.

"Did he know it was you?" Witt asked.

"I didn't show my face until after I knocked him on his arse." She smiled while she unbuckled the top of the gambeson. She'd done it. She'd proved to herself that she could fight men and survive. Only one fight, but she was confident there would be others.

"My Lady," Master Berin blustered, "your language is no better than a gutter rat." Turning to the page who knelt by the squire on the ground, he said, "Take him to the healer. I'll be along later to discuss what to do with him."

"You cannot punish a man for fighting me if he didn't know it was me."

"Your father can do anything he likes. He's the lord. The decision is not mine to make."

"I can beat more of these men, and you know it."

Berin sighed and placed a hand on her shoulder. She shrugged the hand away. He spoke in a low voice. "I've known since you were a little girl that you would be better at combat than any of your brothers. I've known you were unhappy unless you were riding, falconing, or shooting a bow. I also know you were close to Steffen. He was a good man."

"And Father returned his kindness by letting the Paladin burn him." Tears blurred her vision.

"Lord Cederic had no choice."

"He had every choice. You said it yourself. He's the lord."

Berin appeared unsurprised. Evelyne was certain he had heard this argument already. Probably from her mother. "Your father has your best interest—"

"Because of our antiquated traditions, my idiot brother"—she pointed at Erik's retreating form—"may play at fighting all day. Give me one fight with him. I'll show everyone what I can do because right now, I don't give a shit about customs or conventions."

Berin grasped her arm and pulled her close. He spoke in a harsh whisper. "Do you care about the people who work your father's lands?"

"Of course, which is why Steffen should be alive now and…" She couldn't bring herself to say the next part out loud. And Annika should still be at the cottage.

"If word was to reach the king's ears of your behavior, your father could lose his place in the kingdom. Lose his seat on the king's council or, worse, lose the manor. All it takes is for one of the other major lords to whisper how your father cannot handle his manor affairs, and everything and everyone could belong to another family."

"You've no doubt listened to too many stories."

"You may think unchanging loyalties hold this kingdom together, but that is an untruth. Every harvest, every battle, every marriage, every child born to a lord, every rumor, every tithe to the temple, all of it plays a role in keeping the peace. And every one of them can be the single liability which ends a dynasty."

"Don't place such a burden on me." She glared at him. "All I ever wanted was to be like my brothers. To stand at my father's side. Women fight in other kingdoms, so why not in Valmora?"

"Because this is Valmora, and those are our customs."

"Perhaps I need to live somewhere other than Valmora." She wrenched her arm away, turned on her heel, and stormed toward the stable. Sitting on a stool, she removed the gambeson and placed her helm on the ground next to her. She asked a groom for a cloth and wiped down all her equipment to keep it from rusting. She pulled a sharpening stone from her waist pouch and set to work sharpening her blade, checking for nicks or edge damage needing repair.

When finished, she headed to the laundry vats with her padded gambeson and trousers in hand. She began the exhausting work of shoving the clothes in the giant vat. The washing women stared at her in disbelief. One tried to take the clothes from her, but she shrugged her away.

Annika would have done this work herself. It was time Evelyne learned what life without privilege entailed. The lye soap burned her skin as she plunged the garments in and out of the solution. She pounded them against the cleaning stones. Her skill was limited. Her gambeson looked clean, but it didn't smell clean. A girl motioned to a vat of water. When Evelyne dipped the jacket, she smelled the lavender. So that was how they took care of the residual stink of combat.

At first, she felt embarrassed by the work, realizing that anyone who saw her would think her a servant, but soon, she felt empowered. She could wash her own clothes. She'd watched Annika and Steffen care for the geese, repair fencing, cord wood, thatch the cottage, make rope, and dozens of other tasks she'd paid little attention to before she'd met them.

She threw the gambeson over a drying line and noticed Dodd approaching with several other men in tow. He wore bright clothing and polished leather shoes. When he drew close, she could smell the olive oil he used to slick his hair. Something was afoot. Timothy followed at a distance. She smiled and nodded toward him.

"Lady Evelyne. We are heading to the village for a few drinks." Dodd patted the slimmer, more handsome young man on the shoulder. "Finn leaves with you in a fortnight. We plan to send him off in style."

Some friendly banter ensued while Finn blushed at the attention.

"I doubt having a lady with you would give him the best experience."

"Horse shite," Dodd roared. "You bested Braden. He's lying about in the dorms getting plenty of attention from the young serving girls. If you were Lord Witt, you'd be enjoying a round of drinks. You deserve to be one of us, if only for a night."

"Thank you all, fellows." She shook her head. "I believe being with me this evening would only bring you bad luck." And she had no joy in her soul. She had fought to prove to herself that she could do it, but celebration seemed wrong.

"As soon as your father hears of your exploits today, there will be much consternation," said Timothy.

"Yes." She looked at her thin shift and leggings. "I'd best make myself presentable for my beating." She reached out and grasped Finn's forearm. "I look forward to your loyalty, Finn."

"You shall have it, m'lady." He swept into a low bow.

The men moved on toward the village. Timothy gazed back at her over his shoulder.

Would Steffen have congratulated her on that takedown? She heard him in her head saying, "You think that's a fight? Wait until you're in mud up to your arse and see how slow your movements feel."

Then she thought of Annika. Where was she? Was she still alive? Would Evelyne ever see her again?

Chapter Thirty-nine

Y ou have been given a reprieve." Lothaire stood in the doorway of Annika's cell. "If you will only work with Elder Braga. Tell her what she wants to know about your gifts. You can become a part of our temple family. A significant part, I am certain."

"I will never join the temple," Annika replied. How could she forget the role the temple had played in the deaths of her parents?

"Your father would have told you to do what was necessary to survive. Would he not?"

His assured manner and the mention of her father drew her anger to the surface. "Don't talk about my da. Ever! You have no right to tell me what he would have wanted. You killed him." She jumped to her feet and stomped her foot in anger. Pain reverberated through her leg. Tears waited at the edge of her eyes. She wiped them away. She would not cry in front of Lothaire.

"I've known plenty of men like your father. Good men. Pragmatic men. Not lofty idealists. They all have one thing in common, self-preservation." He leaned closer, his gray eyes clear. "He sacrificed himself so you could live. It was the only way. Now I need you to sacrifice yourself for the good of the temple. For the good of Valmora."

He snapped his fingers. A servant appeared with her gittern.

A lump formed in Annika's throat, and it was hard to keep her tears at bay. She grasped it and held it close. Eyes closed, she touched the strings and the wood. Something was left of her life.

"I insist you play." This time, his voice wasn't so honeyed. "I carried it all the way here from Marsendale. The least you could do is let me hear you play the damned thing."

Slowly, she shook her head. She'd throw it in the kitchen fires before she'd play for him. She glared at him, and he returned the glare for several minutes.

"So be it." He grabbed her, ripping the gittern from her hands and placing it on the bed. He pulled her roughly from the room and down the hallway, stopping at a door large enough to push a wagon through. The carvings on the door were a tangled weave of saints, snakes, fairy-tale creatures, and stories from the Enlightened Book, all staring at her with frightening realism. Two male servants in simple white tunics stood on either side. Opening the door took them both straining against its weight, revealing a cavernous room behind it. A half dozen men and women, in both religious and learning robes, stood quietly; fabric masks covered their faces, only their eyes visible.

Lothaire walked her closer to the assembly. She felt fear inside her building. Who were they? What did they want with her? She struggled, hoping to break free, but Lothaire's grip tightened.

"Your honors." He bowed, still clutching her securely. "This is the girl."

She could see some of them shining. What were they trying to do to her? Make her tell her deepest secrets? Trying to get inside her head? Convince her they were friends, like Lothaire had tried?

He pulled Annika close. "Show them what you can do," he whispered. "Or they will make you wish you had burned with your father."

"I don't know how I did those things," she replied, panic building in her voice.

He pushed her forward into the midst of the elders and masters. She stumbled and landed heavily on one knee on the stone floor. Dread filled her as she looked at the masks surrounding her.

"You're sure she survived the flames with her own gifts? No one else was there who could accomplish this feat?" A woman spoke clearly and in the same intonation of Lothaire's convincing way, her voice melodic and pretty. Annika could barely make out two dark brown eyes from behind the mask's opening.

"I am certain of nothing, Elder," Lothaire replied. "I can only tell you what I saw. The flames died as soon as they were lit, and she was untouched by them."

"Lothaire…" A man this time. "If you've called us all here on a wild tale, there will be consequences."

"I saw it with my own eyes," said Elder Braga. "And…the girl is capable of multiple gifts."

A man, from the looks of his hairy fingered hand, stepped forward and grasped her free arm, pushing the sleeve of her robe up to her elbow. He twisted her arm back and forth. He did the same thing with her other arm and stopped.

"She's marked." The man had a gravelly voice, and his breath smelled of garlic. His accent she knew well. Her father's own accent. He was a commoner from the midlands, maybe from one of Marsendales's surrounding villages. The thought of her father hurt once again.

"What is it, Master Malleous?" asked Braga.

"A Weyan symbol perhaps?"

"Much more important than that," said the woman with the dark brown eyes. Her accent was unfamiliar. She drew closer and ran a finger along the ink. Annika shivered at her touch. "An ancient symbol," she drawled. "The crown of the Council of Twelve."

The man who smelled of garlic laughed. "The Council of Twelve? Master Nicholina, the Council of Twelve is an ancient fairy tale."

A tall thin man spoke next. "Master Malleous, there are many accounts of the Council translated from scrolls found in Iola and the East."

"A thousand-year-old utopia story that couldn't possibly have been as powerful as the accounts," replied Master Malleous.

"I wouldn't be so sure," said Master Nicholina. Annika couldn't decide if the woman's gaze was curiosity or if she was scheming.

"Regardless, why does a girl from Marsendale have such a mark?" asked Lothaire.

Braga regarded him as if she had forgotten he was in the room. "Why does the Paladin of the Realm carry the mark of the Two-Faced God?"

Lothaire clenched his jaw and pulled the collar of his tunic, covering a mark on his neck. "I was born with a mark resembling the Two-Faced God."

"She wasn't born with this mark," said Master Nicholina. "She was given this on purpose."

"Which begs the question, why the daughter of a goose herder would be marked with the crown of an ancient polity?" Elder Braga wrapped her bony fingers around Annika's chin and turned her head upward.

A long string of questioning followed by the members who were masters, knowledgeable men and women without gifts or so she assumed. They asked her which astrological sign she was born into. What year? Where was her mother born? After this question, several of the men referenced a large tome, and a debate ensued about which latitude her mother's home resided upon. None of these things made any sense to Annika, and the hours of inquisition took a toll on her.

They'd asked her the same questions Lothaire had and more. When had her gifts begun? Why didn't her parents give her to the temple as proscribed? What was she able to do?

She'd answered honestly. There was no use in being deceitful. What could she say that they would be more afraid of than the fact that she could apparently douse fire with her mind?

Her legs shook, and she felt slightly dizzy from standing so long. She swayed in place. Elder Braga and her velvety voice finally silenced the rest and began the same barrage of questions over again. Annika's answers became terse and short, until all she said was yes, no, I don't know. She was surprised at her own distemper. She had been afraid of these people when she was first brought here, but now she found them petty and annoying. Without the threat of the sword, the flame, or eternal damnation, they could not scare her.

Then Braga and the other elders began using their gifts on her. The gravelly-voiced healer touched her and searched for broken bones and mental deficiencies. Another healer tried again to see if the first man had missed something. Whatever powers they used left Annika further drained and ill-tempered, as if they had sucked the energy from her rather than using their powers to heal her.

"Enough," Braga commanded. "This is your last warning. Tell us how you can have more than one gift. Was your mother a witch? Did she do something to you as a child? A ritual. A seance. A sacrifice." She drew out the word *sacrifice*.

Annika shuddered. Her mother had taught her to sew, to sing, to make cheese, to wash, to prepare a pottage. She'd also taught her to hunt rabbits, watch for the changes in the weather, and tell directions by the sun and stars. She didn't tell the council those things. They were personal. Only for her…and her father.

Braga used her honeyed voice to sway her to answer. Much like Lothaire's gift, and like him, she glowed fiercely, but Annika told the same answers again and again. They could reach in her mind and pull her insides out, but they'd get nothing more since there was nothing more to tell. She did not know how she had more than one gift, but she knew someone who might know. Zuri's face came to mind and the image of the barrel and harp on a swinging wooden sign.

"You hide something, girl." Braga walked around her. She snapped her fingers.

A different man, this one in a dark sackcloth mask, came from the shadows carrying a rod. He bound her wrists and ankles and pulled her next to a table, lifting her on top. Someone grabbed her shoulders from behind to hold her still, and the first man stood over her and waited. Now she was afraid. This was not the threat of gifts that so far were unsuccessful. This meant pain.

Braga nodded. The man lifted the rod and swung round. He struck the bottoms of her feet with a loud thud.

Searing pain shot through her. She screamed, a sound she'd never heard herself make came from deep within her.

Braga asked again, "What are you hiding?"

Annika said nothing. She wouldn't let them kill Zuri as they had her father.

Braga nodded to the man. Annika braced for another strike. She clenched her jaws together so hard, her teeth ached. The second strike was worse than the first. Her feet throbbed, and pain radiated through her leg bones. Her scream deafened her own ears.

"What are you hiding?" Braga asked again.

Annika felt a darkness closing in on her vision. She was close to fainting. She'd done it when she'd worked too long in the fields one summer. She panted and leaned against the chest of the person holding her. The brute raised the rod to strike again.

"Elder, this is pointless. She knows nothing." Even in the throes of her pain, she recognized Lothaire's voice. He stepped into her field of vision. "She is more valuable to the temple as a willing servant of the Maiden. I will help her on this journey."

"This is none of your concern," Braga replied. "Your job is done. The Maiden needs your gifts elsewhere. There are plenty of sinners who need to return to the Maiden's breast."

Annika watched his hand open and close in a fist. He turned to her as he was dismissed. She could see the helpless expression, but she didn't want his help. She wanted none of them to help her. As Braga nodded, she tensed and struggled. She wished she could cut the ropes away as she had doused the flames of her pyre.

Whack.

She screamed. This time, she felt the familiar tingle of her gift. She saw the elder's mouth move and watched her nod but heard only a ringing. When the rod struck again, Annika felt nothing, and a deep silence engulfed her.

Her mind felt disconnected from her body. She saw the room from above as her consciousness rose from her corporeal self, rising through the roof of the temple. She flew in the sky and watched the valley spread out below. The wagons. The people small as ants. The men on horseback. She soared over the thick forests and patches of beans, oats, and barley. The fields passed below her. Greens, golds, blues. She flew like a bird, only faster, much faster, so fast, the landscape became a blur until she stopped on a wall walk at the castle in Marsendale.

Evelyne stood in front of her, her hair in a small bun at the base of her neck rather than in a long braid. A bruise bloomed on her cheek. Annika whispered her name. She turned toward her and stared, wide-eyed. She'd heard her. She reached out. Annika didn't care if this was a vision or a dream. She was happy. She tried to grab Evelyne's hand, but the vision yanked her back. She returned much faster. Instantly, she found herself on the table, reaching her bound hands in front of her. The throbbing, searing pain roared back.

Then the room went black.

❖

Annika!

Evelyne searched around. She waved her arms through the empty air. Annika had stood here on the wall, whispering to her. Evelyne had thought her a ghost until the castle surroundings had disappeared, and she'd seen an immense room with strangers. Before her had lain Annika, her feet bound and bloodied. Black and blue and swollen. A man had stood over her with a wooden staff. She'd tried to move between them but could not. The vision had rooted her to the floor, watching, until she'd returned home in a burst of bright light.

Was it a vision? Was she going crazy? Annika was alive but was being tortured, or was Annika a ghost, haunting Evelyne for her part in the death of her father? She had heard such stories. People who did evil things were pursued by madness until they took their own lives. She rushed from the wall, down the closest wooden staircase, taking two steps at a time. She ran through the gatehouse, ignoring the guards' calls for her to stay inside.

Her father had forbidden her to leave without his permission. She didn't care. There was only one person who might believe her. She could see the smoke from the forge as she approached the village. She leaned against a piling to catch her breath.

"Lady Evelyne." Hilfa nodded while she worked the bellows. "The gossips have a lot to say about you today."

"I saw her, Hilfa. I saw Annika." Evelyne's voice trembled as she spoke.

Hilfa stopped her work. "Where? Is she here in the village? Maiden, she won't have a place to stay."

Evelyne paced. "She was in a great room, surrounded by elders... others. Someone was striking her. Her feet...they were...it was terrible."

"Calm now, m'lady." Hilfa directed her to a bench to sit upon. "What do you mean, you saw her? Was this a dream?"

Evelyne shook her head and stared at her palms, trying to understand what had happened. "I was on the outer wall, and there she was, in front of me, like a reflection on polished steel. A vision swallowed me, and I saw her. Bound. Injured."

"I've heard Talents can see people and places, but I've never heard a story such as yours."

"Did you know she was a Talent, Hilfa?"

Hilfa lifted her head and extended her chin. "I did. And I don't regret it, temple rules be damned."

Evelyne rubbed her hands repeatedly. "I need to stop them. I need to help her."

"You aren't going to do anything. You need to return to the castle." Hilfa wrapped a powerful arm around her. "You don't know if what you saw was real or a daydream."

Evelyne ran her fingers through her hair and let out a long sigh. "I know it was her. I don't know how she did it, but she took me to her. I have to find her."

Hilfa nodded. "When you do, you tell me. I'll go get her." She stood, her back to Evelyne. "I owe as much to Steffen."

Steffen. Evelyne felt the loss again as strongly as the day it had occurred. She couldn't lose Annika as well. She ran back to the castle, ignoring the guards who yelled at her again. She headed for the chapel. Once inside, she bellowed for Theobald. She stopped at the feet of the Maiden's statue and stared up at the serene face.

"I'm asking you for your help. I'm asking you to save someone who only served you."

"Lady Evelyne." Elder Theobald strode from an entrance to his private quarters. A young innocent helped him on with his over-tunic. "Maiden bless you. What is the matter?"

Evelyne touched the statue, something she wouldn't have dared do before all that had happened. "Where did Lothaire take Annika?"

"I beg your pardon?" He sounded insulted.

She turned on him, her anger spilling out. "Where did they take her?"

Whether because of her height or her anger, he cowed at her demanding tone. He stumbled backward slightly. "I do not know. But your tenor, in the house of the Maiden, will displease your father. Leave now." He pointed to the door.

She left, and as soon as she was outside the doors, she put her face in her hands. She needed to find Annika. Someone was hurting her, and Evelyne couldn't wait and let them kill her the way they had Steffen.

"M'lady," came a whispered voice beside her. The young innocent. He looked back inside the chapel before he spoke again. "If you were to provide a donation to the temple, I might have the information you request."

Evelyne understood. She pulled a gold crown from her purse and pressed it in his outstretched hand. She doubted the coin would ever reach the temple coffers.

He fidgeted. "They left for the temple across the valley."

"Thank you."

He nodded and disappeared inside the chapel doors.

Chapter Forty

Evelyne stared at the open chest. Most of her clothes were impractical for any journey. Delicate embroidery. Long lengths of lacing. Drooping sleeves to catch on every branch. She dropped to the floor. The idea that she could leave to save Annika was harder in application than in her mind.

After she'd spoken to the innocent at the chapel, she was so intent on leaving, she had made her way to the stables and placed a saddle on the fastest palfrey before a stable hand had blocked her from the bridle tack. Now she sat on the floor of her chamber, taking stock of her clothing. She'd borrow something from Timothy. She'd need food. How to get it? Nan would know she was up to something. She should also find a map and a compass. Master Jacob had a compass in his possession. One that sat in water and spun to show the North Star. She wasn't sure there was another in the entire castle. Though she didn't know how to use it or where to find it.

She'd leave at night. More dangerous for the horse but safer for her. Meaning she would need a weapon. A real weapon. Steffen's knowledge would have made a difference. He'd lived off the land and had been on the road during battles. He'd know what she'd need for the trip. Every time she'd traveled anywhere, she and her sisters had sat in a covered litter or wagon, followed by servants, staying at other castles or manors. She wouldn't even be able to stay at an inn.

She found Timothy in the armory. "I need you to bring me a sword and some arrows. Later, when no one is around."

He scowled at her. "Trying to go hunting? You'll only get in further trouble."

She looked around to be sure they were alone and lowered her voice. "I know where Lothaire took Annika. I'm going to find her."

His eyes widened in surprise. He shook his head. "You have truly lost your mind." He glanced over his shoulder at others in the room. "You can't save her, Evelyne," he whispered. "She's a rogue Talent. She's in the hands of the Paladin and the temple. Even if you could find her, what would you do once you arrive? Plead with them to release her?"

Evelyne felt her face warm. "I don't know yet, but I have to try."

"Do you understand what could happen to you? Even if your father forgives you, do you think the temple will be satisfied with returning you without severe punishment?"

She ran her fingers across the glimmering steel of a finely crafted, cross-hilted dagger. Could she use it when the time came? "I don't care what happens to me." Could she bring herself to tell Timothy the truth about her feelings for Annika? Tell him she loved her? "She doesn't deserve to be tortured or die." She slipped the dagger inside her long sleeve and held it against her skin.

"You don't know they are torturing her," he said.

She turned back to him. "I do know." She didn't elaborate.

He came close and spoke in soothing tones. "We'll ask Elder Theobald. I'm sure he will know something. If he doesn't, I'll ask him to write to Elder Braga and ask about Annika."

"Theobald is afraid of them. He'll do nothing of the sort." Evelyne looked at the swords. Too big to hide in her tunic. "I plan to leave at the new moon. I can't wait any longer."

"This is insanity."

"Call me insane if you wish, but I am leaving. You can help me or not." She felt his eyes on her as she left the room. Now she had to find supplies. She wouldn't have time to tell Hilfa. She'd give Nan a note for her. Realization struck her: Hilfa might not be able to read.

Fear seeped in at the edges of her thoughts. She had no idea what she was doing and no one to help her. And what would she do when she arrived at the temple? To Timothy's point, she couldn't just demand they release Annika. She could forge another document from her father, but would they acknowledge it? And what if she could free Annika somehow? Where would she take her? Her stomach roiled. She would have to assess things as they happened. All she knew was, she had to do something.

❖

There was a knock at Evelyne's chamber door. She opened it to find her father staring back at her, accompanied by two guards and an elderly servant woman she recognized but didn't know by name.

"Come with me. Now," her father ordered.

She followed him, the gaggle of others behind her. No one said a word as they moved through the corridors. Only the sound of their footfalls on stone and the sounds of fabric and leather followed her. She became nervous when they passed the great hall and didn't enter. What was this about? She'd already been punished for cutting her hair and fighting with the men. He'd overlooked her trip outside the castle when she'd proclaimed she had been called by the Maiden to visit the village temple, the best lie she'd ever created.

They led her into the far tower overlooking the river below. She was rarely in this part of the keep. As far as she knew, only rooms for servants and viewing galleries for the men-at-arms were here. A peculiar place for them to discuss her disobediences, if indeed, her father intended to speak to her at all.

The lead man opened a door and motioned for her to enter. She stepped into a tiny room with only a stool and a bed frame with a threadbare straw mattress.

"I've tried to be understanding, Evelyne." Her father stood in the doorway but didn't enter. "I have prayed for your soul more than you will ever know. Your mother asked me to forgive you your actions, that you're hotheaded like Witt, but Witt is the lord heir, and you…" He looked her up and down as if examining a horse for purchase. "You are complicating our lives."

"I don't understand." She looked at the undecorated walls. "Why are we here?"

"Timothy came to me with a fairy tale. One in which you would attempt to demand the release of Steffen's daughter." He looked uncomfortable as he said Steffen's name.

Timothy, the only other person Evelyne had ever cared about, one of the few she'd trusted. How could he have betrayed her? She felt nauseated. "No. No. He's wrong. I have no intention of doing such—"

He silenced her with a raised hand. "Don't lie to me. How selfish can you be? You endanger not only yourself but your family in this endeavor. I've had word that this gossip has even gotten as far as Lord Tomas. He wrote to me, worried you might bear infantile heirs." He rubbed his eyebrows. "I told him all was well. Now even I am concerned with your health."

"I am not unwell, Father. I only wanted to take Annika with me to my new home."

"You are never to speak of her again." He slammed his fist against the door frame. "You are to stay here until your marriage train is prepared. The servants are packing your things and the supplies you will need for the journey. A messenger left this morning to your betrothed, telling him to expect you within a fortnight. Daniela will be outside the door to provide for you should you need anything. These men will also be here. They will attend you throughout your journey to your new home."

The door slammed shut, and the sound of an exterior bolt followed. She rushed to the door and pushed, finding it wouldn't budge. She pounded a fist on the wood. "Please, Father, don't do this," she yelled.

No one answered. She continued to yell and pound until her hand throbbed and her voice became hoarse and sore. Panic swelled in her, and her mind raced. She tried another round of drumming on the door with her fists, shouting demands and curses at whoever might be on the other side. Eventually, she gave in to exhaustion, slumping with her back against the door.

As darkness fell, she noticed there wasn't even a candle in the room. When she could see little more than shadows, she lay down. Finding the bed too short for her, she turned on her side, pulling her knees to her chest. Tears of frustration fell, and she sobbed without restraint, knowing no one could hear her.

There was no fireplace, no blanket to cover her, and no sisters to cuddle for warmth. What would happen now?

Chapter Forty-one

Annika curled into a ball on her mattress. Her feet throbbed. They were swollen to twice their normal size and looked as dark as ashes. The skin on the bottoms had split open, the cuts oozing blood and pus. She'd stopped using the chamber pot and pissed herself because the pain of walking was too much to bear. The Confessa had not sent a healer. At the burn, Annika had healed Matilde, but she didn't know how she had done it, so there was no way to heal herself.

Without a healer, she might die of infection. She remembered her mother's death, slow and terrible. Instead, she longed for a quick end. Burning on the pyre now seemed a better choice. Terrible pain for a few minutes before welcoming whatever lay in the afterlife, the celestial expanse or the fields of heather of the old gods.

She watched a rat squeeze under her door and roam around the edges near the wall. It stepped over her shoes and sniffed at some spilled candle wax before moving through another impossibly small crack until all she could see was its hairless pink tail slowly disappearing into the darkness. If only she could make herself so thin, she could squeeze through those cracks. Or better yet, become a rat and scurry away without notice.

She clung to one glimmer of pleasure while she lay in her own filth. For a fleeting moment, she had seen Evelyne. She didn't know how it had happened, but she was certain it had been real and not a dream. What's more, Evelyne had seen her too.

She heard the door open, but she didn't look up. Most likely, it was Helena. The girl was kind, checking on her, trying to get her to eat, but Annika had no appetite. She'd even stopped drinking. What difference did any of it make?

But it wasn't Helena. "Maiden's blessing," said Lothaire.

She curled farther in on herself as he spoke, as if she could shut out his voice if she tried hard enough.

He lit the stub of a candle on the floor and moved closer to her. He winced, no doubt at the smell. She'd long gotten used to it. He lifted the hem of her gown, taking a better look at her feet, she supposed. "Why have you not healed yourself?"

She closed her eyes. *Go away.*

"Braga is testing you. She wants to see at what point you will use your gifts."

He said gifts, not gift. She had forgotten that was why she was alive. Because she was some sort of freakish Talent. As if being half-Weyan hadn't always been a burden; now she had to add "the Talent who wasn't like the others" to her list of rude titles.

"She can go to the underworld. You can too," she muttered.

"They will be here soon to interrogate you. I don't know what Braga has planned for today, but I suggest you heal yourself beforehand."

"You're the Paladin. Can't you make them stop? Or better yet, can't you kill me now?"

He touched her knee. Her eyes flew open. He squatted next to her. Concern was on his face. She crawled from his touch, pressing herself against the wall behind her. Pain stung her feet as she moved.

"You know everything about people's minds. Surely you know I would want to die after all I've been through."

He sat on the floor, placing his back against the low bed frame. "My father willingly gave me to the temple. He would have never thought to hide me. He'd have killed me himself if I'd stayed any longer in his household. My mother was too afraid of him and his temper to disagree with him on anything. She stood with my siblings in the doorway of our home, crying. As if crying would help anything."

He stuck his finger in the hot wax of the candle, as if trying to stop his pain with more pain. "Your father offered his own life for yours. His life. Oh, to have had my father say anything at all. He lifted me under the arms and placed me behind the innocent who came to retrieve me. He turned his back on me and pushed my mother and brothers inside the cottage and closed the door. I never saw any of them again."

"Go to them now. You're the Paladin. You can do anything you wish." She hoped her voice betrayed her lack of sympathy.

"They died of plague. Too afraid of healers to ask for help." He set the candle on the floor. "Your father made a mistake in hiding you, but he was a good man. Even I can admit that."

"Until you ripped him away from me," she replied coldly.

His jaw twitched. "What if we could go somewhere together?" he asked. "Leave Valmora. Together."

"Is this another test? Because I'm tired of tests," she replied. "You're the Paladin. The defender of the faith. The Maiden's knight. The king's holy guardian. Did I miss a title? Helena made sure to tell them all to me. You believe what the temple tells you, or you wouldn't burn children at the stake."

"I believe in myself." He snuffed the candle wick with his fingers, dropping a curtain of darkness. "I've been contemplating my purpose. The temple formed me. Molded me. Made me a blunt tool. You will be too, if you give them what they want, but if you don't, you'll be dead. Haven't you ever wondered what happens to most Talents? Did you think they all became members of the order? Why do you think you have a healer in Marsendale who was born in a place a hundred miles away?"

Annika was too tired to respond. She'd let him ramble on if it meant keeping her from thinking about her pain.

"Because most don't survive their seventh birthday. I was one of a hundred children taken from their families and brought to the temple orphanage in Sevenshadows. Only two of us were alive the next year. The rest died during tests of their gifts. Most were barely Talents. They could cure a cold or sense a bad person. The merchants nearby know what goes on there. They whisper to one another about saving their children. They pay large ransoms to spirit their children away to the Concordant Kingdoms or Iola. But out in the countryside, people don't know any better. They hand their children over. Proud of their service to the Maiden."

There were no rogue Talents in Valmora because they were all dead before they came of age. Was being with her father all those years worth his death? Obviously, her father had thought so. If she died now, would any of it matter? "Why doesn't the king stop them?" she asked.

"You overestimate his power. As long as the kingdom prospers, he has no reason to confront the temple. If he did, a schism might form between church and state."

"Why not leave? If you hate what you do, don't do it anymore."

"I have never wanted to leave...until I met you." He looked at her in the faint light from the opening in the wall. "I am certain you are much more powerful than you know. I've seen it. You have three gifts. Three. You don't even understand how rare that is, do you? Perhaps one person in five hundred years has more than one gift. The council will kill you if they cannot find a way to use you, and I don't want you to die, Annika."

His honesty was making her uncomfortable. "What does it matter? I have nothing to live for. My father knew the darkness in men's hearts. I thought the temple was different. I thought the pious were better than us common folk. Doing good in the world. Until I met you."

He stood. "I'll send someone to heal you and bathe you."

"Wait." She raised up a little. The movement sent a wave of pain through her legs. She would sell herself to the gods of the underworld because anything was better than a lingering death at the hands of the council. There had to be another way. "If I decide to go with you, how will I know what to do?"

Let him think she would consider his offer. Maybe he would intercede on her behalf with the council and save her from another round of pain. But she would never go with him. She'd make certain of that.

Lothaire seemed pleased. A smile crossed his face. "Be ready at any time."

Chapter Forty-two

Her eyes were puffy and sore from crying. She admonished herself for being weak and backed away from the door. The lock mechanism made a scraping sound. She stood and backed to the far wall, clenching her fists, ready to charge from the room if possible. She blinked when the torchlight fell on her, and her anger fell away when she saw her mother.

Evelyne ran to her. "Mother." She hugged her and pressed her face to her mother's shoulder, bending down to do so.

Her mother pushed her back slightly to look into her eyes. She placed a finger to her lips, signaling for Evelyne to stay quiet. She gestured for Evelyne to sit on the bed while she herself took the stool. A servant affixed the torch to a wall cleat and closed the door. Her mother spoke in a hushed tone. "I'm sorry. I came as soon as I could. I wasn't informed of your whereabouts until after your father brought you here."

"I hate being locked in here."

"I heard what you were planning. What were you thinking, Evelyne? That you would run off and somehow convince the temple to release the girl?"

"Annika…her name is Annika."

"Annika," her mother conceded. "Did you know she was a Talent?"

"No." Evelyne looked away and pushed herself against the wall. "Yes," she admitted. "But I didn't care."

Her mother leaned forward. "You should care."

"Only because the temple tells us we should be afraid. Do you think a girl, twelve harvests old, who can heal farm animals deserves to burn at the stake?"

"Annika is not twelve, Evelyne."

"No. That was Minerva's gift, a girl in Welford. She tended oxen with her family. She healed a beast, and the temple burned her as her reward." She began relating the stories she had read in the legal documents in the library. "A girl of thirteen was burned for telling the weather before it happened. A girl of fifteen burned for healing a man who fell from a bell tower and broke his back. A boy of fourteen burned for healing his mother and his newborn sibling."

"Enough." Now it was her mother's turn to look away.

"No, it's not enough. They were children. What threat were they? And the judges were men. No confessa or innocents were there. Men, like the Paladin, in armor and carrying weapons, tied Minerva to a stake and burned her for healing oxen." Evelyne stood and paced. "You know what I think? I think the temple wants to keep Talents all to themselves. The temple elders think they are the only ones who should have these powers. So if you don't submit, they burn you. And now Steffen." She slammed her hand against the stone wall.

"I know it seems cruel, but there are reasons for what they do. The temple oversees Talents to protect them. Being in the temple provides structure and gives moral sanctity to the use of their gifts. I know you think I'm a useless woman, a wife, a mother, but I've sat at your father's side for many harvests. Listened while distinguished men have discussed important things in my presence, ignoring me as a woman. What I've learned about Talents, whether the ones given by the Maiden or those inherent in us all, is that without guidance, humans wield power foolishly and cruelly."

Evelyne pressed her hands together and groaned. "There is nothing cruel about Annika." She took a step toward her mother. "Release me, let me go to Annika. I don't want to marry. I don't want any part of the manor anymore. Let me go."

Her mother grasped the Maiden on her necklace and rubbed it. "Your father says you will either marry or he will lock you in this tower for the rest of your life. Branded a madwoman."

Evelyne spread her hands in front of her. "Mother, look at me. Can you not see me? Can you not see who I really am? You know I'm not mad."

"What I see is a heartbroken young woman whose first love hasn't gone the way she expected."

Evelyne froze. "You knew?"

"Of course. I know what love looks like. I love your father immensely, despite what you may think of marriage. Things are much different behind closed doors than in front of them. I hoped you would warm to the idea of being a wife, a mother. I wanted you to experience the joy as I have."

Joy? Nothing about being married and stuck in a role unsuited for her felt like joy. "I feel only the constriction of these four walls when I think of marriage to Samuel." She moved to the window and looked across the estate to the golden fields beyond. "Either choice is a dungeon."

Her mother stood and moved closer. "Your father wants what is best for you, for all his children, but he has many things weighing on him. Things you won't understand for years to come." She looked sad. "I have more freedom than you seem to believe."

Evelyne remembered the day in the charcoal fields. "I didn't know you managed the forests."

Her mother smiled. "Ah, yes. The day I saw you covered in black dust."

"How did you know it was me?"

She reached out and stroked Evelyne's hair. "I would know you anywhere. You can't hide from a mother in a floppy hat and dirty face. I can see any of my children walking at a hundred paces and know you are my child."

The thought made Evelyne feel warm inside. "Small freedoms or not, I feel nothing for the role I was born to play." She placed a hand over her mother's. "I wish I could explain myself better."

Her mother dropped her hand and moved back to the window, the sunset light falling on her face. "If you insist on leaving, you must understand, you will never return here again."

Evelyne frowned. "What do you mean?"

"You will be shunned, your name forever in the temple ledgers as one who will receive no sustenance nor work nor assistance of any kind. Theobald will send the notice to every temple in Valmora. You will lose your title of lady. Your name will be erased and never uttered by your father, your siblings, nor me."

This was unexpected, but what had she thought would happen? They would let her rescue Annika and take her to Samuel's manor where they would live happily ever after like in one of Winifred's romance stories? Never see her sisters again. Never speak to Old Nan. Not know where her next meal would come from. She had not planned for this. Not even thought about it.

"Are you saying, if I choose to leave, you will let me go?"

Her mother nodded. Evelyne could see the tears glistening in her eyes. She clung to her necklace.

Evelyne stepped to the bed and sat on the edge, head in her hands. Was this any different than leaving for Samuel's manor? His father's land was far to the east, farther than any other point from Marsendale. How often might her husband allow her to travel home? Once she was bearing children, the options to travel would dwindle even more. The unknown would greet her there. Was he a kind man, or would he beat her? Would she have any say in the affairs of their demesne, or would she sit idly, running the household? There was no way for her to know because she did not know Samuel, and he did not know her.

But she knew Annika. Secrets or no, she loved her. Annika and Steffen were warmer to her than her own family. They saw her for who she really was, and they let her put them at risk. Steffen was what she wanted from her own father, a mentor, proud of her strength rather than ashamed. He'd died for his daughter, and Evelyne would risk everything for her as well.

"I wish to leave," she said resolutely, though fear coursed through her body.

Her mother nodded.

Evelyne stood and hugged her. She held tight. This might be the last time they were in each other's presence.

Her mother pulled back and patted her hands. "Let me speak to your father first." She walked to the door. "I will send someone when it is time."

Chapter Forty-three

Evelyne had barely slept all night. She was too anxious. Her mind filled with things she had never had to think of before. What would she need to take with her? How was she going to make money on the road? She could hunt, so she wouldn't starve, but would they let her take her bow and enough arrows? She'd need clothes less auspicious than her usual outfits. Traveling alone would attract unsavory types, mercenaries, and conmen...and women. If she wore her typical clothing, they'd think her a wealthy woman. While that came in handy with guards around her, alone, it would be as if she was a slow deer in the sights of a hunter.

And what would it be like to be without her sisters? They'd slept in the same room. Ate at the same table. Laughed at the same gossip. She'd never slept alone, save for a nap, in her whole life. A lump in her throat forced her to swallow. She hoped she would not see disappointment on her father's face. Her whole life, all she'd wanted was to fight in his service, to be one of his trusted representatives like Witt and Erik. Now she would be the greatest disappointment in her family's recent history. Shunned.

There was still time to change her mind. She could submit to her duty and ride to Samuel's manor, give herself willingly to the service of her family, as her mother had done. Perhaps Samuel would be a better man than she imagined. Progressive and open to her ideas and whims. She paced from one wall to the opposite repeatedly in the dark until she collapsed in exhaustion on the bed, falling into a disturbed sleep.

She opened her eyes to the dimly lit room when she heard the latch on the iron lock slide open. She waited for the door to open, but it stayed closed. She pushed to her feet and tentatively tried the door pull. The heavy oak door swung open to reveal an empty hallway.

Whoever had granted it, she wouldn't refuse this gift.

She made her way through the hallway and down the stairs, seeing no one else. Predawn meant few people would be up and moving about, but the complete lack of servants or guards seemed too convenient... until she attempted to enter her own chamber. Old Nan met her in the corridor. Several small bags and another larger one sat on the floor at her feet.

"M'lady." Old Nan huffed and hustled toward her, holding a bag in one hand and her skirts in the other. When she reached Evelyne, she wheezed slightly and tried to catch her breath. She handed over the bag. "I've made your favorites. Fig tarts. There's a little jar of honey to lie over them."

"Thank you, Nan."

Nan looked around furtively and leaned in closer. She reached under her tunic and took out a small, folded piece of parchment and held it in her gnarled fingers. She placed it carefully in Evelyne's hand. "Hurry now. I've packed your bags. A boy is waiting for you at the stables with a horse."

Evelyne tucked the note in the bag and tied it to her belt. She felt slow to gather her things. She didn't know what they had packed for her, but now she would have no choice. Whatever was in them was what she would have in the future. All she would have.

She put her hand on the door to her chamber. Inside, her sisters slept, unaware she was leaving them. She wished she could say good-bye. She glanced at the turn in the hallway that led to the men's wing. As much as she'd fought with Witt and Erik, they were her brothers. She hoped they would grow into good men.

When she arrived at the stables, two horses, fleet of foot, were saddled and ready to ride. Dodd came out from behind one of them, checking the bits and straps before swinging into the saddle.

Evelyne stared at him.

"You didn't think I or your mother would allow you to go alone, did you?" He pulled on the reins and turned his horse toward the open gate in the outer wall.

"When did I earn this loyalty, Dodd?"

"When your mother paid me a shiteload of silver." He smiled, his tongue lolling in the gap of his missing teeth.

"You'll pay more than the underworld price for this."

"Gods be damned, then," he replied.

Evelyne tied her bags to her horse. She carefully unwrapped

something in waxed cloth. A short sword in a plain leather scabbard and a matching dagger, the one she'd stolen earlier from the armory. She stared at them, pulling them from their scabbards and examining the edges. Good quality steel. Perfectly weighted for her. Tears were building. She hoped her father had gifted her the weapons or perhaps Witt, but more than likely, Dodd had lifted them. She carefully rewrapped them and tied them to the saddle along with her bags.

"Evelyne!" Matilde ran toward her, stumbling in her night shift.

She knelt, and Matilde flung herself into her arms. She squeezed Evelyne's neck tightly. Evelyne squeezed back.

"Winifred is crying. She says you are leaving?" Matilde pulled back and looked at her with her big brown eyes. "Are you leaving? You forgot. You promised to take me hunting after the festival. Where are you going? Are you going to get married? Will you be back soon?"

The rapid questions swam in Evelyne's head. "I am leaving." She tried to make her voice light. "I am going on a hunt. I'll be gone a long time. Dodd and I are traveling a long way for a special beast."

"I could come with you. I'm good with my bow."

"Yes, you are good with a bow. Mother and Father won't let you come with me this time. The beast we track is dangerous." She touched a finger to Matilde's nose lightly. "But I expect you to practice every day, so one day, you can join me."

Matilde hugged her tightly. She pulled away and dug in a small pouch on her hip. "Here." She handed Evelyne a small carved horse. "He's good luck."

Evelyne smiled and placed the tiny wooden statue in her own purse. "Make sure you tell Winifred and the others that I love them."

"I will. I will go practice my archery now." She ran off as quickly as she'd arrived.

How nice to be unaware of what this moment meant for them both. Evelyne took one last look around the grounds. So many memories. So much discontent, and yet, she was happy here. What would it be like outside the walls? She tucked her tunic into her belt, raising the hem. She grabbed the reins, placed her foot in the stirrup, and swung her leg over the saddle.

Dodd led the way through the gatehouse and down the familiar path to the village. What would it feel like to ride through the village for the last time? She felt ashamed. She had expected one day to ride out in her knightly kit and be proud. But that childhood dream was never to be. They hadn't gotten to the edge of the village before Evelyne saw two figures in the main square, standing with a cart and work pony. Hilfa and Jack.

"Are you off to a festival, Hilfa?" she asked as they drew closer. Blacksmithing tools and a travel forge filled the cart.

"We're coming with you." Hilfa crossed her arms.

"How do you know where I'm going?" She glanced at Dodd. He looked at the lightening sky.

"You're going to find Annika, and I'm coming with you."

"This is folly, Hilfa. I'm going to attempt to free her from the temple. The Paladin will surely be there. I don't have any idea what I'm doing. Why risk your life with me?"

"I owe it to Steffen," Hilfa replied pointedly. She turned at the sound of someone running toward them. Finn bent over and took great gasping breaths as he came to a stop.

"Are you here to tell me to hurry my departure?" Evelyne asked.

"What? No." He smiled proudly, patting the travel pack on his back, his accent thick. "I'm supposed to be in your service, m'lady. Remember?"

She winced at the honorific. "I'm no longer a lady...or a lord, for that matter. I'm sure my father released you from my service, Finn."

"Mayhap, but when I heard Dodd was going with you on a quest, I knew I had to come along." His youthful eagerness almost lifted her spirits.

"This is no mythical quest, Finn. You need to return to the castle."

"I decided as soon as I heard we were going to save a damsel in distress."

Hilfa groaned and shook her head.

"You'll get yourself killed, boy," Dodd grumbled.

"Better yet." He stood taller. "A bard will sing songs of my deeds."

Evelyne wished she felt as confident. "I have no idea what I'm doing. The elders might burn me for heresy if they catch me. I've been shunned. I'll be allowed no work, no food, no pity. I appreciate everything you are trying to do, but I can't cause your deaths." She addressed her comments to all of them.

"Your mother compensated me well enough. I'll take my chances," Dodd said, patting a fat purse on his belt.

"You don't have any say over what I do." Hilfa gave her a pointed look. "Do you now, Evelyne?"

Point taken. She had no title. No lands. No place to call home. She was shunned. They could do as they liked. But what of Jack?

"Jack, you have no reason to do this. Stay. Make a go of the forge."

He barely looked up, his hair in his eyes. "Annika was always nice to me."

She had no counterpoint. "Then let us get some horses. I can't have all of you walking."

Dodd shook his head. "We'll not be able to get horses, nor anything else, while we're on your father's lands. Word's already traveling. Shunning works fast."

She hung her head. Leaving was harder than she had imagined. She looked around at their small group. At least she wouldn't be doing this alone. Now all she had to do was find Annika and rescue her.

CHAPTER FORTY-FOUR

Lothaire's word was good. He sent a healer who tended her feet, but Braga changed tactics and started a different type of interrogation. Several of the elders used their gifts at the same time. All of them healers, trying to search with tendrils like fingers, poking inside her skull. She didn't understand, but they could untie muscles and then heal them, so they kept fishing in her mind, untying connections and healing them.

There were moments when she couldn't feel anything and others when the pain was agonizing. Whatever the purpose, they dragged her back to her room and left her facedown on the bed, where she lay uncovered and half-asleep. The throbbing in her head was unbearable.

When she heard the door's lock fall, she knew it was Helena. Unlike the guards, Helena didn't throw the bar hard against the braces. Annika opened her eyes.

Helena placed a bowl of pottage and a pitcher of goat's milk on the floor near the head of the bed. She was pretty on the side Annika could see, the one not marked by the pox scars. This was her chance. Annika pushed herself up. The spinning stopped after a few moments.

"Are you feeling all right?" Helena asked politely.

Annika nodded and stood. "Helena, I've soiled the bed again." She tried to look ashamed. "Is there any way to get a new cover and fresh straw?"

"Of course." Helena reached for the knife that hung on her belt and leaned over the bedding. "Let's get this off and put the straw in the corner." She cut through the linen, ripping the seam, and pulling out the straw.

Annika moved to her blind side. She swallowed hard, her mouth dry. She slowly reached down and grasped the jug handle. She'd only have one chance. She struck Helena on the side of the head, dropping her to the bed, face-first. She checked to make sure she wasn't dead, gently stroking her wet hair. "I'm sorry, Helena. You've been kind to me." She stared at the pool of milk on the sheet. What a waste. She was already thirsty, and she wouldn't have time to find anything to drink.

She swapped clothes, dressing Helena in her own reeking gown, and laid her on her side, facing the wall. She covered her with the thin wool blanket. Standing at the door, she took one more look around. Her mother's gittern sat in the corner where Lothaire had left it. All she had left from her life was a mark on her forearm and the instrument. She grasped it and held it like she was hugging another person. So many memories. So much serenity in its strings. She placed it on the ground.

Good-bye, Mother.

She stepped from the room, locking the door behind her.

Dressed in Helena's innocent's robes, she moved silently along the corridors, weaving from shadowed corner to shadowed corner, careful not to make any noise. The others would be at the communal meal, listening to the droning chants of an elder. She approached a cross corridor that led to the council room. All she had to do was make it another one hundred steps, and she'd be in the public space where, with some luck or the Maiden's help, she'd be able to slip away with other community members as they came and went.

As she was about to step into the crossway, she heard someone. "I'm running out of patience." Braga's clipped voice. "You sent a healer to the girl, disobeying my direct orders."

"I've done everything I've ever been asked to do for the temple." Lothaire.

"You mean for the Maiden," Braga corrected.

Annika heard Lothaire growl his next response. "I mean for you and the council. I'm not sure what the Maiden wants from me anymore."

"How dare you? Speak more like this, and you'll end up nothing more than a morality tale in the Book."

"Let me take her to Tarburg. I'll present her to the king. The masters in Sevenshadows can help me convert her to the path of the Maiden. She is too valuable to kill."

From the sounds, they were drawing closer. Annika slipped inside the nearest doorway and closed the door softly behind her. A healer's library from the looks of the tables of glass jars, the herbs drying from rafters, and several sets of shelves full of books. She heard footsteps. They were getting closer. She moved behind a tall bookshelf and tucked herself in the corner on the floor, making herself as small as she could.

She smelled the mildew and dust from the surrounding parchment. The floor was dirty, gritty on her hands, but she didn't dare rub them. The door opened, and her heart felt like it was going to beat out of her chest. She wouldn't let them take her again. She had Helena's knife. She slipped it from its sheath and waited.

"She bears the crown godsmark," said Braga as they entered the room. "Perhaps it is a coincidence, or mayhap she's descended from the Council of Twelve. Either way, she is a danger to Valmora and a danger to the temple."

"You pointed out yourself that I wear the mark of the Two-Faced God. Why am I not a threat?" asked Lothaire.

"You survived the trials as a child. The king wanted you as Paladin. You've shown nothing but loyalty to the way of the Maiden."

"And if I was to choose to leave the temple?"

There was silence.

"You would suffer the same fate as the girl. Don't throw your life away on a fool's errand."

"Give me more time."

"Do your duty, Lothaire. The pyre is ready, and the executioner is ready to behead her if she once again extinguishes the flames."

"Please," he said, his voice pleading. "I know I can help her."

"She is an abomination. A threat to our way of life. Her beauty sways you. Or perhaps she has another Talent. One that can influence the minds of men. You see a harmless young girl." Her voice rose. "I see a hideous monster in human skin waiting to tear down the walls of our sanctified and holy mother temple."

"Enough."

Annika heard steps, shuffling, the clinking of glass, a soft gasp, and a dull thud. She opened her eyes and peeked through the books. Lothaire moved through the room and out the door. Annika waited, unsure if Braga was still in the room, but she heard nothing.

She stowed the knife and stood. As she came around the bookshelf, she saw Braga in a heap on the floor in a pool of blood. She gasped and leaned down to check if she was still alive. Her chest didn't rise or fall. Lothaire had killed her. As she looked at the old woman's serene face in death, she felt little pity. Braga had caused her so much pain.

And yet, she couldn't leave her here without saying something. She lifted her head and made a silent prayer to the Maiden to take Braga to her breast and wash away her sins.

Outside the door, she no longer heard voices.

She had to leave...now. If they found her with Braga's body, she would never survive the day.

She took a few breaths to steady herself before opening the door just enough to peek through the crack, carefully looking for anyone who would recognize her. There was no one. She snuck from the room and rushed toward the main hall.

Once inside, she mingled with a family paying tribute as she made her way to the exit. She ducked her head and kept her hands tucked in her sleeves like the other innocents. No one stopped her as she slipped through the main doors into the reddening light of sunset.

❖

They'd been on the road all day. Evelyne had listened to Dodd tell tales about his prowess with women until the sun was low on the horizon. Finn had hung on every word. Most of the time, Evelyne had rolled her eyes. She was certain they were mostly lies, but she wasn't going to point it out while he was willing to help her.

Another surprise of the journey, Finn played the recorder. And well. His music was uplifting on a day of slow going. She had thought about riding ahead, but she felt an obligation to all of them for risking their lives with her.

As dusk fell over the rolling hills, Dodd took them off the main road. Evelyne hadn't even seen the path; the brush hid it well. Creaking and thumps from the cart worried her, but the pony was surefooted on the rough trail. Dodd stopped his horse and dismounted in a small clearing.

"Why are we stopping? We need to get to the temple," she asked.

Hilfa unloaded gear from the cart. "I love her too, but I can't take another step tonight."

"Dodd, you and I can ride ahead."

He tied his horse to a small tree and stretched. "We don't have the luxury of swapping horses at every village like your father. These animals will have to do us. They need rest." He unbuckled the saddle, placing it on the ground. "And so do I."

Finn followed his lead, laying his pack on the ground. Jack removed the harness from the pony, letting him lower his head and graze.

"They might kill Annika before we can get there."

"She might already be dead," said Dodd.

The thought struck her like an arrow.

"We've no way to know." He pulled the bit out of his horse's mouth. "You won't get there at all if you push everyone too hard."

She glanced down. Her horse's head hung low, pulling against her reins. He was already looking for something to eat. His neck glistened with sweat, and foam gathered at the edge of his mouth. She slapped her hand on the pommel of the saddle. She wanted to yell at them all, order them to keep going. Ride all night. She looked around. They were all tired. She understood this, but it took everything she had not to ride her horse and herself into the ground.

"Jack, gather some tinder for a fire. Evelyne, you're good at sniffing meat. See if you can shoot us something to eat. Otherwise, we have some oats and a few vegetables from Nan, but I'd like to keep them for later."

Dodd was the most experienced member of this band of misfits. No matter their status yesterday, he was now the most obvious choice to keep them on task. She tamped down her desire to lash out and did what he told her.

Three roasted squirrels later, the fire burned more slowly. She'd ridden since she was younger than her memory, and yet a full day on the road made her legs ache and her lower back hurt. She stared at the glowing embers of yellow and orange. "I hate not being able to do anything," she said. That was the truth. She needed to do something, and here she sat, eating a squirrel.

Dodd looked at her across the flames. "Welcome to a warrior's life. Hurry to the battle. Wait. Wait some more. Have a giant mess of a fight. Lie around, recover, wait some more."

Jack seemed worried by the words.

Dodd continued. "Sieges are the worst. You spend most of the time worrying you don't die of the flux."

She'd made her choice. There was no going back to her life as it was. She was beginning to understand what she'd given up. No tent. No servants. There was no one to draw water for her. No one taking care of the minor details. Her hands were filthy. There was dirt under her nails. One thing she was glad for was the shortness of her hair. She'd pulled it back and tied it behind her neck. If nothing else, it would stay cleaner on the road.

She dug through her satchel. Someone had packed her several clean shifts, a handful of rags for her monthlies, and in the bottom, a comb and a few other grooming items. If only someone had packed Witt's tunic and leggings.

She unsheathed her knife and unceremoniously cut several inches off the bottom of her tunic and shift, exposing her ankles and lower leg. Better to be deemed wanton than to stumble about while hunting or fighting. What would her mother think of her now? She remembered the note Old Nan had given her when she left. She dug in her belt purse. Not unexpectedly, the handwriting was her mother's.

> *I've sewn a sapphire in the lining of your tunic. Spend it wisely. If you travel to the border with the Concordant Kingdoms, you will find my brother, Tybalt, in Merkvald. I have sent a message to him as well. This has been the hardest thing I have ever done, besides burying your tiny siblings. I wish you the grace and steadfastness of the Maiden on your journey.*

Had she made the right decision in leaving her family? Evelyne wiped away a stray tear.

Hilfa looked at her sympathetically. "You all right?"

She nodded and tucked the note in her bag, neatly folded. She felt something thick in the bottom of her pack, wrapped in a piece of linen. Removing the cloth, she stared at her book of training drawings, bound together with green embroidery thread. At the bottom of the first page, a small note was scrawled in careful lettering.

> *You'll need this for hunting in the kitchens.*

Evelyne smiled. Winifred. For all her love of gossip and romance, she knew what mattered. Evelyne would miss her fiercely.

"Why were you willing to be shunned?" asked Jack. His question was barely a whisper. He picked at a piece of bread.

Why had she done it? Left them all behind. Her mother, her father, Winifred, Birgitta. Tildie. Timothy. "Because I love her," she said.

No one spoke.

"Does that bother you?"

Hilfa answered. "Not at all." She threw a bone on the fire. "I wonder when someone will love me as much. Here's to hope."

Smiles all around met Evelyne's gaze.

Dodd turned to Finn. "Like I was saying earlier, long campaigns are right miserable. I'll take a quick death myself."

Evelyne stared at her dagger. How would she face death? Would she cry out? Would she foul herself? Or would she meet the Maiden with courage, as Steffen had? She tried spinning the knife by its point on a flat piece of wood. She'd seen Timothy do this trick many times. Timothy. She still couldn't believe he'd betrayed her. She would have been proud to have him at her side when she confronted the Paladin.

Chapter Forty-five

In the morning, they rose and continued to the temple. The first sign of something wrong was when a group of heavily armed riders overtook them, forcing them to move to the side of the road. As they passed, Evelyne noted their mail shirts, covered with well-worn tunics. Each of the men eyed Dodd and Hilfa in particular. He returned the scrutiny.

"Hedge knights?" asked Evelyne once the men were far enough away not to hear them. "I didn't see any manor colors."

"Mercenaries," replied Hilfa. "I've worked on many a knife for the likes of them." She didn't say it with any respect in her voice.

Dodd nodded in agreement.

"Mercenaries on pilgrimage?" asked Finn. "I guess they have a lot to atone for," he added lightly.

What were mercenaries doing here?

Soon after, a large wagon covered in heavy fabric, pulled by a line of four horses tied in a row, a man riding the first, passed them heading away from the temple. Half a dozen masters sat within, while several guards walked on either side. The wagon groaned and rocked on the uneven ground. The guards' eyes narrowed at her band of misfits.

But true chaos reigned at the temple. Evelyne and the others moved to the side of the path and stopped as more masters and elders readied to leave. Guards stood watch in front of the gates to the temple, not relaxed, very much at attention. A gaggle of innocents cried softly together at a well to the side of the entrance.

"What in the bloody hell?" asked Dodd.

Another group of men and women mounted in the courtyard and rode past in a great hurry.

Evelyne's throat closed tightly. Were they too late? She dismounted. "Wait here."

"Not bloody likely," said Dodd.

Finn motioned to her. "Let me, m'lady. This is where I shine." He gave a big grin and walked toward the guards at the gate.

"Not a lady anymore," Evelyne muttered. She tried to contain her nervousness. She stroked her horse's neck to soothe the animal. The mare's ears flicked back and forth, aware of the commotion and Evelyne's tension. She watched as Finn approached the guards. They gestured. He raised his hands and moved toward the innocents by the well.

"Where'd you find him?" asked Hilfa.

"He's like a puppy," said Dodd. "Won't leave my side. Thinks I'm some sort of legend."

"Who might have given him such an idea?" asked Evelyne drolly.

He shrugged in response.

Evelyne's gaze roamed every face she could see. Hoping upon hope one would be Annika. She gripped the handle of her dagger until her knuckles hurt. If one of those guards said Annika's name aloud, she would be on them in a moment. The rage inside her was difficult to quiet. Nothing she wanted to do was rational or logical.

Before long, Finn returned. He shuffled out of the way of another trio of riders. Evelyne looked around to make sure no one was nearby. "What did they say? Is she in the temple?"

Finn shook his head. "The guards wouldn't talk, told me to move on. But the ladies were more helpful. I told them a sob story about needing indulgences to save my immortal soul. How I'd heard the Paladin was nearby. He's here."

"What of Annika?" Evelyne asked.

"A girl arrived with him, and this"—he gestured to the chaos—"is for her. They said she killed an elder."

Evelyne gasped. It made no sense. Even if she was in mortal danger, Annika wouldn't have killed an elder. She'd stood on the pyre at the castle and waited to die.

"They've sent guards to look for her." He paused. "Well, for a girl with blond hair. Pity any girl with fair hair today."

"Where do you think she'd go?" asked Hilfa.

Evelyne looked at the paths leading away from the temple. The one behind them led west, back to Marsendale. Had Annika come that way, they would have seen her. The only other visible path headed north along the ridge top.

"I know where she is going," said Evelyne. "To the Giant's

Bridge." She turned to Jack. "Take the cart and go back to the last bridge we passed. See if you can move underneath and wait near the creek's edge. If we haven't returned on the morrow, go back to Marsendale and wait."

Jack frowned. "I'm not afraid."

Evelyne put a hand on his shoulder. "I know you're not. The cart won't make it on that path, and Hilfa is going to need those tools. You're doing something important."

Hilfa nodded and helped Jack turn the cart around.

Evelyne watched as he walked the pony and cart back down the hillside. In the distance, she noticed a rider in a cloak. Sitting atop his horse but not coming closer. He seemed out of place, but with all the commotion around the temple, he was probably waiting for someone. She was getting jumpy. "Hilfa, ride with me. Finn, ride with Dodd. It will be faster."

❖

All night, Annika had stumbled over downed trees and large stones. She'd chosen this path because she knew anyone looking for her would assume she'd taken the main road back to her home. Even if she could hide well enough to make it to Marsendale, what would be there for her?

Her father was dead. Evelyne prepared for marriage. She'd seen her in that moment while the committee tortured her. She had been with Evelyne on the wall. At home. But only for a moment before the pain had torn her away. Part of her hoped it was a dream. She wouldn't want Evelyne's last image of her to be in that room.

Now she truly was a rogue Talent. With Braga dead and Lothaire obsessed, she had no choice but to run. Her first regret was not stealing a container for water. She'd drunk at the well before leaving the temple grounds, but that was many hours ago. Now that the sun had risen, she was thirsty. She listened for an underground stream but heard none.

She did not know where she was going, how she would feed herself, or when her journey might end, but she would try to survive. The only thing left to her was herself.

Between the trees, the ruins of a gatehouse appeared in front of her. The design was square and simple and much older than the one in the castle. So old, in fact, it was crumbling in several directions, but the archway was intact. She must be close to the aqueduct, as Evelyne had called it. Through the gate, the path was smooth. In places, stones lining the ground stuck out at angles, pushed skyward by roots.

With no villages, no streams, and no idea where to go, she doubted she would last a few days. Why had she come this way?

Evelyne. She wished she could go back. Accept any offer Evelyne gave her. Stayed in her cottage instead of going to the harvest celebration. Run away with her father. Her chances would have been better. But if she hadn't gone to the burn, would Matilde have fallen in the fire? Would she have died?

What was the use of reliving something she couldn't control?

At the end of the path sat a small fortress, squat and flat. A short stone bridge led to the center of the building. Looking to her left, she could see the valley through the trees. Wreckage of the aqueduct entered one side of the fortress and extended out the other. She imagined what it must have looked like when the ridge was cleared of trees and the bridge extended from side to side along the valley. She supposed it was like looking up at the temple, but this was much more impressive.

She crossed the bridge, careful not to trip on debris, and entered the structure. Inside, the walls were in good condition. Weeds and vines and even a tree had found their way inside, creating great cracks in the floor and walls. Sunlight fell through holes in the ceiling. The channel where water had once run split the room in two, so she followed it to the right.

She moved to the corner and saw water trickling down the face of the stone. The roof must hold rainwater. She knew it might make her sick, but she was thirsty enough to cup her hand and drink several cool sips. The liquid was soothing. Enough to make her feel better, at least.

Faint sunlight fell on the opposite side of the room. Paintings covered the wall, half missing, but the remainder were painted in bright reds and oranges. A naked woman's body lounging on a bed. Her hair dark and curling. Her eyes had no pupils, only the whites were visible. How had such a thing lasted for a thousand years when all the rest of the culture had withered to dust?

Here was a moment in time, frozen for her to observe. Was it a portrait? A representation of a god? A manual of some sort? A decoration? There was no one here to ask. No clothing or tools, nothing but stone. All stone. Nothing left of the people or their culture. Were they giants? Or gods? She touched her inking. What would they think of her? A girl curled amidst the rubble of their magnificent accomplishment.

She continued to the far end of the building where the aqueduct ended abruptly. The next nearest section was half its original height below her, the deck now jagged pieces of rock and stone, overgrown with greenery. She hoped she could find a way down that didn't involve climbing…or falling.

She turned back and entered another room closer to the northern end of the building to look for a staircase or other entry. This room felt eerily familiar. The moss on the walls, the shapes, even the smell.

Of course, this was the room in her vision. When she'd met Lothaire.

In her panic, another vision came. It took her in a flash to a kitchen in a tavern. A woman stood stirring something over the fire. The woman stopped, dropped the spoon she held, and turned toward Annika.

Zuri!

Though her mouth didn't move, Annika could hear Zuri's voice clearly, as if she was in the room with her. "Come to me in Tarburg."

Before Annika could say a word, the vision whisked her over a great city, larger than any she had ever seen. Across fields of grain, forests, villages, and then she was face-to-face with Lothaire.

He looked startled. "Annika. Where are you? I've been searching for you."

She wanted out of this vision, but she did not know how to stop it. She felt along the wall behind her and dislodged a piece of stone. She clamped her hand around it until pain shot through her arm. That pain ripped her from Lothaire even as he reached toward her as Evelyne had.

She was back in the crumbling fortress. The stone fell to the floor as she opened her hand, the blood bright red.

Afraid, she whirled in place. But there was no one. Only soft sounds of dripping water and birdsong.

CHAPTER FORTY-SIX

To Evelyne's chagrin, nothing about the path was faster on horseback. Overgrown bushes, fallen trees, and displaced rocks covered the road.

And now she stared at a fork in the path. She dismounted and walked around, staring at the soft earth. She was an excellent hunter, but someone else had always done the tracking for her. It had never occurred to her to learn that skill. Now she wished she'd paid attention to the small things that had made her life so easy.

"Which way?" asked Hilfa.

"I'm not sure," said Evelyne.

"We can split it up. Finn and I can take the left, and you and Dodd take the right."

Evelyne didn't like the idea of separating. Leaving Jack behind was bad enough. She felt the need to stay together. But before she could say more, she heard movement behind them.

Five men on horseback, taking more risks and riding much faster than they had. As they drew closer, she recognized the leader.

Lothaire.

"Out of the way," called one man with him. The mercenaries.

Why wouldn't he have king's men with him?

She surged forward, grabbing the reins of Lothaire's horse and pulling it to a stop. The mercenaries drew their swords.

"Lothaire, you bastard." All she could think about was watching Steffen burn and knowing it would have been Annika as well, had the temple had its way.

"Lady Evelyne, I almost didn't recognize you." He bowed his head. "Since we meet in this unusual location, I assume you know where Annika is."

She knew she'd made a mistake as soon as she looked him in the eyes. "I think she's headed for the Giant's Bridge." The words fell from her lips like water.

He turned to one of his companions. "Which way?"

One with a soft voice responded, "That way," and pointed to the right.

"No!" Lothaire's gift no longer held her. She had led him directly to Annika. She yanked hard on the reins. "She's done nothing. Leave her be."

He leaned down toward her. "Haven't you heard? She killed Elder Braga." He smirked and kicked her in the chest, knocking her to the ground. Dodd, Finn, and Hilfa drew their weapons. "Take care of them."

Lothaire spurred on his horse. The beast leapt over her as she lay on the ground. She curled into a ball and waited for the strike of the hooves, but the animal cleared her easily. She scrambled to her feet and rushed for her own steed, putting her foot in the stirrup before someone yanked her backward.

It was the soft-spoken mercenary who had pointed the way. His helm had a nose guard draped in chain mail, making it hard to see his features, but she saw the broadsword he drew and swung. She leapt backward, out of range. Her sword was still wrapped in its scabbard on her horse. She had no chance of retrieving it.

Another swing, another leap. All so fast, she didn't have time to think. She couldn't dance away from all the attacks. She had to act. On the next swing, she moved out of range and on the backswing, she grasped the broadsword by its blade. Her leather gloves took the brunt of the edge, but she could feel the pain building in her fingers where the blade bit into her hand. She threw herself forward, knocking the man off his feet, and drew her dagger. As he fell, his helmet came partway off his head. He pulled it the rest of the way off.

When their eyes met, Evelyne knew in her bones she was facing another woman. She could feel it. A woman like her but truly living a man's life. The dagger shook in her hand. Kill a woman? Not some angry, brutish man-at-arms, but one of the few other women in her world who had chosen a man's occupation?

The pause was enough to give the woman motivation. She stood and ran full tilt at Evelyne, her sword wielded like a pike. This time, Evelyne slipped and fell, and the mercenary moved in to strike the final blow. But she couldn't stop her momentum as Evelyne rolled away from the strike and took her feet from underneath her.

Evelyne jumped upon her and drove her dagger into the side of her neck. The dagger met with resistance as it pierced the skin, then sank in and through to the other side, cutting the woman's windpipe on its way. A hard scrape—the bones in the neck—a slight resistance from the skin on the other side. The woman's eyes, wide in fear, reflected Evelyne's own visage. When would the gurgling sound stop? Evelyne withdrew the dagger, and blood pulsed and spurted from the woman's neck.

She'd killed someone. A woman. She'd killed a woman.

It was done now. She couldn't take it back. The overwhelming smell of blood surrounded her, and she leaned away and retched. The bile burned her throat, and the smell, mixed with the smell of blood, made her retch again.

Evelyne heard movement. Someone was behind her. She would die because she couldn't muster the energy to fight back. She waited for the blow but heard a cry, then a bearded man fell in front of her. His brown eyes were open, but he looked at nothing.

A firm hand grasped her shoulder.

She craned her head around and saw Timothy's comforting face. He leaned down and helped her to her feet. He forced her clenched hand open and took the dagger. He wiped the blood on his tunic and sheathed it at Evelyne's side.

"Go," he said in a gentle tone before he turned back to help the others.

Yes. Annika was still out there somewhere, most likely as scared as she was. Evelyne wiped the vomit from her lips and nodded. She mounted her horse. She looked back for a moment, long enough to see Hilfa strike a man's helm with both her hammers.

Maiden, protect my friends, she thought as she turned and rode after Lothaire.

❖

Annika woke with a start. She had fallen asleep against an interior wall after searching for and finding no way down the mountain. The slope on the western side was too steep for her to climb. She would backtrack to the path she had seen that led down to the valley. The risk was great that someone would find her, but she needed food and water, even if she stole it. She wouldn't leave until nightfall. She could hear her father saying it would be safer under darkness.

Safer from men, but what of wolves and bears? She shook her head. She could only worry about one threat at a time.

"There you are. I was worried about you." Lothaire stood in the doorway, backlit by the late afternoon sun.

Annika stumbled to her feet, pressing her back against the wall.

"I have something for you." He swung her gittern around from his back and pulled its strap over his head. He held it out to her. "I couldn't let you lose it."

Her thoughts went to Elder Braga lying in her own blood. If she refused him, would he do the same to her?

He laid it on an empty plinth, the statue that once stood there now shattered pieces around the base. "You should be happy. I went to your cottage and retrieved it before they set it ablaze." He took a step closer. "Are you not pleased?"

Ablaze? She sobbed. Now she truly had no place to return to.

"Here, here." Lothaire took another step toward her. Approaching her like someone would a skittish animal. "It's all right. I'm here now. You called to me, and I came. I knew you would."

She had never meant to call to him. She should never have tried to control the gifts she didn't understand. "Who am I?" she asked.

"Who are you?" He laughed. "Annika, tender of the fowl."

"Tender of the *foul*," she murmured as she remembered the night she'd met Evelyne. Fearless and strong Evelyne. She would know how to escape Lothaire. "Who am I that you would kill to possess me?" she clarified.

"You are the most powerful Talent in a millennium. And even if you weren't, you are the most beautiful."

Coming from him, the words felt wrong. She didn't want his affection. She moved to the opposite doorway, but he was faster, grabbing her wrist and pulling her backward into his arms.

She struggled to get free.

"I will help you. I will teach you how to control your gifts. How to use them." His expression above her grew manic. "Together, we will be unstoppable."

"I don't want to be unstoppable."

He laughed. "You don't know what you want. You're just a girl. You will learn to obey me."

"If you care for me…" She was taking a chance that the look he favored upon her was the same as Evelyne's. "If you love me, you will let me go."

He laughed again. "Love you? You can't love a Talent."

"Some of us can." Evelyne stood in the opposite doorway. Golden sunlight bathed her from behind. Her sword appeared alight with fire.

Was this a vision? Was she conjuring Evelyne from memory somehow? How was it possible they were all together in this place?

"So nice to see you, Lady Evelyne."

Lothaire saw her too. Then Evelyne really was here. Thank the gods.

"Haven't you heard? I'm no longer a lady. My family shunned me. Renounced my name," Evelyne replied.

Shunned? She'd given up everything. That couldn't possibly be true.

Lothaire swung Annika to his side, holding her by the wrist. He drew his sword with his other hand. "Evelyne, if you leave now, I will forgive this disobedience. I'll even force your father to retract your shunning. You can start your life over again."

"I'm done with men telling me what I can and cannot do. Neither you nor my father will ever tell me what to do again." Evelyne pointed with her sword. "I won't let you hurt her. And that is me telling you what I'm going to do."

"You're injured. How long do you think you'll last against me?" He waved his hand. He held his sword pointed toward the floor as if unconcerned by her defense.

Annika saw the blood dripping from Evelyne's left hand.

"Don't relinquish your life for this girl." Lothaire stepped closer. "Why don't you go home, ask to serve the Maiden, and forget this ever happened?"

Annika watched Evelyne's sword arm lowering. She blinked as if to clear the confusion that filled her mind. Lothaire glowed.

"He's using his gift on you," Annika yelled. "Please, Evelyne, leave before he kills you."

She shook her head. "I won't leave you." She raised the sword slightly and no doubt fought to concentrate. "I won't let you hurt her."

He stepped closer, pulling Annika with him. Why wouldn't Evelyne stop looking at him? "I don't want to hurt her." His voice was patient and soft. "I want to help her."

"No." Evelyne shook her head. She seemed confused. "You're going to hurt her, aren't you? You murdered Steffen." She sounded unsure.

And in that moment of confusion, Lothaire brought his sword up, and Evelyne stood still, almost unaware. Annika gasped. She had to do something to stop him. Her dagger. She had been so afraid, she had forgotten it. She drew the blade and sank it in Lothaire's sword arm. He groaned and released her. She stepped back toward the end of the aqueduct, hoping to lead him away. He turned and followed, the dagger still stuck in his upper arm.

No longer under his gift, Evelyne swung at his back, but Lothaire ducked away from her at the last moment. She stumbled on the miss as her sword pulled her forward. He thrust at her. She jumped away. He pulled the dagger from his arm and threw it off the ruins. He pushed on at Evelyne and swung. She stepped behind a column. His blade rang against marble; chips of the wind-worn stone flew in the air.

He swung on the other side, and she ducked again. With a loud crunch, his blade struck stone instead of flesh. Annika watched helplessly. Where were her gifts now? She concentrated, but nothing happened.

"No one has ever loved me." Lothaire swung angrily this time. Evelyne blocked his strike with her own sword, the blow forcing her backward. "Even before they knew I was a Talent. That I was special." He struck again.

Annika watched agonizingly as Evelyne stumbled under the blow. Was he toying with her?

"No one loved me."

Evelyne panted from exertion.

"Women flock to me like bees to a skep, but they don't love me. They love what I represent." He struck again, taking Evelyne to her knees. "They loathe who I really am." And he thrust his sword into Evelyne's side. She fell back against a pile of rubble, holding her wound.

"No," Annika yelled. She looked over the edge of the aqueduct. "If you kill her, I will leap."

He turned back and walked toward her, leaving Evelyne sprawled against the stones. "Only one person can possess you. Me." He kept coming. "Together, we can smite kings and queens. Create our own kingdom where we are free to be our true selves with nothing holding us back. No petty rules and religious orders. No more being their instruments of destruction and healing."

Annika moved closer to the end, sliding her foot a little farther over the edge. "I don't want to smite anyone. Don't come any closer." She moved as far onto the edge as she dared, looking down. Below her, the ruins stuck out of the ground like jagged teeth. If she was lucky, she would hit one and die instantly. She stared out across the plains. All she had to do was jump. She wiped one of her palms on her tunic. Everything would be over quickly. All of it done. No more fear. No more pain. Only the end. She tensed her legs and tightened her arms, readying herself for the leap.

"No!"

She turned to meet Evelyne's gaze.

"Annika, don't listen to him." Evelyne seemed to struggle to talk. "I loved you before I knew about your gifts. I'm not afraid of you nor piteous nor envious. I simply love you."

Lothaire lunged, grabbing hold of Annika before she could move. She struggled against his grasp. He leaned in near her face. "Fine. We will die together."

Love. Love equaled death. Love equaled momentary glimpses of happiness, only to be brought back to reality. She looked from Lothaire to Evelyne. One loved her enough to sacrifice everything for her, and the other wanted to kill to possess her.

A rock hit Lothaire in the side, knocking the breath from him. He released her and spun to face Evelyne, who could barely stand. She leaned against the nearest wall as Lothaire stormed toward her. He pulled his sword arm straight back at the elbow. He was going to finish her.

And Evelyne was too weak to fight back.

She smiled at Annika. That beautiful, roguish smile.

It was Annika's turn to say what she wanted.

"Stop!" Her voice rippled through the air like waves, the sound carrying across the valley below. Everything around her, Lothaire, Evelyne, dust, leaves, they all paused. She walked toward Lothaire while his arm was frozen in midair, his face contorted with anger. She reached out and touched his inking, visible just above his collar. She could feel his heartbeat, see the red of his blood, the pink of his muscles, and the whiteness of his bones. A bright light filled her vision. Lothaire and she faced each other as they had the first time they'd met. The past vision had been right here, a future she hadn't known was coming.

"Who are you?" he asked.

"I'm no one important."

"How can this be?" He seemed confused.

"The gods work in complicated ways." And she released him. The present came quickly back into focus. So dark, she had to blink a few times until her vision cleared.

Lothaire knelt on the floor. Crying. "You've taken my power." He covered his face with his hands.

"You're free," she replied. "You can start your life anew. Be anything you want."

"I don't want to be merely anyone." He stood. "I wanted to be more. I wanted to teach them all a lesson. To show them what genuine fear could be. I knew you were someone special when I first saw you. Impenetrable. Unswaying. Now you've taken it all from me." He lunged for her neck. His hands tightened. She clawed at them, trying to make him release her. Even without his gifts, he was incredibly strong.

"I'm no one now," he growled.

She felt energy coursing through her. "Release me."

He pulled his hands back. His eyes went wide. He was frightened, as Elder Braga had been in the castle. And before he could try again, Evelyne threw herself against him and pushed him away before she collapsed to the floor in a heap. He stumbled backward until he was at the very lip of the ruin. He seemed to balance on the very tip of his shoes for a moment, as if he was trying to fly, before he plummeted out of view.

Annika didn't bother to look. She had seen the ragged stones below. All she cared about was Evelyne, sprawled on the floor before her, blood pooling underneath her.

"No, no, no." Annika dropped to her knees. She ran her hands through Evelyne's hair. "I need you. I need your strength. You must stay with me."

She was tired. So tired from the gift she'd used on Lothaire. But she had to try. She placed her hands over the wound on Evelyne's side and willed herself to heal. She begged her mother, Zuri, the Maiden, and the old gods. Anyone who would help her with this task. She'd do anything, say anything, to heal Evelyne.

When the feeling came, the light blazed, and she felt something else, someone else, and the light grew so bright, she could no longer see. When it stopped, she fell backward.

Evelyne stirred. Annika crawled back to her, kissing her forehead, her cheek, and finally. Her lips. She examined the cut in the fabric of Evelyne's tunic. Where the wound had been, there was flawless skin. But on Evelyne's neck, there was a fresh godsmark. The Two-Faced God. Lothaire's mark.

CHAPTER FORTY-SEVEN

Evelyne opened her eyes. The sun was shining so brightly, she couldn't see anything else. No, not the sun. A fire? Then someone leaned in front of the fire, and she blinked several times before she could see.

The Maiden. I've died, she thought. I am dead, and I have reached the heavens. Praise Her.

Then the Maiden reached out and touched her cheek. Her touch was warm. She was saying something. "Evelyne, I was so worried."

Not the Maiden. Annika.

Then she felt the kiss. Soft and warm. It woke her from her confusion. She reached out and pulled Annika down to her. Pressing against her. She wanted to stay this way forever.

Annika broke away. Evelyne could see the blush on her cheeks. That was when she realized others were staring at her. She lay on a blanket with a soft tunic under her head. She heard birdsong and could smell something delicious cooking. She remembered. She reached for her side, sliding her hand under her ripped tunic. No pain. No blood. No wound.

She raised herself and waited for the dizziness to subside.

"Ah, decided to join us, eh?" Dodd smiled at her with his broad, toothless grin.

She looked around. Hilfa was working on weapons, caring for them. Sharpening the edges and checking the hilts for loosened guards and pommels. She nodded at Evelyne and winked. Evelyne smiled in return.

Finn raised a bowl of pottage to his lips. And on the other side of the fire, Timothy sat with his head down and his hands clasped as if in prayer.

"The Paladin?"

"Dead, I hope," said Dodd.

Dead. So she hadn't dreamed it. She'd killed the Paladin. The temple's warrior. The king's man. If she had held any hope of one day serving the king, she could no longer. Her stomach turned when she thought of the mercenary woman she'd struck through the neck. So much blood and stench. She looked at her hands, lowered her head, and prayed for forgiveness.

Dodd pushed the wood into the fire gently, bringing the flames higher. "We stripped the mercenaries of anything that could identify them. Buried the bodies off the path with stones atop to keep away predators and buried the clothes farther along the ridge."

Annika handed her a bowl of pottage. "Eat. You need your strength."

She did as she was told. The whole while, she kept her eyes on Annika. She was alive. They were both alive. She stood but wobbled a bit. Annika grasped her to steady her. She handed her bowl to Annika and kissed her gently. "I'll be back in a moment."

As she approached, Timothy looked up. She sat next to him. "Thank you for everything you did."

He didn't look pleased. "I betrayed you when I should have stood with you. I acted like a boy. A foolish boy."

"You came in the end."

"I was jealous, Evelyne. I didn't want to see you reunite with Annika. I did everything because I was jealous. I wanted you to love me, not her."

"I do love you."

He looked surprised.

She nudged him. "I love you like a brother. I love you more than a brother, certainly more than I love Erik, but not the way I love her."

He nodded. "I understand." He brushed some dirt from his tunic. "Maybe I don't understand, but I will try to one day."

"I need someone to tell me what happened while I was with the dreammaker."

Timothy recounted the fight with the mercenaries. How they'd found Annika among the fortress ruins. He'd thought Evelyne was dead at first.

"I thought I was dead as well." She looked at Annika. She smiled, but she looked tired.

"I was worried," said Timothy.

"About me?" Evelyne joked. "It was only a scratch." But she

knew it hadn't been a scratch at all. She'd felt the blade cut through her. Heard the crack of her ribs. Had seen the blood flowing freely before darkness had taken her.

They sat silently together for a while, watching the others put away their things and prepare to rest. Was there anything left to say? It would take time for her to trust Timothy again. She returned to where Annika sat, her legs tucked underneath her, and one hand holding her up. Evelyne sat beside her, and Annika rested her head on Evelyne's shoulder.

"You look like a painting of a god resting. Waiting for an unaware human to stumble upon you and let you play tricks on them."

Annika placed a hand on Evelyne's thigh. Evelyne felt a thrill course through her. "This god is way too tired to play games," she said.

Evelyne drew Annika down so her head lay in her lap. "Then sleep. Tomorrow, we will begin anew."

❖

Morning came too early for Annika. She awoke wrapped in Evelyne's strong arms. Underneath the blanket they shared, Evelyne's scent filled the warmth. She couldn't describe it, but she would know it forever. Evelyne's body touched hers from her head to her feet. Nothing had ever felt so comforting and secure.

Evelyne moved away, and Annika felt cold. She wanted to reach out and pull her back, but that was selfish. With daylight came the realization that one challenge was over, and another was just beginning.

Timothy sat upon his horse. He spoke to Evelyne in a low voice when she reached him. Annika couldn't make out the words, but she could see the disappointment on Evelyne's face. Evelyne nodded and patted the horse's hindquarters, and with that, Timothy rode toward the temple.

"Where is he going?" she asked when Evelyne returned.

"He is my father's squire, and he must do his duty," Evelyne said with sorrow in her voice. "He is returning to Marsendale."

"Will he be in trouble?"

Evelyne shook her head. "I do not know." Emotions warred on her face before she returned her attention to Annika.

"We need to take our leave of this road before someone comes this way," said Hilfa while she adjusted the saddle of a former mercenary's horse.

"With the Paladin missing and Elder Braga dead, the king will send men after her," Dodd said, pointing at Annika.

"I'm taking her to Weya," replied Evelyne.

Dodd groaned. "Weya?" He picked his blanket from the ground and rolled it. "I hate cold weather. Makes my knees ache."

"I'm not asking any of you to go with us. I can't speak for Annika, but your debts to me are settled."

Annika smiled. There was the Lady Evelyne. Taking charge. She looked handsome doing it. Annika almost hated to spoil things. "I must go to Tarburg."

The look of shock was everywhere around her, especially from Evelyne.

"What?" Evelyne turned to face her. "Is this in jest? It is way too early in the morning for it."

Annika shook her head. "I must find a woman, Zuri, in Tarburg. She knows things about me. About my gifts. She can help me. I am certain."

"Are you daft, girl?" asked Dodd. "Did you not hear me? Everyone from the Dragon's Back to Gravesend will search for you."

"He's right," said Evelyne. "We need to take you to Weya. Get you somewhere safe."

Annika stepped away abruptly. "You'd take me to a place I've never been, where I know no one, and leave me to my fate?"

Evelyne gaped several times, opening and closing her mouth.

Annika lifted and shook their shared blanket. "I must go to Tarburg. If I must do it alone, I will."

"I'll go with you, fair maiden." Finn covered his heart with his hand. "Anything for a lady."

Annika smiled. "Not a lady, Finn. A mere goose girl."

He shrugged.

Evelyne drew close and spoke in a low tone. "Annika, please. If we go to Weya, I won't leave you there. I will stay with you. You will have someone. You will have me."

"I must tell you something." Annika took hold of Evelyne's shoulder and held up a small mirror to show her neck.

The godsmark was dark and clear. Evelyne looked confused. "What does this mean?"

Annika put her hand on Evelyne's forearm. "Something happened when I stopped Lothaire from killing you. I marked you with the symbol of the Two-Faced God. His symbol."

"Are you saying I have his gift now?"

Annika shook her head. "I don't know."

Evelyne scowled. "If not a gift…"

"Lothaire was no longer the Paladin when you killed him." Annika thought of his last words. "Somehow, I stripped him of his gift. I thought it would make him happy if he was no longer a Talent. He hated it so much. Hated himself. When I thought of it, it happened. And when I healed you, his mark appeared on you."

Evelyne stared quietly at the inking, running her fingers over the blackness.

"What if it will harm you, Evelyne?" Annika gripped her forearm tightly. "Being with me kills the ones I love."

"You saved my life." Evelyne guided Annika's hand to her lips and placed a gentle kiss on Annika's palm. "I'll take the consequences of the mark, whatever they may be. And I'll not leave your side. Not ever again."

"Not to interrupt, but I'm coming with you." Hilfa stood, arms crossed, giving Annika the look she had given her every time she was in trouble as a child. "Your da will haunt my dreams for the rest of my life if I don't. We'll need to find Jack on the way. He's got all my tools."

Annika ran to her and accepted the hug she gave. To her amazement, they all chose to come with her to Tarburg. Each for their own reasons, she was certain. Coin was Dodd's motivation, and Finn… she was worried he'd get himself killed. And Evelyne now had what she wanted, a band of fighters with whom to serve something greater than herself.

Annika worried her cause was selfish and not worthy of their devotion. They were refugees heading to the maw of the dragon. The very center of Valmora. Home to the man who ruled them all, who most likely was already setting bounties on her head.

Not knowing how to ride, Annika stayed firmly on the ground walking with Hilfa and looked at Evelyne astride her horse. Her tunic ripped and dirtied. Her hair wild and tangled. Her face smudged with dirt. But pride emanated from her. From all of them. As they moved down the mountain path to the valley, Annika looked at the sky. It was a beautiful blue day.

She grasped her gittern and played. This time, the tune was a hopeful one.

About the Author

Suzanne Lenoir is originally from the East Coast (USA) and is currently a resident of Cincinnati, Ohio. Her most vivid childhood memories are of exploring medieval city walls, feeling the coolness of dark, ancient churches, and staring at arms and armor while dreaming of being a knight. Her debut novel, *A Talent Within*, combines her love of YA fantasy with her interest in medieval history. Suzanne is a technophile, video gamer, history buff, and avid reader, who loves EDM and builds model siege engines. She lives with her adventurous, spreadsheet-loving wife and her blind, toothless Chihuahua. Find out more at SuzanneLenoir.com.

Young Adult Titles From Bold Strokes Books

A Talent Within by Suzanne Lenoir. Evelyne, born into nobility, and Annika, a peasant girl with a deadly secret, struggle to change their destinies in Valmora, a medieval world controlled by religion, magic, and men. (978-1-63679-423-5)

Take Her Down by Lauren Emily Whalen. Stakes are cutthroat, scheming is creative, and loyalty is ever-changing in this queer, female-driven YA retelling of Shakespeare's *Julius Caesar*. (978-1-63679-089-3)

Two Winters by Lauren Emily Whalen. A modern YA retelling of Shakespeare's *The Winter's Tale* about birth, death, Catholic school, improv comedy, and the healing nature of time. (978-1-63679-019-0)

Boy at the Window by Lauren Melissa Ellzey. Daniel Kim struggles to hold onto reality while haunted by both his very-present past and his never-present parents. Jiwon Yoon may be the only one who can break Daniel free. (978-1-63679-092-3)

Three Left Turns to Nowhere by Jeffrey Ricker, J. Marshall Freeman & 'Nathan Burgoine. Three strangers heading to a convention in Toronto are stranded in rural Ontario, where a small town with a subtle kind of magic leads each to discover what he's been searching for. (978-1-63679-050-3)

#shedeservedit by Greg Herren. When his gay best friend, and high school football star, is murdered, Alex Wheeler is a suspect and must find the truth to clear himself. (978-1-63555-996-5)

The Infinite Summer by Morgan Lee Miller. While spending the summer with her dad in a small beach town, Remi Brenner falls for Harper Hebert and accidentally finds herself tangled up in an intense restaurant rivalry between her famous stepmom and her first love. (978-1-63555-969-9)

Bury Me in Shadows by Greg Herren. College student Jake Chapman is forced to spend the summer at his dying grandmother's home and soon finds danger from long-buried family secrets. (978-1-63555-993-4)

I Am Chris by R Kent. There's one saving grace to losing everything and moving away. Nobody knows her as Chrissy Taylor. Now Chris can live who he truly is. (978-1-63555-904-0)

The Dubious Gift of Dragon Blood by J. Marshall Freeman. One day Crispin is a lonely high school student—the next he is fighting a war in a land ruled by dragons, his otherworldly boyfriend at his side. (978-1-63555-725-1)

Jellicle Girl by Stevie Mikayne. One dark summer night, Beth and Jackie go out to the canoe dock. Two years later, Beth is still carrying the weight of what happened to Jackie. (978-1-63555-691-9)

All the Worlds Between Us by Morgan Lee Miller. High school senior Quinn Hughes discovers that a broken friendship is actually a door propped open for an unexpected romance. (978-1-63555-457-1)

Exit Plans for Teenage Freaks by 'Nathan Burgoine. Cole always has a plan—especially for escaping his small-town reputation as "that kid who was kidnapped when he was four"—but when he teleports to a museum, it's time to face facts: it's possible he's a total freak after all. (978-1-163555-098-6)

Rocks and Stars by Sam Ledel. Kyle's struggle to own who she is and what she really wants may end up landing her on the bench and without the woman of her dreams. (978-1-63555-156-3)

CPSIA information can be obtained
at www.ICGtesting.com
Printed in the USA
JSHW022110200723
45010JS00001B/3

9 781636 794235